COMING HOME

BY

RICHARD TURNER

Published by Richard Turner

First Published, 2015

ISBN 978-0-9934834-0-0

For ordering information please email:
cominghomeanovel@gmail.com

To my mother, whose love of pre-history provoked mine.

Acknowledgements

I gratefully acknowledge the faith of my wife and children in this book. Particular thanks are due to my editing and publishing team, Will and Katie, without whom this book would still be a forgotten disc.

I also gratefully acknowledge the many authors in the field of pre-history whose works I have so enjoyed and which have inevitably influenced mine. Yet I must emphasize that his book is a work of fiction; the views expressed in it, correct or erroneous, are my own.

CHAPTER 1

Berin's heart was pounding so loudly, he was sure the sound would carry to the deer. The buck lifted its shiny black dew-dropped muzzle from the brook, twitched its ears, and turned its head to look back along its flank, directly at Berin's hide in the sedge at the edge of the marsh. Berin froze. His muscles corded; his knuckles whitened about the spear's shaft.

He pressed himself to the ground, seeking to merge his mired body with the rank grass, to hide his intrusion. In the reduced-scale world closely focused in front of him, a snail grazed on a blade-shaped leaf of woundwort, slowly sliming its yellow-grey body forwards from its shell, eye stalks searching. Berin prayed. A beetle climbed laboriously to the spiked flower at the top of a sedge stem, balanced precariously, rolled upside down as the breeze bowed the grass towards Berin, and retreated. The buck flicked its short tail at the biting fly on its rump, stamped its hind foot and snorted indignantly at its failure to dislodge the nuisance. With a resigned shake of its antlers, it bent once more to its drinking. Berin blessed the local deity, promising an offering. He inched forwards.

If only I had Belu's spear, he thought, I could throw from here, sure that I would make a kill; or my bow. I should have been more careful not to wet the string. Even with those light arrows of Ermid's I could wound the buck from here, at least enough to give me a chance with the spear.

Berin fingered the finely tooled flint spearhead. One of my best, he thought, but I am close to the edge of the cover. It will be a long throw. Will the point be good enough to make a kill? Berin muttered the hunter's prayer.

1

A jay's screeching alarm call slashed the tendrils of Berin's thought. The buck started, straight-legged, quivering, poised for flight. Berin burst from cover, hurling his spear as he rose from the swamp, shrugging rush and weed aside. The spear flew true. It struck the buck behind the shoulder, reaching for the heart, yet failing, the flint point splintering on the ribs, turning to gouge the soft pinkness of breath itself. The buck staggered, sagged at the knees in shock, then suddenly aware of foul man scent, scrambled in panic along the stream bed towards the beckoning shelter of a nearby thicket.

Berin followed, fumbling in his haste to loose the knife held by a thong around his neck, leaping the stream to land where only moments before the buck had drunk. He had no need to read the spoor so clearly marked in the lush grasses of the stream bank, or the pink frothy gobs, for Berin could hear the buck's thrashing flight. Through the whipcords of his own adrenaline- powered elation, he could feel the buck's panic, sense its life force melting. Brambles snatched at Berin's arms as, impatient now for the kill, he ran alongside the stream, slipping through nettles into the pebbly bed of the brook, clambering up again, pulling on a willow root, with the wet earth smell strong, the blood lust burning in him.

The buck's headlong flight stopped at a low wall of chalk at the far side of a grassy bowl rimmed by alders. It turned to face its tormentor and stood its ground, quivering. Berin advanced, knife in hand. The buck trembled, its forelegs buckled and it fell to its knees in supplication, pink froth at its nostrils. Berin circled, warily, seeking a chance to close and deliver the death cut. The buck struggled to rise, tossing its proud antlers, defiance flashing momentarily in its eyes, spraying its white chin patch pink at each laboured breath. Berin pounced. Seizing the buck by its horns, he pulled back its head and quickly drew his knife across the exposed throat. Warmth flooded over his right hand and forearm. The buck kicked weakly, and the bright brown-blue sheen of its eyes faded.

Berin's blood lust died. Suddenly aware of his tiredness, Berin sat back on his heels. It had been a long day since he had left his father's house on the high chalk land to the south, soon after the early morning meal. He had picked up the buck's spoor close to the edge of his clan's hunting grounds and had tracked it for several miles beyond the escarpment, down into the marsh land that bordered the Great River, where few men ventured. Now the late afternoon autumn sun cast long shadows, throwing the lush green foliage in the dell into sharp contrast with its dark echoes.

Berin walked to the stream, knelt and drank. Conscious of the cloying gore and the mire from his passage through the swamp, he washed himself in the shallow, still waters, relishing the cool freshness. The blood from his own scratches mingled with that of the buck and the stirred whirls of sediment in the pool.

Berin returned to the buck, rolled it over and carefully, so as not to damage the hide, pulled out his spear. Ruefully he examined the spear head. The flint point that had taken him so many hours to fashion, had done its work well, but in doing so had been destroyed.

Belu's point would not have broken, Berin mused. What would I give for a spear point or knife, or best of all an axe formed from the bronze that gleamed so softly, yet with such power. With such an axe I could carve fields from the forest, build stockyards for the herds and long houses to

3

shelter the wives and strong sons that such abundance would bring. If only I had the cattle to trade.

A gust of wind swirled crisp leaves around his bare legs, reminding Berin of his near nakedness and of the advance of evening. It would not be wise to be unarmed in the outlands at night. Berin straightened. He had left his pack and clothes under the rowan at the edge of the marsh. He would have to return there before dark, or he would never find them. He scrambled up the chalk and flint littered bank to get his bearings. A hare started from his feet and bounded ahead of him up the slope, zig-zagging, now around, now under the juniper bushes that dotted the hillside.

Berin shaded his eyes against the sun as he breasted the top of the slope, to find an open area of grassland studded with occasional clumps of hawthorn, blackthorn and birch, interwoven into impenetrable thickets with brambles. Turning from the sun, Berin gazed over the broad valley of the Great River. The lands on its far bank were lost in the greying northern skyline. In the middle distance, occasional stands of beech swelled majestically above tossing green gold cuffs of birch, alder and willow, and marked low hills within the wet lands of the valley floor. One, higher than the rest, and crowned by a distinctive beech grove, Berin recognised as the steep hill that rises from the bank of the Great River at the furthest settlement of the men of the line of Harac.

On the far eastern skyline, illuminated full face by the sun, were the chalk uplands that swept down to meet the hills of Berin's homeland, to which the rise on which he now stood was an outlier. Plumes of smoke, whipped ragged at their tops by the wind, and occasional chequered fields, marked distant settlements. Berin could just see the fold in the escarpment which hid the great hall of Dorn the High Chief. The chief's great house was set on a terrace above the ford, below which the river rushed white and shrill, yet impotent, to its perpetual bad tempered meeting with the chalk hills at the gorge. Many times, when Dorn had sought his father's advice at the Council of Elders, and at the time of festival, Berin had made the journey from their long houses, along the escarpment to the ford. Between the hall of Dorn and the hill on which Berin stood, lay miles of wet land, marsh and mist-shrouded osiers, sedge beds and bulrushes surrounding ponds and bordering meandering streams, a haven for the myriad water fowl that each year sought its sanctuary from northern storms.

Berin identified the gully he had used that morning to climb down the escarpment to the marsh and fixed his bearings with the touch of the wind on his cheek and the direction of the lengthening shadows. Reassured, he hastened back to his prize, hefted it onto his shoulder and set off on his return journey.

Berin splashed into the stream. It ran from a rush-bordered pool, overhung at its shadowed eastern end by a gnarled and very ancient willow, the writhing roots of which crushed a massive sarsen stone in a timeless embrace. A spring bubbled gently from beneath the stone. Despite the breeze that had chilled Berin earlier, the pool was still, darkly reflecting the willow and a background of evening sky.

A place of peace, a place for reverence, thought Berin, recalling the promise made as he lay in the sedge. Surely this is the place the Spirit would choose. But what should I offer. A promise made must be kept or it will be bad luck. I have only my knife.

Berin fumbled one-handed with the thong holding his flint knife. It was a fine blade, with a beautifully worked bone handle. He had made it as a youth as he learned to knap flint from the old master himself, old Anoeth of the ford. Many hours had passed choosing the flint nodule, roasting it, selecting the hammer stone and the exact spot to strike off the first shard. Many more hours had passed in the delicate flaking of thin slivers, each press of the rounded bone on the nascent blade an agony of suspense lest the whole should crack along some unseen flaw, all to the litany of deprecation from old Anoeth. Berin remembered how he had worked on, ignoring the jibes, the cuts to his fingers and to his thighs beneath the leather apron on which the masterpiece took shape. Finally, Anoeth had grunted a grudging approval. But Berin had seen the twinkle of pleasure in the old man's eyes as he fingered the completed blade, a twinkle dimmed for ever by Anoeth's subsequent blindness, except, that is, in Berin's fond memory.

Well it will just have to be the knife, thought Berin grimly. So much for hasty promises, then touched his greenstone and amber necklace for luck, just in case the spirit knew his thoughts.

"Oh Spirit of the Spring, accept my token," intoned Berin and threw the knife into the pool below the sarsen stone.

A curled dry leaf fell and danced like a boat on the ripples.

"Hold!"

The command rang out thinly but firmly on the brittle evening air. Berin, bowed under the weight of the buck as he climbed the gully, stumbled to a halt. The command brooked no denial. Berin, proudly born and not inclined to take orders, especially on his own ground, was tired to his bones and only too glad to stop and set down his burden. Besides, he had recognised the voice of the youth who proudly fulfilled the man's task entrusted to him, and had no wish to be felled by a well directed pebble. Oranc's skill with a sling was known throughout the chalk lands as far as the ford over the great river. Oranc hadn't recognised him with the buck on his shoulders, half hidden as he was by the juniper scrub. Berin had no wish to chance his luck.

"Easy, Oranc, it's me, Berin. Lend a hand here."

"Berin? Oh it **is** you! Thank the Mother. Quick. We must get back home."

"I'm ..."

"The Afon'ken are raiding. Look! Do you see? Smoke... lots of it... from home!"

Berin's blood chilled as he glanced southwards, at the same moment, pitching the buck from his shoulders. He straightened with a groan that was more worry at the confirmation of Oranc's news than relief from his burden. A dark smudge amongst the indigo clouds which shaped the southern sky had to be acknowledged, however unwillingly.

"I was just about to turn back when I heard you coming up the dene."

"Let's go. Do our kinsmen gather?"

Without waiting for an answer, Berin forced his tired limbs to a bruising pace along the familiar path along the crest of the escarpment. Oranc, though rested, had to stretch his young legs to keep pace.

"How many are there?" gasped Berin. " Where's Ermid? Did Aedd and Amren come in with him? What about Naf and Brys? Is Belu with my father? "

"Father just managed to get away from lower garth. He was the one who warned us. I don't know about Naf and Brys. Aedd was arming himself as I left. Amren chased what cattle he could on to the top and went on to Ilws to fetch our kin. Belu was with your father when I left," panted Oranc. "My father was all in. You know how he puffs and groans when he has to run. Hard to make sense of what he was saying, it all came out in bits, and he didn't wait to count them, but he thought a score or more."

Never in such numbers before, Berin worried, against our seven, eight with Oranc. At least we were not taken completely by surprise. I hope its only cattle they're after. By the Gods I wish I still had my spear unbroken or my bow-string dry.

The spit thickened in Berin's mouth, caking his lips. He felt the familiar burn as warm lung tissue wrested desperately needed oxygen from the chill evening air. His exhaled breath steamed behind as his booted feet pounded the rhythm of his heart and lungs. The string of the useless bow slung across his shoulders burned a weal above the collar of his kidskin shirt; it stung with the salt sweat running from his face. The stiff ox-hide quiver of arrows slapped against his leggings, keeping time with the pack slung on the other side.

Olwen's face formed in his mind's eye, dancing before him. She must be safe... she just had to be. Fleetingly he recalled last night, when his hand had stretched stealthily to her in the warm but darkly discreet shadows of Ermid's hearth. She cared for him as he did for her. How else should he interpret the answering pressure of her fingers on his.

"Berin!" Oranc's strangled gasp ripped Berin back to the present. Berin turned to see Oranc at full stretch on the track, his youthful features contorted in pain. Swiftly he turned, ran back and knelt at the boy's side.

"Oranc. What is it? Are you badly hurt?"

Chest heaving, Oranc struggled to his knees, head down, his shaggy mane of dark hair hanging over his face, which had assumed an alarming tinge of puce between the dirt, streaked and smeared by sweat and now tears. He fought to recover the breath pressed from his body by his fall.

"Your own mother would find it hard to love you the way you look right now," Berin grunted. "Come lad, rest a while. We will be no use to them winded."

Berin sat on the bank beside the track, drawing up his knees and dropping his head between them. With his surging breaths more controlled, he discarded bow, arrows and pack. No use to me, he thought ruefully, they'll only get in the way. He fumbled in his pack for the water skin. He lifted his head, swilled out his mouth and drank deeply. Without saying a word he passed the water to Oranc.

About them stretched the north pasture, open undulating grassland studded with thickets of juniper, but cleared of its timber by his ancestors many generations before. Here herdsmen and traders travelled the ancient way from the west on its route to the ford, and to the Mother alone knew where beyond. Below the crest on which they sat, just in front of the beech trees whose tops could be seen bushing darkly from the steep narrow valley beyond, wicker hurdles set to keep out straying stock, marked the first of the fields where, only a few short days before, Berin had worked alongside his kinsmen at the harvest. A few hundred paces down the valley, where it widened as though spreading to give birth to the rivulet that grew into Afon'panw, lay home.

Rolling clouds of smoke billowed upwards, pursued, overtaken and finally shot through by a rush of sparks and smuts. Swifts and martins, interrupting their migration, wheeled and dived, now fiery red from sunset and fire, then blacker than the coming night, beaks agape, gorging on seared and roasted insects at an unexpected farewell feast. A waft of burning drove Berin to his feet again, Oranc at his side.

"Bastards," growled Berin, sick anger rising in his throat. "We'll skirt around the top of the beeches and see what's happening. Pray they are all safe."

Swiftly Berin and Oranc moved down to the fields, opened the hurdles and skirted around the head of the valley to the spur above the settlement. Crouching low as they approached the brow, even though prepared, both started involuntarily at the scene of devastation.

Aedd's and Brys's hearths were no more than charred, smoking posts. Three figures sprawled in stark rigid poses at the entrance to the settlement, where the gate hung agape as though astonished at what had happened before it. One figure staked to the ground by a spear, fingers clawing the shaft in a last vain attempt to undo the immutable, would clearly never rise again, much to Berin's satisfaction as he failed to recognise the sightless staring corpse as one of his kin. But icy fingers of apprehension climbed his spine as unwillingly Berin dragged his gaze to the remaining bodies. Familiarity struck as a hammer blow.

"Belu!" he gasped, "Belu and Ermid."

"Father...?" Oranc wailed. "My father! Oh no...."

He sprang to his feet, Berin grabbed him and wrestled him to the ground, clamping his hand over Oranc's mouth. Oranc convulsed and moaned through Berin's tightly clenched fingers. Berin tightened his grip.

"Quiet," he hissed, his mouth pressed close to Oranc's ear. "We cannot help them now, but there may be others that need us. Be still! Be still in the name of The Mother. We are in real danger." Oranc sagged sobbing to the ground.

Below them in the valley the men of Afon'ken were looting the longhouses, dragging out the bolts of soft woven wool, furs of wolf, fox, and ermine, and bundles of cured sheep and cow hide. Others drove pigs from their sties and turned out the milch cows, sending them with a whoop and a slap on their rumps on their way down the valley, where a haze of chalk dust marked the passage of stock and men. All the raiders had plainly drunk deeply from the ale pots.

The leader, a tall, rangy figure paced to and fro' in the open space at the centre of the settlement, shouting at his men. Berin stared, struck with equal parts hatred and awe. The man was clad in a leather tunic which was sewn with rings and plates of bronze. Across his shoulders was a sash from which hung, at his left side, a wide, double-edged blade, fully one pace long, fashioned, but for the leather-bound handle, completely from bronze, whilst on his back hung a round wood and ox hide shield studded and rimmed with bronze. The raider's long sandy hair was braided and covered by a leather helmet strengthened with bronze bands. His under tunic and breeches were of fine wool, and the latter were tucked into soft leather boots. As Berin watched, one of the raiders brought a cloak of blue wool and fastened it about the leader's shoulders with a fastening that gleamed yellow and orange as he turned, catching the last of the sunlight. Not even at the High Chief's hall, not amongst all the travellers along the West Way, had Berin ever seen such a warrior, such wealth.

A flicker of movement down the slope amongst the beeches caught Berin's eye.

"Oranc. Oranc," he hissed, "get your sling ready, we may need it."

The sobbing next to him stopped. Oranc turned his tear stained face to Berin. "I'm ready" he replied, slipping a smooth pebble into the soft leather pouch of his sling. The set to his features marked his transition from boy to man more than the coming of age ceremony ever could.

"Wait here. I'm going down through the beeches to see if there's any trace of our people. I thought I saw someone move down there, but you stay here. I'll be back for you." Berin smiled. "Good lad," he said, reaching out a hand and grasping Oranc's upper arm in a firm parting embrace, almost finding tears of his own.

It was dark in the beech wood. A ring dove clattered through the upper branches as Berin paused beside one of the smooth trunks just inside the wood, to allow his eyes to accustom themselves to the gloom, and to listen. His boots crunched on the dry husks of last season's beech nuts, but there was no sound from the valley. Quickly he glanced to where he had seen the movement. The ground between the beech trunks was open, but for occasional holly bushes. It was also empty.

They'll be at the flint mine, if they're anywhere, Berin thought. They could defend themselves there. Only one or at most two could pass at a time through the entrance to the caverns.

Berin started to descend crabwise down the steep valley side, slipping and sliding from tree to tree as he stumbled over roots and moss-covered boulders hidden beneath the leaves, making his way to the head of the valley where countless numbers of his forebears, as he himself had done, had dug for flint in the hillside. A low whistle sent him crouching behind the roots of a fallen tree and into the hole torn from the earth as the tree had toppled in some long forgotten gale. Berin scrambled up the side of the dip and peered cautiously from beneath the bole.

Forty paces below him, a dense patch of holly trembled, heaved and finally disgorged a hirsute giant of a man. A mat of red hair, part brow, part beard, fell to massive shoulders on which it was barely distinguishable from the fox fur of his jerkin. His meaty right hand held a spear, whilst his other hand was hidden by the wood and ox hide shield. White scars of fresh cut wood showed that it had recently been put to good use. From a curling belt that barely constrained the belly above, hung the great greenstone axe of Aedd. As Berin now rose from concealment, the beard below the red veined nose, that certainly had seen many a pot of ale pass beneath it, was slashed by a toothy grin.

"By all the Gods Berin, it's good to see you," Aedd growled." We really need you. Any news of the men of Ilws?"

Berin closed the remaining gap between them in a sliding rush of leaves and mould that broke as a wave against Aedd's boots.

"None. You've sent for them? "

13

"Aye and to Dorn. Amren went straight to Ilws from the south garth. I sent Alen to the ford, but he can't bring them before nightfall. Amren's had time enough though. They should be here now. They'd better come soon or it will be too late. We've been pressed. But for them being distracted by the ale pots and plunder, we would be fighting yet."

"I saw Belu...," Berin's voice faltered "...and Ermid."

"Their leader, a big bastard with a great bronze blade did for them. Mother its sharp, and heavy! Look!" Aedd held up his shield. "There was no holding him. Belu, Mother rest him, spitted one nicely before that bastard got him."

"And the rest, are they all right?"

"Your father is wounded in the shield arm, but his greater hurt is for Belu. Naf is over there, see, down behind that elder. He's keeping watch on the other side. Well he's not so pretty now; took a nasty slash on the face. We got all the women and youngsters in the mine. Your father and Brys guard the entrance. Don't know about young Oranc. We sent him to look for you along the escarpment. Did you see him?"

"He's back there on the ridge. He's not wounded but he hurts for Ermid. I thought I saw someone down the valley."

"Aye, Olwen. She went back to look for Amren's youngest."

"And you let her?" Berin's voice broke with shock and anger. "You let her? You let her go back down there, alone, to those animals? Do you know what they'll do to her if they catch....?" The enormity of the thought choked Berin to silence.

Shamefaced, Aedd mumbled "She was past in a flash. I tried to stop her... I did. Your father bade me to stay. For the greater good he said."

"Damn Father and his greater good. Give me your spear."

"I don't know that I ought. I have to guard...."

Berin grabbed the spear but found it immovable in Aedd's grasp. Angrily Berin stared at Aedd. Aedd felt the pain and fear for Olwen behind Berin's glare. Slowly his fingers relaxed.

Berin turned and, spear in hand, ran off down the valley, careless of any attempt at concealment. Slowly Aedd slipped his axe from his belt, stroking the smooth greenstone head that had outlived so many fine ash handles. There'll be work for us before long, he concluded grimly.

Oranc watched Berin enter the beech wood and started at the clatter of a ring dove bursting from the tree tops, veering and swerving then veering again, curling away with the wind as it caught sight of the men in the valley, and of Oranc in his hiding place on the spur above them. The men of Afon'ken were picking up loads of the looted wool, furs and hides and following their murderous companions and the stolen livestock down the valley. Their drunken shouts carried to Oranc, watching in sick despair at his own impotence, as they staggered and stumbled past the crumpled, grey-haired corpse of his father. The few raiders that remained were firing the looted houses and the grain stores. Oranc's hatred flared anew with each thrust of the burning brands.

A shrill scream pierced the air. A child, its smut and tear-stained face contorted in fear, tottered on unsteady legs from the porch of the house closest to Oranc. Flames rose high from the thatch. Olwen, braids flying, her normally fair and peaceful features hard, sharp and pale, two spots of red, high on her cheeks marking her distress, burst from the dark doorway and snatched up the child Cas, youngest son of Amren. She ran from the burning house towards the dark shelter of the beech wood. Alerted by the child's scream, the two fire-raisers, who had set the house ablaze, lurched drunkenly to intercept her.

Oranc started to his feet, sling at the ready, even though far out of range. A cry of anguish forming at his lips was bitten back as the first of the pursuers fell writhing to the ground, a spear point protruding from the small of his back, bright arterial blood pulsing into the tired thin grass at the edge of the settlement. Berin vaulted over the hurdle fence that bounded the homestead, stepping between Olwen and the second of her two pursuers.

"Great Mother! Berin!" Oranc exclaimed.

Berin shouted. Oranc could not hear what, but the message was plain, for his outflung arm was pointing towards Oranc. Olwen hesitated, as though trying to find words, but Berin had already turned to face his adversary. Olwen turned and ran, with the wide-legged, hip-swinging gait of her sex, for the fallen hurdle that Berin had indicated and the last frail hope of sanctuary offered by Oranc's sling.

Berin fixed his eyes on those of his opponent, who, seeing him alone and unarmed, was advancing on Berin with a wolfish grin of anticipation. Berin edged towards the fallen raider, hoping to retrieve Aedd's spear. Seeing Berin's intention, the man of Afon'ken, his spear probing before him, moved in a scuttling crouch to put himself between Berin and his goal.

Berin began to back away, dodging from side to side to avoid the spear thrusts, each accompanied by a predatory grunt of effort from his pursuer. The marauder's eyes widened then slitted in certainty, as his body bunched for the death lunge. Berin felt the hurdle at his buttocks. "Mother!" he cried, and threw himself backwards over the fence, expecting at any and each of the long drawn-out fractions of an instant during which he tumbled, the searing thrust of the spear point as an all too brief prelude to oblivion.

Oranc switched his gaze from his sister panting so painfully slowly, child in arm towards him, to the plunderers' leader, who strode straight-backed and authoritatively through the smoke around the side of the house so recently set ablaze, calling to his men. At the reply, he drew the long bronze blade from its sash and, throwing back the cloak, unshouldered his shield. The tall man dropped into a long legged lethal crouch, the stance of a killer.

Berin had backed from sight to the certain fate that Oranc had read in the malevolent pursuit, but which mercifully had been hidden by the outstretched branches of the outermost beech. Sick at heart for his friend, white-faced, trembling with the responsibility that he now knew was his alone, Oranc saw the man with the great bronze blade round the corner of Amren's grain store. The man turned and loped after Olwen.

Olwen, now flushed from exertion, began to climb the ridge. She was tired, tired by her dash for freedom and the weight of the child, but also inwardly exhausted, bereft of

17

all thought and feeling by the pain and fright of the day, her actions now purely instinctive survival. The smooth going of the settlement had given way to the tussocked grass of the hillside. Olwen scrambled upwards, grasping , pulling , panting, no sight but the rank grass stems, no sound but the pounding of blood in her ears, the sobs of her snatched rasping breaths and the sobs of the child, no smell but that of her own fear. In her tiredness, Olwen tripped and fell forward.

With a shout of triumph, careless of all but what he now saw as a prize beyond all others that day, the raider redoubled his efforts. He was nearly up with Olwen and Cas when Oranc let fly. The round flint flew true. Some instinct, or perhaps the brief flitting shadow as the pebble crossed the last sunlight, caused the man to look up and raise his shield. The flint splintered on the bronze rim. A sharp shard pierced the soft jelly of the man's left eye, reaching deep to cut a white flash of pain of an intensity that until then the man had only known by inflicting it on his victims.

With a roar compounded of rage and agony the man clapped his shield hand to his injured eye, dropping to his knees with the shock. In his fury he looked up, searching for his assailant. Oranc, fitting a second pebble to his sling, quailed and stepped back, as though physically struck by the intensity of the venomous hatred that beamed from the single eye. Despite himself, he turned in panic, seeking flight, forgetting Olwen, Cas, Berin, forgetting Ermid, nothing mattering but the urgency of self preservation. A great roar filled his head as he tripped and fell.

"Will you lie there all day!" grumbled Aedd, stepping across the hurdle fence to retrieve his axe. White and trembling, Berin rose to his feet. Shakily he took the offered arm. Straddling the fence, he stumbled over the corpse of his assailant.

"Thank you Aedd," he said, searching out the blue eyes beneath the heavy brows, indicating the fallen raider.

The roof timbers of Amren's house collapsed in a shower of sparks, sending out a wall of heat. The two men retreated, Berin pausing briefly to retrieve Aedd's spear. Crossing the path taken by Olwen a few short lifetimes earlier, Berin looked once more towards the ridge.

" Olwen! Olwen and the boy?" Berin turned quickly; his blood chilled at the sight of Olwen fallen so close to the enemy. He was out of spear throw.

With a loud roar, the men of Ilws swept down over the brow of the ridge, Amren at their head. The leader of the men of Afon'ken rose from his knees, shield and blade raised in defiance. Then, realising that most of his band had already staggered off under the weight of booty and ale he turned and ran down the hill, nursing his injury. Amren knelt by his child and gently hugged him. The tide of rescue swept past them, and Olwen and Oranc who both slowly, almost unbelievingly, sat up, found each other and embraced. The few fire-raisers that remained rallied briefly to their leader at the entrance to the settlement, but seeing the numbers and fury of the newcomers, they fled before them, down the valley that led to their own Afon'ken.

Berin and Aedd, Amren and Cas, Olwen and Oranc gathered at the broken entrance to their shattered home, each searching for, and finding reassurance in the eyes and physical presence of their kin; each making their own silent tribute to Belu and Ermid, the dead of Com; each knowing that the world that they had known was irrevocably changed.

CHAPTER 2

The flickering flames of the camp fire sent the men's shadows skipping through the beech colonnades in poignant contrast to the flinty set to the two men's features, each mirroring the other's grief and lineage though not the passage of time.

"Well what are we going to do about them then? We can't just let the bastards burn us out, steal our stock, kill us..." spluttered Berin. "Father, we must stop them. We must fight."

"Dead... my Belu is dead," muttered Com, hunching his shoulders and pulling his cloak tighter about him, nursing his bound left arm in his lap. "That's what fighting brings...the death of loved ones." He bowed his head, overwhelmed by a desperate void, his eyes, dulled and dark-ringed, fixed on the crimson caves amidst the dancing flames, searching out memories of his first born. From within the nearby entrance to the flint mine came the shushed wails of sleep-starved, frightened children and a low persistent keening, the timeless, desolate, declaration of inalienable, unbearable loss.

"Not just Belu... Ermid too, don't forget him; and if we hadn't fought, there would have been a lot more of us dead," retorted Berin. "We were lucky poor Ermid gave enough warning to get the women and children away, and raised Ilws by sending Amren. Look, until today they've just run off a few cattle, but today was different. There were more of them, meaner, led by that big bastard who killed Belu. He's not from Afon'ken. He's an outlander. It's changed, Father. It's all changed. They mean to run us off completely. They won't stop until they have our land. Next time there will be even more of them. More of our dead unless we do something."

"It is for Dorn to keep the peace," responded Com dully. "The High Chief punishes all who break the peace of the West Way."

"Well where was he today, eh? He's done nothing," stormed Berin, "nothing since we went to see him last year when those bastards raided us. Peace of the West Way be buggered. What West Way? When was the last time a decent herd passed? Years ago, that's when. Dorn does nothing, nothing for us. He's..."

"Silence!" roared Com, at last turning his face to his son, stung from his miserable introspection. "You forget yourself."

"Father, forgive me. You are not alone in your pain. Belu is .... was my brother. Ermid... well, I hoped you would ask..."

"And Dorn is your High Chief, to whom you owe service and respect," interrupted Com grimly, shaking his head and returning to his reading of the flames. "We will return Belu and Ermid to the Mother, as is fitting," he continued, "then I shall plead our case with Dorn."

"But Father, we must defend ourselves. We need..."

"Go, go now in silence, lest I forget myself too."

Tight-lipped, near sick with anger and grief, trembling as much from frustration as from tiredness, Berin turned from his father. Unable to face grieving widows and mewling children, he chose the path down through the beech wood.

A camp fire beckoned from the remains of the settlement. Berin approached the group of men who sat talking quietly, bunched to one side of the fire-lit circle, as though afraid of being overheard by the still forms on litters raised on trestles at the limit of the firelight. His boots scuffed puffs of white ash, which rose to mingle with a pervasive stench of burning that hung like a misty shroud around the charred skeletons of the longhouses. Here and there, glowing embers shed sparks and spluttered briefly into flame, as whispers of the night breeze played about them. Smoke rose from still smouldering grain pits.

"You all right, Berin?" growled Aedd. "Have you eaten? Here, take this", he added, proffering a hunk of flat coarse bread and an ale pitcher.

Wearily Berin shook his head. "Father won't listen," he replied. "He thinks only of Belu. He talks only of the High Chief and his law. We are to fulfil the last rites and then he's off to beg help from Dorn. Has Alen come back yet?"

"I haven't seen him. If Dorn hasn't raised the levies, I hope he has the sense to stay at the ford 'til morning. I don't want him out there in the dark."

"Now that Dorn should deal with 'em an all," interposed Han, a man of Ilws, raising himself from his heels. "We've all given him service many a time. Aye, and provided food and ale for working parties. Remember the flood that washed out the stones at the crossing. Who put them back, eh? Then we chased them rustlers and there were those new fields we cleared for him on t'other side of Great River. He should raise the levies and sort these bastards out, so 'e should."

Aedd grunted. "Well he didn't do much the last time those Afon'ken bastards came up here. As for raising levies, as I remember you weren't too keen last winter when the outlanders stirred up Afon'panw."

"Aye, abed with his new wife he was," grinned Cadw cheekily. "On a nest of fox furs. Didn't see him nor her twixt the first snow and the last melt."

"Well I still say the High Chief should protect the likes of us," shouted the discomfited Han above the barracking laughter. "This is different. Not just a few cows and sheep and a broken head or two. There's men dead. Blood to be paid. 'Course 'e must settle it."

"How's Com's wound?" asked Aedd gently, turning from the argument.

"Not good. He can't grip or move his fingers. It's a deep slash, to the bone. Rh'on bathed it with woundwort water and pinned the edges, but he's in a lot of pain. Is she here?"

Aedd nodded towards a cloaked figure bent over one of the litters, wringing a cloth into a bowl. Berin followed Aedd's glance then hurriedly looked away.

"And Naf, how's Naf?" Aedd asked, filling the awkward silence as rapidly as it developed.

"Oh Naf's all right," replied Berin, relieved. "Just a flesh wound. It smarts and will scar badly, but he's lucky. He must have turned the blow just enough. He was chatting up Cigfen when I left, and she was making such cow eyes at him. I don't know how he does it. How are things here? Did you set guards?"

"Aye, but I doubt that them bastard's will be back tonight. That big outlander will have no stomach for a fight for a while. I put Amren about a thousand paces down the valley. I'll send Brys to relieve him. Kar is out on the ridge.

Young Cadw here will change with him. Madwyg. Elin and Anwen I sent back to guard against trouble at Ilws. The rest, except for Oranc are here. Where is Oranc by the way?"

"I left him to comfort his mother and sister, but Dana knows, he would be better here than with the old women at the mine," replied Berin.

Aedd glanced up sharply at the cutting edge to Berin's voice. "He's a brave lad. There's not many would have stood against that outlander," stated Aedd firmly.

"Well he surely saved Olwen and Cas," said Berin gratefully.

"Maybe he's done for that big sod of an outlander. Wounded eyes often fester," Aedd added hopefully.

"How badly did they hit us?" asked Berin.

"Brys's and Amren's hearths are gone completely. Mine too. We won't know for certain how bad the rest are until sun up," replied Aedd. "We saved a good part of your father's house, although it's a right mess. Ermid's is looted, but the fabric seems to be sound. Most of the grain pits are all right. A few over at my place and at Brys's were burnt out. Some grain at the top of others is scorched, of course. The pigs and the milch cows are gone and I suppose most of the stock from the valley pastures. They've taken all the cured furs, most hides and all the cloth. Your father's hounds are done for. Put the dog out of his misery myself a while back. The bitch lay dead at your father's door. My little bitch has run off, damn her useless yellow eyes. Always said you can't train a bitch with pale eyes. The cattle Amren drove before him from the lower garth should be on the top, and the sheep. We'll not starve, this winter, but there's precious little to trade come the festival."

"And their dead?"

Aedd jerked his thumb over his shoulder to the ruins of his home. "Down my old barley pits. Burned the bastards, then filled the embers in on top of them. Let the bastards lie with what they did," he growled. "Well, what would they have done with us," he retorted in answer to Berin's shocked expression. "Vermin, that's what they are, just vermin."

"Berin, they are ready now," said Rh'on softly, taking his elbow. "I have done all that I can to prepare them for Dana. I think that you should have this," she added, holding Belu's spear out to him.

Berin looked at his mother, seeing with a start, transparency at the temples and wispy, greying hair which false memory counted so full and lustrous black. He searched her eyes for unfathomable answers; he read defeat in the dark dullness. Where for all his life he had been accustomed to see joy or anger, he saw uncertainty and hesitation, where none had ever been admitted in Rh'on, comforter, healer, lore-keeper and mother. As her chin creased in response to a quiver at the corner of her mouth, he took her in his arms as she, head bent to his chest, sobbed bitter tears to his heart, yet held herself stiff-backed against his comforting hands.

"Your father wants Belu to take it with him, but I..."

"I know. It's all right. Don't..."

"No. Let me go on. Please. I think that you.... I mean... we need it. The Mother cares for her own. We can find another spear for Belu's journey. I want you to have it," she pleaded, raising her red-eyed, tear-streaked face as she straightened, stood back a pace and gravely handed Berin the spear.

Berin, suddenly formal, reached out and grasped the smooth ash handle. The bronze leaf at its tip gleamed dully in the firelight. "Thank you mother."

"Your father will agree when he is himself again. He misses Belu so." A partly strangled sob burst through her tightly bitten lips.

Rh'on turned to the men, silent spectators, unwilling voyeurs to the unfolding play. "Well, which of you fine men will bring me a torch?" she asked breezily, not entirely masking the underlying brittleness. "You Arec, will you help me? I must search out a jar of ointment before you light me back to the others."

Berin walked over to the litters on the edge of the firelight and stared down at his brother and Ermid. In the uncertain light they lay still, eyes closed, as though resting. Each was washed and groomed; even Ermid's habitual three day grey stubble had been shaved. There was no sign of their wounds. Each was freshly dressed and cloaked. Belu wore his favourite necklace of polished shale, gleaming black against the paleness of his kid shirt, next to the clan necklet of greenstone and amber. His cloak was fastened with the curved bone pin which he had made for his mother, and which she had always worn. A woven rush basket holding two bread cakes was placed at his feet with a pitcher of water. His best bow and a dozen arrows, six tipped with barbed bone and six with finely shaped flint heads lay at his side. Belu's belt held the flint knife with the wood and leather handle which Berin had made for him last winter. From the same belt hung the dark green-grey stone axe head on its sturdy ash shaft.

Images of Belu haggling for the axe with the trader from the West Way flickered in Berin's mind's eye. What stories the trader had told. Tales of the axe stone quarries, of a great chief and his quest for the blue stones in the mountains of the West. Tales of outlanders who come to the mouth of the Great River from across the salt sea, bringing bronze to trade for furs and hunting dogs.

Dorn has copper and gold, Berin remembered, a copper amulet and a gold ring, but no one else; such is the importance and wealth of Dorn of the Ford. No one else has it. Dorn has bronze. Axe heads, spears, daggers; such wealth. Belu had hunted long and hard for three winters for the soft white winter pelts of the stoat before he had a trade for the spear head at last winter's festival.

Now, at last, I have bronze too, Berin thought, as he first stroked and then thumbed the smooth hardness of the spear head, wondering at its ability to renew and hold point and edge without shattering. Suddenly shame flooded him, blooding his cheeks as he glanced involuntarily towards Belu, as though caught in an act of betrayal.

The whole clan assembled at the place appointed by Com for the burial of his son. Two pits side by side, stark white slashes in the green turf awaited their offering at the highest point of the chalk uplands within Com's land, overlooking the broad valley of the great river, the rolling pasture and wooded valleys falling away to Afon'ken and in the foreground, the open, juniper-pocked, stock-shaved ridge of the West Way.

Com climbed the nearest of the twin mounds of chalk taken from the pits. The wind whipped his grey hair, tangling it in his beard, stirring his cloak. Scudding clouds dispersed, hurried on and then mantled the sunlight. Rain spots flurried through the company, impartial in their choice of resting place.

"Belu and Ermid died for us," he cried. "We gather here as is our custom to add their deeds to clan lore, to remember their bravery and sacrifice and to return their bodies to Dana, the Earth Mother, who gives us life."

Rh'on came forward and stood at the head of the two litters on which Ermid and Belu lay. Head tilted back, eyes wide and unblinking beneath the wreath of barley straw, interwoven with red poppy and blue "sheep's bit", she intoned the familiar rhythmic verses of the clan lore.

Rh'on told of the Earth Mother's secret valley in which Man and Woman and their children roamed at will, naked as their companions the animals, which neither threatened nor feared them. She told of warm sunny days and moonlit nights; of cool sweet spring water, honey and fruit in abundance; of sturdy, well-favoured sons and lithe beautiful daughters.

Rh'on's face hardened as she recounted in erratic, discordant strains, the fall from grace. How Woman, tiring of fruit and honey, begged Man for meat; how Man called the hare to him and when it came to him, trusting, how he killed it and fed it to Woman.

She wept at the telling of the harsh rhymes which told of the punishment; of near perpetual darkness, unremitting snow, rivers and mountains of ice: of Man and Woman dying and their children starving for countless generations as the fruits withered and the bees shrivelled in the penetrative cold: of how the children of Man and Woman found only meat to eat: of how, since they too were meat, they suffered from fierce attacks by wolves, by bears the size of two men and by giant cats with teeth the length of a man's arm.

Rh'on smiled as she told how the Earth Mother finally relented; how she sent the descendants of Man and Woman fire from the heavens to warm them and flint from her bosom to guard them. In lyrical verses she recalled how their ancestors followed the reindeer along their migration along the chalk uplands, how they gathered fruit, roots and seeds along the way.

Rh'on's voice trembled a little as she recited the verses which recorded Dana's greatest gift, the gift of barley. How every spring their forefathers would find barley growing again at each of their camps, especially around the winter camp of Harac in the shelter of the gorge, below the ford used since time began by the reindeer to cross the Great River.

In reverent tones, Rh'on recalled Harac's covenant with the Earth Mother. His promise to honour all living things; to take only that which was needed; to kill only to eat; to return to her when called by Death the reaper.

Then cattle, sheep and pigs had renewed friendship with the descendants of Man and Woman, and dogs too, who at first had crept close to share the warmth of Harac's hearth in cold winters, also had come to be his friends and to share his work and meat. But the hare and his friends were still afraid and other meat-eaters remained jealous and unforgiving.

Rh'on named the line of Harac, whose high chiefs rest in the long barrow above the gorge, from Cadwen, Harac's firstborn son, clearer of the forests, the mightiest axe-man in all chalk land, to Cwl, Cadwen's grandson, the builder of the stones at the crossing, and so on through time. With each name, she recited a précis of their deeds, a description of their sons, landholding, wives and other children. Finally she came to Com, youngest son of Herget, brother of Hwlch, who was the father of Dorn.

Rh'on stopped. Her head dropped forward, her shoulders slumped with exhaustion. A collective sigh escaped the gathering.

Com raised his good arm. "My eldest son Belu fell at the gate to our homes, Ermid at his side," he proclaimed. "Though attacked by many times their own number, they fought bravely with bow, and when all arrows were used, with spears, killing one and wounding many. Their heroic stand allowed the remaining fighting men to gather and arm and to bring the women and children to safety. Their lives were sacrificed to the greater good. I ask that they be committed to the Earth Mother."

Rh'on prostrated herself at the feet of the litters. Arms outstretched, she grasped the turf, digging her fingers through the sod to the soil beneath. "Oh Dana," she intoned, "guide Belu and Ermid to your secret valley and receive them there with honour. May their journey be swift. May they find sweet water, plentiful game and good company on the way."

At a signal from Com, who stepped down from his white podium to take Rh'on's hand as she regained her feet, two men strode to the end of each litter and lowered them into the pits. Rush mats were placed over the bodies. Slowly, carefully, even gently, as if to avoid awaking the still forms, chalk rubble was filled back into the pits.

As the sods were replaced on the twin chalk mounds, Alen, who had returned just as the sun slanted through the beech wood, ashen faced with exhaustion, bruised and scratched from his headlong flight to the ford, turned away from the wounds to Mother Earth and buried his tear-streaked face in his father's belly. "They wouldn't come, father," he wailed in disbelief. "They wouldn't come."

CHAPTER 3

"Father, if it must be, let me go in your place," pleaded Berin earnestly, his eyes resting uneasily on the drawn, dark, pain-smudged face of Com. "You must rest. You're badly hurt."

"Aye, badly hurt I am, but the wound you see is the least of what pains me," Com replied grimly. "No, if there are hard words to be spoken between me and my cousin, I'll do it myself."

"But..." Berin started to protest, only to be interrupted by Com.

"Berin, my son, it seems we are much at odds these last days."

Dutifully Berin kept his silence, swallowing unspoken words, failing to stomach the acid anxiety they would have expressed. He turned from Belu's grave and watched the last of the line of returning mourners sink from view below the brow of the hill.

"Ah, you see things so clearly, so simply," continued Com. "Would that I could only see it so," he sighed, gently curbing further interruption, less by the touch that he now gave to Berin's arm, than by the new softness of his tone. "All my life, and for all the generations before me, who have followed the Mother and farmed our land, the sons of Harac have given hospitality to travellers on the West Way and traded with them. We have lived in peace, each on his own farmstead, harming no one, our hearths open to all. Now you want me to call all our folk to one settlement, to build a wall around us, to go with suspicion, aye, even fear, on our own land; to bar the gate at night and turn strangers away. It is not the way of Dana. Berin listen to me," he added softly, taking his son more firmly by the arm to emphasise his need for empathy. "Soon my time will be done. I feel it. What has just happened is not of my time, but the beginning of the next. Yours! You will be the leader of the clan soon. I have failed you. I have never even imagined that the task would ever fall to anyone but Belu, and after him, to his sons." A shadow flitted behind Com's eyes as he hurriedly continued. "You have not been prepared...not as Belu was. You will learn the pain and loneliness, yes and fear of decision, a fear so much more desperate than that dispelled so easily by action. You must learn to act for the greater good of all your people, who will look to you for guidance. It may be that you will choose to dispose as you ask me to order now. I hope not. It is not a life I would lead. You must... Ah well, time enough for that. I am master yet and must act as my head tells me. I will see Dorn tomorrow. I shall take Aedd."

"Father, please let me come with you," Berin begged, the words conjuring a memory of a small boy at the longhouse doorway calling to father and son, first bow and arrows fisted proudly.

"Berin, you must stay. Our people need guidance. There is much to be done. No, I'll take Aedd as my shield bearer."

Com turned from the living son to the dead. "Go in peace Belu, go in peace. You were ever a great joy to me." He started down the hill side, stopped after a few paces and half turned, shy of his tear-streaked cheeks, to Berin, who remained motionless at his brother's side, ever the acolyte, even to the dead. "I would like very much to raise a cairn over him when we have time. Yes, it would look well, a white chalk cairn on the roof of our land, a roof for our loved one."

"Now Aedd, be careful to watch for fever," whispered Rh'on. She glanced towards her husband and son in earnest conversation at the doorway, where other, busier figures were occasionally silhouetted, as she wrapped the honeyed barley cakes, which Com liked so much in a rush mat, before placing them carefully in the satchel which Aedd was holding open for her. "At the first sign, make an infusion of these," she said, thrusting a small leather pouch after the barley cakes, "and make him drink it. You might have to hold him down, he hates it so; such a baby."

"I'll look after him; he'll be all right," answered Aedd steadfastly, shouldering the satchel.

"I know you will Aedd. Bless you. And take care of yourself too."

With a fond smile of farewell, he turned and picked his way through the bustling workmen, adze chippings and fallen reeds from the thatchers on the roof.

"Ah Aedd, there you are. Well now, we might as well be off."

Aedd looked admiringly at his chieftain. Com was dressed in his

finest for his visit to Dorn, the High Chief; white kidskin shirt, brown, black and grey striped woollen tunic, kid breeches tucked into calf-high boots. A blue woollen cloak hung to his waist and was pinned at the throat with an ivory pin, made from a boar's tusk, with a single gold band at the broad end. Around his neck he wore the amber and polished greenstone necklace of his clan, symbolising the wealth of the tribe; amber from the north; greenstone from the west. A leaf-shaped bronze dagger was thrust through his belt. Aedd picked up Com's bronze-tipped spear and round ox-hide shield from where they rested against the door post.

"Aye, lets see what they've to say for themselves," Aedd replied stiff lipped.

Com and Rh'on embraced briefly; she looking intently, lingeringly, into his eyes, extending the moment, fixing his face in her mind; feeling his pain, hurt, anger, anxiety; sensing the approaching vacuum, the ebb; regretting, reliving, holding.

"Take care my love," she whispered. "Go with the Mother."

"Aye," he replied automatically, almost absently, as though already in Dorn's hall; as if knowing that his life's remnant was already beyond reach, in the fast stream, speeding, swirling, rushing forward to the falls. "Aye, you too."

Com and Aedd started with measured pace up the slope of the valley side, treading their own black shadows, retracing the mournful steps of yesterday to the level of the West Way. As they reached the ridge, Com paused briefly to glance towards his son's burial place on the height.

"Tell me again what Alen said," Com asked, turning right to follow the ancient route to the ford over the Great River.

" It was Urak that told him," answered Aedd, "or so I guess. A tall thin man he said it was. With long black hair, greasy like, and black eyes set right in his head."

"Yes, that will be Urak," answered Com.

"Well, Alen gets to the ford about dusk. He runs straight to Dorn's house and meets Urak at the gate. Alen explains what's happening, well that is after he gets his breath, and Urak pulls him through the gate and takes him over to his own quarters. A couple of Urak's men are there, drinking and gaming and he leaves Alen with them, telling him to stay put and he'll go and organise things with Dorn. Well there's a right carry on outside. Men yelling, dogs barking and all the geese honking. One of Urak's men goes to the door and there's men running everywhere, getting armed, torches and so on. Then it quietens down. Alen begins to fret a bit because he wants to go with them and then Urak comes back. He said we'd have to look after ourselves as best we could, he was sorry, but Dorn had sent the men off down the river to drive off some raiders. Well Alen starts to create about seeing Dorn. Urak says he's resting and not to be disturbed and that Alen can see him in the morning. Alen takes no mind, so one of Urak's men smacks him around the head. Urak tells him to mind his manners and to stay where he is until morning. Urak sends one of his men out on some errand and sits with the other for a bit then leaves. The one left on his own sets to drinking and after a while, falls asleep. Round about first light, when its all quiet, Alen slips out and comes home."

"Hmm," muttered Com, "you're sure he said that Dorn sent the men down the river?"

"That's what he said."

The ground began to drop away from them into a thickly wooded narrow valley. The two figures hurried on, the open grassland studded with juniper bushes giving way to a trail which became more marked as the valley steepened and the track had to cling to the hill side for support. The white transparency of autumn elder at the wayside contrasted with the blue-black umbrellas of berries and below them, the stately grandeur of golden beach. Nature's beauty went un-remarked by the two men, each lost in his own single mindedness.

As the ground levelled, the way became diffuse, a clearing through the woods rather than a path. The sounds of habitation, a barking dog, shrill-voiced children at play, the scolding mother, came to them on a light breath of air, pungent with wood smoke. Rattling leaves at their feet obscured and sometimes revealed a more persistent sound of hastening waters. Long legged pigs snuffled for beech nuts, looking up, runny nosed, to inspect the travellers with watery eyes from beneath floppy ears, their fat unshaven cheeks pouched with beech nuts.

The valley of the great river suddenly opened, very narrow and bright before them, the hills of the opposite bank close enough to shock in the clear autumn light. Harvested fields spread along the river side dotted with farmsteads; sheep and cattle grazed the stubble, fattening themselves, careless of approaching winter sacrifice. As they turned to follow a well worn path downstream, they saw ahead of them the long houses of Dorn's settlement set on a wide flat terrace, between the tumbling wooded hillside at the start of the gorge, and the scurrying river below the ford. Overlooking the peaceful scene from a shelf on the far side of the valley was the House of the Dead, the white-capped resting place of the chiefs of the line of Harac.

As they entered the settlement, they collected a train of children, chattering, screeching and wondering at the strangers and their mission. Small round bellied toddlers, snotty nosed and dirty kneed stared suspiciously, bellicosely from darkened doorways, or buried their heads in their mothers' skirts. Babes in arm spat out milky teats, round-eyed in amazement. One child, older than the rest ran on ahead to the great hall of Dorn.

They were met at the entrance to Dorn's compound by a bondsman who took arms and satchel and, depositing their belongings in the porch, and held back the hide curtain for them to enter.

"Greetings cousin and to you Aedd of Com. Come cousin, sit beside me here." Dorn indicated a lambskin-covered seat beside the hearth. "Urak told me you were attacked. Tell me. What happened?" Dorn's cragged and lined face struggled with displaying both pain at the obvious distress of his friend and counsellor and relief at his safety and presence once more at his hearth. Dorn was large-faced man, once large in body, but now stooped at the shoulders which were brushed by silver grey hair, held back from the high forehead by the band of kingship. Although still spare limbed, he was enfeebled by running so willingly the race no one wins.

"Will you take some mead, some barley cakes," he asked in a deep voice. "Come, I'm sure Aedd will. See to it Branwen," he said, the last in an aside to the dimpled, merry-eyed youngest daughter, the product of an afterthought shared with his third, and prettiest wife. Branwen rose from her place at Dorn's side. "Go with her Aedd. You are wounded Com. Sit, sit. Do you want for anything? Shall I send for Urak to doctor it?"

"Thank you, no," said Com stiffly, grunting with relief as he bent to the lambskin, cradling his arm in his lap, motioning Aedd to follow Branwen, then, when they were alone, looking directly at Dorn and adding "and I'm not sure that honeyed drink is fitting accompaniment to the bitter words I must speak." He almost relented at the look of hurt in his friend and patron.

"Belu's dead. Ermid's dead. But for their sacrifice we would all be dead and none but the crows would watch the West Way and farm the headwaters of Afon'panw. Our messenger to you returned alone, crying you would not come. We bury our dead and rebuild alone."

Dorn started. His face paled. "Oh, not your Belu, my dear friend. I am so sorry," he said flatly, numbly. Then, after a pause, remembering in shock..."Would not come. What story is this?"

"Why would you not come?"

"As to would not, I must suppose that we could not. Why even now our men still search the gorge for raiders. I sent them out before your message came. Would I had not. I knew nothing of your plight until yesterday morning when Urak told me of your messenger who came with the night and would not wait. We could not have helped; cannot even now, not until the men return. I am sorry, Com, truly sorry," Dorn said earnestly, leaning over to grasp Com's good arm, willing him to read sincerity in his words. "I know how you loved the boy. I did too."

The pain and affection were palpable, and could not be ignored. Wearily Com turned to his cousin. "Alen, Aedd's boy, our messenger, says he told Urak, who took him to his quarters and left him there. He thought your men were being armed to come to our aid, but Urak told him that you had sent them off down river and that we would have to look after ourselves as best we could."

Dorn shook his head. "Well I don't understand. That night I do remember ordering out the levies, but precious else. I had another of my headaches, drank one of Urak's potions and knew no more. I'll send for Urak. Branwen. Ah, there you are child," he said as she appeared around the wattle screen, "Send after Urak, and I want to know the moment, the moment do you hear, that the levies get back. Oh, and where's that mead?"

Branwen glided out to return shortly with a pitcher and a basket of barley cakes and cheese.

"These are bad, bad times," said Dorn, filling the silence left by the departing girl. "Unrest everywhere; everything is changing. No trade along the West Way. Haven't seen an axe peddler for two seasons now and the last even half decent herd was this past festival, and that from up north. Precious little reaches us on the river; only the old folk of the river still bring their furs, but nothing from downstream. The outlanders stop at Aberken now and trade up the Afon'ken valley. Senot and his people grow stronger by the day from the bronze trade. Bronze, always bronze. Men will do anything for it, it seems. These outlanders bring it by the boatload and still it is never enough."

"Senot! We should move against him," raged Com suddenly. "It was his men who raided us. He killed Belu. We should avenge ourselves."

"I fear it is too late," answered Com sadly. "He is already too strong. He has allies all along Afon'ken and he has made friends of the strangers too I hear."

"Aye, 'tis true," muttered Com darkly. "One led the raid on our hearths."

"Then it is already worse than I feared," replied Dorn. "Tell me. Tell me all that happened, though it pains you." He poured from the pitcher and handed the beaker to Com, who held it slack handed, untouched, the liquid surface a screen to recall for unfocused eyes the events which already were being buried in memory.

Dorn listened attentively, unmoving, not interrupting even prolonged silences, embroidered, but not broken, by the hiss of sap in the fire, the muffled chatter of women beyond the screens and the distant living sounds of the settlement. Agonisingly, scene by terrible scene, the whole story of the raid and its aftermath emerged.

"Berin's right you know." Com looked up startled at Dorn's words, shocked into physical response. "Oh please don't misunderstand," Dorn went on rapidly, "I am no admirer of disrespect and he must learn to guard his tongue if he is to serve in Belu's place, but there is a wisdom in that hot head of his."

"What do you mean?"

"Well it's true that this last raid is different. Senot means war. He's never dared before. It shows how close his links are with the outlanders, how strong he feels. That alliance has made him bold. Now Senot wants it all. He's always wanted the ford and the river traffic. He means to drive us out and take our land and he's using the strength of the outlanders to do it. He can't force the gorge, for all his bronze, but if the West Way were to be unguarded, if you and the men of Ilws weren't there, he could come in the back way. So, he hoped to drive you off, or kill you all. That was no raid for cattle. That was for bodies, dead or alive. Why else did he press on to the settlement, to you and the womenfolk when he had won the stock in the bottom valley pastures so easily. Why risk more, when so many head had been won so cheaply? Yes, Senot meant to kill you all. He will not be pleased that his men were diverted by ale, and by cattle and plunder, however rich the spoils. He will keep coming back until he succeeds."

"So what about Berin's idea?"

"Yes, I think we must try it, and quickly, for Senot will try again before the snow falls. But a ditch and bank should only be the start. A ditch and bank, with a stout palisade on top, maybe another ditch and bank in front; space inside for your stock, but not too big to defend, that is, with the help of your neighbours, and I shall send you some bondsmen. It must be on a height with steep slopes, well provisioned and with plenty of arrows and sling stones; shelters too, firewood. We can't match them in number, spread out as we are, but with time to rally, it's a different matter. Berin's idea will give us that time."

"And what of water? Without water they can defeat us in days, if help is delayed, or busy with its own attack," countered Com, with heavy irony that Dorn chose to ignore.

"Yes, that is a problem, but you cannot defend your present hearths, nor can you live for ever in the mine. We must find an answer."

"It will take forever to build," muttered Com, his stomach cramping, hot juice searing his throat at his new responsibilities. I'm not a man of war, he thought in panic. Mother, how is it come to this. Can we not go on in peace, as it has always been? Why in my time?

"... with Tarok's men from the outstation, now that the harvest is done, we should be able to raise say, three score for the building and still leave enough to guard the gorge and outstation." Dorn's suddenly revitalised voice pressed for Com's attention. "Why, we should be able to manage a fair sized bank and ditch in the space of a moon. We could use hurdles until the palisade is finished."

"Berin suggested that the hill just south of the settlement would be a good spot. It is very steep on three sides. The fourth leads along a ridge to Ilws. It would be very close to the houses," contributed Com, slowly thawing before Dorn's warming enthusiasm, yet feeling detached from the unfolding conversation, as though an observer.

Aedd enjoyed the cakes and ale, which Branwen brought to him, blushing and simpering, pushing her shoulders forward, as she bent before him, to loosen her breasts and tighten her cleavage, then skipping off to giggles and mirth in the kitchen. A stretch of the legs and a rest from the women's teasing tittle-tattle, that's what he needed now, Aedd thought. Strange, he mused, as he lumbered to his feet and set off slowly through the gate, taking the steep, pebble strewn path to the ford, how since his dear Grainne died in childbirth five winters ago, he had little patience for women's company. Women's talk was full of constant empty headed prattle. They invested shallowness and superficiality with seriousness. Duplicity was the norm in their dealings with each other. They pretended abject surrender to tempt confessions of weakness before striking for the throat. Branwen may, or may not want him, but Aedd knew that she wanted to boast to her peers of his reactions to her, more than she wanted the reality, if she even knew what that was.

At the ford, dug-outs were drawn up on a small beach. Huge sarsen stones, great knobbly brown leviathans, breasted the current, offering dry passage to the quick and nimble, and one a launching pad for a small, white throated, brown bird, bending and flexing its knees in pre-dive exercises.

Set back above the ford, where the river path hugged the narrow grassy flat between river and terrace, was a low bothey formed from alder saplings planted in a circle and

43

bent in an inverted bowl to the smoke hole at the apex. The frame was roofed with hide. At the entrance, a skeletal old man sat blind, but wise beyond his lost sense, in a welter of flint chippings. Flint nodules were stacked waist high about him. From time to time he took a flint from the largest pile, lovingly caressing its curves and patina, rudely exploring its crevices and cracks with horny finger and thumb, before placing it on one or another of the smaller piles. His eyes were stark white, quite sightless in cicatrixed sockets, which were folded into a furrowed face.

Aedd walked slowly towards him. "Aedd of Com," the old man said clearly, "you are well. Clearly unfit sacrifice for Afon'ken and no doubt still choosing greenstone for your axe before good honest flint, thereby taking food from the mouth of an old man who has done you no harm."

"Anoeth, you old rogue. So you're not dead yet. You've tricked another young girl to mince your food for you, and not just that I'll be bound."

The old man chuckled, revealing four blackening yellow stumps, barely straining the dark, gummy cave of his mouth. Then as quickly as the smile had risen, his face fell, a crumpled parchment of experience.

"You were attacked. How is everyone?"

"Oh, so you know."

"Aye, word came down from the big house, but not how you fared. I am glad to know you are well."

"Belu and Ermid are dead. Com and Naf wounded, Com bad. Most of us are burned out. Much of the stock's gone. We sent here for help and my young 'un comes back and says the men of the ford won't come. What's going on Anoeth? What's going on?"

44

"Belu and Ermid you say. May they rest with the Mother. It's a bad business Aedd, a bad business," he said, shaking his head. "Two good men dead and ours all out chasing fancies."

"Why didn't they come?"

"Couldn't, could they. They were all out chasing cattle thieves. Pah! A chill is all they're likely to catch. They'll never catch no cattle thieves. Ain't none and never was."

"What do you mean?"

"Well stands to reason, don't it. If you want to stop honest folk from helping their friends, you get 'em running, for good reason mind, or so they're to think, in the opposite direction."

"The levies were tricked you mean."

"Aye, that's right. All our enemy's got to do is stir up a few cows, a bit of yelling and bellowing like, then off. Don't even need the cattle, only hold them back, travel too slow with them. All our men are then out blundering about down river and you lot are left to look after yourselves."

"Well I'll be damned. The cunning bastards!"

"You'll take some ale with me Aedd." It was more statement than question.

"You've never heard me say no."

"Ened, Ened, come here girl."

The skin door of the bothey was pulled back. A slim girl came forward and knelt at the old man's side. Her knee caught at the hem of her simple woollen shift, tightening it over burgeoning buds. A flint scrap pressed a white dent into the other uncovered begrimed knee. She shifted

45

slightly; the flint stuck to her skin, the skirt released, lay wrinkled on her thighs, freeing her breasts. She glanced shyly at Aedd, brushing lank black strands of hair back from a face smudged as grimy as her hands and knees. For a moment Aedd read something, some sort of expectation, a flash of hope in her dark brown eyes, before they were turned down.

"Ale girl; a pitcher and two bowls."

Quickly the girl rose to her feet which were spread wide and callused, feet unused to shoes. As she turned to her task the rancid pungency of unwashed womanhood caught Aedd's breath.

"I knew it, you old devil," said Aedd, a little later, wiping the froth from his lips with the back of a sleeve, as the girl retreated to the door of the hut.

Anoeth was silent as he took a long pull from his bowl.

"Ah, no one makes ale like Cigfen. And thank you for the kind thought. If it were only so, but I fear it would be the death of me, even if my old friend could raise himself for the occasion. Bless the Mother for memories. No, she's a good girl. Looks after me well enough and helps out baking the flints, as she is now. Glad for that, I am. I kept burning me self. Not the same since the second eye went."

"She's not from around here."

"No. Tarok's wife sent me her bond from the outstation. He laughed. "Broc, who brought her, reckoned Tarok wanted to keep her for himself. Ened's a bit of a beauty by all accounts, not that I'd know; a black night and the inside of a flint mine, they're each the same to me.

46

"Where's she from" Aedd asked, draining his bowl with relish and refilling it from the pitcher.

"Tarok's missus bought her from the river people. They picked her up near dead with fever close to the headwaters of the Great River. At first they thought she were touched by the Mother, she raved all sorts of mad tales, Broc said. She don't talk much here though, which suits me fine. Just gets on with her work; gets me grub. She's a good girl. Ain't you Ened?" he added, as the girl came out of the hut carrying a leather bucket. Ened smiled quickly in response, as she glided down the path to the river.

"Pour me some more Aedd. Tell me what happened."

Aedd's face hardened. At first grimly then simply and sadly Aedd related the events of the past few days. Anoeth listened intently.

"Aye a bad business Aedd. Times are changing. No saying where it will all end. Nothing comes up the river. The outlanders have stopped coming. Not much from the west neither. We still have the flint traders, the amber and wool trade from up north. The river folk bring their furs still, more to the outstation than here. In fact Broc was saying that there's more of them, seems they're pulling back from the headwaters. There's raiding parties out there, though what they'd want in that wet wilderness I don't know....must be something bad going on out west to stop the traders getting through, and the river people too. They're pretty wild them lot and don't scare easy. Still, what should I care; flint's my business. Here, the traders brought me some good stuff the last time, you can tell by the ring to it."

He picked up two partly shaped axe heads and struck them lightly together. "See, much better than the stuff you get here, but they have to go deep for it. They can't tunnel like we can into the side of a hill and follow a seam. They have to dig all the way straight down until they finds it. When it gets real deep they lose a lot of men. The pits fall in as they try to follow a seam out from the shaft. What a life."

"Hi there, Iowerth, over here," Aedd yelled to the man leading a band of two dozen weary, begrimed men, shambling their way up the riverside, shoulders slumped, spears trailing, shields slung across their backs.

"Why it's Aedd, Aedd of Com. Well I'm blessed. What are you doing here?"

"Did you catch them?"

"Nah, didn't even frighten them. All the way down to Aberpan and it's as peaceful as the grave. None of the farmsteads lost anything, nobody heard anything. In and out of the water enough to give me ducks' feet. Ruined a good pair of boots. Only thing missing is old Cerdic. Probably drunk under a bush. Conwen and his men are looking for him now. Cerdic will be right pissed off though. Two of his clamps are burned through. He must have left them for a while for that to happen."

"Who's Cerdic," asked Aedd in an aside to Anoeth.

"Charcoal burner. Lives out on the slopes this side of the river. Where the gorge begins to open out again."

"Give me some ale Anoeth, for pity's sake," asked Iowerth, throwing himself to the ground next to Aedd, dismissing his troop to their homes, "I've a tongue in me like a boar's brush."

"Ened, Ened, bring more ale," called Anoeth, "and another bowl. Damn me, where is the girl."

"Drawing water at the ford when we passed, and having a bath too by the looks," Iowerth reported then leered at the girl straining at the handle of the full bucket. Her shift clung damply to her thighs, vee'ing tightly as she stumbled lop-sided, white knuckled, as much at Iowerth's too obviously carnal interest as from the weight of the water in the pails. The berry tipped breasts trembled and thrust aggressively at the damp loosely woven material, threatening to burst free of the constraining neckline. Her hair, black as jet and shining wet, was combed back from her face to hang as a mourning veil around one side of her neck, to rest on the initial swell of her breasts. Her neck was arched and finely formed, though starkly emphasised by straining tendons. Her face was fine boned with a delicately chiselled nose, large eyes, glinting, darting, searching for neutral ground, avoiding contact, a generous mouth now clamped in determination and annoyance. Aedd shifted his seat. Such stirrings had become unfamiliar enough to discomfort him with their return.

"Ooh, lend her to me Anoeth," Iowerth groaned. "What a waste on an old man."

"Ened, fetch a bowl for Iowerth and more ale whilst you're about it."

As she bent to retrieve the pitcher, Iowerth rounded his eyes, gawking at the round mounds of her buttocks stretching the fabric of her dress.

"Anoeth, the pick of Lunger's litter for one night with Ened," Iowerth pleaded.

"Away with you. What would I do with a hunting dog. And who would face Angharad? Not all the hunting
49

dogs in Britain would be worth a tongue lashing from that shrew of yours. It's time you put her with child."

"Aye, so I would if I could only get near her. How a maiden so soft and fondling, so mooning, promising and generous, becomes a wife so waspish and tart beats me."

"What, beats you too?" laughed Aedd.

"Perhaps that's the trouble. You should try that the other way around Iowerth," cackled Anoeth.

"What are you doing here Aedd?" asked Iowerth, ruefully changing the subject.

"I escorted Com. He came to ask Dorn why our plea for help is refused." Iowerth looked up questioningly, eyebrows raised.

"We were attacked two days past by the men of Afon'ken. Belu and Ermid were killed. But for Ilws coming when they did, we would all be done for."

"Mother!" exclaimed Iowerth. "Belu and Ermid. Oh damn. I'm sorry. But what's this about help refused?"

"When they attacked, I sent Alen to Dorn for help. He came back alone first thing the next day. Poor little bugger was proper upset. Said you lot would not come. Com was right put out. We completed last rites as fast as decent, if you know what I mean, then came straight here this morning, despite his wound. He copped a bad one on his shield arm. Big bastard of an outlander with a great bronze blade, fully a pace long. Mother it was sharp, and heavy. I had real trouble with him, I can tell you. Anyway, turned out you were all out down river."

"Here, is that Conwen?" asked Aedd, pointing towards a column of men approaching the ford."

"Aye, looks like someone's hurt. Who's that between the poles?"

Aedd and Iowerth got to their feet and walked down to meet the approaching men.

"What's up?" Iowerth asked the grim faced leader.

"Cerdic," replied Conwen. "We found him all right. A bit late for the poor old dotard though. His throat's been cut."

"Urak, there you are at last. Where have you been? Something terrible has happened. Afon'ken raided Com's people. Belu and Ermid are dead, our cousin wounded, their homes are plundered and burnt."

Urak strode quickly to Com's side, dropping to one knee in polite greeting to an elder, his thin face drawn into a mask of concern.

"It hurts me to hear of my cousin Belu and kinsman Ermid, and to see you so sorely wounded. Please, let me attend to your wound. I'm sorry I was not here to greet you, I have been making an offering to the Mother."

"It is fine, thank you Urak," Com replied. "Rh'on is skilled in your arts and has seen to it."

"Then a draught of mine to alleviate the pain."

"Urak," Dorn interrupted. "Com's hurt at this moment lies elsewhere. He feels betrayed because we did not help him and angry at our treatment of his messenger, the boy Alen. I remember you asked for the levies to be raised, that Cerdic had brought news of raiders at the southern end of the gorge, then....well your potions are very effective. What happened after that? Please explain to Com; I will not bear his displeasure any longer."

"Surely," answered Urak, rising to his feet, slowly pacing back and forth.   "The lad arrived at the gates not long before sundown, out of breath and very upset. I took him to my quarters to settle him down and listen to his story. You had one of your headaches; I wanted to spare you. When I had heard his grim news and realised the gravity of it, I tried to tell you of the new development, but the sleeping draught I had prescribed for you earlier was taking effect. You had just ordered the levies to defend the gorge. I had to make a decision for the greater good."

Com grunted. Urak glanced towards him inquisitively and continued. "Either I tried to recall the levies in darkness, causing great confusion and leaving us exposed to a threat in the south, to send help, which might in any case arrive far too late to do any good, or I left things as they were, in the hope that Com would cope, as the Mother be thanked he clearly has, though at great sacrifice. When I returned to my quarters, the lad became abusive, hysterical. One of my men, too zealous in my defence, slapped him to quiet him. I have since dealt with him. Father, Com, forgive me if I did wrong. I am shaman. I am no warrior."

There was silence. Urak stopped pacing and relaxed, confidant, almost languid in manner and gazed open-faced at his father and at Com sitting beside him. Dorn looked first at his son, then at Com. Com, sensing his cousin's rising expectation, looked up from the fire which had held his attention these last minutes.

"Hmm. I think you acted for the greater good, Urak," Com said, a wry smile of self mockery cracking the set of his drawn features. "You have shown judgement that I would wish for my own son, though I cannot admit that I have enjoyed the result."

"Well that's settled," said Dorn, with obvious relief, sitting back and relaxing his tensed frame. "Some mead Com, then we will eat, for my stomach tells me the day is well advanced."

"Aye, I'll drink with you cousin. As to eating, perhaps a little broth and I'll retire early."

"Are you ailing? We have tired you. I am sorry," replied Dorn.

"No, no," answered Com testily. "I have no appetite."

"There is..., well another matter I would raise with you..." said Dorn, looking up at his son and motioning him to the door. As Urak left, he continued ... "it is the question of a husband for Branwen."

Com was suddenly alert, but answered impassively. "Oh and, what do you have in mind for her?"

"Well, I thought of Berin, actually, if you agree. It would be a good match. She is obedient, well taught by her mother before she died, Dana rest her, and pretty. He's now heir to a chieftaincy and by all accounts a young maiden's dream. It would strengthen our bonds, something worth considering in these days," he added slyly, cocking his head on one side to gauge the reaction to his words. Com was nodding, Dorn noted, barely perceptibly, but nodding all the same. Good, thought Dorn, he's hooked.

Dorn needs me to guard the back door, mused Com. Let him dwell on that thought. Com was too experienced as a trader to agree at once. He allowed the silence which followed Dorn's suggestion to draw on until it became uncomfortable. Com finally broke the stillness.

"It is as you say, cousin, a good match for the children. But think, should you risk your daughter with us at what has become a frontier settlement, full of danger from raiders? We are few and Berin is poor, the poorer for our losses to the raiders. Even with my help he would have difficulty to raise the bride price fitting for the daughter of the High Chief."

"On the subject of bride price, cousin, I think we can come to a private arrangement. I have been considering making you a gift of cattle to compensate for those lost in the raid. A generous gift, say two hundred head, would allow Berin to meet his dues without leaving you uncared for."

Com's eyes glistened; but for his injured arm he would have rubbed his palms together, they itched so unbearably. He remained impassive, willing his features to betray none of the elation he felt. Where's the catch? he thought, there's always a catch.

"The girl, of course, is well provided with the usual personal and household goods, you need have no fear on that score."

Com wondered if she counted amongst her personal possessions the famous and fabulous collection of jet and amber jewellery, which her mother, a woman from the north, had brought to her marriage bed.

"Of course, I am very fond of her," continued Dorn, and I would want her safety to be of paramount importance. I thought I would leave ten men with you when the stronghold is finished."

Ah there's the rub, thought Com rapidly. They will outnumber us and be beholden to him. I will be little more than a dupe, keeping his back door safe, whilst taking all the risks on us.

"But cousin, I must rely on my fighting men to obey me instantly. With them thinking always to guard the girl, there will be confused loyalties. I could not guarantee the safety of the West Way with such men."

Sly old fox, thought Dorn, wishing he had offered only five men, as he began to realise that he was going to be bested. "I would make it clear to them that they are to obey you," he said.

Com pretended to mull over this suggestion, sucking his teeth and pursing his lips in an outrageous charade. "But if you were attacked too, what then of their allegiance?" Com countered, scenting victory.

The silence lengthened. What had started as a convenient way of alleviating a nagging feeling of guilt for his friend's recent losses, at the same stroke securing his flank and strengthening his control, was turning into an expensive exercise. Damn him, Dorn raged inwardly. The West Way must be secured or the gorge cannot be held. Without the gorge, the house of Harac must fade into obscurity. It's clear, the price must be paid.

"Very well Com, you shall have their bonds. Not for nothing are you known as the fox of the West Way. But you owe me a favour, a very big favour."

For the first time in days, Com laughed. "You shall have a fine son-in-law."

Berin bent and retrieved his pack, quiver and arrows. The carefree hunt, and indeed the panic which had followed it, seemed a lifetime ago; he was almost surprised to find his possessions in the same state in which they had been left so hurriedly. He restrung his bow with the new string, which he had brought with him. For a moment he considered retracing his hurried steps of the day of the raid to the escarpment, where he had left his kill; then shrugged off the idea. Crows and foxes were sure to have eaten their fill and he could not fancy their leavings; besides there was no shortage of meat at the settlement, yet.

It had been a busy day, he reflected. The settlement was rapidly returning to a semblance of normality. The gaunt, charred skeletons of the burnt-out houses had been pulled down and all the debris piled to one side, on the ruins of Aedd's longhouse. Berin wanted to bury the Afon'ken corpses deep and had half a mind to start the next midden on the site. His father's house stood firm, cleansed of all trace of the interlopers. Ermid's house too was restored. The main structure of a new house for Brys was complete to the ridge pole, but still wanted thatch and walls. The corner posts of Amren's new house had been set in pits and back-filled with rubble. Berin had postponed the start of Aedd's new house until his friend's return. No doubt Aedd would want to grumble about the choice of site. Enough timber and straw for thatching had been collected to complete all three, and when he had left the settlement, the men had been happily hard at work, adzing the raw timber to shape, whilst boys and womenfolk cut to length and bundled the thatching straw.

There had been no sign of their tormentors. A scouting party sent down the valley had brought back a bundle of cured hides, a lame cow and two pigs, and a report that all was quiet. Guards were set, and a relief rota organised. The clan was coming to terms with its losses and working well at returning to normality; all in all, a satisfactory day. Tonight the clan would return to sleep in the two surviving houses, their first night out of the flint mine since the raid.

Berin sat on the bank and watched the sun dropping slowly over the ancient West Way, savouring the last, rich, warm, golden light on his face. He plucked a straw and chewed it reflectively, turning over in his mind and ordering the mountain of tasks to be achieved in the new day.

There was a rustle and Olwen sat beside him. "It's so peaceful now, it's hard to believe all that happened," she said.

"We will none of us be the same as we were," he began, but faltered. Berin had not heard her approach, so locked was he in his own thoughts. Now the warm womanliness of her so close to him drove all careful consideration from his mind, constricted his throat and dried up conversation. I must say something, he thought desperately, or she will think me a fool. But he had no wish to talk of the events that were better pushed from memory. He wanted only to talk of Olwen and himself, but words failed to form; his mind was a total blank. He could feel a heat emanating from her, smell a heady muskiness the meaning of which, though unclear, was unmistakably exciting. She said nothing, just looked where he looked, content simply to wait, a silent companion. Her slim, down covered forearm lay so close to his, it burned. He could feel his hairs standing from his gooseflesh, extending, reaching to touch her. He inched his arm towards her. A warm answering pressure assured him that his touch was welcome. Slowly he extended his fingers, sliding his hand sideways across hers, taking it, twining fingers with hers, pressing, touch answering touch.

He turned to her, taking the straw from his mouth. She lay back on the bank, still holding his hand, but cradling the back of her head on the bent elbow of her other arm. The pose flattened her breast, yet as Berin was now so aware, emphasised her nipples, pressing to escape through her shift. Her expression was serious. Not stern or unhappy, but concentrated on the here and now. He noted for the first time a faint brush of freckles across the bridge of her finely chiselled nose, a fading summer's souvenir, and down on her cheeks. The evening breeze waved wayward strays from her hair across her lips. He brushed them away with trembling hand. She pursed her lips, lifting them to his fingers, her eyes fixed on his.

Berin leant over her, replacing fingers with lips of his own. Sweet, soft and cool, lip to lip they hung, time suspended, all senses concentrated on the interpretation of the new wonderful textures. Olwen's lips trembled. Berin's tongue tip traced their inner edges, followed each slight parting, every offered opening, lightly at first, calling appeasement, then firmly, erect, proudly demanding surrender and at last claiming possession as Olwen opened her mouth to him. Olwen brought her arm from behind her head to hold him, pulling him hard to her, pressing her vanquished mouth to his, excited beyond all measure at her own capitulation.

Berin's fingers, so gentle at her lips, traced the angle of her jaw to test the baby soft down on her cheek, then down the vulnerable line of her throat, crossing quickly, on quivering tips, the plain beneath to cradle the swelling of her breast. His fingers and palm held her, warm and fluttering. Berin wondered at a texture at once so firm and soft, elastic and yielding. He lifted his thumb slowly to brush the nipple, standing proud, lifting the material of her dress with its hardness. Olwen moaned, sucking at his mouth, yielding yet further to his predatory lips and tongue.

Berin drew back. Eye to earnest eye they gazed at each other. He became aware of a huge tenderness in himself, awed at his new-found sentience; she became conscious of the fragility of her control over her own feelings and over both of their actions. Berin moved his hand to her neckline, taking the drawstring between finger and thumb. Olwen covered his hand with hers; not resisting, simply making a quiet statement.

"Berin! Berin!" The call hung quavering high in the air, insinuating between testing fingers, and shared heartbeats, demanding attention, calling for postponement of further surrender and possession, now temporarily mortgaged to prolong bewitchment.

Berin stood and called out "I'm over here Oranc," then turned to help Olwen to her feet, she, shy now, half turning away as she smoothed her skirt.

"Oh, er.. right." Oranc glanced quickly at his sister, colouring at the realisation of his obvious intrusion, then continued hurriedly. "You'd better come down. Sorry, but Han and Auron are arguing again. Han wants to go home for the night, says he's been away for too long and that Auron should stand his watch. 'Course Auron says he just wants to bed his wife."

Berin turned to Olwen with a wry, apologetic grin. "Sorry, I'd better sort them out."

"Yes, you go on," she answered.

Berin held her gaze for a long moment before striding away, Oranc at his side. As they sank from view below the brow of the hill, Olwen gazed after them, hugging her knees to her breasts against the evening chill and in simple delicious delight.

CHAPTER 4

Aedd held out the steaming bowl to Com in his bed. Com grimaced and pulled himself up on his good elbow.

"Must I?" he sighed.

"I promised Rh'on you would drink it if you got feverish," Aedd answered.

"Aye, I suppose you're right. It's been a very trying and tiring day. I suddenly feel very old," Com said and reluctantly took the bowl, sipping and shuddering as Aedd fussed with the pillows and bedclothes.

"I'll leave the taper burning. There's a spare beside it and red coals in the hearth if it burns out," added Aedd, turning to go.

"Stay a while Aedd," suggested Com. "I'm glad that after what you and I have learned today, our doubts are set at rest and our friendship with Dorn is as it has always been. I just could not believe that my cousin would ever refuse us help."

"Well I'm not too happy. They never found a sign of those raiders. What's more, it's a sight too much of a chance that Cerdic being the one to give the alarm and then being found with his throat cut.

"Aedd," said Com sternly, "surely you aren't suggesting that Dorn has betrayed us?"

"No more I am, but someone may have betrayed him. That there Cerdic is the key, but he's dead, so I expect we'll never know."

"You may be right," answered Com thoughtfully, "but do not talk of this again to anyone. It is very important that we keep our good relations with Dorn at the moment. The safety of the settlement depends on it. You must not say or do anything to upset my plans. Swear it Aedd!"

"I swear." Aedd looked enquiringly at his chief as he made the expected response, but saw only that the pained look of distaste at the medicine had been replaced by the crafty look of the trader hiding his final price.

"I think I will sleep. Go now Aedd, thank you. Remember, not a word of your suspicions to anyone."

Aedd dropped the hide door curtain behind him, shutting out the wan light from the taper and hearth, which anyway could not compete with the darkness of the night outside. He made his way to his own guest accommodation, took off boots, breeches and shirt, stacked charcoal from the pile onto the hearth, and doused himself from the bucket which stood next to the duckboard over the drain in the corner. He checked for a spare taper, then lay down on the straw palliasse, covered in a quilt made from fox and hare pelts.

Tired though he was, sleep eluded him. Something is badly awry, he thought. Somewhere there is a clue, but where. Cerdic gave the alarm; the alarm proves to be false; Cerdic is murdered. Com is convinced that Dorn is alright; so too he is, there's no malice in the old man. But is he being tricked and by who? That clever son of his, Urak, perhaps? But why? He is shaman, lore keeper to the high chief, already rich and privileged. Urak's explanation that Com told sounds so reasonable. Aedd shook his head as though to shake some sense into his jumbled thoughts.

A movement at the hide door sent the flame at the end of the taper sputtering, shooting swirls of black smoke to the high pitched thatch, flickering long shadows, which bent and bowed where roof met wall. Ened stood at the entrance, the hide falling behind her. In the flickering light of the taper and the dull glow of the charcoal in the hearth, her form, which Aedd knew was softly rounded, appeared angular in the sharp contrast of light and shadow. Strangely this effect obscured her outline, disguised expression, yet also set her apart from the grotesque dancing parodies of her body, which shadowed her on wall and pitch of the guest room.

She stood silent, looking at him. Finally Aedd asked "What is it Ened, what do you want?"

"My master sent me. I am to tell you that he has learnt that Cerdic is named as the messenger who brought the warning, but Cerdic did not pass the river road the night of the raid."

Aedd's brow furrowed deeply as he wrestled with the new information. So Cerdic didn't pass the river road that night. Suddenly it was clear. No Cerdic, no warning and they were betrayed, betrayed by Urak. It had to be, but why? Hot anger welled up to be checked and dampened by cold determination. What does Anoeth know? Can it be proved; the word of a blind man against that of the lore keeper, the son of the High Chief. Who would believe it? Would Com? The old fox is hatching something and wouldn't thank me for such news. He doesn't want trouble. Mother! it would be trouble all right. Urak, curse him, if it's truly him I could slit the bastard from crutch to throat, Aedd thought viciously.

The girl stood waiting.

"Did he say anything else?"

Ened cast her eyes down, looking at him from under lowered lids "..er and.. and.."

"Yes, what is it girl," Aedd prompted impatiently.

"... and I am to stay if you want me to."

The words spoken so softly struck Aedd like an axe blow, leaving him breathless. The silence lengthened. Aedd looked at the sad-faced girl, who started to tremble under his gaze.

"Were you to be free of your bond, what would you wish?"

Ened, eyes still cast down, shuffled from one foot to the other, hands clasped in front of her, fingers entwining nervously.

"Come Ened, answer me," Aedd said after a while.

"Sir, I would wish to go home," she said softly, lifting her head defiantly, tears streaming down her cheeks, sobs wracking her slight body. "I would go home!"

Aedd allowed the girl to cry unchecked for some while then said gently, "Ened, come here, sit by me. Where's your home? Tell me about it?"

Ened stared at him from red rimmed eyes, surprised at the gentleness of his voice.

"Come," he said, "come here, sit," patting the furs at his side. Hesitant, doe-like, she stepped across the space dividing them. She sat shivering on the edge of his bed. Her skirt rode up goose-fleshed thighs.

"Where do you come from. Tell me of your home, of your people."

Ened looked at him with doubtfully. Aedd straightened to ease a cramp. She started. Aedd smiled reassuringly.

"Go on," he said.

Ened was tense. She found it hard to grasp that this man did not immediately seek to touch her. Falteringly she decided to take him at his word.

"Sir, I... I am of the line of Swlys. I come from...from a place far off in the west," she began hesitantly. Then, realising that Aedd really did want to know and that his request was not a gambit, a preamble to the expected advance, she continued with a little more confidence. "We live by a spring in a wide valley, surrounded by hills and forest. The waters that come from the ground are warm; a gift from the Mother. My people live much as you do. We raise sheep and cattle, keep pigs and geese, grow barley, hunt and fish and gather wild fruits and roots, just like your people. We collect wool and weave our cloth, cure hides and furs, brew ale. We make tools of stone and bone. We trade, for axe stones, greenstone and flint, and we trade at the western sea for salt and I've heard for bronze too."

"What? You trade at the western sea for bronze? Who with?" Aedd interrupted, wondering that the outlanders had reached as far west as the western sea.

"Why Sir, with the men from the end of the earth," replied Ened. Seeing Aedd's puzzlement, she explained. "If you travel westwards from my home for...oh, a moon, always keeping the sea on your right hand, you come to a wild high rocky cliff. There, they say, for I have never been there, that the sea is on your left hand too. It is the end of the world. In that land, it is said, men dig stone from the streams and rivers and from the earth, and with fire and magic, turn them into bronze. So it is said..." she added defensively as Aedd looked doubtful..." for it sounds a fable to me, yet so it was told me by my father, and his father as a young man, went there and saw for himself.

"You mean they were not outlanders?" interrupted Aedd.

"Oh no, I don't think they're outlanders. Folk say they look much as we do and live as we do. They follow the Mother, which the outlanders don't. No, they're not outlanders."

"You said once, "Aedd asked, intrigued. "Do you not still trade with them?"

"I don't think that there's been trade with them in my lifetime. I haven't seen them, but then I've never been to the sea. Anyway, everything stopped... changed when the troubles started." Ened stopped talking, her head fell forward, her long black hair covering her face like a curtain drawn on an inner sorrow; a stifled sob escaped her.

Aedd reached out and smoothed the hair at the back of her head. Startled, she jerked away. Aedd pulled back his hand as though burnt.

"Tell me of these troubles you talk about," asked Aedd gently. For a moment he thought she would not continue, then she wiped her eyes with the back of her hand and faltering a little at first, she went on.

"Men came from the high chalklands in the east. They asked our young men to help them. They wanted them to drag great axe stones, the size of two men, up the river and beyond, to their own land. They paid in axe heads, so many of the young men were eager to go. One year, when our men wanted to return for the harvest, the

66

easterners refused to pay them, bound them and forced them to work. Then war parties came for the rest of us. We were taken by surprise, but in any case we could not resist, because most of our warriors were already taken. The men were forced to work on the stone gangs. I watched my brother clubbed down and dragged off as he tried to defend my father. I don't know where they are, or even if they are still alive."

She sobbed, low harsh cries of misery wrenched from deep within her slight frame, which trembled and heaved. Aedd sat forward and folded her in his arms, cradling her head on his chest, gently rubbing and patting her back. She cried unrestrainedly, soaking Aedd's chest. Tenderly he held the girl until she had cried herself to silence. Taking several shuddering deep breaths, Ened continued as if to exorcise her memories.

"The women and children were driven for two days and then herded into in a big round pen, with a ditch and a bank with a fence beyond that. There were guards on the bank; it was impossible to escape. They gave us no food or shelter. The sick and weak died and were thrown in the ditch. The next day, outlanders came and bought us, just like cattle. My mother and sister were taken in a different group to mc, the Mother alone knows where and what's happened to them. I'm so frightened for them; the outlanders are so different. It was said that instead of honouring the Mother, they worship the sun." She shuddered at the heresy.

"I was bought with four others, by a huge outlander. Our wrists were tightly bound with rawhide thongs and we were all roped together by the neck. I was the first in line. We were marched northwards and eastwards through the chalk lands, and forced to carry the outlander's packs. He and his men beat us if we stumbled or fell. The first night the outlander set me apart from the others, tying me to a tree. I think he meant to save me for himself, but he was greedy and wanted to enjoy the others too, I think, before giving them to his servants for their pleasure. It was my good luck. He... he stripped and baited the other women, forcing them...whilst his men held them, he made them... ugh, it was so horrible!" She hid her face in her hands as though to shut out the images, still so real. After a while, during which Aedd simply held her close, she dropped her hands and continued.

"I found a flint in the tree roots and hacked at my bonds. I cut my wrists and fingers as I did it. All the time I thought he would come and find me out. I watched while he did it to them and ..." she sobbed, harsh retching sobs from the depths of her soul. Aedd was at a loss, so deep and lonely was her grief "... and I'm so ashamed. I just hoped that he would go on long enough for me to get away. I ran off into the dark. I ran and ran and ran. For a while their shouts were so loud that I was sure that they would catch me, then they faded, but still I ran. It began to rain and soon I was soaked. My feet were bleeding. I crawled into some thick scrub. I must have slept for a while, because suddenly it was first light. I felt awful. My head ached and I felt feverish, really ill. I just kept going. I avoided all people. How could I know if they were friendly, or if they would hand be over to the outlanders? Where should I go? I had no family, no home."

The plaintive tone reached inside Aedd. He bent his head to her and kissed the top of her head, hugging her to him, resting his cheek on her hair. She lifted her face, searching his. With his thumb he rubbed away tears from the corners of her eyes, gently rubbing her cheeks.

"The river people found me. I was near dead they said. I had wandered into a marsh and was raving with fever. They thought at first that I was mad, touched by the Mother, and I suppose I was a bit. They were really kind. They saved my life, nursed me back to health, but they are very simple and poor. They live by hunting, fishing and gathering roots and berries. I had few skills that they could use and winter, which is a very hard time for them, was coming, so they sold me. Tarok's wife, the lady Mygrwn bought me to attend her. She's kind. But that Tarok...he wanted me, you know, like the outlander. I could see it, the way he looked at me. I'm glad Mygrwn made all that trouble, glad she sent me away, glad she gave me to Master Anoeth."

Aedd said nothing. The silence lengthened. He stroked her back.

Ened felt the warmth of his arms about her. The sharing of her experience had drained her, yet she was comforted for the first time since she had been wrenched from her home. This huge kind man gave her warmth and a feeling of security. Her mean bed of bracken and cow hide in Anoeth's hut seemed a poor cold substitute.

Ened broke the silence. "Will you send me away now?"

"No Ened, I'll not send you away," Aedd said, taking her chin in his hand and tipping her head back, raising her generous mouth. "No, I'll not do that."

Aedd lowered his lips on hers. She was completely passive. Her lips full, but unresponsive. Aedd's hand moved down her throat, brushing the top swell of her breast with stealthy finger tips, teasing the bud which tightened involuntarily at his gentle touch, before cupping the fullness in his palm. Her lips yielded under the pressure of his. His tongue probed gently, seeking passage, touching teeth, which parted slightly. His thumb trapped her now bursting nipple, she shivered, and opened her mouth wide to him.

"Take off your dress" Aedd commanded softly.

Ened rose from the bed and started to undo the drawstring at her breasts.

With trembling fingers she pulled the drawstring and slid first one shoulder, then the other free, before dropping the dress in a crumpled heap at her ankles.

Aedd was breathless. Ened stood naked before him, hands held loosely at her side, open to his gaze, ready for his pleasure, but so vulnerable. Aedd's excitement mounted as he appreciated her beauty: the proudly jutting breasts, crowned by dark nipples, the narrow waist, slightly flaring hips, small tightly rounded belly flattening to the dark triangle between her thighs where, in a gap silhouetted by the back light of the guttering taper, her secret lips pushed flower-like through her tightly curled brush.

"Come here," said Aedd, throat dry, feeling his voice to be little more than a croak. He pushed back the coverings, reaching for her as she came to join him, taking her gently by the nape of the neck with one hand, the better to possess her mouth, the other at her waist, pulling her to his manhood. At the first touch of him, she shrank back, but as he gentled her, caressed her back with long, soft, open-handed strokes, then the backs of her thighs and her buttocks, kissing her open mouth, nibbling her lips, thrusting his tongue deep within her, she found herself pressing against him, seeking his hardness.

Aedd's hand traced a course from breast to bush, her thighs spread when his questing fingers found the nub of her wanting. She groaned. Divorced from reality, almost from each other with the intensity of their individual needs, Aedd stroked and caressed, touched and probed and Ened accepted, received and opened, excitement mounting, each height surpassed by the next excitement until, when unbearable, Aedd rolled between her thighs spread wide in welcome, seeking and finding entry in a panic of sensation that mounted, bucked, tossed and swirled them both to the inevitable abyss.

Aedd struggled upwards, up the dark tunnel, clawing through the clinging spiders' webs, to the faint flickering light ahead. He felt a great urgency, as though pursued by something extremely evil, but anonymous, close behind him. He felt a desperate need which was not defined, beyond reaching the light before being caught. As he struggled and broke each sticking strand, another, thicker, always thicker and stickier strand wound around him, obscuring light, pulling him back. He was abruptly aware of a long bronze blade in his hand, glinting in the faint gleam from the end of the tunnel. The restraints parted and he staggered into a dark cave. Silk shrouded cocoons swung from ropes, spinning slowly to reveal the faces of Ermid and Belu. A scuttling sound made him look around. A huge spider, black and bulbous, suspended on hairy cantilevers, was squatting over the desiccated cadaver of Cerdic the charcoal burner. The spider turned; its head was a monstrous parody of a human shape, its face a grotesque distortion of Urak's.

Aedd awoke, bathed in sweat, breathing deeply. Immense relief flooded him. Ened lay spooned in his lap, her head pillowed on his arm, her hair, outlined by the flickering taper, tickling is face. He lifted his head to look at her. She was breathing deeply and evenly, fast asleep, long eyelashes resting on her cheeks, a faint suggestion of a smile at the full, generous mouth giving the appearance of being content. He tried to steady his breathing, worried that he might wake her. Aedd sighed. The girl stirred, rolled over towards him. He turned on his back, relieved as the blood returned to his arm where she had lain. She snuggled into his shoulder, one breast crushed to his ribs, throwing a long lithe leg over his. He felt the prickle of her bush at his hip and the stirrings of renewed desire. He allowed it to subside, content to hold this girl-woman in his arms, to breathe the fragrance of her and of their love making.

Aedd could not remember ever having enjoyed such a feeling of well-being. The girl had reached a part of him he had thought long dead and buried. She had touched deep within him the raw nerve that needs the soothing, caring companionship and understanding of a woman. She had stimulated and then satisfied an excitement that he had thought a part of his youth, now far behind him.

In the morning, he must go at once to Anoeth. Anoeth must sell me her bond, he thought desperately, I'll promise him anything, but I must not leave without her.

Berin could not sleep. The longhouse was alive with a constant background murmur compounded of regular breathing, coughs, snores, interrupted by conversations conducted in heated whispers, the sounds of half the clan at rest. From time to time a child woke in fright at some memory of the past few disturbing days, to be shushed and comforted. Thoughts of what had to be done tumbled and churned in his mind with half resolved problems and plans. Even the soothing memory of that afternoon with Olwen failed to help him sleep. In fact too detailed a recall had quite the opposite effect.

Berin decided to inspect the guards. He sat up and pulled on boots and jerkin. He wrapped his warmest cloak around him and picked his way through the sleeping forms to the doorway, an oblong of paler black in the dark interior.

A watch fire burned near the entrance to the settlement. Auron sat silhouetted against the light, cape pulled close around him, a hunched, disgruntled figure. Berin gave him a cheery greeting as he passed, not expecting much of a reply, bearing in mind the harsh words which he had been forced to use to Auron at dusk; nor did he receive more than the expected resentful grunt.

Berin strode on down the valley, checking each guard in turn, glad to be in the open. All was quiet, with scarcely a breath of wind. The moon had not yet risen. The clear night sky displayed a cascade of stars. Berin paused to sniff the air; another moon and such a night would bring frost, he reflected. He climbed the steep ridge just down the valley from the settlement and was puffing and blowing long before he reached the top. Just the place for our defences he thought, anyone attacking will be at our mercy, just as I told father. Why won't the stubborn old fool listen. He's so set in his ways.

"Who's that? Berin, is that you?" Olwen's voice called softly.

"Yes, it's me. Hey, what are you doing up here."

73

Berin climbed towards her. She was sitting, rugged in a cloak, a darker shade of darkness, topped by the pale gleam of her face, on the upper lip of a small dished depression, just a few paces across, little more than a zone of inflexion on the slope of the hillside. His boots splashed water as he crossed to her.

"Oranc wanted to stand watch with Naf and he went off without his cape. I took it to him. But I couldn't sleep anyway," she said, head on one side. "The night is so beautiful out here, so peaceful. I wanted to be alone for awhile, away from all the other people."

"Oh," he said, "I'm sorry," he said, feeling suddenly foolish.

"Not you, silly."

He stretched himself beside her. "I couldn't sleep either. Too much on my mind, I suppose."

"Like what?"

Berin was silent. How could he answer. His thoughts of her had been thoroughly erotic and disturbing; yet so much easier to deal with than the reality. Here he was with her, alone and once more tongue tied.

"Er...about rebuilding... about what to do about the Afon'ken people. How we're going to get through the winter," he said, sticking to safe, unromantic themes.

"Oh and not about me?" she mocked.

"Yes of course...all the time...." he confessed, further speech drying in his throat. Unsure of what to say or do, but knowing that he could not simply allow the silence to lie between them, he opened his cloak. She came willingly into his arms. He closed his cloak around her, cocooning them both in a private world. Her cold nose pressed against his cheek, wisps of hair tantalised his forehead.

Her lips kissed his jaw line, moving around, searching, as they lay back on the slope, finding then opening under his lips. This was so much easier than words, Berin thought, tasting her, inhaling her scent.

"I love you Olwen," he heard himself say, surprising himself with his audacity, suddenly fearing rejection.

She considered this, trying hard to see him, to read his face in the faint starlight, then apparently satisfied answered very seriously. "And I love you Berin of Com of the line of Harac. I have loved you for as long as I can remember."

Relief swamped him. "I want you to be my wife" Berin said. He felt unreal, disoriented. Had he really just said that?

There was a long silence. Olwen's shoulders shook. He lifted his hand to her face and touched tears. Confused, Berin asked. "What is it? What's the matter?"

"I have loved you as a chief's son, but I never thought you would be his heir. Now, after Com, you will be chief in Belu's place. I have hoped more than I can tell you that one day you would want me, but never did I once think to be wife of a chief." Olwen sniffed, rubbed her eyes on a corner of her cloak. "You know that such marriages are arranged with great care, with much more thought than is usual for the rest of us. Why even the High Chief himself must consent to a match for people of the blood. Am I worthy? Will Com accept me?"

"Don't cry. I'll make him agree. But why should he not accept you?"

There was a long silence. Berin simply held her close.

"I could not bear it if I were thought unfit, I want you so."

Berin claimed her lips, nibbling them with his own, sliding his tongue between them, pushing, prising, demanding. With a soft moan Olwen surrendered, opening to him, one hand behind his neck, pulling his urgent mouth to hers. His hand went to her breast, fumbling with the folds of her cloak.

"Wait," she whispered. "There," she said, after a while, reaching eagerly for his mouth again.

Berin's hand found not only her cloak unfastened, but that she had loosened the drawstring of her dress. He slowly pushed aside the cloth to free Olwen's passion, marvelling at the smooth warmth he found. Olwen shivered at his touch and pressed closer to him. He possessed her breast and its bud, uplifted in anticipation of his touch, smoothing with his finger tips, cupping with his full hand, taking the burgeoning berry between finger and thumb, excited by the response this induced in Olwen. Impatient at the feeble resistance still offered to his roaming fingers by her open neckline, Berin pulled the dress from her shoulders, Olwen his willing helper, bending first one elbow and then the other, pulled the dress to her waist. Both breasts now open to his attention, Berin tenderly suckled first one and then the other. Olwen moaned, pressing her nipples to his searching lips.

He held her to him, wrapped her in his arms, pressing the warm soft woman-scented length of her to him, moulding her softness to his strength, aching as she pressed against his hardness in eager response. He smoothed, gentled, stroked the full length of her, lingering to grasp her buttocks, pulling her centre against his, then stroking her thighs to the hem of her skirt. Hesitant, he pressed upwards. Olwen's thighs trembled at his touch and fell apart, allowing his hand passage between them. Emboldened, Berin advanced tenderly, wondering at the softness of her inner thigh. His hand was trapped by the tightened hem of her skirt. Impatiently, Olwen lifted her hips, tugging at her skirt, bagging it with her dress top, already at her waist. Berin started at the unexpected springiness under his hand. New lips parted, moist to questing fingers, a new bud swelled, slipped and thrilled. Berin nibbled at her lips, her neck, biting gently down her throat to her nipple. As he took it again between his lips, greedily this time, Olwen arched her back, thrusting her breast and its bursting fruit to his mouth, groaning, as she buried her face in his shoulder.

Her fingers hurried his, fumbling at his belt. Impatient for fulfilment she reached for his manhood, encircling him with her fingers, pulling him, guiding him within her, spreading herself in joyful welcome. Berin felt the hot entrapment; all his senses now focused in his manhood, he lunged forward, careless of the weak final barrier, unwanted by either of them. Olwen felt the tear, the sharp small pain quickly lost in the greater, rapidly growing sensation. She met his full thrust, countered, rocked and surged in a wild back and forth rhythm, ancient dance steps of the Mother's favourites, until with a cry and spasmodic, decreasing strikes, Berin subsided.

Now Olwen wrapped him in her arms and cloak, held him close to her, gentled him with long caresses, for she had felt, deep within her, the explosion of his seed. She was woman, one day she would be mother. She was content, secure now in the certain knowledge that in surrender, hers was the ultimate victory.

Anoeth chuckled, rocking on his heels, well pleased with himself. "So old friend," he cackled, "and now you want her bond. A few hours of pleasure and you're ready to beg for her. She must be good. Perhaps I should keep her. What about me, eh, what about a poor old man left all alone, no one to look after him? Play on friendship and take an old man's last comforts in his old age, would you? What are you going to give me for her, eh?"

"Your sister's girl will look after you as she's done these past three years, though why anyone can spare any time for such a cantankerous old bugger is beyond me," answered Aedd, growing a little gruff at the old man's pointedly accurate remarks, then adding quickly, in case the old man took offence, "you can have all I've got."

Anoeth, recognising the mood change, reached forward, groping, searching to grasp Aedd's arm. "If I hadn't meant you to have her, I wouldn't have sent her to you, just to torment you. But you can do something for me in return. I need an apprentice. I can't manage no more, now that the other eye's gone. I want to pass on what I know before it's too late. Find me one, Aedd. The girl's yours Aedd, but find me someone to follow on, someone who can come to love the flint as I do, not too old, not jumped up and cheeky, but biddable and willing to learn. Someone like your Alen."

Anoeth fell silent, then added "Aye, your Alen, he'd suit just fine."

Aedd's face creased in thought. It was a wonderful opportunity for Alen. No one knew the working of flint like

Anoeth. With a real skill like that Alen would be provided for life; but his own son in exchange for the girl? No, that's not the real balance, he rationalised. Think of the good side for each of us. Aedd calculated, sure now that the old man had trod the same mental path before him. The farm he could manage, except at harvest. Ened would be just as able as Alen, more so for a good few years yet, until he's full grown. Alen would be safe at the ford, safer than at Com's outpost, and he can keep an eye on what's going on, keep track of Urak.

"You can have him back for the harvest," Anoeth wheedled.

"Then give me your hand on it; it's a deal," answered Aedd. They solemnly shook hands, both clearly delighted.

"Ened, you strumpet, come here," Anoeth called. She ran over to kneel respectfully at his feet, looking back over her shoulder at Aedd, whose wide grin and brief nod told her all that she wished to know.

"This ruffian wishes to buy your bond from me; do you object? No of course you don't. Well fetch it then, be quick!" Ened rose and ran to the hut.

"Who's that," Anoeth called as booted feet crunched on the gravel path to Dorn's compound.

"Aedd, Aedd, are you there?" a voice called.

"Yes, over here," Aedd answered. "Who are you, what do you want?"

"I am Creggan, I wait on Dorn. He sent me to tell you that you are to come at once. Com wants to leave."

"Come here Creggan. You can witness this."

Ened returned carrying a length of plaited leather which, kneeling once more, she thrust eagerly into the old man's hand.

"Give me your hand girl." She held out her right hand and fumbling a little in his blindness, he tied one end of the thong around it. "Come over here Aedd, where I can reach you."

Aedd stood next to the girl, who turned to look up at him with shining eyes. "Give me your hand Aedd. Here take this," Anoeth said, thrusting the other end of the plaited leather into his hand.

"Ened, I give your bond to Aedd of Com. You will obey him in all things. Now make the sign girl."

Ened turned to Aedd and bending low, touched her forehead to his booted foot.

"Is it done?" asked Anoeth.

"It's done," answered Creggan, adding "Aedd, you must hurry."

"You go ahead Creggan, tell them I'm on my way. Ened go and pack my things," responded Aedd, untying the leather thong and handing it to her. "Put this in my pack."

Creggan hurried off on his errand. Ened turned to Anoeth and, taking his hand in hers, kissed it. "Thank you, oh thank you!" she said.

"Yes, yes, be off with you," the old man replied, "your master wants to speak with me."

"Anoeth, what is this of Cerdic," Aedd asked when they were alone.

"Aedd, as my eyes have dimmed, the Mother has blessed me in other ways. I can tell the footsteps of all who pass this way. I knew it was Creggan before he spoke. I recognised you yesterday as you approached. I sit here all day and much of the evening. I tell you Cerdic did not pass that evening."

"Could you be mistaken?"

"Do you think that I wouldn't like to be? You know what it means. Shh! don't even whisper it, even though we're alone. There is great danger. It would be death to make the accusation."

"But Dorn is a fair man."

"Aye, fair, but blinder than me where his sons are involved. Send me Alen, we will watch together. He shall be my eyes. Don't fear for him my friend. My life before his, I swear. Take the girl away. She knows too much to be safe here. Swear her to silence."

"I must go now. I'll send Alen to you. Stay in peace."

"Go with the Mother, Aedd."

CHAPTER 5

The defining moments of my life have always arrived unannounced and gone away again unrecognised until their effect is felt long afterwards. The day Pippa tipped her cousin Wayne from her tricycle after he had wrestled it from her on her fourth birthday was such a turning point. None of us, not Sarah my wife, nor Emily, her sister-in-law and certainly not I, had recognised it though. We had been too concerned with soothing Wayne's hurt and ruffled feelings, and calling for tokens of forgiveness. Even the injustice of the action and justice of the reaction had been ignored, sacrificed at the altar of family togetherness. I should have known. I should have recognised the signs of what was to come in Pippa's defiant stare and Wayne's glowering pout.

Now, nearly ten years later, my daughter stood before me, wearing the same defiant stare. God, she was lovely. The reflection of her mother was so faithful that it mocked my practised self-deception and pulled at the sutures of that deeply hidden wound. Her long, corn-coloured hair was tousled. Wisps were plastered against her sweat dampened temple, others strayed across her freckled cheek and nose. She brushed her hair away from her face with an impatient grubby hand. Her developing breasts pushed at the torn, begrimed brown and white check of her school dress. Her knees were dirty, but not too dirty to hide the angry red grazes.

"Dad?" she wailed, voicing the despairing tone of youth faced by the adult inability to understand.

"So what happened?" I asked, reaching out to her. She came into my arms and I hugged her. She was tense, the muscles of her back were bunched and hard. She rested her head on my shoulder. I stroked her hair, smoothing it over the back of her head.

"Tell me."

"Wayne...."

"Oh not again..."

Pippa pulled away. She gave me the look. The one calculated to freeze me in my tracks... a real pillar of salt job.

"Oh great...just great. You never listen to me."

"I'm sorry sweetheart...it's just... Well you know the hard time I get from the wicked witch of the west each time you and Wayne fall out."

Pippa giggled. The transformation of her features was instant and dramatic.

"We did more than fall out this time, Dad."

"Go on. Tell me," I sighed.

"I decked him," she said, with too much satisfaction to be ladylike. She rubbed her hand. I took it in mine. The knuckles were grazed and swollen.

"Is it OK?" I asked, stroking her fingers gently with my thumb. She winced.

I tapped the ends of her finger tips. She didn't react, so at least there was no fracture.

"And what does he look like?" I asked wryly.

"Not too good. I split his lip."

"Pippa!"

"Well he asked for it."

Her eyes blazed as the memory of her anger resurfaced. I felt what Wayne must have faced and was sorry for him.

"What started it?"

She shrugged. "We had this debate in school... about if we should be a republic. I spoke for keeping things the way they are. I mean if it isn't broke why fix it....and well so much of our history links us to England. Many of us originally came from England, like you Dad. Wayne took the other side. He said we don't need the Queen. The whole idea of the monarchy is outdated. It's not democratic. We've got loads of Australians from Greece and Italy and Asia. We are part of Asia, he said. What does the royal family mean to them? I said what about Princess Di? The whole world is interested in her.

Anyway, that was cool. It was just his point of view and I could accept that. But afterwards, outside, in the school yard, he had a go at me Him and his mates..."

"He..." I corrected instinctively.

"Dad..." she warned.

"He said that Di screws around, just like in the soaps...and her mate Fergie. Why would you want them to represent your country. Then his mate Max started on about Charles and ... what's her name...Camilla. But he was really rude. No... really rude."

She sniffed. I sensed that I wasn't going to get a verbatim report. Pippa could be quite prudish sometimes about protecting my sensibilities.

"Anyway, Grant said that whilst we were talking, Di was probably having it off with some wog. Wayne said only a Pommie loser like me could admire Diana. Then he sort of sniggered and asked if I'd like him to suck my toes... so I hit him."

I thought of my daughter being taunted by that bunch of larrikins and felt the anger surge within me. At that moment I could have hit him too. I looked at her and she started to cry.

"It's all right," I said inadequately, patting her back. But it wasn't, and I knew it.

"You had better go and clean up. I'll fix us our tea."

"Lunch time dinner and dinner time tea," Pippa echoed the old family joke. As she said it, she was her mother and the pain of her loss bit savagely and deep.

"Oh Dad..." she said, seeing my pain, sharing it. "I'm sorry... I didn't mean to..."

The 'phone rang, loudly, insistently. "I know Kiddo, I know."

I picked up the 'phone.

"Do you know what your little tart has done," Emily screeched at me. "She's cut his lip...broken his crown. It cost two hundred dollars. She's out of control. You aren't fit to bring her up. I'll get the 'Socials' on to you. She needs a lesson that one and I'd like to give it to her...." I held the receiver away from my ear.

"The wicked witch of the west?" Pippa grimaced.

"The very same," I answered.

"John...John are you listening to me?" the 'phone squawked stridently.

85

"No. No I'm not and I don't think I will ever again. Your little shit of a son got what was coming to him and he should just be thankful that I wasn't there," I said and hung up.

"Thanks Dad," Pippa grinned from the doorway, giving me a look that made parenting, especially single parenting, worthwhile.

"What are you plotting tonight?" I asked some time later, reaching for her empty plate. "Have you got much school work?"

"Nope. Just some Italian vocab to learn. I'll do it in bed. Dougie's coming round. We'll hang out down at the Coffee Shop." She paused, and looked at me, suddenly serious. "If that's all right Dad? You OK on your own? I mean..."

"Yeah. I'm fine." The lie came easier with practise. In fact I felt so confident about it that I embellished it. "I've some quotes I have to write up."

She pursed her lips and frowned. Acute scepticism was written into the curve of her eyebrows.

"I thought Steve was supposed to do all that. You work too hard," she said, sounding more like her mother than she could ever have imagined.

"He's working late on the planting at the new shopping mall. Besides I like to keep a close eye on new clients."

"Well... if you're sure."

"I'm sure. Don't nag."

"Here, let me wash up then"

"Done."

She started to stack the plates and clear the table. She was right of course, just like her Mum. I was working too hard. Work was one way to take my mind off Sarah. Falling into bed exhausted was better than falling into bed drunk or using that other chemical cosh the doctor insisted I use in the long nights after she let go. Pippa was right. I didn't have to work so hard. Steve could cope on his own, with everything except the design and planting plans, which were my domain. He was beginning to have some original in-put in my patch too. I didn't have to work so hard, but I wanted to.

The door bell rang. Dougie's six foot stack of trainers, bulging calves, board shorts, T-shirt, toothy grin topped by flaxen thatch, filled the door frame.

"Hi Mr Allen. Pippa there?"

"Sure. Come in."

"Hi Dougie. Be with you just now. I've got to wash up for Dad." Her smile warmed me, even though it wasn't meant for me.

"Go on, off you go," I said, taking the dish mop from her hand.

"You sure?"

I can raise my eyebrows with good effect too. Pippa took the hint. I watched from the doorway as the two of them jostled and kidded down the veranda steps and garden path to the street. My long-legged, lissom beauty; my God, for a fleeting moment I was so jealous I actually felt a sharp pain in my chest. She had it all to come; all the sweet excitement; the cosiness; the warm trust.

I pushed the black thoughts of happiness ripped apart by a premature and unjust death into the dishwasher with the plates and finished the pots and pans that Pippa had started. What was I going to do about the Wayne - Pippa strife? I mean, how could Wayne think of her as Pommie? I didn't even think of myself as a Pom, and I was born there. I had very few memories of the place and fewer of the people; no one with a face, not even Mum and Dad; not from that time. Mum and Dad had not spoken of England, or of family. I used to get a card and a parcel from Gran at Christmas and on my birthday. They stopped when... when was that? I was still in junior school anyway. There were some warm, but flimsy mind pictures of Gran's beamed kitchen, her smile and hug, and threepenny bit she'd give me to run down to the village shop to buy sweets. I still can not smell baking without thinking of her. I remembered feeding the chickens off-cuts of cabbage and cauliflower and the magic of a new laid egg nestling in the straw. I remembered the icy touch of linoleum on the feet and steam clouding the bathroom and the running jump into bed to huddle down and find the hot water bottle. I remembered Dad sitting with some papers at the kitchen table, his head in his hands and Mum standing beside him, rubbing his back like she did to me when I'd hurt myself.

After that, all memory was Australian. Even the boat trip, a hazy recollection of a sort of extended stay at a moving Butlin's holiday camp seemed more a part of Australia than England. I certainly felt Australian, looked like and spoke like an Australian, supported the baggy green and the green and gold and always had; not from peer pressure, not from a convert's zeal; I simply always had for as long as I could remember. My British passport was an accident of history; the result of indolence compounded by sloth. First Dad and then I simply hadn't bothered to do anything about it. It had never seemed necessary….and I had never experienced any animosity. There simply is no such thing as anti-Pom sentiment at large. No this was just the particular polemic cosh chosen by Wayne to bash my beautiful daughter. Kids!

I wiped down the table, took a beer from the fridge and wandered into my den. I pulled a file from the cabinet, sat at my desk and started to check the estimates. They covered three new jobs, one private, a complete redesign and planting of a big old sloping plot in Mosman, and two municipal works, with maintenance contracts thrown in. My landscape architecture consultancy was going well, but more than half of the revenue now came from maintenance. I would have to start thinking about taking on more permanent staff. I switched on the computer and brought the spread sheet up on the screen.

Greg Hawkins and his wife Liz wanted to restore their Mosman garden to its original splendour. A tall order, since the previous owner had been a devotee of native species. The original owners at the turn of the century would certainly have used imported plants, shrubs and trees to recreate an English country garden. I also reckoned that although they were interested in the effect, they were less than keen gardeners in the hands on sense. So, no tender varieties. Liz Hawkins particularly wanted a rose garden by the terrace.   I pulled down my trade catalogue. Vigorous, hardy, traditional colour…. mmh… the *Queen Elizabeth* seemed to fit and they were a good price. Nice fit with the name too. Liz would like that… unless she was a republican. No, she hadn't seemed like that; much more likely to use Greg's business connections to angle for invitations to Government House. A real Mrs Bennet, that one. Anyway, what was the republican type, if there was one?

The public debate, what there was of it, seemed to me to be highly politically charged and bad tempered in the usual Australian way. The republicans were strident. They laid claim to modernity, to the Asian connection, to a hi-tech vision of rapidly expanding model Asian economies. The traditionalists were painted as blimpish, but they had a point when they highlighted the corruption and inherent instability of many Asian governments. To me it came down to a low brow and fairly blatant grab for more power at the centre; a bid to reduce the powers of the State Governments. I couldn't see the point of changing something that worked well and had given us stability in government for a century. We were independent. We certainly had our own confident sense of national identity. Why should we deny the historical links with Britain when the forging of that chain was inseparable from the forging of our own nationalism? You can't deny history, only rewrite it. But for all that, I couldn't see any point in falling out about it.

The screen door slammed shut followed closely by Pippa's bedroom door. I knocked on the door.

"Are you OK Pip?" I asked. "What's the matter?"

She didn't answer, but I heard her sobbing so I opened the door. Pippa was lying full length on the bed. Her shoulders heaved with her sobs. I sat on the side of the bed and rubbed her back. It was as hard as a plank, the muscles knotted.

"What is it? Tell me."

She turned her tear-streaked face to me. Her eyes were already swollen.

"I hate him. I never want to see him again. Never!"

"Who?"

"I mean... he...he... ohh!"

"Who's he?"

"Dougie."

"Dougie?" I echoed. "But..."

"I never ever want to see that gutless... Ohh !" She rolled over and pummelled the pillow with tight fists.

"What's he done?"

"Nothing," she mumbled into her pillow. She sat up. "He did nothing," she shouted at the wall. "He just sat there...and...ohh!"

Pippa flung herself into my arms and I held her tight against me, feeling her shake with hurt.

I held her and stroked her hair. Her heaving sobs slowly lessened. I fumbled in my pocket and pulled out a cleanish handkerchief which she grabbed and blew into vigorously.

"I hate him. We were sitting in the 'Coffee Shop'. Everything was fine. Then Wayne and his mates came in. They sat at the next table and started cracking on about Poms...about Poms being losers...at cricket at rugby. Then they started barracking Dougie about going out with a Pom...what was it like going out with a loser? He went red but just took it. I stood up to leave and they said go on, get out. Go to England. Be a real Pom. I went and Dougie stayed. I thought he was special. I thought he was my friend. I hate him. I hate it here since Mum died. It's all changed. It's all gone bad," she said, in a small, shaky voice.

So much hate, so much hurt in such a small sweet package. It wasn't right.

The telephone rang. I gave her a hug and went through to my den.

"Mr Allen? It's Peter Mariner speaking…Principal at the High School."

"Yes."

"It's about your daughter, Philippa."

"Go on."

"I feel a bit awkward about this. There was an incident at school this afternoon; with one of the other pupils. Are you aware of it?"

"Pippa told me that she was hassled by some of the boys after school. I wasn't going to report it. She seems to have taken care of it."

"That's just the point. How she took care of it, I mean. A boy's parents have laid a formal complaint. I am obliged to hold an inquiry. I must ask you to keep Philippa from school until the matter is resolved."

"You mean she's suspended?

"Mr Allen, let's not call it a suspension at this point in time. The inquiry will establish the facts and decide an outcome."

"What about the boys?"

"As to the boys, from what I know, there is no suggestion that the boys used violence. Or have I got it wrong?"

"No, not from what Pippa told me. But there was a lot of verbal abuse and extreme provocation."

"Mr Allen, the rules are very clear. Violence is not acceptable at my school, ever. I'm sorry, but I will get to the bottom of the incident, believe me. But meanwhile I think it better if you keep Philippa at home."

"It seems I have no choice."

"Neither do I Mr Allen, neither do I. I like Philippa and I sympathise with her...and with you. She's... you both must have been under a lot of stress recently. I'm sorry."

"Who was that, Dad?" Pippa asked from the doorway.

"Mr Mariner. The wicked witch from the West has made an official complaint. You're to stay back from school until there's been an inquiry."

"Sorry Dad," Pippa said.

I looked at my daughter, still beautiful despite the tear swollen eyes and hangdog expression. "It's okay Kiddo," I said. "You've not done anything wrong. Not in my eyes."

The man is probably right, I thought. Pippa is under enormous stress and I'm just burying mine in the business. My priorities have been all wrong. Pippa and I needed some time, away from it all; away from the familiar environment and the daily reminders of her mother, my wife.

"Maybe we should both take a break. Let's go away for a while," I said, warming to the idea even as I had it. Steve could handle the business for a while. I wasn't short of money.

"Where to, Dad?"

Cairns, Noosa, Byron Bay flitted across my mind and then inspiration struck.

"Well, those toads keep on told you to go there, so why not. Let's you and me go to England?"

Pippa screamed. "You don't mean it. You do! Oh my God you do," she shrieked, jumping up and down and hugging me all at once, her eyes shining, the smile back on her face. For the second time that day, parenting was really worthwhile.

CHAPTER 6

The flight entered limbo after about the first ten hours, when I seemed to become welded to the seat. The first section was properly entered in my memory bank; seven hours or so to Singapore, chatting to Pippa, a passable lunch, a few drinks, a movie. But after Singapore it became a confused blur of lights turned on and off, flickering video screens, crying children, snatched sleep, passing trolleys and meals at what seemed to be the wrong time. Pippa loved every minute. She accepted each drink, each meal, examined each tray, the packaging and contents with minute interest. She watched each movie and must have listened to each music channel several times over. In between times she tidied up our seating area and chatted to her neighbour, Mrs Paxton, from Brisbane via Singapore, en route to Galashiels in Scotland to see her latest grandson; or simply read her book, her reading light a bright lonely cone in the dark cabin.

The captain's reassuring drawl announced our imminent arrival at London Heathrow. The cabin staff fussed, collecting headsets, setting seat backs upright, putting up tables, waking reluctant passengers, chasing last minute visitors from the loos, before settling in their seats and fastening their safety harness. Pippa turned to me with a bright smile and squeezed my arm.

That London August morning dawned bright and sunny: a complete contrast to the clichéd cold misty grey of memory: a complete contrast to our wintry departure from the other side of the world. We walked for miles along girdered, carpeted corridors, shepherding Mrs Paxton and her suitcase on wheels, which she dragged behind her like a dog out on a walk. We left Mrs Paxton when she had to join the long queue of Australians at immigration. We lined up with a collection of souls that truly demonstrated the spread of *Pax Britannica* and sailed past the desk for EU passport holders with a nod, a smile and a cursory inspection of our British birthrights.

"Dad," Pippa whispered hoarsely as I stretched for her bag on the luggage carousel. I decided to save myself a hernia and let it go around once more.

"What sweetheart?"

"I've just remembered. I kept some grapes and an apple from dinner. I'll have to dump them before the fruit fly control."

"No worries, Pipsqueak. I don't think they have it here."

Pippa gave me a look that would have been very old fashioned, if she had been old enough. I was just debating whether the look was caused by my reversion to her childhood nickname or by the incomprehensible irresponsibility of officialdom in London, when her bag came past again. As it happened, there were no controls of any kind. A few customs officers chatted amongst themselves as we trolleyed past, unaccountably feeling guilty, though for no good reason and then we were cast up on London's shore before a wave of faces intent, so it seemed, on anyone but us.

I had heard somewhere that you could expect non stop good natured banter from London taxi drivers. Ours must have had an off day. He was as taciturn as he was morose and slid the glass partition shut the moment Pip and I settled back in the seat. We didn't care. I was as excited as Pippa. We eagerly pointed out sights to each other; the black cabs, double-decker buses, National History Museum, Harrods.

The hotel in a side street off Piccadilly was not as grand as I'd expected for the price, but Pippa was delighted with the view across the roof tops and fire escapes and with a new collection of freebies in her bathroom to pick through. She was also delighted with the bedside gadgetry of radio clock, light and dimmer switches, and the TV and mini bar. All had to be tried and tested.

"Cool," she announced at last, settling with a sigh on the bed happily munching on potato chips and swigging on diet Coke from the mini bar.

"Get yourself cleaned up and unpacked. I'll see you in an hour and we'll take a look at the town," I said.

Her reply was unrecognisable through the chips and Coke, but I took it for a yes. I went back to my room and set about shaving and showering away what I could of the effects of long distance travel.

My plan was to spend a few days seeing the sights in London, before picking up a hire car and running down to where Gran used to live, the one reference point I had in England. I had only the faintest idea of where it was; Bernton, somewhere in Berkshire. I had spotted Berkshire in the atlas at home, but had not been able to locate Bernton. I needed a good road map.

A very cheerful, pretty and efficient girl at reception arranged for a hire car to be delivered to the hotel early the following week. I wandered over to the lobby kiosk to buy a newspaper and to see if they had a road map. Princess Diana's face smiled from the magazine rack. The newspapers were full of her romance with Dodi. I bought a paper, a very detailed road atlas and a London guide. The coins were strangely familiar, but I struggled with the unfamiliar notes. Everything seemed to be very expensive; about the same price in pounds as I would expect to pay in dollars back home.

I knocked on Pippa's door. "Open up, it's me," I called.

She came to the door, fresh-faced, eyes shining, hair still slick and damp from the shower. She hugged me tightly.

"Oh Dad ... it's so great; really great to be here with you."

"My pleasure," I answered, and it was.

"We've work to do," I said, tapping the London guide. "You find what you want to see and we'll arrange an itinerary."

"Aw Dad, you pick. I want to read the scandal," she said, taking the paper from my hand. "It's just been on the news. This Di and Dodi thing is the business, I tell you what. She's snogged him. They're off to Paris today. They say she's going to stay with him."

She flung herself on the bed and began to turn the pages. I sat in the chair by the window and sifted through the attractions listed in the London guide. Of course it would have to be the big tourist things first; Tower of London, Tower Bridge, Houses of Parliament, Buckingham Palace. Would Pippa go for the National Gallery, the Tate, the British Museum? Maybe if I mixed them in with shopping. Better leave that for next week and focus on the touristy things over the week end.

"Dad....? I don't really understand this. Why would it be a problem for Di and Dodi to get married?"

"Married?" I asked. "Who says they're going to get married?"

"There're lots of different stories here. One says Dodi's friends say they're planning to get married. Princess Di's friend says it's a load of nonsense. She's just having a fling on holiday. Some woman in America claims that Dodi is engaged to her. This article says that Princess Di would have to give up the princes if she did because you couldn't have the heir to the throne brought up by a foreigner and the future head of the Church brought up by a Moslem."

"It sounds like a lot of press talk to me," I answered. "They'll say almost anything to sell papers. I wouldn't believe half of it"

"But look at the pictures Dad. He's all over her."

"Poor boys," I muttered, looking at the selection of photographs, some obviously staged, the principal players waving at the camera, others, in their intimacy, showing a complete disregard for the watching telephoto lenses.

"What do you mean?"

"Well how would you like it if pictures of your Mum with a man that's not your Dad were splashed all over the papers?"

"At least they've got a mum," Pippa said mournfully as her eyes filled.

I cursed myself for a fool. "Come on, places to go, pizzas to eat. How about a feed at Planet Hollywood before we start the sights?"

I awoke, completely disoriented, to loud knocking at the door.

"Who is it," I grumbled, fumbling for the bedside light switch.

"Dad...Dad. Let me in."

I struggled to focus on my watch; seven on a Sunday morning. What could she be thinking of. I grabbed my dressing gown and opened the door. Pippa stood there, tears streaming down her face. "She's dead," Pippa sobbed.

"Oh sweetheart," I said, pulling her through the door and closing it behind her.   "I'm sorry. I didn't mean to upset you...." I mumbled, shaking my head at my stupidity the day before.

"No...no you don't understand. It's Di. Princess Diana. She's dead. It's on the news. She and Dodi were killed in a car crash."

        I switched on the TV. We crawled into bed and I hugged my daughter to me and watched and listened as the awful events of that Paris night unfolded.

My first sight of a nation in shock was the efficient receptionist of yesterday reduced to a sniffling wretch, stemming her tears with a tightly balled tissue.

The mood in the Breakfast Room, cheerfully decorated in sunny yellow and green, was sombre.

"Isn't it awful," confided the waitress with a sniff, before asking "Will that be tea or coffee?"

Tourists and Londoners milled outside Buckingham Palace when we arrived. Some clustered around a notice posted on the railings. Many laid bunches of flowers. Most simply stood in silence and stared at the facade.

"Why ain't there a flag," a little girl asked her father.

I looked at the palace roof. The flagpole was bare, and lonely.

The morning papers and the TV became our focal points as the days passed. Diana's death was all absorbing, not just for us, but for anyone who was in London at that time and, if the media reports were to be believed, for everyone in Great Britain and a great many more around the World. We watched in silent misery as her body was brought home. We cried out together in angry disbelief at the revelation of the driver's drink consumption on the fatal night. We postponed our departure to the country because, for some reason I could not explain, I felt the need to sign the book of condolence at St James's Palace and Pippa wanted to lay flowers at Kensington Palace.

Waiting, standing in line is something we are all used to. We have all grumbled and shuffled along in theatre queues, at sales, football matches and airports. I have never stood and waited as long as Pippa and I did outside St James's Palace. The queue, four deep, stretched for a mile. Yet there was no whinging. I heard not one word of complaint, though our section of the crowd contained the very old, the very young, City types and country folk, rich, poor, tattered and smart. There seemed to be a complete cross section drawn from every type that the polychrome multiracial community of modern Britain could offer and many tourists too. An elderly, but still sprightly moustachioed man in his cavalry twills and sports jacket shared his barley sugars with all who could reach. When a Harrods van distributed drinks and sandwiches, a dishevelled Afro-Caribbean type with matted dreadlocks, his toes poking through worn trainers, made sure that all around him were taken care of before he satisfied his own thirst and hunger. No, there was no complaint about our lot; but there was complaint.

Deceived and spurned by Charles; stripped of her title, Her Royal Highness; stripped too of the protection she so obviously needed and which would have saved her precious life. The brave princelings forced into stiff upperlipmanship attendance at Church. How unfeeling of the Queen to stay on holiday and not grieve openly with her people. No flag at all at Buckingham Palace. The Royal Standard proud, unyielding above Balmoral; so immoral. Queen of Hearts, we love you and spurn those that spurned you, for you are Diana, the people's Princess.

"Glad she's dead, they are. Shame on them. Now she's out of the way. Convenient like, I say. Ohhh very convenient, isn't it?" a stout lady from Wales muttered darkly between tight lips.

"I mean man, what are they to me," Dreadlocks explained. "Di cares; all this landmine stuff. She cares about us blacks; about our bro's man, in Africa like. Know what I mean? She ain't scared to touch some nigger with Aids."

And at last, quietly ushered to a desk and the tyranny of a blank page, watching other mourners pen their laments, wondering what they were writing, feeling that Diana was so close, just the other side of the wall.

Kensington Palace was such a crush that when we left, it was a relief to escape to our hotel. There the grief was more evident, more public. Grown men wept with their women and children. The scent of the serried ranks and banks of flowers was overpowering. The poignancy of the messages, of the balloons, the ribbons, the Teddy Bears, the guttering candles in their jam jars, was too rich to bear; but

102

Diana was not there. No matter how hard I listened, how hard I focused, she was not there amidst the avalanche of love, loss, sympathy and condemnation.

CHAPTER 7

We decided not to stay in London for the funeral. The media were predicting crowds in the millions and we had had enough of the emotional overload. The day we left, the tabloids were crowing that they had compelled the Queen to listen to the will of the people, return to London and fly a flag at half-mast from Buckingham Palace. The press seemed to be rabble rousing, just like the Aussie press would have done back home. I hadn't expected it of the British. I was surprised. I mean, in Australia we knew that Charles was unpopular, because of the break up of his marriage to Diana and that there had even been suggestions that he should abdicate in favour of William. Many Australians, perhaps even a majority, questioned the relevance to modern Australia of a distant Royal Family in England. But that was Aussies in Australia; until my own experience in London, it had never occurred to me that the monarchy as an institution and an instrument of government might not be universally popular in England.

Bernton turned out to be easier to find in reality than it was on the map. My memory of it being in Berkshire turned out to be wrong. When I couldn't find it in the road atlas I turned to the index. The only Bernton listed was in Oxfordshire. I decided to head there anyway. We stopped for lunch at a pub beside the Thames. Pippa threw the remnants of her bread roll to the gliding swans whilst I watched the river throw itself over the weir. The pub was old. Older by several centuries than any building in Australia and was probably considered old when Cook sighted Botany Bay. Sitting in that place, the sun on my back, watching the glassy water spill into froth, gave me a sense of timelessness. The weir and lock must have been built at natural shallows. The shallows had probably been a ford and so a meeting place used by travellers ever since there had been any.

"The landlord said that they moved to 'The Crown' at Bernton."

The mention of Bernton woke me from my reverie. I turned on my bench. A portly man, wearing a loud check jacket and a Panama hat was setting a gin and tonic on the table before his blue-rinsed lady.

"Excuse me," I said. "Did you mention Bernton?"

He eyed me suspiciously, glanced over at Pippa and obviously concluded that I was not a threat. "Yes I did. Why do you ask?"

"Oh, I'm visiting from Australia. My family originally came from a place called Bernton, but I thought it was in Berkshire. The only Bernton I could find on the map is in Oxfordshire. I wondered if it was the right place."

He swigged from his pint, set it down on the table and wiped his tobacco stained moustache. "There's only the one," he said jovially, his eyes twinkling behind frameless glasses perched on a nose that had clearly passed over many a pint before the current one. "Kings come and go. Governments change. People move on, but places don't change. Bernton is still Bernton."

I must have looked very puzzled, for the man's companion interrupted.

"Get on with you Bertie. You're confusing the nice young man." She sipped elegantly from her glass, leaving a smudge of lipstick on the rim. Her gold charm bracelet rattled down her skinny parchment-covered arm. "It was Mr Heath," she explained. "Always was a meddler. Took part of Berkshire and gave it to Oxfordshire, the same time as he invented all those other counties. Silly old fool; just trying to look modern by changing things that had been there for a thousand years and didn't need changing. Like this Mr Blair and his New Labour. Thinks he's changing things. He'll learn." She smiled. "So you were right. It was in Berkshire; now it's in Oxfordshire."

We left the pub and followed the road along the side of the Thames. The river ran deep and wide behind the weir. Motor launches puttered up and down the still reach. A rowing eight pulled energetically, like a giant pond skater. The far bank, marked by willows, edged water meadows, which ended abruptly at a steep wooded hillside. A white slash in the green showed the scar of an old quarry in the chalk. The road cut into chalk as we left the river, climbing a steep hill through a beech wood, sunlight dancing through the bright green tree tops. We burst through the edge of the wood into high open fields. The Thames valley spread out before us, a wide open expanse of farmland, scattered villages and occasional tree-topped hills.

I picked up the sign to Bernton and turned off the main road into a different century. A narrow road threaded its way between black and white half-timbered thatched cottages, red brick houses with tiled roofs, past a grand manor house set in manicured lawns behind black iron gates and alongside a fenced paddock, where several horses, grazing contentedly, looked up curiously as we passed. I stopped at the Village Shop and Post Office.

"What do you reckon?" I asked Pippa.

Her wide grin and shining eyes were answer enough.

A bell tinkled overhead when I opened the door. "Good afternoon," I said as I stepped inside, with Pippa close behind me.

"No its not! Bloody awful. Damn the Post Office, its month end routine and its bloody forms."

The woman's face that regarded me from behind the counter had seen good service. It was lined, true, but as much from years in the sun and from laughter as from anything else. Grey-blue eyes twinkled behind half frame reading glasses and gave the lie to her severe tone. She caught sight of Pippa, peering around my side.

"Come in. Come in," she cried, "or the draught will have my forms all over the place."

The bell rang again as I shut the door.

"Now, what can I do for you?" the woman asked, dragging wisps of grey hair from her forehead. "Sorry about that, by the way. I always get in a bit of a state doing my returns."

I smiled and said "I feel the same way about my GST returns; I think you'd call it VAT." I was rewarded with a heart warming wide mouthed smile.

Er... we're looking for accommodation. A holiday let or bed and breakfast. We, that is Philippa, my daughter and I are visiting from Australia. I thought you might be able to recommend somewhere."

"Mmmh... lets see. The Crown does rooms, but they've been full since the dig started. We've got some archaeologists in the village. They're excavating the old Iron Age fort up on the hill," she added, by way of explanation. "Mrs Bynam does B and B and Mr and Mrs Trevose were converting a stable, or something. I'm sure she was planning to do holiday lets. They've had a bit of trouble keeping up with the mortgage since he lost his job. I don't know if it's ready yet. Can you give me a minute? I'll give them a ring."

"Oh that's very kind."

"No trouble. Hang on a tick."

She dialled. "Mary? It's Madge. No I'm not nagging you about stuff for the craft stall at the produce show. Yes, I'm sure your cushion covers are just the job." Madge rolled her eyes. "I know they take ages, but that's not what I want to talk to you about. I've.... Yes.... Yes Mary.... Mary there's a man and his daughter in the shop. They're looking for accommodation. Have you got any rooms free?"

Madge covered the mouthpiece. "She's a nice old bird, but she does go on," she whispered.

"Right... Okay... fine, not until Tuesday. I'll tell them. Yes Mary. No I haven't forgotten." She replaced the receiver and began to dial again. "Sorry about that. She's only got a double and that's not until Tuesday when... Ah Viv... it's Madge... Yes fine thanks... Look here, is your holiday let ready yet? ...Not quite, what a shame....It's just that there's this nice man and his daughter in the shop, from Australia. They're looking for somewhere to stay.... I see... yes, well I'll send them along then... It's ...?" Madge looked at me enquiringly over her half frame glasses.

"John Allen," I said.

"It's a Mr John Allen and his daughter Philippa. Okay. That's all right...anytime. See you at Harriet's tonight. 'Bye."

"Viv... Mrs Trevose, says that they aren't quite ready. Something about some tiling in the kitchenette and

108

some painting to be finished, but you're welcome to have a look."

"Thanks, it's very kind of you. How do I find them?"

"Here, I'll show you."

Madge came from behind the counter and walked to the door. She pointed up the road. "Carry on to The Crown at the T - junction. Turn left and then immediately right. The Trevose's live in Lower Farm House, about fifty yards on the right, opposite the village hall. You can't miss it," she added confidently.

I thanked her and followed her directions. Lower Farm House was set back from the road behind lawns crossed by a sweeping gravel drive. To me, as an Australian, it was a bitsa sort of a building; bits of this and bits of that added over the ages to make a harmonious whole that seemed to have grown from the ground instead of being built on it. The main part was half timbered, with a tiled roof. A thatched, timber-clad barn extended from one side and a red brick and timber wing formed an L - shaped addition to the other. A woman came to the door as the car wheels scrunched to a halt on the gravel. A black Labrador barked loudly and deeply from the safety of the entrance hall. A Springer Spaniel danced around me, yapping its challenge.

"Quiet! Freda, Meg. Here. Sit! That's enough. The dogs fell silent and crouched at her feet.

"Hi," I said. "John Allen. I've come about the accommodation," I offered my hand. She wiped some flour from her fingers on her apron. Her hand was cool and firm in mine.

"Vivianne Trevose," she said. "And this must be Philippa."

Pippa dug me in the ribs. "Pippa," I said. "She prefers to be called Pippa."

"Well then Pippa it is," she laughed. "How old are you. You look about the same age as my Melanie."

"Fourteen," Pippa replied shyly, conveniently forgetting the six months to her next birthday.

"Close enough. Melanie is nearly fifteen."

Pippa looked really smug.

"Come this way." Vivianne Trevose led us past the end of the barn to a smaller weatherboard and tile building set on staddle stones. The dogs followed until a pigeon took off with a loud clatter from an apple tree. Both dogs gave chase.

"It's an old granary," she said, as she led us to the steps.

"Look Dad, the house is resting on giant mushrooms," Pippa said in a loud stage whisper.

"Yes, they do look a bit like that, don't they, Vivianne laughed. "They were meant to keep the rats out when it was used to store grain."

The door at the top of the steps opened into a sitting room, with a kitchenette and breakfast bar on one side and three doors on the other. A man in overalls was bent over the sink.

"This is my husband, Leslie," Viv announced as the man straightened and turned towards us. He was tall and lean with a mop of ginger hair and an unruly beard. "Les,

110

this is Mr Allen and his daughter Pippa. They are looking for some accommodation."

"Hello," he said and made to offer his hand, then noticed that it was covered in grout. He withdrew and shrugged, embarrassed. He nodded, as though offering an alternative to a hand shake. "Just finishing off," he said. "If you don't mind the odd job still to be done or left undone, you can have this place. It all works. Hot water, cooker, bath and loo," he said walking across the room and opening the centre door. "And two bedrooms," he added, opening the other two doors.

Pippa darted into the nearest bedroom and bounced on the bed. She looked around her at the high vaulted timbers and beams, grinned and practically hugged herself with delight.

"Viv will give you bedding, crocks and cutlery, pots and pans and a TV," Leslie Trevose added, as if he thought he needed to sell the idea to me. How little he knew Pippa and the way she could twist me around her little finger. Pippa's look told me that we would be staying.

"And I've got a heater I could put in for you. It might get chilly at night soon. How long do you want it for?"

"Oh at least a month."

The Trevose's glanced at each other. Viv looked embarrassed. "It's a bit pricey. You see we've spent a lot on it and Les has lost his job. We thought we could let it self-catering for two hundred pounds a week in the high season. Would four hundred pounds be too much?"

Leslie looked agitated. His wife glanced towards him. "Mum can go in the spare room like she did last time. She may not even come," Mrs Trevose said.

Leslie still seemed agitated. I don't think it was his mother-in-law's accommodation he was worried about. Pippa had that look on her face; the one that the dog used to have when it was trying to teletransport food from my hand to its mouth.

"Fine," I said. "No problem. Would you like it in advance?"

Leslie visibly relaxed and Pippa whooped in delight.

"Come and have a cup of tea. I'll sort out the bits and pieces for you whilst the kettle's boiling."

The kitchen was stone flagged, with low beams. An oak dresser filled with blue and white china occupied one wall. A young girl wearing jodhpurs and polo shirt sat on the Aga, her knees drawn up to her chin, her heels resting on the chrome rail at the front. She jumped down when we came in.

"Ah Melanie, there you are," Vivianne said. "This is Mr John Allen and Pippa. They're going to live in our granary for a while."

"Hi," Melanie said, shyly. Pippa and Melanie measured each other up. Whatever alchemy was involved, the correct signals were given and received. Both broke into broad grins. "Cool," Melanie concluded.

Viv filled the kettle, lifted the cover and set it on the Aga. "Have you given Pepe her work out yet?" she asked.

"Just going to, Mum," Melanie answered. "Do you want to come?" she asked Pippa.

"Where?"

"To my horses. It's not far. Just down the road. The paddock past the shop."

Pippa's eyes widened. "Those horses are yours?"

"Two of them are. Well, one and a half really, 'cos Charlie Brown's only a pony and is getting on a bit. Do you ride?" she asked.

Pippa looked crestfallen as she slowly shook her head.

"I'll teach you. You can ride Charlie. He'll teach you more than I can. Come on. Come and meet him."

Pippa glanced at me. "Can I Dad?"

"Of course," I answered. I wouldn't have dared answer differently.

"Be back at seven at the latest", Viv called, as the two girls rushed from the room. "You'll have dinner with us this evening, won't you," she asked. "It's only a bit of steak and kidney pie, but you're very welcome."

"If you're sure, I'd love to."

"That's settled then," she said as she made the tea. "Then there's no rush."

Leslie drained his glass of wine, stood up from the kitchen table and rummaged on the dresser until he found pipe and tobacco. "If you're going to smoke that thing, you might as well take John down to the pub," Viv said, beginning to clear the table.

"Don't you want a hand with the dishes?" I asked.

"The girls will help me. Go on."

"Well, if you are sure," I said. "Thanks very much for dinner. I enjoyed that. It was very kind of you."

Leslie's aromatic pipe smoke hung on the still air on the way to The Crown.

"It's a lovely spot," I said, to make conversation, but meaning what I said.

"Yes, it is, isn't it," he replied. "I'm so glad that I'm back in UK. All the times I was overseas, it was the thought of Viv and Melanie living here that kept me going. That and the quality time we could have together when I was on leave."

"Oh. You worked overseas. What did you do?"

"I worked in the oil industry. Pipe line projects mainly. Nigeria, Iraq, Turkey, Saudi, Romania. Russia was a job too far for me. When the last contract finished unexpectedly, Viv and I decided that I should stay at home. Now I do a bit of consulting. We'll try and build up the bed and breakfast business. Things are tight, but we'll get by. What about you?"

"I'm a landscape architect. I design parks and gardens, public spaces, that sort of thing."

We turned into the pub. A few couples were eating. Four youths were clustered around the dart board. Leslie ordered a couple of pints and we sat at a table in the window recess. "Maybe you could help me out," Leslie said after taking an appreciative pull at his beer.

"Glad to. How?" I answered.

"There's a corner of my land behind the granary that's just rough ground. A bit of a bog at one end. Maybe you could advise me on how to develop it."

"Sure. I'll take a look..."

A loud tap on the window pane behind my head startled me. Leslie waved and beckoned. I turned around, but saw only a shadow gliding towards the door.

"Here's Rebecca. She's the archaeologist in charge of the dig up on the hill."

Rebecca was ... well... breathtaking. She was tall, and lean and built as though she spent a lot of time digging. She wore muddy boots, a red checked shirt worn outside dirty jeans and tight T-shirt, which did nothing to disguise her figure. If her shoulder length hair was described as corn coloured, then her eyes had to be cornflower blue. She greeted the youths playing darts, and ordered a pint of bitter at the bar.

"She has that effect on everybody the first time," Leslie joked. I realised I had been staring too hard. I looked away as she turned from the bar.

"Hi Les," she said, pulling up a stool. "Who's this," she asked, fixing me with a frank stare.

"Ah... this is John, John Allen from Australia. John, meet Rebecca, our grave-robber in residence."

"You're a shit, Les," she said laughingly, "but I've had much too good a day to care."

"You mean the excavator I hired for you didn't break down."

"No, actually it worked fine."

"There's nothing wrong with the permits."

"No."

"What could be better than that?"

"This," she said, reaching into her top pocket, placing a polythene sample packet on the table.

"What's that?" Les asked.

"Bronze age pottery shard," she announced triumphantly.

"So?"

"It's only what I've been looking for ever since I started this dig. It's only the first sign of pre-Iron Age occupation at this site ever," she said scornful of his ignorance. "It's only the first lead to support my opinion that this and probably many other Iron Age forts were developments of Bronze Age or even earlier settlements, if not strongholds. It's only my damn PhD thesis," she said, almost angry now.

"So it's quite important then," Les announced with a straight face.

"Oh you really are a shit Leslie Trevose," she said affectionately.

"Could you explain, please," I asked.

Rebecca examined me coolly, searching for latent mockery. She must have been satisfied there was none, for she smiled.

"Received wisdom told us that there were a series of invasions of the Celtic people through the Bronze and Iron Ages. Each technological advance or fashion in say pottery or even funeral customs, is supposed to be introduced by a new invasion. The hill top forts were built during all this mayhem, or at least the Iron Age part of it." She paused to drink from her pint. "An alternative view, that I find it easier to agree with, is that ideas disseminated, but people essentially stayed put. Sure there were some turf wars, territories lost and won, slaves taken, that sort of thing, otherwise there would have been no need for defences, but no mass extinctions. No complete eradication of existing culture, just gradual change. "

"So how can you decide from the archaeological evidence," I asked.

Rebecca shook her head in frustration. "The problem is that the archaeological evidence always highlights the new superimposed, literally, on the old," she answered. "It's almost impossible to show from published data how technologies might have overlapped. Think about it. We mostly find either grave goods, or what's left of them 'cos they're often already looted, or disturbed by ploughing; or we find discarded rubbish. Neither can be representative of what was actually happening. I mean, imagine you had the only bronze axe in a group still making flint tools. You'd take damned good care of it. Pass it down father to son. People only throw away the broken or commonplace.

"Makes sense to me," I agreed.

"On the other hand, some ritual, which we can only guess at, might force you to part with your most treasured possession as an offering to the gods, or whatever. I mean if everyone acted that way looking at it now, in the twentieth century, you could get the idea that everyone is as rich as Croesus."

"But how can you hope to prove your theory?"

"Oh, it's not just my theory. Lots of archaeologists think that way. It's really hard to prove just with artefacts, but actually there is some good evidence to support us, well in general, anyway. You might even have read about it. It was in all the papers."

"Give us a clue, Rebecca?" Leslie asked.

"A research group took DNA samples from a Neolithic burial in Somerset and compared it with mouth swab samples from the population in the local village. They found a match. Imagine that. After more than four thousand years. After the Celts, the Romans, the Dark Ages, Saxons, Vikings, Normans, plague, rebellion, famine, civil war, the dislocations of the agricultural and industrial revolutions, one family had stayed put. Wow!"

Rebecca tossed her hair back, as she exclaimed. She was so beautiful and animated, so alive it was almost incongruous that she should deal daily with the affairs of people so very long dead.

One of the young men at the dartboard left the pub pursued by raucous comment about his prospects with his date. His friends called Rebecca over to take his place. She did so with alacrity. I watched her play. So did every other man in the pub.

"Who are they?" I asked.

Leslie regarded me sardonically. "Her students. Nice lads." He indicated his empty glass. "Fancy another?"

I felt very mellow when Pippa and I said our thank yous and goodnights at the kitchen door. The granary was warm and welcoming. I watched the late news on TV whilst Pippa used the bathroom and made ready for bed. The news was full of the Queen's imminent return to London and the Prince William and Harry walking amongst the flowers at Balmoral. I went to Pippa to tuck her up. It was a little routine we had adopted since Sarah died.

"Dad," she said as I sat on her bedside. "You know we were planning to use Bernton as a base and tour around."

"Yes..." I answered, half suspecting what was coming.

"Well can we just stay here for the rest of our trip. I mean this little house is so gorgeous and Melanie and Viv... Oh don't look at me like that. She told me to call her Viv... Anyway they are just so cool and I want to learn to ride so can we, can we, pleeease dad?"

Memories of the day just ending flooded into my mind; our first view of the village, the friendly reception everywhere we turned, Pippa's new love affair with Charlie Brown, the pony and her instant rapport with Melanie. "If you want to sweetheart," I said.

"Oh you're just the best Dad a girl could have," she said, throwing her arms around me.

But later, as I lay in bed listening to the silence, pictures of my evening in the pub flickered across my mind and it was clear to me that quite apart from the business of digging for our roots, I didn't mind staying in Bernton either.

CHAPTER 8

I awoke at dawn to the brash squabbling of starlings under the eaves. They left on some airborne mission and I rolled over and dozed for a while to the sound of pigeons cooing contentedly in the ash tree next to the granary. Then Pippa awoke me more thoroughly with a mug of tea. I stared blankly at my watch. Seven o'clock. Pippa was already showered and dressed and looking very fresh in jeans and polo shirt.

"C'mon Dad. It's a lovely sunny day. Don't forget you're helping Mr Trevose today. Breakfast is all set. Do you want an egg?"

"Hmm..." I grumbled, never at my best first thing in the morning.

"I'll take that as a yes," she said and left.

I drank my tea and listened to Pippa clashing pans in the kitchenette. The smell of coffee and toast drove me to the bathroom. Sunlight streamed through the open windows. I showered and shaved and dressed in comfortable shirt and jeans. Pippa hugged me when I sat at the table.

"What have you done to your hair?" I asked. It was pulled back from her face and tied in a pony tail.

"Oh Dad," she exclaimed. "I'm going riding... I can't have it falling all over the place." The tone was that of an exasperated teacher to a pupil who failed to recognize the obvious.

A clattering on the steps announced Melanie's arrival. She burst through the door, clutching riding hats and elastic-sided boots.

"You should find something to fit you in this lot," she said. "Hi, Mr Allen," she tossed over her shoulder as she set to work fitting out Pippa. Suitably attired, and admired, my daughter tumbled out of the door with her new friend. I tidied away the breakfast things and sat down in front of the TV with a second mug of coffee. The news was full of plans for Princess Diana's funeral. The Queen was returning to London. The Union flag would fly at half-mast from Buckingham Palace. Apparently, normally the only flag that flies over a Royal palace is the Royal Standard and that only when the Monarch is in residence. The Royal Standard is never flown at half mast. The King is dead! Long live the King! So much for etiquette. Her Majesty would address the nation. She was reported to be saddened by the people's collective misunderstanding of private grief and mourning.

"John? Are you there?" Leslie called from outside. I switched off the TV and joined Leslie outside. The morning had the feel of a summer's day reluctant to admit that autumn was on the way. The dew was heavy and sparkled in the sun. The air was damp and fresh, with a slight chill. We walked around the side of the granary, beneath spreading dog roses and into an orchard. The trees were old and gnarled. Some still bore fruit, mainly apples, and the long rank grass was cluttered with windfalls. The ground fell away slightly, then rose steeply in a bank on which patches of chalk showed white through the brambles and nettles. The ground at the foot of the bank squelched with sodden leaf mould from which clumps of sedge and occasional willow saplings grew.

121

"So what did you have in mind, Les?" I asked.

"Dunno, really, except that it's a bit of a waste of space and an eyesore the way it is. I thought that I might be able to make a bit of a pond."

"Yes, you should be able to do that. It looks like a natural spring that's just become silted up. You could strip out the older and diseased fruit trees. Some of them are in a bad way and a real breeding ground for fungi. Replant them with new varieties. Cut and harrow or rotavate this old grass and re-sow it as a wild flower meadow. I hate to use poison, but I'd get some systemic weed killer on that brush on the bank, especially the brambles. You could replant it with... oh I don't know, Cotoneaster or Juniper if you want to keep a sort of wild look. If you could get hold of some boulders, you could have a rockery at the back of the spring. With the help of a pump, you could have flowing water too. Maybe even a cascade. Use the silt you dig out from the pond to make some raised beds. Hold them back with timber. I usually use old railway sleepers."

"That sounds really great," Leslie enthused, "I've got some old beams in the barn," then added in a crestfallen voice, "but it would cost a fortune."

"Not really. Not if you do it yourself. Hire one of those small tracked excavators, you know the ones they use for putting in cables, and a chain saw. Oh and some wire slings to pull stumps. You should be able to hire everything you need on a day by day basis."

"I know where to get all that, and I've got my own chain saw. But I'm not sure that I..."

"I'll help you," I said, surprising myself, then warming to the idea. Why not? Pippa would be off all day every day with the horses if this current new interest

122

developed as all her crazes had in the past. It was just the sort of design work I liked and it would be good to get back to the labouring side of my job, an aspect of my work I had left behind years before. It would be a great way to de-stress.

"Would you really? Do you mean it? But what about your holiday?"

"Pippa's not too keen on touring old ruins. I think she means to attach herself to Melanie and Charlie Brown. It'll give me something to do."

I spent the rest of the morning checking the fruit trees, felling those which were too old or diseased and sawing them into logs. When Leslie called me to lunch, I had developed a fine sweat and blisters between thumb and forefinger. Leslie poured me a beer which I drank gratefully. Melanie and Pippa tumbled into the kitchen, enveloping us all in horse scent.

"Dad it was just great!" Pippa exclaimed. "Melanie reckons I'm a natural. Charlie is just the greatest pony... except of course for Pepe. You should have seen Mel jump her. I mean... it was like so high," she said, rounding her eyes and holding her hand at a wildly improbable height.

Viv sent them off to wash their hands. I sat at the table. Viv bustled around the table, passing bowls of home made soup, crusty fresh bread and a cheese board. I was content to rest for a while. My muscles were stretched. I had justified my lunch. Sitting at the long oak table in that beamed and flag-stoned kitchen, I had a great feeling of continuity, that I was part of a succession of similar meal breaks stretching back over the centuries.

"Digger arrives at two," Leslie announced. "I've borrowed a rotavator from Fred Simpson. I'll pick it up with the trailer after lunch."

"It's ever so kind of you," Viv said, "what with you being on holidays. I feel really guilty now, charging you all that money for the granary."

I looked up from my plate. "Just carry on feeding me like this and I'll be looking around for extra jobs for you when this one's over," I said. "Look, I'd have had to pay a fortune to stay in a pub or hotel."

"But it isn't even finished," she started to say, flashing an angry glance at Leslie, who was shifting guiltily in his seat.

"Then there are the riding lessons..." I interrupted, "and well... besides I need something to do whilst Pippa is off with Melanie."

"Well, if you're sure," she said, suspiciously, only partly mollified. "Les, you'd better finish off in there today."

"I'm sure," I said and I was.

I made good progress with the excavator. The mounds of silt, clay and rubble grew and water bubbled from below the bank. The sun was warm on my back. My nostrils prickled at the smell of diesel exhaust, a smell that I have always associated with hard work. I manoeuvred the excavator to the head of the depression, close under the bank. I lowered the bucket, but it scraped against something hard. I pulled it back a little and tried again, but with no luck. I kept the downward pressure on and drew the boom in slowly. Suddenly the bucket bit deep. I emptied the bucket and returned it to the soft spot. The bucket jarred and bounced off something very hard. I revved the engine and powered the bucket down to the full extent of the boom, and lifted it dripping water and gravel, swivelled and dropped its load on the waste pile.

I closed down the engine and slid down the newly excavated bank to check the obstruction. I didn't want to break one of the bucket teeth. A large boulder protruded from the side of the excavation. Water swirled and bubbled from beneath it.

"Everything okay," Les called from the excavator, which ticked and clicked as the engine cooled. "I heard the engine rev and then shut down," he said anxiously, no doubt worried about the deposit he had paid to the hire company.

"Yeah," I answered. "I just wanted to check out this boulder, so that I don't wreck the bucket."

"Suits me," he grinned.

I splashed water on the rock and rubbed it clean. It glistened a light brown in the grey sludge.

"Looks like a sarsen," Les called.

"A what?" I replied.

"A sarsen stone. There are lots of them in this part of the world. Lumps of sandstone left by the glaciers, I'm told. There's one in the roadside up by the church. The landowners used to use them as boundary markers."

"Anyway, whatever it is, I was right. There's a spring here all right. Look at that," I said, pointing to the water welling up from beneath the stone.

Part of the bank beneath my feet gave way and slid into the water. I flung myself back, scrabbling for a hold on the loose gravel I had dumped from the last bucket load. My fingers closed around a stone, it was sharp and completely different from the other rounded pebbles. I washed it off in the pool. It was about ten centimetres long and finely edged, like a knife blade, with what seemed to be a tang at one end.

"Hey, look what I've found," I called and scrambled up the bank to join Les.

"Wow," he said, taking it from me. "That looks man-made. Look at these chips along the edge and this could have been a handle," he added, pointing to the tang.

"We should show it to Rebecca," I said. "It might be important."

"You're right. And we'd best stop digging until she's seen it."

Rebecca was crouched in the bottom of a trench scraping the loose soil with a trowel.

"Hi," I said. "I've got something to show you."

"A pint of bitter, I hope," she laughed, staightening her back with a groan as she rose from her knees. "I'm, parched." Her face was flushed from the heat and from bending. It contrasted with her red hair.

"I'm afraid not," I laughed, and held out the flint to her.

Rebecca paled. I swear that she shook as she took the flint in her hand. Her eyes glittered. She turned the flint over and examined it closely.

"Where did you get this?" she asked excitedly.

"I found it in Leslie's orchard, at the base of the bank. I was excavating a pond on what looked like a spring..."

Now her eyes glistened. She leapt from the trench, threw her arms around me and kissed me full on the lips. My heart pounded.

"Oh you darling man!" she exclaimed, releasing me to examine the flint more closely.

My chest still felt the soft pressure of her breasts. My lips still tingled with her kiss.

One of her students wandered over. "You don't kiss me when I find you things," he grumbled. "What is it, anyway?"

"You don't find me anything like this," she answered. "A late Neolithic tanged flint knife. It's about the best example I've seen. Beautiful workmanship," she added, rubbing her thumb over the blade.

"If I get a kiss every time I find something, I'll start digging again right away," I joked.

She laughed. Her generous lips spread wide to show her even white teeth. Her eyes glinted. "Deal," she said, in a challenging tone, "but you must show me where you found it. Now!"

CHAPTER 9

Com and Aedd, with Ened at his side, returned to the settlement around noon. As the little party breasted the brow of the hill, allowing them their first glimpse of the settlement, Com grunted in approval. In the valley, smoke rose languidly through the thatch of Com's and Ermid's longhouses. Both bore signs of re-thatching, pale-yellow fresh straw contrasting with the deep-brown weather-beaten and smoke-stained old roof. A new longhouse was being thatched and was two thirds complete. Two thatchers were on the roof, balancing precariously on the roof poles as they tied, beat into shape, combed and finally trimmed the bundles of straw passed up a ladder by two boys. A stack of neatly measured and cut bundles lay at the foot of the ladder. A fourth house was nearing completion. The main roof beams were in place, showing pale fresh adze marks, and the builders were swinging acrobatically through them, wedging and pinning in place the poles which would support the thatch. Small boys were daubing the hazel branch hurdles which formed the walls with clay, smoothing it with palms wet from time to time in a bucket of water. Two youngsters, naked but for loin cloths, trod and puddled clay in a shallow pit, where a young girl, at their shouted demand, added either water from a bucket or dirt from a pile adjacent to the pit. Young, unformed, lissom girls, calling to each other with eager laughing voices, carried water from the stream, some to replenish the clay pit, others to their mothers busy with the myriad of domestic chores that formed the substrate of survival.

In front of Dorn's house, a bondwoman knelt, grinding corn, rubbing the rounded stone back and forth with a slight rolling motion on the quern stone, deftly flicking the grain under the moving pestle with practised fingers which somehow escaped bruising. On the sheep-dotted hillside, a boy shepherd was watched over by his sheep dog. Pigs foraged amongst the beech trees. Around the houses, neatly cropped stubble fields, soon to be ploughed for spring planting, spread up the hillsides.

"Look how peaceful it is, Aedd, practically no sign of the burning. They have worked wonders in our absence."

Aedd nodded in agreement. Looking at the tranquil scene below it was as if the events of the past days had never been. A sudden presentiment sent a shiver through him, making him reach for Ened, hugging her to him, as though seeking to ward off evil with the power of his growing attachment to the girl. In that moment, Aedd saw the view clearly for what it was, an illusion. The real world would never be the same as it had been a few short days before.

Rh'on came out of the house and looked up as they descended the final slope. She waved in recognition, a touching girlish gesture, thought Aedd, although it appeared to be lost on Com.

"Welcome home my husband, and you too Aedd. Who is this? You too are welcome," said Rh'on in greeting.

"Rh'on, this is Ened, I have taken her bond," answered Aedd, a little awkward and embarrassed, because Rh'on was looking at him with smiling, quizzical, but at the same time knowing eyes.

"Well then you should be ashamed of yourself Aedd. Poor girl. Why did you not dress her? Why, the first frost is just around the corner and no shoes on her feet?" She took Ened's arm, and smiling gently said "You come with me. When I've attended to my husband, we'll see what can be done. Com are you well?" she asked, turning back to her husband, a worried frown chasing the banter from her face. "How is the wound? Come, let me attend to it. Come inside, all of you. Berin! Berin!" she called, "your father is home. Cigfen, fetch me woundwort and hot water. Oh, and some fresh dressings. Gwyn, some of the beef stew, bread and ale for our travellers. Quickly girls! Com, you have a fever; come and sit down. Aedd, did I not tell you to give him the infusion?"

"Er... I did," protested Aedd, but his reply was lost in the bustle that suddenly developed around them. Ened clung nervously to Aedd's arm.

"Gwyn, make some fresh fever infusion for the master."

Com sat on his customary cushioned stool, relieved to be home again. Rh'on took his arm on her aproned knee and gently started to remove the bandages.

Berin appeared at his father's side "Hello father, welcome home," he said.

"You've moved very quickly here, Berin," Com complimented, "we'll soon be back to normal at this rate."

"Thank you father," answered Berin, beaming at the unaccustomed praise, "everyone has worked really hard. But tell me, what did Dorn have to say?"

Com winced as the last of the dressing stuck to the wound. "It seems they thought they were under attack when young Alen arrived there and Dorn had already sent the levies to defend the gorge. He was very upset, very sympathetic, a good friend. Oh, and he thinks you're right. He is sure that the attack was meant to drive us from our land, capture or kill us, not just a cattle raid."

Berin smiled. At last, he thought, someone is seeing sense. "He thinks that the attack on us is part of a plan by Senot to take the ford and control of the trade routes for himself," Com continued. "Because the gorge, which is so easily defended, stops him coming upriver, Senot must outflank Dorn and come through the backdoor, us. We have to build a stronghold, just like you said, but Dorn wants it even bigger and better than you suggested."

Com broke off with a groan, paling and holding himself rigid as Rh'on soaked away the last of the bandages. The wound was red, angry and swollen, yellow-green pus oozed from the gash in the tightly attenuated, hot skin. Tenderly, Rh'on bathed it in the woundwort solution, careless of the drips in her lap, which soaked her skirt.

Rh'on began to re-bandage his arm. Com continued, "I put your ideas to him, you know, about the south ridge. He's going to help us build it. There will be working parties from the ford and Tarok's outstation arriving soon."

"Did you tell him that we need bronze; that we can't fight men like that outlander and win with our flints; how a hunting spear is good for only one thrust."

"No Berin, I did not. Dorn is already more than generous. I cannot ask him for bronze, which anyway he does not have in any quantity. Senot monopolises the bronze trade as you well know."

Berin caught a sharp glance thrown at him by his mother and choked back the irritated response which he was about to make.

"No more talk for the moment, Berin," she said gently enough, but with very firm undertones, as she tied the end of the bandage. She took the steaming bowl from Gwyn and handed it to her husband. "Here, drink this. It will save you from the fever. Then you must eat and rest."

Obediently, Com drank, but with obvious distaste. "There is much to be done Rh'on. I can't rest now."

"You'll rest," she said, "even if I have to tell Aedd to put you to bed."

"Don't worry father," interposed Berin, "I'll take some men off the building and make a start on the stronghold, at least mark it out, so that we are ready for the working parties, then later, when you are rested, you can come and see what you think."

"All right, Berin, thank you. Yes that seems to be the best solution," quailed Com, already resigned to Rh'on's nursing, "but there is something else I must tell you."

"Later Com," Rh'on commanded firmly. "Your wound is infected, you have a fever and are like to die sooner rather than later if you don't take heed," she added, bustling him to his couch. "Off you go, Berin. Bring the master some stew," she flung back over her shoulder at Gwyn as she fussed Com from the room, "then help Ened to serve Aedd."

Aedd was wiping the bowl with the last of the bread when Rh'on returned. Her forehead was creased, she seemed much less self-assured, more vulnerable.

"I did dose him that brew of yours," Aedd said hurriedly in case he was to be blamed for Com's deterioration, which clearly was giving Rh'on cause for concern.

"Yes, I'm sure you did, Aedd," she said absently, her mind elsewhere.

"How is he?"

"Oh, not well, not well at all. In fact if he does not rest he is going to be very ill indeed. The wound is badly mortified, you see. Normally woundwort would have prevented mortification, but for some reason it hasn't this time. I'm worried."

Then she smiled a bright and brittle smile. "Now Aedd, why don't you go off after Berin while I attend to Ened. There are a few things we must do."

When Aedd approached, Berin was directing Amren, Brys, Han and Arec. They cut stakes from hazel bushes which they had dragged up the hillside, and drove them into the turf to mark out a trench along the contour, just below the lip of the hill.

"Hey Berin, How's it going?"

"Fine. Well fine here. Look I told the old man to see about bronze weapons." Berin fumed. "Why didn't he talk to Dorn about it? You were there. It was you who told me how Belu died because he couldn't free his spear point after the first thrust. Why didn't you make him ask?"

"That's not fair, Berin, I don't need this. I don't deserve to be spoken to like that," Aedd answered indignantly.

"Oh I'm sorry Aedd. I just hate the fact that my father can be so blind."

"Dorn too. Listen I've much to tell you, but for your ears only."

Berin looked askance at his friend, who clamped his lips in a thin line and jerked his head to one side, a firm refusal to talk further except out of earshot of the others.

"Amren, take charge here," called Berin, "carry on along that line. Send someone for picks and shovels." They walked around the hill, out of earshot of the others. "Now what's going on Aedd?"

"There was no attack on the ford. The levies were sent off on a wild goose chase, deliberately, to stop them from reinforcing us. We were betrayed."

"What, who by? By Dorn? Why?"

"No not by Dorn. He had been given a sleeping draft the night of the attack. He had no idea of what was going on. He is very sympathetic and concerned. I think Urak is behind it in some way."

"Urak? But why? That's ridiculous. He's shaman, lore keeper, a man of power in the tribe, Dorn's son. Does Com know your suspicions? He said he had something to tell me."

"No, I don't think so, no, in fact I'm sure he doesn't, but he wants to believe Dorn, that all is in order. I think he's doing a big deal with Dorn, maybe that's what he wants to talk to you about."

"Well we must tell him at once. Come on." Berin turned to make off down the hill, but Aedd grabbed him and swung him round to face him.

"No, Berin. I have no proof. Besides, I'm sworn to silence. I wasn't to tell anyone of what I suspect."

"You'd better tell me it all, Aedd. Everything."

"Well when we got there, your father goes into a huddle with Dorn. I wander down for a natter with Anoeth. As we were talking, the first of the levies come back. Then along comes Conwen with the rest of the men and they're dragging a body, Cerdic, a charcoal burner who works in the gorge. They'd found him with his throat cut. That evening, as I'm looking after your father and he's telling me about Dorn and Urak's explanation of what happened to Alen, he lets slip that Urak claimed Cerdic brought the warning of the raiders in the gorge. Then, and this is the bit your father doesn't know, Anoeth sent word that Cerdic, who was supposed to have brought the news, had not passed the ford that night."

"But that means Urak must be lying. If there was no warning, then the levies were sent to the gorge deliberately to prevent them helping us. Cerdic was murdered to prevent him giving the game away. We are betrayed. I must tell father!"

"Berin !" hissed Aedd, " be quiet. How can you tell him? What can you tell? That a blind man did not hear a man pass his hearth? That the son of the High Chief, shaman and lore keeper of the tribe is conspiring against the High Chief and his own tribe? For make no mistake about it, Dorn's concern is real and he is no part of this plot. Listen! One man is already dead, murdered to preserve this secret. Would you want me, or Anoeth to follow him to the Mother? Would you want to be disgraced for accusing the son of the High Chief of treason?"

"But what are we going to do, Aedd, we must not allow this scum to hurt us further."

"Well...he hasn't hurt us at all yet. The levies would not have arrived in time to alter the result, though he was not to know that, and we now suspect him and he doesn't know that either. I'm sending Alen to Anoeth as apprentice. He will be our eyes."

"Good, good. That will also give you reason to visit. We must keep watch on Urak and keep faith with Dorn and

Tarok. With a strongpoint here, we hold Dorn's rear. With their help we will survive, without it we are all lost."

Berin gazed out over the loved clan lands, his attachment to them almost palpable, so strong his feelings of being rooted in this space..

"We must get this strongpoint built immediately. Senot will try again. We must assume that he will know about our plans soon. He will try to attack before we can finish it. Damn, we need bronze weapons, but I suppose that is impossible. Senot holds the bronze trade with the outlanders, and he's hardly likely to trade any with us."

"Berin, my bondwoman, Ened...."

"Bondwoman? What bondwoman? Who's Ened?" Berin looked at his friend quizzically.

"Er.. er," Aedd spluttered, looking sheepish.

"What have you been up to now?" Berin continued to probe.

"I took her from Anoeth. He wanted her out of the settlement. For her protection, like."

"Is she pretty?" Berin asked, grinning broadly.

"Some would say so," Aedd answered reluctantly.

"So it's just protection then. Nothing to do with your comforts, I suppose."

"Suppose what you like. Nothing to do with you is what it is," Aedd answered firmly.

"Anyway she told me of some people in the far west who make and trade bronze. Not outlanders, but people like us who follow the Mother."

"What? Do you think it's true?"

136

"Well, she says her father told her, and that his father had actually visited them and watched them make it."

"Where can we find these people," Berin asked excitedly.

"The end of the earth, she said. A moon's travel from where her folk live near the West Sea. But there's no trade now, anyway, not since the troubles started a few years back."

"Oh?"

"Some chief in the high chalk land far to the west of here is raiding down as far as the West Sea, taking slaves. Outlanders are mixed up in it, trading bronze for slaves. They take the women, and the men are sent to work for the chief."

"Doing what?"

"Dragging great stones on rafts up the river and then overland. She said the stones were as big as two men."

"But what for?"

"Nobody knows. But the slaving explains why we haven't seen any trade along the West Way in a long time."

"The Mother knows how I'd like to make contact with those bronze traders. But we daren't even dream about it at the moment. We can't spare anyone and anyway we've nothing to trade, even if we could keep clear of the war bands." He hit the palm of one hand with his fist in frustration and turned to stare westwards.

"What an adventure. Would you come with me?"

"You couldn't stop me Berin."

Berin turned back to the work party. "Oh not like that, Brys. That's no way to use a pick. Have you ever seen

anything like it Aedd? Here, give it to me," Berin chided as
he grabbed the pick from Brys. Swiftly Berin checked the
antler tine, the drilled stone weight and the ash handle,
then hefted it over his head, left hand at the end, right
hand at the head of the shaft, just below the weight. As he
swung down, his right hand slipped along the shaft to his
left, so that the pick head described an arc, centred on his
shoulders. The tine buried to the weight in the turf, and
weathered chalk below. Berin levered up on the handle,
freeing turf and chalk.

"That's how you do it. Let the pick do the work. Now let
me see you try."

"You see father, if we run the ditch around like this,
right on the shoulder of the hill, stack the dirt on the uphill
side and then take the shoulder of the ditch out too, adding
it to the bank, why any attacker will be faced with a bank
at least his own height, nearly twice in places."

"Hmm, I see, but how do you stop the spoil falling back
into the ditch?"

"Well we make a wide level base as we go and pack the
dirt down on to it, with that big stamp over there, " Berin
explained, pointing to where Han and Arec stood on a
wedge of excavated chalk rubble, tamping it down with a
huge log, two side branches of which had been retained to
provide lifting handles. "We make the bank narrower as we
go up, but we also drive in stakes, and fill in the gaps with
brush and hurdles, to retain the dirt until its packed solid.
It's working well where we've started. Come and have a
look."

They walked around the south western slope which faced
down the valley. The men of Ilws and Com were digging a

138

trench around the contour. Twin lines were marked out on the hillside with stakes. Aedd and Amren, both stripped to the waist, were working in opposite directions with the picks. Han, Arec and Kar stood by with shovels and the log stamper.

Com watched in silence for a moment, then asked "Who's on watch? Most of the men are here or working on the house."

"Brys is one, with his wound he's better on light duties and then I'm using Oranc, Cigfen and Blodwen. I thought using the women to watch during the day would release the men to work. The men will stand their watch at night though. They always have their weapons nearby, I've insisted on that. When are the other working parties coming? There's so much to do, even on the houses."

"Tarok's men will take a day or so to gather and at least a full day on the march. Anyway, they should be with us tomorrow. It's a pity they can't come direct, but the wetlands are impassable. None can travel in them, you could lose an army there."

Berin thought back to his recent experience and agreed. He had only hunted the fringes of the lowland but that had been bad enough.

"Dorn's men march today, we should see them this evening. We should kill an ox."

"I'll arrange that now. Hey Kar," Berin shouted, "get down to the settlement and organise an ox roast. We're expecting company." To Com he added, "How many are coming?"

"I expect a score from Dorn, nearer to two score from Tarok. Dorn is worried about a threat to the gorge if he takes too many away from the ford."

"With near four score, counting our own, we should finish at least the first defences within a moon, but they will need feeding. We haven't enough."

"Don't worry Berin, Dorn is sending us a very generous herd, very generous indeed. In fact I am quite pleased about our arrangement. But water, what about water for the stronghold. As I said to Dorn, it could be days before relief came, especially if there were simultaneous attacks at the gorge and here."

Berin walked around the hill to the depression where he had lain with Olwen. Was it really only last night? "You see the water in the dip?"

"Yes, but that's not enough."

"No, of course not, not as it is, but why does the water collect there, on the side of a hill? I suppose that it is run off and dew which collects on the clay base of this hollow. See where I've dug into it here. Well the clay stops the water from running out. If we made a series of these, only much bigger and deeper, or made a ditch inside the top bank and lined it with clay, we would have enough water for us and even enough to leave some for the stock."

"Yes, I think you could be right Berin. Water was always my worry, even after Dorn persuaded me that you were right and that we had to build a stronghold. Yes, you have coped extremely well while I have been away. The settlement is cleaned up and the new houses progressing well. All in all, most satisfactory."

Berin basked in the uncustomary praise.

"Now I have some news for you," Com continued. "Let's walk a while." He steered his son further away from the work party, until well out of earshot. "Dorn is sending two hundred head," he continued when satisfied they could not be overheard. Berin whistled. "Yes, very generous, I agree," continued Com. "Much of them on your behalf."

"On my behalf father?" puzzled Berin.

"Yes, Dorn..." Com hesitated for a moment to find the right words, "...Dorn has a daughter, Branwen, a delightful girl, pretty, obedient, well-trained and no doubt a good dowry from her mother. Dorn and I have decided that you shall take Branwen to wife."

Berin was stunned. He felt himself pale, weaken as the blood drained, as Com's news sunk in. "But I don't want her. I want..."

"Hear me out Berin. Dorn is sending me ten bondmen as part of the dowry. He's giving their bonds to me, they'll be yours when you inherit. Think what that means. We have always been small in numbers, but with ten bondmen we have security and a decent work force at last. Think what we can achieve."

"But...but I want to take Olwen for my wife."

"Olwen? What.... Ermid's daughter? Oh a pretty and sweet girl. I can understand her turning your head, but not a match for a chief's son, no connections or bloodline to compare with Branwen. Wait a year or two and take her as a second wife."

"Father, don't you understand? I love Olwen. I mean to make her my first, and only wife."

"Berin, Berin my son. Think. Two hundred head of cattle. Ten bondmen and the High Chief's daughter. A pretty thing she is too…"

"I won't do it. I've already asked Olwen to be my wife, and she's agreed."

"You are my son. You will be chief in my place when I return to the Mother. You must think of the greater good of your clan. You shall do as I bid."

"I shall wed Olwen. You don't understand. I love her!"

Berin thought his father was going to have a seizure. Com's face purpled. He spluttered with rage. "Love!" he spat, "what do you mean love. What do you understand about love. Don't presume to tell me that I don't understand. I understand that you have no sense of responsibility to your people, no love for your family or for their honour or for their lore. I understand the lust of a young man for his doxy. Would that I could disinherit you, but you are all that is left me. A son who will gladly put his hussy before the good of the clan. I'll not have it. You will obey me in this matter."

Eye to eye they glared at each other, spittle dribbling slowly from the corner of Com's tight set mouth. Berin fixed his father with a look of such malevolence that it would have frozen the midsummer's sun, but Com faced him, so strong was his own conviction, and it was Berin who turned on his heel and walked away.

Berin pounded the ground in anger. Although the sun had long since set on the evening of his most recent and damaging confrontation with his father, Berin's fury had not cooled with the night air. His hurt was like a deep wound in his chest. His lungs ached, trying to heave short breaths around the nauseous lump in his throat. His stomach cramped with the deep seated sobs wrenched from him by his anguish, once he had found isolation, here in the furthest watch post down the valley.

Slowly, as the penetrative silence around him had its affect, until his own distress was the only anomaly in the general peace, his breathing steadied and some sense returned. Guiltily he remembered Oranc's shocked expression as he had curtly ordered him back to the settlement. The resentful glances, turned shoulders and choked-off responses when he had rostered night guards, checked progress and organised work parties for the following day, had told him that he had been savagely unreasonable. Damn, he thought, shaking his head in abject misery, what am I going to do.

A twig snapped behind him. Suddenly alert, hairs rising on his nape, Berin crouched, reaching first for his spear then turning to face the sound, searching the darkness. A second twig snapped, closer, a branch rustled. Berin masked his face behind his cloak to hide its paleness and firmed his grip on the spear shaft.

"Berin" whispered Aedd's voice, "Berin, where the hell are you?"

There was a loud thump, a surprised yelp, instantly suppressed, as Aedd measured his length on the hillside and a slithering rustle, growing louder as he slid down to the thorn thicket where Berin kept watch on the valley below.

"Oh damn, where is the silly bugger?"

"Over here you great lummock. Quiet, you're making enough noise to wake Senot himself."

"Oh, right," said Aedd in a loud whisper, picking up his shield and pulling his axe from between his knees, where it had swung on its thong during his fall. "All quiet?" he asked, as he squatted beside Berin.

"It was until just now," replied Berin dryly.

"I'll bugger off back up then," Aedd answered gruffly, straightening his knees and ponderously rising to his feet. "Some folks don't deserve company. You've been sore all evening, like a bear that sat on a bee hive and can't reach its own arse."

"Oh stay Aedd. I'm sorry, all right? Berin reached out to touch Aedd's boot.

"Here, I brought you some grub," Aedd said, mollified by the gesture, untying a cloth from his belt and passing it over.

"Er.. thanks Aedd, but I'm not hungry, I couldn't," Berin replied, his stomach knotting.

"Waste not want not." Aedd wolfed alternate mouthfuls of still warm beef and bread. "Lacks salt and about three days hanging. Mother it's tough. What got into you tonight?"

Berin was silent for so long that Aedd wondered if he should leave after all. When he finally spoke it was in a very quiet, sad, flat voice, which alerted Aedd to the real depth of his friend's hurt.

"Olwen. I want to take her for my wife. Father has done a deal with Dorn. They are agreed that I shall take Dorn's daughter, Branwen, to wife."

"So that's what you were arguing about on the hill. I've never seen anyone as angry as you two. Why not take

144

them both? Wed Branwen as they want, then after a while take Olwen as your second wife. There are plenty as do."

"Oh Aedd, not you too. That's just what father said at first. But you don't understand. I feel so...so much for Olwen. I love her. I don't want others, only her. I want our children to succeed me, I want her as my first, my only wife. I love her Aedd. There's more," he added after a brief silence, "I have asked her to wed me; we are already lovers."

Aedd silently put his arm around his friend's shoulders. "Well you're in a pretty mess then, aren't you. But what can you do? Persuade your father to change his mind?"

"No, father will never change his mind now. Too much has passed between us. I was a fool, I lost my head with him. Besides, he has done a great deal with Dorn. Two hundred head and ten bondmen."

Aedd whistled. "Now that's a deal." No wonder the old fox didn't want me upsetting things with Dorn, he thought.

"Father is determined that our connections with Dorn and his people must be strengthened. So is Dorn. It's mutual security really. Dorn needs us to defend the West Way. We need his strength. The ten bondmen are the decider. Cattle we can always get back, but labour, fighting men to face this new threat, that's something different. No, father will never change his mind."

"Then Dorn must change his."

"No, the High Chief cannot. It would stain his honour, besides, father would never let him out of a deal like that."

"Berin," Aedd said steadily, "do you remember what you told me this afternoon. You said we must hold true with Dorn and Tarok, that we are all lost without their help.

145

Don't you already know the answer? Don't you already know what you have to do?"

Berin's shoulders heaved. He took a deep breath and sighed. "Just don't say for the greater good Aedd." There was a long silence. "How am I going to tell her?" Berin asked finally. "What can I say?"

"I don't know my friend, I don't know. Look, I'm going back now. Can I get you anything? Who is your relief? I'll send him down early."

"No relief Aedd, I'll not go back tonight. I have much to think about."

"I'll see you tomorrow then."

"Yes."

Aedd struggled up the slope, a rivulet of rolling pebbles small flint fragments and pieces of chalk marked his passage for a while, then as Aedd's deep breathing punctuated with occasional grunts of effort and the sound of rustling bushes receded, so did the stone fall trickle to a stop. Berin welcomed the silence, wrapping it as a bandage around his broken dreams.

Aedd scouted back from Berin's hide for several hundred paces before dropping back down the slope to the familiar valley path alongside the brook they called Afon'panw. It was only then that he realised that in the confusion of Berin's pain, he had forgotten to tell Berin that Urak had arrived at the settlement with the working party from the ford. Ah well, he thought, poor bugger has enough to worry about at the moment. I'll keep an eye on Urak, though he's not likely to be up to anything tonight.

As he walked, he allowed his thoughts to drift to his own good fortune. Ened seemed to have made a great impression on Rh'on, who was treating Ened, bondwoman though she was, as one of her own family. She had taken Ened to her own quarters and found shifts and shoes for her and assigned one of the divisions at the rear of the longhouse for their own use, for however long it took to rebuild a house for Aedd. As she said, with a wink to them both, it would give them a measure of privacy. Aedd hurried his pace at the memory and grinned as he caught himself out.

He was glad that Alen had taken it all so well. He seemed genuinely pleased at the idea of going to the ford to be Anoeth's apprentice. Alen had always enjoyed working flint and in fact he was already capable of fashioning quite passable tools. Alen's enthusiasm had reached fever pitch when Aedd had drawn him aside and, in hushed tones, outlined the other part of his assignment. He was a good lad. He would keep his mouth shut. Alen could go back to the ford with the drovers who were due tomorrow.

The glimmering of several camp fires beckoned as Aedd rounded the right hand bend in the valley, opposite the spur in which the stronghold was being built. The occasional figure moved between the fires, briefly blotting out the friendly glow, but as Aedd drew closer, he saw that most of the visitors were wrapped in groups around the fires. Bursts of laughter and occasional song drifted down the valley, showing that a pot or two of ale had been downed after a days march.

"Halt!" came the challenge, "who's there?"

"Aedd of Com," Aedd replied, adding "Who are you?"

"Creggan, we met at the ford this very morning."

"Ah, that's right. Listen Creggan, you'd better know that we have scouts out, so don't go spitting them on that pig

147

sticker of yours, when they come in tired and thinking of their beds. There's Berin, he's furthest out, down the valley on the east side, where it gets steep. The brook makes a bit of a bend to the west there and opens up a wide meadow. Kar is up on the top, behind us here and Madwg is on the other side, past where we're building the bank and ditch. Pass it on to your relief. Oh, and no one is to go down the valley. I want to know if anyone tries. Who is your relief?"

"Darak"

"Pass on what I've said to him."

"Aye, I'll see to it."

"Good man."

Aedd walked on into camp. "Hey Aedd, have some ale with us," Iowerth called.

"Aye thanks I will," Aedd replied, taking the proffered bowl and squatting beside Iowerth.

"Hear you took the bond of that little beauty Ened, you lucky bugger."

Aedd nodded, wondering what was coming.

"You'd best watch out for Tarok when he gets here. He was very smitten with her. Mad as hell he was when his wife sent her away. He'll be madder still when he doesn't find her at the ford, especially when he discovers Anoeth passed her bond on. Reckon he thought she'd be safe with the old man, safe for him on his visits, if you know what I mean."

"Thanks, I'll keep her out of his way."

"Look Aedd, I don't owe Tarok no favour. I witnessed Ened's bond being passed to Anoeth, just so that you know, in case he tries something."

148

"Aye, thanks Iowerth, Aedd said, draining the bowl and clapping him on the shoulder."Thanks."

Aedd strolled on up to the settlement. Urak's bondsmen slouched against the entrance to Com's house. Aedd greeted them as he advanced, but there was no response. Aedd checked for a moment, more in surprise at their rudeness than for any other reason, then, realising that they were making no effort to make passage for him, he continued deliberately and determinedly on his course. At the last moment, when collision seemed inevitable, they moved aside reluctantly to let the big man through to the porch, where a dim light flickered around the edges of the door curtain.

As Aedd raised the curtain Com was saying "... and these are my new wards, Olwen and Oranc. Oranc is the brave lad who felled the outlander with a sling shot." Olwen bobbed on slightly flexed knees as her name was mentioned. Oranc stared impassively at Urak, who was sitting at Com's side at the hearth, a bowl of mead in his hand.

"Ah, Aedd, "Com said, "come and join us. Urak has been asking me about our dispositions. I've told him that he should ask Berin, or you. Where is Berin, by the way?" Com asked testily, his face clouding. "I wanted to talk to him about work parties for tomorrow."

Aedd sat on the skins which were scattered around and between the stools on which Urak and Com were sitting. He accepted a bowl of mead offered by Gwyn, who returned to the shadows at the end of the hall.

"Berin is scouting the valley. He intends to stay out most of the night, I think. He wants to make sure that our scouts and sentries are on their toes."

"As Urak is come now," Com continued, "he suggests we should build the cairn as soon as possible, then he can dedicate it and will not have to stay longer than necessary. He feels that his father needs him at his side, which I can quite understand. Aedd, if Berin's not back by first light, you'll have to organise the men. At least a score for the cairn, then we can complete it in a couple of days."

Aedd protested. "But Com, that will mean stopping work on the ditch and bank. Surely we must organise our defences before all else."

"Aedd, without the caring hand of the Mother to support us, all our enterprises are doomed to failure," Urak interrupted in quiet, measured tones. "It seems that because of circumstances prevailing at the time, our good friends Belu and Ermid were sent on their journey with a minimum of respect to the Mother and consideration for the relatives. We must make amends. We must not risk offence. Aedd, do not forget the grieving father and mother and brother, the son and daughter, their grief must have a focus. What is two days in a moon? We will build the cairn, sacrifice to the Mother and dedicate it to the memory of her servants. You have also started the defences without sacrifice. I understand your haste, but we must not lose the Mother's favour."

Aedd looked nonplussed towards Com, but he was smiling and nodding in agreement.

"Come now Aedd, Com has brought me up to date on progress in the settlement and the fortifications. You have solved the water problem I hear. Excellent. But what of your defences now, at this moment, how are we protected?"

"We have scouts posted to watch the valley, and the tops on either side; a line of pickets across the valley where we are building the stronghold and the main force is camped between the settlement and the picket line."

"Good, good, but is it necessary to watch the tops? What about the West Way?"

"We think it is necessary to watch the tops, there's always a chance that they will try to sneak around in the dark whilst we concentrate our efforts on the easy route up the valley."

"But surely it is very difficult to pass? The valley sides are thickly wooded."

"The sides are, Urak," Com contributed, "but not the top. It was cleared long since. Oh parts of it have grown back, but it's quite open. We use it for summer grazing, you see, and that keeps it fairly clear. Once on the top, a body of men could move quite easily. Of course, getting down the side would be a problem, because there are only a few places where they could pass and so we watch those."

"And where are these places? Where do you place your scouts?"

Aedd thought rapidly. I must answer, or he will suspect that I know something, but I cannot give our men away to Urak and risk yet more slit throats. "Below the pickets, the scouts have freedom to choose their own positions."

"Oh, why is that? That sounds uncontrolled to me."

"It's hard out there; hard on the nerves. The scouts are hunters, only this time the quarry is man. The choice of hide depends on many things, the wind, moonrise, rain, dew or frost, the wild animals. It is a dangerous game and a wrong decision may mean death. They must each have the choice." Aedd noticed that Olwen had gone very pale.

"What about the West Way, is that guarded?"

"There are several shepherds in the hills. It is very open up there. They would be sure to spot any party of men and would alert the night watchman. No, an enemy could not come at us undetected from that direction."

Satisfied for the moment, Urak turned his thoughts to Oranc, from all that he had heard about the battle at the house of Com, the immediate cause of the set back to his plans, "Well cousin I thank you for your offer of hospitality. Your wards, are they staying here?"

"Why yes. I thought it better to bring them under my wing, and then Ermid's house can be used communally until the other houses are completely finished."

"Then it would be a pleasure if they would attend me during my stay. Could that be arranged?"

"Why of course, yes, an excellent idea."

"I thank you. If you have no objections, I would like to retire now. With respect cousin, I suggest that you do too. You look very tired and worn."

"Your lodging is prepared. Olwen, Oranc, look after our guest. Show him to his quarters. Here, take his satchel, Oranc, light the way Olwen."

Olwen took a taper and Oranc picked up the satchel. Urak rose and followed them out of the main hall, through the wicker screen set in the dividing wall.

"Such a charming man," Com said approvingly."

Oh Com, how can you be such a fool, thought Aedd, biting his tongue, knowing that what he had to say would go unheard. Instead of the bitter truth he desperately wanted to reveal, he asked blandly, "How are you feeling Com, how is your wound."

"To tell you the truth Aedd, not good. I will go to my bed as Urak suggests. Gwyn," he called, "Gwyn, light me to my bed, there's a good girl. Then you can go." Com shuffled off behind the serving girl to his sleeping quarters, a stooped, rapidly ageing figure.

Aedd slipped out of the door flap to answer a call of nature. Urak's retainers were still at their posts, literally, lounging against the supports of the porch. Aedd wasted no breath on them. He walked to the privy at the edge of the settlement. The fires in the encampment were dying down and with them, the sounds of merriment. The new moon was rising, a thin sickly crescent; a chill breeze from the north east threatened a cold night for the watchers. Not for me, thought Aedd contentedly, not now with Ened to warm me.

As Aedd returned, the door flap of Com's house was suddenly swung back. Urak, momentarily illuminated, stepped out and allowed the hide door to fall back into place. Aedd froze, pressing himself to the wall of Amren's new house, peering into the shadows, scarcely illuminated by the faint moonlight. He could see nothing but a deeper shadow, which might have been the porch, or the grouped figures. He could hear nothing but the fluttering of dried leaves as the breeze swirled and made them dance madly across the hard packed earth between the houses. The door flap flared again, was briefly blocked by a man's figure then blacked out completely. Aedd heard footsteps scrunching through the fallen leaves towards him, then turning at the end of Com's house to head up the valley. I wonder what all that was about, he thought. Anyway, both of them have gone up the valley, so there is nothing to worry about for the moment. He's probably sent them back to the ford on some errand.

Ened was waiting for him in the storeroom which Rh'on had had cleared out for their use. Her face lit up from within as she saw him. As he sat on a stool with a grunt of tiredness, she knelt at his feet and pulled off his boots.

"Look Aedd, look what Rh'on gave me," she said standing up again in front of him, smoothing the fine spun cream coloured cloth over waist, hips and thighs, "and two others, one brown and one green, and look," she enthused, standing on one leg, holding up a booted foot for his examination, "I've never had boots before. They pinch a bit though," she said, reaching for her toes, balancing precariously, then falling giggling to the sleeping furs.

Aedd smiled inside and out at her lying there, so ingenuously, hair flung as a mane around her head, one boot on, one boot off, lissom legs spread wide as she had fallen, skirt hitched to the tops of her thighs. Aedd raised his finger to his lips with a nod towards the wall. Her face at once became a mask so serious that Aedd started to giggle. He undressed quickly, pinched out the taper and scuttled under the coverings. Ened was there before him, completely bootless and dress-less, open mouthed and breathless.

Berin had attuned himself to the sounds of the night. Up the slope, behind him, a branch tapped intermittently on a tree trunk, as occasional gusts swirled in the bowl of the valley, each seeking to regain its parent breeze at the top of the hill, but like a naughty child at bed time, lingering long enough to dance and play with the remaining leaves. Must be the rowan, Berin reflected. Sounds around him became familiar, not threatening, as much a part of his temporary woodland existence, as the gentle sound of his stubble rasping on his cloak with each new breath. Berin amused himself identifying the creatures of the night. Near at hand, the overloud busy crackling of leaves and shrill squeaking betrayed quarrelling voles, oblivious to his presence, intent only on territorial supremacy. Further off, he heard the delicate prancing advance of the roe deer. Berin could almost see its damp nostrils dilate and twitch, its eyes round, its ears turning this way and that, alert to any and every danger. Even so he was startled by its stiff-legged turn and sudden headlong brush-crashing dash as it caught his scent on an eddy. Later, from down the hill, towards the meadow, he detected the amiable shuffling amble of a badger. Berin did not see or hear the wild cat which watched him for a while before delicately, paw by slinking paw, it went about more important business.

Towards dawn, at the first paling of the stars in the eastern sky, Berin drifted towards sleep, in his imagination lying in Olwen's arms, head pillowed on her breast, suffused with the heady scent of her womanliness. His tired, hurt conscious mind, drubbed by the use he had made of it since he learnt of his father's awful decision, finally bowed to the sub-conscious and found relief in happier memories.

The long quavering call of an owl, come to hunt the shadows of the bottom meadow as the tops of the hills lightened under the rising sun, sent the voles scuttling for cover beneath a fallen tree, all quarrels forgotten, and brought Berin to his senses. Swiftly, yet hardly moving his body, Berin checked around him, first the valley, then the slopes on either side, then the slope behind. All was still. Slowly he stretched beneath his cloak, first one leg, then the other, then his arms. Mother, my feet are cold, he reflected. The clap of a pigeon's wings as it broke cover from a beech tree at the top of the ridge alerted him. The bird had been alarmed, but by what. Berin stilled his body. A blackbird's strident alarm call came from further down the ridge. Berin, now fully alert, adrenaline sharpened, grasped his spear, covered his face with his cloak and moulded his body to the ground contours beneath the hawthorn. He peered out through the rank grass stems at its base and through the screen of golden and russet leaves and scarlet berries on a fretwork tracery formed by the tree's drooping lower branches.

The blackbird would not settle in the branches of the old crab tree on the edge of the small grassy clearing. The bird was fluttering, cocking its head repeatedly in the direction from which it had flown in panic. Carefully Berin searched the undergrowth, leaf by leaf, concentrating on the vital hand span above ground level needed to hide a man's body, searching for the face, the paleness, the give-away head movement as the hunter-quarry searched for a watching enemy, searched for him.

At the foot of the sinuous ribbed trunk of a field maple, glorious gold and orange, even in the early half light, tufted, long dead stems of meadow grass, stately cow parsley, imperious even in grey autumn desiccation, and brown pinnacles of dock were strewn with golden leaf fall. It was a place of contrast and shadows, yet one shadow, darker than most, more continuous than most, had neither light nor form to cast it. Berin concentrated, remaining absolutely still, hunter's instinct slowing, stopping all but his acutely sharpened senses, aware of eyes searching for him. The shadow moved, drew back on itself, coalescing, consolidating, then rose, taking human form and substance, evidently satisfied that the way was clear. The cloaked figure beckoned and was joined by a second. The two men, strangers, hurried now, as though, vampire-like, they needed to find shadows in the face of the advancing sun. They passed within five paces of Berin's hide. Their faces, grim and tensed, were beginning to relax.

Berin stayed absolutely still, pressed to the ground until all sounds of the men's passage had long since receded down the valley. Although still in body, his mind raced. So Aedd was right. We are betrayed. Who are those two? I've not seen them before.

Berin slowly rose to his feet, tendons cracking, chilled, cramped muscles rebelling. Cautiously he made his way back up the ridge, snaking his way from cover to cover, avoiding open spaces. Near the top, where the slope slackened, he paused, working his way within the branches of a buckthorn which drooped to the ground, offering complete concealment. Carefully he watched the line of his retreat. Satisfied that he was not followed, he turned and made his way back towards the settlement.

When Berin approached the encampment, men were already on the move, gathering around the fires, coaxing them to flame, stoking them, warming themselves. Columns of blue-grey smoke rose, giving the fresh morning air a familiar pungency.

Berin was relieved to see the huge, easily identifiable figure of Aedd, moving from group to group, greeting, ordering, chaffing, disposing. Good, he thought, we can really get things started, and with Tarok on the way, the stronghold will soon take shape. Then he noticed parties of men taking their tools up the valley, towards the settlement, not towards the ditch on the ridge. He quickened his pace, finally breaking into a run.

"Aedd, hey Aedd!" he cried, "what's going on?" Where are they going?"

"Ah Berin," Aedd answered, "orders from Com last night. He and Urak, oh, he's here by the way, came last night. We're to build the cairn first."

"Oh sacred Earth, what next," fumed Berin. "Is he really so blind? Urak's trying to delay the stronghold. Two men passed down the valley this morning; they must be taking a message to Afon'ken. I must tell father."

Aedd remembered the two bondmen who left the settlement the night before. "What did they look like?" he asked.

Swiftly Berin described them. "Aye, Urak's men all right," Aedd answered grimly. "They left here last night, went up to the West Way. I thought they were going back to the ford, so I didn't bother with them; they must have cut back along the top."

"Right, that's it. Now I'll tell father. He must listen now."

Aedd took hold of his arm. "You've still no proof. I spoke with Urak and Com last night. Urak was asking about where our scouts are posted. You know and I know why he did it, but what if he says he sent his men to check that all is well, or to test the defenses, or to scout for him or a thousand and one reasons a bastard like that can think up. He's the High Chief's son, damn it. You must have proof!"

"Then I'll tell father to stop this nonsense and get on with the stronghold before we're all cut down," said Berin, raging with frustration, seeing and accepting the truth of Aedd's remarks, but liking them no better for that.

"Berin, he's set on this cairn. It means so much to him, to honour Belu."

"And I don't care about Belu, just because I want the living to survive, is that it Aedd? Is that what you think?"

"No Berin. But what's two days. That's all it will take."

"Maybe the difference between life and death, Aedd, that's all, only between life and death."

"He won't listen to you."

"Perhaps I'll be more popular when I tell him that I'll take Branwen. Aye, Aedd, I must. Damn it, I must." Berin turned pain-filled eyes to Aedd, who simply stared back, massive, powerful, but helpless in the sight of his friend's hurt.

"I'll come with you."

"No Aedd. You get the men back to work on the ditch and bank."

"I can't do that Berin, much as I want. I am your father's liegeman and he gave me a direct order. Only he can countermand it."

"Then you had best come with me and see that he does."

Berin set off grimly towards his home, tight faced, a tic playing amongst the balled muscles of his clenched jaw, eyes flashing, yet feeling unreal, detached from events, as though observing them instead of participating. He burst through the door curtain. Urak, Rh'on, Olwen and Oranc sat around the hearth. They looked up, startled as he burst in. Olwen started to her feet, then, remembering where she was, subsided, blushing, relief spreading a glow across her face that was not lost on Rh'on.

"Where's father?" stormed Berin. "I must see him. This is madness, what can he be thinking of."

"Berin!" Rh'on said sharply. "Remember your place. Be silent. Your father rests. Urak has given him a sleeping draught. He is in great pain and needs rest."

"But..." Berin stopped as he became aware of Aedd at his side, squeezing his arm very tightly.

"I'm sorry mother. Please forgive me. I really need to speak to him. I think that..."

"We really think that Urak should pour libation before the cairn is started," interrupted Aedd, tightening his grip on Berin's arm. "And it would be a good idea to ask for blessing on the stronghold too, before we go any further. Rh'on, Berin has been out all night beyond the picket line. You live on your nerves out there. Please understand, he needs rest too; some food and the rest; right Berin?"

"Er.. yes, Aedd. Of course. Sorry mother."

"Gwyn, Gwyn," called Rh'on. "Oh where is that girl?"

"Never mind, Rh'on, I'll fetch him something, said Olwen, rising with a smile, eager to serve her man.

"Ah Berin, I missed you last night," said Urak. "I hoped that you would explain about the defences and the general situation here. As it is, your father and Aedd obliged. It must be very nerve-wracking out there at night."

"It's all right once you get used to the night noises," replied Berin, finding it difficult to keep the enmity and contempt from his voice, masking his true feelings in a yawn that ended as the genuine article.

"Where were you last night?"

"Oh, a thousand paces or so beyond the picket line, in the valley."

"Did you see any sign of the Afon'ken people?"

"No... look... forgive me please, I'm very tired. Mother, will you excuse me to my quarters?"

"Yes of course, Berin. We'll attend to the sacrifices as you suggest, won't we Urak."

Berin turned to Aedd, catching his eye. "Thanks old friend, take care of things, eh?" Aedd smiled his reply.

Once in his private quarters, Berin stripped and sluiced himself from the bucket on the slatted floor over the drain, relishing the freshness of the cool water, and the tingle from rubbing himself dry.

"Berin, can I come in," called Olwen from the door.

Quickly Berin wrapped the cloth around his waist. "Oh yes, yes do," he panicked, not at all sure that Olwen's company was what he wanted just at that moment.

"I've brought you something to eat; some broth," she said, swinging through the doorway, setting the food down at his bedside and rushing to him, throwing her arms around him, pressing herself to him, rubbing her cheek against his chest. "I was so worried about you last night."

Instinctively Berin put his arms around her, felt her quivering, felt her breasts crushed against him, felt himself harden, then, taking her firmly by the arms he pushed her away from him. She searched his face, eyes widening in surprise. Her full lips parted moistly in a smile, a dimple formed in the crease at the corner of her smile, he noticed for the first time. Stray hairs still escaped her braids and chased each other across her cheek. "Berin, what is it?"

"Olwen, there is something I must tell you," he began.

Fearful of what she might learn, she turned away, picked up the bowl and brought it to him and without thinking, he began to spoon the broth into his mouth. He tasted nothing, he could not swallow against the misery that constricted his throat. Silently, Berin put down the bowl and took her by the shoulders, she pressing towards him, he holding her at arms length.

"Olwen, listen to me. My father and Dorn have decided that I shall take Branwen, Dorn's daughter, to wife."

Olwen's face fell, her smile straightened and then turned down, colour drained, leaving her skin with a strangely translucent pallor. Tears welled and coursed unnoticed over slack cheeks. She blinked, as though in disbelief, matting her eyelashes, as she stared into Berin's eyes, searching for, hoping for the lie, but seeing only miserable truth. Still, but for a barely discernible tremor which suffused her whole body, she stood before him, waiting.

"Dorn and Com want to bind our houses closer to each other, for mutual protection. Dorn will send ten bondmen as her dowry. Com says they will give us the labour we've always needed; help us to defend ourselves. Then there are the cattle, two hundred head."

"And you Berin, what do you want?" she asked quietly, resignedly, head slightly to one side, as though pulled by the weight of her braid, eyes never leaving his. "Com and Dorn have decided. Com says this, Dorn says that, what do you, Berin, say."

"Me? I want you."

Olwen blinked again, setting new runnels off across her cheeks, but now there was misty light within her eyes and the beginnings of a crease at the corner of her lips, threatening the dead pan of her expression.

"You have me," she answered very softly, "but you will be chief and you must act as a chief, for the benefit of all your people. What have you decided? You have already decided, haven't you?"

"Olwen," he croaked, tongue filling his mouth, a lump choking his throat, constricting his breathing, "if Com and Dorn quarrel, we are all lost. The men of Afon'ken will take everything. What can I do but agree. I will have Branwen. But it's you I want Olwen. You."

His hands at her shoulders no longer pushed, but pulled, hard. He crushed her to him, held her head against his chest, felt her tears, her lips open, felt the tip of her tongue as she kissed his naked chest, felt her lips move as she said softly, but determinedly "I knew that night I gave myself to you, they would never let me wed you. But you have me Berin, I am yours as surely as if I were your bondwoman."

Gently he stroked her hair, the nape of her neck, conscious of a huge responsibility and tenderness. Olwen sank to her knees before him and touched her forehead to his foot in the ancient acknowledgement of submission.

"Olwen," he gasped.

She looked up at him, eyes shining through their wetness, radiating her love to him. "Whatever happens, I am yours and always will be. Take me as your second wife.... your bondwoman."

She pressed herself against him, holding him around his thighs, pressing her face to him, feeling his hardness pushing through the cloth against her. As much for her own needs as to seal her act of subservience, she pulled aside the cloth and took him in her mouth.

Berin groaned. He pressed both his hands behind her head, holding her to him, knowing he could never give this woman up, never. Olwen, looking up at him at that moment experienced the heady satisfaction of defeat turned into triumph.

Berin, impatient now in his turn to take full promised possession, raised her to her feet, nodding towards the door.

"They're all gone to the libation," she said, but still dropped the inner door curtain, tying it in place with hurrying fingers. She turned and stood before Berin, where he had thrown himself on the couch.

"I promised that I am yours. What do you want with me," she said.

"Show me that which is mine," Berin said, eager for his eyes to share that which his fingers already knew so well.

Olwen untied the waist strap of her wrap-around bodice. Eyes fixed on her lover, eager for his approval, she shrugged her shoulders, discarding the cloth, spurning its protection, dropping it to the floor. Her breasts stood proud. Her fingers moved with a tremor to her skirt and loosened the folds which held it above her waist, letting the material fall.

Berin stared at her breasts, nipples standing, reaching towards him. He stared at her smooth long legs, swelling to firmly rounded thighs which touched each other as though clinging together, seeking reassurance at his inspection. He stared at her generous hips which cradled her secret. Olwen followed his eyes, accepted his unspoken will and moved her hands to hang loosely at her sides, laying her golden fleece open to him.

Berin pulled the cloth from around him, freeing himself to rise proudly. "Come," he said, holding out a hand to Olwen and she came, crouching to his side. He slid one hand between her thighs, which parted to allow him to posses her, feeling her moist and open to him as he pulled her head to his, holding her to him, exploring her willing lips with his, his tongue sucked into her eager mouth. Olwen reached for him, stroked and caressed.

Breathless from his kisses, Olwen slid her mouth to his throat, feeling Berin's life pulse beneath her lips. Berin, unsure of his new found mastery, risked gentle pressure with his palm on the top of her head. Olwen understood and obeyed. Excited at her own submission, she mewled with fluttering kisses across his chest, his lean hard stomach, breathing for a while his man scent before taking him between her lips.

Caress followed exciting caress, each seeking another way to gratify, to provoke exquisite response until, near overcome by the results of their lovemaking, Berin rose to his knees. He took Olwen by the hips, raised her buttocks and thrust himself deep within her ready folds. She moaned her pleasure, pressing herself to him, rearing, bucking, seeking to keep time to his ever faster plunging, joined as one, married as man and woman, coupled as stag and hind, in their joyful ride, bit players in Gaian progress.

Sprawled face down on the sleeping furs, Olwen's rasping breaths, her madly drumming heart, her blood suffused cheeks and bosom, slowly returned to normal. Berin's arm lay heavy across her, his hard hand filled with her breast, his body warmed the length of her.

I knew, the day we buried Belu with father, I knew they would never let us wed, she reflected despondently. But I have him all the same. He's mine in a way no one else can ever have him, she thought fiercely, triumphantly, and I'll have his child, I know I will. She squeezed her thighs together, part delicious memory, partly to hold his seed within her.

She snuggled against him, pressing her buttocks up to his thigh, hugging his hand to her breast. There was no response. Suddenly aware of his deep, regular breathing, she raised herself on her elbows and saw that he slept. Gently extricating herself from his embrace, she covered him, dressed quickly and with a last lingering loving look, opened the door curtain and slipped out.

In the hall, the hide drops to door and windows had been rolled up and shutters taken down. Sunlight streamed in, lighting dancing beams as Gwyn, bent double, head down to the task, ample, tight skirted buttocks raised to the light, swept dust from the packed clay floor with a bundle of broom twigs. She looked up as Olwen came in, a knowing smile playing at her lips.

"Mistress said would you look in on the Master. Oh, and Master Aedd told me to tell you he wants to talk to you. Up at the sacrifice he is."

Olwen moved silently into Com's quarter. Com was lying very still and pale on the couch, eyes closed, veined eyelids fluttering gently in deep sleep. Carefully, so as not to wake him, she stooped and picked up the empty bowl at his bedside. She looked at him anew, alarmingly aware of how easily she could smother him with his pillow, as he lay there helpless. Com, perverter of her dreams. She shuddered, collected herself and shrugged off the fantasy, reminding herself that she had won. She had beaten Com. She, Olwen, had taken his son.

CHAPTER 10

The men stood silent around the perimeter of the trench which Aedd had marked out around the burial mound of Belu and Ermid. Some leant on picks, others on shovels; all eyes were turned towards Urak, who was standing beside the graves, where a small pit had been excavated.

Urak stood with arms spread wide, a pitcher of mead in one hand, sandals removed, bare feet in contact with bare earth. "Oh Earth Mother, Great Dana our protector," he intoned, "giver of life, mistress of all that runs, swims and flies, mistress of sun and rain, of frost and storm, giver of all that grows and fruits, hear our prayer. We are gathered here today to mark the memory of two brave men, to raise a burial mound on their land so they shall never be forgotten."

At the completion of each phrase he poured mead onto the ground, to murmurs of 'So be it' from the crowd.

"Accept our offering of drink and food," he continued. "May those that work here be spared from injury. Bless our endeavours. " A loud 'So be it ' greeted the end of his oration.

Urak signalled to Han, who gripped a sheep by the horns, its head held back, neck exposed. Han slashed the animal's throat. A scarlet flood stained the grass, soaking into the thirsty chalky soil. The sheep thrashed in its death throes, rattling and bubbling from its severed larynx, dainty cloven hooves scrabbling frenetically. Han bent its head sharply back, snapping vertebrae with a loud crack. Swiftly he gutted and skinned the carcass, wrapping the head and contents of the body cavity in the skin and placing the parcel reverently in the pit at Urak's feet. Urak

168

raised his arms once more, calling out "Oh Dana, it is done."

Ceremony complete, Han picked up the carcass and, knees bent to the slope, carried it down the hill to be prepared for the feast. Urak moved away from the crowd. Ignorant peasants, he thought, how stupid to be impressed by such trivial barbarities. Still, one must be thankful. One couldn't invent a better way for them to be controlled. Tarok and Dorn were subjugate to Dana... and therefore to him. He loved to make Tarok cringe in a fervour of religious guilt; such delicious revenge for the slights of childhood bullying. Even Senot, with all his power over the trade in bronze and with that over men, was his to persuade if he could convince him that he, Urak, was favoured by the Earth Mother; and then, his to control. Urak shivered at the prospect of such power, a feeling as erotic as bending one of his catamites to his will.

Rh'on approached him, looking a little pale, he thought.

"I always feel that the Mother would be just as happy with some mead and barley cakes, at sacrifices" she said. "Is the blood-letting really necessary?"

Urak looked at her sharply, feeling as if she had just glimpsed a corner of his mind. "It records our fall from grace, and, by feasting on the sacrifice, Harac's covenant," he said officiously, recognising and irritated by his own pomposity.

"Yes, I know. It just seems such a shame."

Over her shoulder, Urak noticed two mired, caped figures hovering on the edge of the crowd, trying to catch his attention.

"Excuse me Rh'on, it's an interesting point, perhaps we can debate it later. I believe my man wants to talk to me."

169

Urak turned and strode across to his servants, drawing them away, out of earshot.

Aedd watched the meeting, angry at his inability to hear what they were saying, knowing that it was treason, yet powerless to denounce them.

"You wanted to see me Aedd?" Olwen asked.

"Oh, Olwen, yes. Here, wait a bit. I'll just get these fellows started." Aedd called out. "Hey Amren, take charge will you. Remember, lift the turf first, lay it grass side down, then pack the chalk."

Turning back to Olwen he whispered. " It's Berin. We talked a lot last night. He's very upset; he's... well he's in a bit of a fix between his father and you and... I'm not doing this right. Look..."

Olwen laid her hand lightly on his arm. "It's all right Aedd. I know. We've talked and it's all right, really." She smiled at him wistfully. "I must be and therefore shall be happy with what I have. Berin can be reconciled with his father. He will be a good chief you know Aedd, a very good chief."

Aedd looked at her, concern written in his expression, seeing a deep hurt, yet, curiously, sensing it was overlain by a secret joy. "Well, forgive me for butting in," he said gruffly, feeling clumsy, an emotion rare in him, despite his bulk. "It's just that I care a lot about him, I don't want him hurt, or you."

"That's all right Aedd, thank you. But you know I really love him. I'd never hurt him."

Aedd turned away, feeling strangely inadequate before the soft intensity of Olwen. Aedd looked towards Urak, still talking to his bondsmen. "Then you'll be ready to help him? …with him over there?" he said, nodding towards Urak

"Urak? What about him?"

Aedd glanced swiftly around to check that they could not be overheard. Satisfied, he continued. "Com's told you to look after him, hasn't he?"

"Yes."

"So you're around him a lot of the time. In his quarters too?"

"Well yes, with Oranc. Look here, what is all this about?

"Berin and me think he's… well.. let's just say we think he's up to no good. We want to keep an eye on him, so we need to know where he is, where he's going, what those three talk about. Will you help?"

"Berin didn't say anything about it," she answered, then thought, well it wasn't exactly a burning issue when we last talked, was it, and giggled. She noticed Aedd was looking at her strangely. "If I can, Aedd, I will. Of course I'll help."

"Be careful not to make him suspicious, or talk about this to anyone but Berin and me. It's better you don't know any more. He could be…well… very dangerous."

As Aedd spoke she glanced towards Urak. Her spine chilled. She wanted to run, to hide. Urak was watching her with an expression of such malevolence, she was sure he had heard her speak, or read her mind. She felt stripped, defenceless.

CHAPTER 11

Pippa and I joined the Trevose family to watch the funeral. The sombre mood was heightened by sitting in their best room, a room for formal occasions, a room chilled by its location on the north side of the house, a room so different to the comforting clutter of the warm kitchen. Viv began to sniffle into a balled tissue when the gun carriage emerged from the gates of the drive to Kensington Palace, the first flowers were thrown in its path and the first anguished cries rose from the otherwise silent crowd that lined the streets a dozen deep.

"How could they treat her that way," Viv wailed.

I turned to ask her what she meant, but Leslie, with a frown and a tight lipped shake of the head, warned me to silence. The view changed to the Union flag at half mast over Buckingham Palace and the black Royal party standing outside, waiting for the cortège to pass. The Queen bowed her head as Diana's coffin passed. The TV commentator remarked on the gracious gesture.

"Huh!" Viv exploded. "That's the least she can do after all her family did to poor Diana."

Leslie silently passed her a handkerchief to supplement the now useless tissue. I didn't really understand the depth of Viv's feeling, or its cause, but clearly it was not the right moment to explore her reactions to the drama unfolding in front of us. I had watched and listened to the Queen's address. I had been moved by her pain at the reaction of the press to the attempt by immediate family to comfort and shield the young princes in the privacy offered by Balmoral. The pictures of Charles guiding young Harry and the boys' obvious attachment to their father seemed so at odds with Viv's scornful attitude, a stance that seemed so out of character with the warm friendly person which first impressions had led me to believe she was. Clearly, there was much I did not know or understand about Viv...and people's attitude to Diana and the monarchy.

My turn to pass on a handkerchief came when the solemn princes fell into step behind the gun carriage as it passed St James's Palace. Pippa and Melanie sobbed at the close up of Prince William's tightly set features. My throat tightened when the specially composed words of "*Candle in the Wind*" echoed through that tensely silent sitting room and Earl Spencer's voice caught as he paid tribute to "....my sister, the unique, the complex, the extraordinary and irreplaceable Diana...." Viv clapped. Viv clapped along with the crowds watching events in the park and with the mourners in Westminster Abbey.

"That's shown them," she muttered with grim satisfaction.

I was simply sad; sad for the end of a life; sad for the fairy tale with the unhappy ending; sad for my lack of understanding.

I swung the axe and sliced through the last of the roots beneath the stump of the old apple tree. I reached for the wire sling and loop it around the stump. I climbed wearily out of the hole.

"Take a breather," Leslie said, offering me a bottle of mineral water. I drank gratefully and greedily and sprawled on the grass. Leslie pulled out his pipe.

"Thanks for taking the hint... earlier, in there during the funeral," he said quietly, stuffing his pipe from a tobacco pouch. "She's a great admirer of Diana. Always has been, ever since the wedding. Viv was really upset by her death. It all came as such a shock, you see," he added, pausing to light his pipe. "Better just to keep quiet. She'll bang on otherwise and get all worked up."

"But why does Viv blame the Royal Family? Where's the sense in that?" I asked.

"Oh I don't suppose there's any great logic to it," he said, cupping a match over the pipe and puffing. Leslie sucked on his pipe. "I think Diana comes across as a victim," he said at last. "It's just her way. You know that look from under the eyebrows routine. For there to be a victim, someone has to victimise her."

"Now who's applying logic," I laughed.

"Okay, okay," he admitted. "But ever since the Squidgy tapes were released, Viv's been ready to believe any conspiracy theory. And they are getting ever more loony. Have you heard that the Egyptian press reported that the Royal Family wanted Diana out of the way because she was going to marry Dodi; absolutely unacceptable to the royals, of course, because he's a Muslim. According to this particular plot, the Court used MI6 to set up the accident. Have you ever heard such twaddle? But Viv believes it."

"What does Viv believe?" Rebecca stood above us, blotting out the sun, which shone through her hair, making her look as though she had a halo. Even then I was biased.

"That Di's death was a plot by MI6," I said.

174

Leslie frowned, as though I had revealed some terrible family secret. Rebecca laughed.

"Stuff and nonsense," she scoffed, dismissing the idea and the topic.

"Look here," she said, holding out her hand, kneeling down between us. "This is what we found when we sieved that pile you excavated."

Her grubby palm held a few pieces of broken pottery, a piece of what looked like the end of a knitting needle and an arcuate fragment crusted with verdigris.

"Do I get a kiss?" I asked hopefully.

"Do you hell. I found them," she answered emphatically, but her eyes held a promise, or so I imagined.

"Then at least explain."

"These are almost certainly late Neolithic pottery," she said, poking the fragments with her finger tip. "They're just like the ones we found in a burial up on the escarpment. This is part of an awl. Bone. Looks like Neolithic.... and this is part of a bronze pin."

"So...?"

"So this site was occupied in the Upper Stone Age and in the Bronze Age. It may even be a transition site, because this pin looks early."

"And that's just what you need to prove your theory," I said quietly.

She looked at me intently, looked for a moment as though she was going to say something deep and meaningful, then laughed. "Got it in one," she said. "It could just be what I was hoping to find. That is if Mr morose Trevose here lets me dig up his orchard."

175

"Dig away," he said equably. "Dig away. Start on the old apple stumps."

"You're such a shit, Leslie," she said, thumping him on the shoulder. "Just one trench from the bank to...let's see...well... about here."

"Rebecca?"

"Yes?"

"That flint knife I found. Could I have it back to show Pippa?"

"Sure. For you, anything."

Leslie rolled his eyes and was rewarded with a kick from Rebecca's muddy boot.

Somehow I had missed the announcement of Mother Theresa's death. When I heard, I felt a pang of guilt, as if I had failed her, failed a life so full of real practical meaning to so many. I was still sitting in front of the TV, cradling a malt in one hand and caressing the flint blade with the other, paying only passing attention to 'Newsnight' when Pippa popped her head around her bedroom door.

"Dad?"

"Yes sweetheart."

"Melanie's got to go back to school on Tuesday. Can I go. To school, I mean, with Melanie."

"I don't see why not, if they'll have you. But are you sure you want to? This is supposed to be a holiday."

"Oh Dad. You're so dumb sometimes. What am I going to do when you're fixing the garden or talking archiwotzit with Rapunzel... oops sorry Dad. That's what

176

Melanie calls her. Says she lets down her hair to catch a man. Anyway Viv says its fine. She's fixed it with the Headmistress."

I had that old familiar feeling of being outsmarted and outflanked by the female cavalry, again.

"Well okay, if that's what you want."

"Thanks Dad. You're the best." She danced across the room and planted a kiss on my forehead and was gone again before I knew it, leaving a lingering washed clean scent.

Rapunzel indeed ! I smiled to myself. The name certainly fitted Rebecca. I sipped my scotch. The flint blade was comforting in my hand, like worry beads, its contours already familiar. Pippa had shown just a fleeting interest in it. I was surprised. I had thought that it would have fascinated her, but I suppose she had always been a one fad at a time girl and the current one definitely involved Melanie and horses.

I wondered what, if anything I would find out about my connections to Bernton tomorrow. Viv at supper had suggested that I talk to Mary Bynam, who was supposed to know everything and everybody to do with the village. She'd lived here all her long life. Mary had been really friendly on the 'phone. So friendly that the supper dishes had been cleared away by the time I had returned from Leslie's book-lined study. Mary had been unsure and I thought a little hesitant and reticent when I'd mentioned my parents' names, Louise and Mickey Allen, but then, as she put 'it, her memory was one stook short of a stack. I'd arranged to meet Mary after church. It was a worry, her not knowing Mum and Dad. Maybe my memory was playing tricks with me and it wasn't Bernton at all, but some other place with a similar name.

I sipped my scotch, rubbed the blade with my thumb and thought of Rebecca. I could hear the passion in her voice as she talked about her work. The double burial up on the escarpment. The cleaved skull of one victim, the scored ribs and fractured humerus of the other. The flint arrow and spear points, the pottery grave goods and the polished greenstone and jet. I remembered her puzzled tone as she wondered how such savage wounds could be caused by flint weapons. Such violent times. How people must have struggled, just to give life to the next generation. I thought of the softness of Rebecca's lips and the pressure of her breasts on my chest.

CHAPTER 12

The bells stopped their peal and settled to a single repeated chime just as I turned into the churchyard with Viv. Pippa had left the house early, before I had had the chance to ask if she wanted to come. Leslie hadn't even bothered to pronounce his agnosticism. Viv was glad of my company and promised to introduce me to Mary.

The church was cool and hushed and surprisingly well filled. The organ fluted quietly. We settled into a pew near the back. Viv pointed out Mary, sitting across the aisle a few pews in front of us. She was a frail looking lady, but with a strong face. Viv greeted acquaintances in a pew behind us, turning her back to me to sit sideways, speaking in a hushed voice. I could almost feel the stolen glances of the congregation flicker over me, probing the newcomer.

The looks were kindly meant. I felt that too; just gentle enquiries. A sense of peace washed over me. The church had stood quietly, firmly, through storm and snow, rain and sunshine, for hundreds of years. Thousands of villagers, hundreds of families had passed through its doors, for baptism, weddings and funerals or like this, for Sunday devotions; a tie, stretching back over the ages.

I was surprised when, in the middle of the service, the congregation was invited to turn to their neighbours and shake hands. My dim recollection of childhood services certainly involved no such act. But it was nice to have a complete stranger, who a short time before had been examining me, take my hand and wish me peace. It was like passing a test, a gentle initiation. I was surprised too that the order of service included the Eucharist. My dim recollection was of the initiated getting up very early before

179

breakfast for their special ritual. I stayed seated whilst the congregation approached the altar rail to complete their mysteries. I felt conspicuous and alone.

The priest took my hand as I left the church. His words were banal, but the pressure of his hands, the smile and the look in the soft brown eyes which held mine were genuine. Mary spoke at length to the vicar and some church worthies, including Madge from the shop. Viv hovered on the fringe. I wandered over and inspected the grave stones. Atheson and Elsey figured prominently, reaching back well into the beginning of the eighteenth century and maybe beyond, but the older inscriptions were hard to make out. Then I came to Berry. I felt a surge of excitement. That was my mothers' maiden name.

"John, this is Mary," Viv said.

"Hello," I said, holding out my hand. She looked at me with her head slightly inclined to one side. Her silver-white hair was wispy. Her skin was stretched tight, parchment thin over her temples. Her piercing blue eyes held mine in a very thorough examination.

"Hello," she replied, and took my hand in hers. It felt cold and papery. I felt a slight tremor.

"Look, I'll be off to put the lunch on," Viv announced. "You and Pippa will join us of course, John, won't you? About two, I expect."

"Yes... fine... thanks," I replied. I turned back to Mary. "Did you know the Berry's?" I asked, indicating the headstone. "Berry was my mother's maiden name."

"The Berry's...why of course. Bless my memory. It's worse than a gnat's," she said swiping feebly at some dancing midges.

"Louise Berry..."

"That was my mother's name," I exclaimed excitedly.

"Can't think why I didn't think of her when you telephoned. She went off to Australia after the war. She's the only village person to do that," she said, with heavy emphasis on the word 'that', as though the act of leaving the village was some incomprehensible betrayal.

"She married a soldier. It caused quite a stir with her family, I remember."

"What was his name? Was it Allen, Mickey Allen."

"Oh bless me but I can't remember. It could have been. He wasn't from here you see."

My disappointment must have shown, for Mary clasped my arm. "Madge will know," she giggled.

"Madge, Madge, come here a minute. Come and talk to this nice young man," Mary trilled.

"What do you want now," Madge grumbled affectionately, moving from the group clustered around the vicar.

"This young man thinks his mother could be Louise, Louise Berry who went off to Australia with that soldier. What was his name?"

"Louise who?" she asked. Her eyes rested on mine briefly, then flicked away.

"Berry. You know.... She married the soldier from London. His mother lived in Lavender Cottage before it burnt down. You know..."

"Don't know what you mean. I don't remember any Louise Berry, or any soldier."

"But Madge... you..."

"I said I don't remember," Madge reiterated, glaring at Mary "... and knowing your memory, I don't suppose you know what you're talking about either. Now if you'll excuse me, I've lots to do."

Mary stared at Madge as she retreated up the path through the church yard.

"Oh dear," she said, in a small, lost voice. "It all seemed so clear. I suppose I've just made another muddle."

Embarrassed, I thanked Mary for her help and left her to her bewilderment. I examined my own bewilderment as I walked back to Lower Farm. A family found and lost again, or was it? Mary had been so helpful, so sure of her memory of Louise Berry; her name matching my mother's; my own memory of a link to Bernton, were clues too strong to be dismissed as coincidence. Madge's put down seemed to end that line of enquiry, but Madge's behaviour had been a little too brusque, even for her peppery character. That initial eye contact. She had revealed something of herself, before she looked away, but what?

Sunday lunch with the Trevose family was a protracted and very enjoyable affair. Les handed out large gins, helped to make the gravy and struggled to carve the leg of lamb as the gins took effect. My contribution was to open a bottle of wine; Australian, very familiar and very good. Viv heaped my plate and Les kept my glass well filled. We talked about planting plans for the pond area. The girls chattered away about their morning hack and Mr Belcher's bull, which had spooked the horses with its sorrowful bellowing to the heifers in the next field. My mood of introspection vanished.

After the girls had rushed off to their next equine date, Les and I dried dishes as Viv washed.

"How did you get on with Mary? Was she any help," Viv asked.

"Yes..yes she was..." I hesitated.

"You don't sound very sure."

"It's just that Madge was so odd."

"What do you mean?"

"Well... Mary was telling me about Louise Berry, a local girl who married someone from outside the village and went off to Australia. Louise Berry was my mother's maiden name, so it all seemed to fit together. I was really excited. I really thought I was on to something. Madge shut Mary up. She more or less said that she was a silly old woman who had lost her marbles. Mary was quite distressed."

"That doesn't sound like Madge. She's normally very protective of Mary. They've been through so much together."

"Mmmh... that makes Madge's behaviour really peculiar."

"You should talk to the vicar," Les said.

Viv and I looked at him askance.

"If your mother was married in Bernton, it should be in the parish records," Les responded.

"Of course," I cried. "Why didn't I think of that."

The three of us strolled in the orchard after lunch. I meant to demonstrate my planting plans, but I was distracted by Rebecca's buttocks, tightly wrapped in jeans,

183

waving above the top of a trench. Rebecca, on elbows and knees was carefully brushing the bottom of the trench. She was so engrossed in her task that she failed to notice our arrival. I watched the smooth white skin where her T-shirt pulled away from her waist, revealing the top of her briefs. I watched until I felt her vulnerability and reviled myself for a peeping Tom.

"You don't even have Sunday off," I said, to announce our presence and to cover my confused feelings.

"Oh...hiyah," she called, turning her head and wrapping me in the warmth of her wide mouthed grin. She straightened her back and flicked back her hair, an action which set her breasts jostling beneath the 'Archaeologists dig it' slogan on her T-shirt.

"Not when it gets this exciting," she said. "Look." She pointed to the bottom of the trench. I peered and squinted, but saw only earth.

"Er... exciting? What exactly am I looking at?" I asked.

"Look....here... and here.... and again here," she said, picking up a trowel and pointing out patches of darker tones in the trench floor. "Post holes. There was definitely a wooden structure here. And I've found a shard of the same pottery we found in the gravel. It's a Neolithic settlement all right," she said, squinting up at me.

"And you think it could be your transitional site?" I asked.

"Exactly. The bronze pin suggests just that, although it could post-date the flints and pottery. In other words, it could have been lost at the spring at a later date and was mixed up with the Neolithic artefacts by your digging."

"Sorry," I said.

"Don't be daft," she said with a smile that made her words a compliment.

"I'd love to excavate more, Les," she said, her expression suddenly serious, her eyes watchful. "This could be a really important site. Will that be all right? You see I'll have to talk to the Prof. tomorrow about funding the extra works. It would be really helpful if I could tell him that I had the landowner's consent."

Les hesitated, looked at Viv and then at me.

"I know you want John to do your garden," she said, "but I won't hold you up. I promise. I'll help with the labour. Oh please."

"How long will it take?" Les asked.

"Only three to four weeks actually on the dig," she said hopefully.

"What do you reckon, John, will it stuff you?"

"As long as I can finish the revetments at the spring, I can't see a problem. We have to do that to optimise the use of the hired equipment," I added.

"Not a problem. The lads were inspired by the finds. They turned out today too. They should be just about finished."

"Cutting down and clearing has to be done, but Rebecca will need to do that too before..."

"I'll help... I'll do it," she promised eagerly.

"She must keep the topsoil separate. If she helps with the labour, it won't hurt to delay planting a month," I concluded.

"Okay then sweetie, go for it, "Les said with a smile.

"You darling man," Rebecca exclaimed, jumping from the trench to hug him. Viv and I grinned as Les waved his hands helplessly, so very careful not to put them anywhere he shouldn't.

Rebecca assembled her acolytes and started laying out the next areas for excavation. I led Les and Viv to the spring. Clear water welled from beneath the Sarsen stone forming a dark pool. The water trickled past a heap of washed gravel where Rebecca's students had so recently been sieving the spoil from my excavation. Les and especially Viv listened enthusiastically as I did my arm waving stuff.

"I can see it, John. It'll be just gorgeous," Viv said.

As we turned to leave, a pungent precursor of autumn, the smell of burning leaves, wafted from the orchard, where Rebecca's crew was burning off cleared brush.

I stayed up late to telephone Australia. Steve reported that all was well with the business. The shopping mall was finished and the invoice sent off. Greg and Liz Hawkins loved my plans. All the earth moving was finished and the planting was about to start. One of the municipal contracts was in the bag. Steve was really cheerful and it seemed to me as if he relished being in the driving seat. I suppressed an irritating feeling of resentment.

My conversation with Peter Mariner, the high school principal was less happy. Mutual understanding was not fostered by the delay and echo induced by the satellite relay. We both interrupted and spoke over each other. But the message was plain. The school governors were determined to make an example. Violence was not to be tolerated under any circumstances. Pippa was to be suspended for one full term. No, there was no appeal and I hadn't helped Pippa's case by absenting myself. Mutual understanding began to fade at that point and disappeared altogether when I learnt that there was some talk about the appropriateness of Pippa being brought up by a widowed working father.

After I slammed down the 'phone, I sat for a while at the desk in Les's study. Les must have caught the end of our exchange, for he soon appeared around the study door with a bottle and two glasses.

"Dalwhinnie," he said. "Single malt... the best of Speyside," and poured two generous measures. "A cure all," he added, settling into an easy chair.

After my first sip, I was more than willing to agree. "Sorry, did you catch any of that?"

"Only the 'anally retentive pompous arse' bit. Do you mean there was more?" he asked with a grin.

I laughed. "There was some more before that," I confessed guiltily. "Enough to stuff my daughter's school career. Maybe even put me in trouble with the Social Services when I get back home."

The door swung wide and the Springer tumbled into the room, followed by Viv and the Labrador.

"Dogs have been out. I'm off to bed. Good night," she said.

"Good night," we chorused.

The Springer fussed until Les stroked and pulled its ears, when it settled itself at his feet. The Labrador grunted and waddled over to stick its snout on my knee. I stroked the smooth coat on the top of its head. The fur was still slightly damp and cold from the dew.

I began to tell Les the whole story. It turned out to be a bit of a monologue, a catalogue of my disgruntlement. I'll say this for Les, he's certainly a good listener. Or maybe he just wanted a drinking companion. Only the bottom half of the bottle was left when I stumbled out of the door and across to the granary, reflecting on the curative powers of malt. 'Settle in with us,' he'd said. 'At least for a term. Pippa can go to school with Melanie. It sounds as if your man is running the business well enough; too well even,' he had leered knowingly. Smart as new paint, that Les.

CHAPTER 13

Berin awoke. Olwen's scent lingering on the furs which covered him brought a slow broad smile to his face; relief flooded across him, a warm wave of comfort. He stretched luxuriously. Memories, flickering part images, disjointed, out of sequence, but graphic, erotic and exciting, tumbled over each other, competing for his consciousness, eager for his attention after his long sleep. Berin felt tumescence returning, but snapped the cord of suggestion. Whatever happened now, he was sure of her love; certain in possession. Now it was time to resolve his row with his father, to get on with building the stronghold, with survival; a time to do.

All tiredness gone, he rose from his couch and dressed quickly, suddenly aware of a huge hunger. He strode into the hall calling out "Mother? Gwyn, Cigfen, anyone here?" But the room was deserted.

Gwyn bustled in. "Ah, master Berin. You'll be hungry I expect. I'll fetch you something."

"I'm starved. Where is everyone?" Berin asked.

"Well the Master's resting still. The Mistress, that Urak, your Olwen and her brother are all out to the sacrifice. They're blessing the work on the cairn," she answered as she fussed and clucked her way behind the screen to the cooking hearth.

Berin scowled, remembering his anger of earlier in the day, then made a determined effort to relax. Tarok should be here today, he thought. We'll get on with the defences tomorrow, with his men. It's really only one day lost on the cairn. A whole day! However he tried to rationalise it still seemed a monstrous waste to him.

"Here you are master Berin. Sit yourself down." She moved a stool to where he sat, setting bread, a bowl of broth and a pitcher of ale before him.

"How's father," he said, picking up the horn spoon, cradling the wooden bowl in his lap, feeling its warmth.

"I'll go and see. You sit there and eat, master Berin. You'll be needing your strength," she giggled.

Berin, wondering just how noisy he and Olwen had been, bent his head to the bowl, glad of an excuse to avoid Gwyn's merry eyes.

"He's getting up directly, master Berin," Gwyn called.

As Berin was mopping the bowl with the last of the bread, Com tottered unsteadily into the room, looking pale and drawn.

"Good morning father. Are you well? How's your arm?"

"Ah, there you are. At last. No I'm not well. My arm hurts like hell and my head aches abominably. Where the devil were you all night?"

"I scouted the lower valley, father."

"Did you have to be out all night? Urak arrived and I was most embarrassed because you had gone off without so much as a by your leave. If it wasn't for Aedd I would have looked really foolish in front of Urak. Such a well mannered, intelligent man, sensitive too. He understood straight away about the cairn. He's devoted to his father, and a credit to him. What was that you said?"

"I didn't," replied Berin, trying to redress a rapidly deteriorating situation, regretting now his mumbled aside.

190

"Yes you did. I heard you say ...if you knew... or something. If I knew what? What do you mean by it, eh?"

"I don't want to quarrel with you father. I... well I want to ... I want you to know that it's all right about Branwen. I'll take her as my wife."

Com looked up, fiercely. "Damned right you will, my boy. How very nice. How gracious. Damn, but I've had enough of your impudence. Of course you'll take Branwen and think yourself lucky. It's not every son that has the offer of a High Chief's daughter. Not many that would turn her down for their slut."

"Oh father..."

"Don't you interrupt me. Don't you ever speak out against me again! Great Mother, why did you take my Belu. If you had to take a son of mine, then why him?"

Suddenly the balm of reason and logic which lubricated Berin's attempt to humour his father, evaporated in the flame of Com's petty and vindictive spite, leaving only the ungreased overheated machinery of destructive rage.

"I will speak out when you're wrong, father. I must. Like the cairn and Urak."

"Ahah the cairn...that I understand. You always resented Belu. Now its Urak too."

"You're mad. I idolised my brother. Oh yes, I loved him, but he is dead. You will jeopardise our security to build a monument to the dead. As for Urak, how easily you are taken in by that piece of bat shit. I can't talk to you about him. You won't ever understand."

Trembling with the pressure of boiling rage, scarcely contained behind close-clamped jaw, Berin turned and strode from the house, pausing only to take his bow and quiver from their place in the porch, leaving Com apoplectic, so strong his frustrated urge to wound, to mutilate, to rip apart the last vestiges of his relationship with his living son. Outside, Berin turned, first one way then the other, seeking escape in action. Finally he ran full pelt straight up the nearest steep hillside, trying to burn off the explosive charge of his fury in physical exertion, desperate to replace the mental anguish, the child of misunderstanding and rejection, the result of his perpetual second place in a scheme of two, with honest physical pain born of rasping lungs and tormented muscles.

Thick undergrowth slowed him at the tree line, but still he struggled on, branches whipping at his face and hands, brambles tearing, grass-hidden roots snaring his feet. The slope levelled. He stumbled into a small clearing where a once majestic oak, now a decaying host to sour smelling, orange-yellow fungi, had smashed lesser trees and bushes in its fall from grace. The up-ended saucer of roots sheltered a dished depression, covered in grass and the bright yellows and oranges of strawberry leaves. Berin flung both arms in the air and screamed, mouth wide and distorted, neck tendons strung, eyes popping. Berin screamed out his rage, his battle cry, his challenge. From the thickly forested slope down the valley towards Afon'ken, a red deer stag roared its defiance.

CHAPTER 14

The herd ambled slowly, splay-footed under its own white cloud of chalk dust, for the most part content to follow the swaying rump of the beast directly in front, content that is but for playful yearlings and bullocks, making determined rocking-horse dashes for freedom from the flanks of the herd, then standing, forlorn, bewildered, bellowing mournfully, before rejoining the security of their fellows. Four dust-stained drovers and their slinking, nipping dogs guarded the flanks, van and rear, chasing back the strays, goading and prodding cows which stopped for snatched mouthfuls of late grown greenery, whipping and raising dust from the hides of recalcitrant bulls.

Aedd strode down the steep slope from the burial site on the hill crest to greet the nearest drover. Olwen kept close to his side, determined to hold on to his bulk whilst Urak was near.

"Where's the boss?" Aedd asked.

"That's me," the dust-covered drover replied.

"Right; there's two stock yards down the valley, just below the encampment, water in the stream; fodder there too. You'd best turn them there," Aedd said, pointing, "about a hundred paces past that bush, then keep to your left, slightly up the hill. Don't want 'em through the settlement."

"Right. I've got that."

"When are you going back?"

"This afternoon, I thought. We might as well go straight back after we've delivered. There's nothing to keep us here and I've a warm bed waiting at home."

"Will you take my lad with you, drop him off with Anoeth?"

"Aye, surely, be glad to."

"Well when you are done, pick him up at the chief's house. He's all packed and ready. They'll give you a drop of ale."

"Now there's a thought." The drover's eyes twinkled; his sticky tongue pushed surprisingly pink through his dust dry lips, tried to moisten them, then retreated in disgust. "There's a thought."

The drover set about turning the herd off the West Way, calling to his mates, whistling up dogs, sending them scampering. Aedd turned to Olwen, "And what about you," he said. "I should stay and supervise the cairn, but I'll see you back to the settlement if you're really worried about Urak."

"No, I'm sure I'll be all right. It was just the way he looked at me back there. I couldn't help it. I just felt so... so threatened," she confessed, shuddering. "Anyway, he seems to have gone now," she added.

Aedd turned and searched the skyline, but there was no sign of Urak, or his travel-stained servants. "Damn, now I wonder where they've got to," he worried, catching a corner of his lower lip behind his teeth and chewing reflectively. "Look, ask Ened to bring me up some grub later, will you?"

As Olwen wandered back to the settlement, Aedd climbed back to the working party on the hill top. "Anyone seen Urak or his men?" Aedd puffed as he came up to them.

"Oh they went off a while back, Aedd," replied Amren.

"Which way did they go?"

"Why, back to the West Way, towards the ford."
Aedd inspected the ancient route. A faint chalk haze still
hung where the herd had passed, but there was no sign of
Urak, or his henchmen. "Damn," he said.

Berin rolled over onto his back on the bank, crushing
grass and strawberry plants, shaking his head as though to
rid himself of the thoughts which had been tumbling
around like pebbles in a whirlpool. Father is not to be
reasoned with, he concluded, still angry, going back over
their most recent argument. Why did he flare so quickly?
Aedd was so right to stop me from accusing Urak. There's
no way that father would listen to me now, he's so taken
with the bastard. What has Urak been saying to him? As
for the cairn, I bet that's Urak's doing too. A whole working
day lost, two if Tarok doesn't get here soon. Anger and
frustration surged through him. Deliberately Berin tensed
and consciously relaxed, muscle by muscle, allowing
rancour to dissipate with their softening. He closed his eyes
and turned his face to the warmth of the sun, the redness
of his eyelids replacing thc heat of his wrath, the dancing
spots his chaotic introspection. The red deer stag still
roared his invitation and challenge from the wooded slopes
of the valley, but gradually Berin's mood calmed, reaching
out, seeking to match the warbling bird song heard above
the whispering trees.

A rustling at the top of the slope brought Berin to the
alert. Cautiously he rolled his head, peering through the
screen of grasses growing at the lip of the depression, past
wrinkled rosettes of next year's foxgloves, his pupils

expanding, compensating after the intense redness, searching for movement in the dark undergrowth.

A doe, soft, wide-eyed, virginal, stepped delicately into the clearing, ears twitching, searching, waiting for the call to be repeated; not understanding, knowing only deep within herself that she must answer the summons. Berin's hunter's instincts were aroused. His angry mood dissipated, his mind now solely concentrated on the quarry. With a slowness and control born of hunts ruined by careless hasty movement, he felt out his bow and by touch, selected an arrow, never taking his eyes off the deer. Almost automatically he registered wind direction on the swaying seed heads of the long grasses. The hind was moving cross wind down the valley and was now upwind of him. Good, he thought. She'll never scent me with the wind in this direction, or see me in this cover, it's near perfect. Searching each leaf and tussock around him before moving, to avoid the flight-provoking snapped twig or rustled leaf, Berin rolled on to one knee, notching the arrow to his bow string. As he tensed to draw, the doe skittered, turned to face upwind, nostrils dilating, ears twitching, then with a leap, crashed off down the valley, the sound receding until subordinated to the soughing of the forest and the birds' warbling.

Disappointed though he was, Berin was too much of a woodsman not to take an interest in the cause of the deer's precipitant flight. His immediate reaction was to stay absolutely still; then, pressing his body back below the level of the depression, he searched upwind. A few hundred paces away, the gloom of the wood lightened at the edge, where in years long gone, trees had been felled to make farmland, land which had long since fallen into disuse, except as rough summer pasture and for hunting. Berin blinked. He concentrated hard on the light, seeking out movement. Had a shadow flitted between those trees? He scrutinised the spot. There it was again, and another. Three men were travelling south along the top of the ridge.

Berin quickly replaced the arrow in its quiver. Stooping, he picked up a handful of moss and smeared face, neck, hands and spear point with the earth from its underside. He wedged the moss around the arrow shafts to prevent rattling and slung his bow across his back. Berin crouched low for maximum observation in the forest and angled off through the trees in pursuit.

The edge of the wood was more a thin immature version of the parent than a sharp boundary. Over the years the forest had gradually advanced over the cleared ground, as first seeds and then suckers had grown and thrived. Quarry and hunter made good progress, the former at a fast walk, certain that they were secure. The pursuit followed in a series of rushes from cover to cover, always keeping brush or thorn between himself and the men.

Berin recognised the steep valley which hid the line of pickets. The leading figure waved the others to a stop and dropped from sight. Berin imagined him snaking forward, searching out the watcher, ears attuned for leaves rustled by limbs cramped from long immobility, the cough, sneeze, or muffled conversation, alarm calls of birds; eyes watching for the careless movement, checking, watching, returning. The scout reappeared and motioned the other two figures, directing them from cover to cover in an arc around him, his real attention on the watcher beyond their sight.

Berin allowed them time to clear the valley and move on before following. He was sure that they would stop for a while and check for stealthy pursuit; just in case the picket was alerted. He was also fairly certain of the direction they would take. He recognised two of the figures as the men he had seen at daybreak. He guessed they would follow the ridge to his hiding place of last night and re-enter the main valley where they had done on the previous occasion.

Berin briefly checked the flattened grass on the far side of the valley, smiling grimly at the correctness of his forecast, before hurrying on, careless now, certain of his objective. He hesitated briefly as he came to the buckthorn where he had waited that morning, checking the way ahead, anxious now to close up. A brief flicker of movement down the slope hurried him on after them, past his hiding place of the night before, to the edge of the forest and the meadow at the bottom of the valley.

A twig snapped loudly under his foot. Berin froze, damning his haste.

"What was that?" Urak's voice called urgently, very close.

Hell, they've waited at the forest edge, panicked Berin, furious with himself for not thinking of it. He sank slowly to earth, already imagining the two scouts fanning out to outflank and take him, noting their silence, their refusal to answer the novice and thereby reveal their position. Heart pounding, dry mouthed, panting softly, eyes searching this way and that, darting from leaf movement to shadow, ears straining, skin contracting, prickling, Berin tensed. A crashing close to his right had him whirling, eyes popping, mouth agape, sphincter loosening, spear at the ready, near sick from the rush of adrenaline. The stag and his new doe cleared the forest edge and bounded away across the meadow. For some time they had been content to move slowly ahead of the man scent to the edge of the trees, but this latest affront, caught between two groups of men at the end of cover had been too much to bear. When the twig had snapped, so too had the stag's nerve.

"A stag and his doe, Master. We've been pushing the doe ahead of us since the top."

"Why bolt now?" asked Urak uncertainly. "What made it bolt?"

"We'd trapped them against the edge of cover. Panicked," said the bondman, his condescension of the initiated to the tyro scarcely disguised. "I reckon its all right to go on. We're expected. We've seen no sign since the picket line. Those scouts you told us about, Sir, are probably only out at night. We saw no sign of them when we come through at daybreak. We'll travel faster in the meadow, then we can be sure to get back and up the top again before sundown, before the scouts are out and about."

The three men rose from cover, barely twenty paces from where Berin lay petrified and moved out into the meadow. Berin retched and retched again, bringing up bitter green bile, the result of sick fear, and of the certain knowledge of Urak's betrayal.

Cautioned by his fright, Berin crept along just inside the wood, every now and again, snaking to cover at the edge of the meadow to check the progress of his quarry. The three men headed towards a solitary oak. As they drew close, a tall figure detached itself from the shadows at its trunk. Berin inhaled sharply. It was the outlander.

Urak could not help staring in fascination at the outlander's empty eye socket. The man had lifted his bandage to underline the meaning of his last remark, to confirm the intensity of his animosity.

"Boy, I want boy. Others, yes, is good market, but I have special plans for little turd who do this." He leered lopsidedly, relishing his vile intent, the whole effect rendered even more macabre by his curiously accented and broken speech.

"I will keep him safe for you, but you must get the job done quickly. You'll have him when the job is done."

"Good, very good," answered the outlander, rubbing his hands and cracking his knuckles. "I enjoy pulling the turd apart."

"But you must attack soon, before they finish the stronghold."

"Is how many?"

"About thirty or thirty five now, more than seventy after tonight or tomorrow, when Tarok's men arrive. You should have attacked again, straight away."

"Is not possible. They is not warriors. The pigs is drunk. Care only for loot. Is stupid. We capture slaves is worth much more, and carry itself. I have much pain. I give some of them much pain." He laughed. "Yes, they share pain with me. Now afraid... of me. Fight better but now is too many enemy for these pigs of Senot. I get my men. They with my friend. I get help from my friend. He trades slaves in west; very good trade. He has many men, good men, not like these pigs. They have bronze, these new peoples?"

"Very few have bronze weapons, only the captains and then not as you. No blades, a few daggers and spear points, maybe an axe or two." The outlander leered at that news, showing yellow teeth. Urak recoiled from the stench of the man's breath.

"I am trying to delay the building," Urak continued. "Once they have the ditch and bank complete, with even thirty men they will cause you great trouble. You must get ready very quickly and be ready to attack at any time on a signal. I will try and make a good opportunity, cause confusion in the camp. We must have a signal."

"Make fire on hill, big fire, much smoke."

"No, they would be suspicious and be ready."

"It will be good. We will camp near here. Be there soon. They have no time. You see."

"All right, but no mistakes like last time. What about at night? If you attacked at night it would be easier."

The outlander started, clearly shocked. "No night, no fight in night. Helos not there to help if wounded, to take if killed. We not fight at night."

Stupid man, thought Urak. More stupid superstitious nonsense. They are all as bad as each other. Our people slavishly follow the Earth Mother, the outlanders their sun god. It's such a missed opportunity, the chances to create mayhem and confusion multiply tenfold in the dark.

"How soon?"

"Maybe a moon, half a moon if goes well."

"As long as that?"

"My man must find my friend, finish business, come with our men. Is long way. I must have our men to keep Senot's pigs fighting. Is another thing. There is woman."

"Yes, yes, we agreed. The men you sell in the west, or to Senot, the women you keep for trade with your people. We share."

"No, is special woman, the one I tell your man to tell you is for me. I see her. She has long yellow hair, is... is tied here at back of head. This one for me. You keep safe. Like boy I not want kill in fight. Want for me, you keep her safe. You know woman?"

So it is Olwen, mused Urak, I thought it must be, and another weakness of yours, he gloated. "Yes, I know her," Urak answered, "I will keep her." As an incentive for your continuing co-operation and my payment, he reflected. Yes, Olwen will be very useful to me.

"The guards, what guards they have?"

"A picket line stretches across the valley about two thousand paces down from the settlement. Below that they have scouts, watchers. I don't think they come this far, and they have watchmen in the settlement and in the fields and pastures beyond."

"They not come here. We watch."

"I must go now. Be ready in half a moon."

"I try good. Not promise. May be a moon."

Urak called softly to his bondsmen, motioning them from the drooping outer branches of the oak where they watched, safely out of earshot. "We'll go back now."

Urak set off across the meadow behind his guides, thick green tussocks catching at his feet, wetting his boots, a beige sea of seed heads rising waist high on ungrazed stalks. How strange these outlanders, he reflected. So rich and powerful, with gold, bronze, ships and well armed, trained warriors, yet so savage and uncouth, so superstitious. Our people are bad enough with their touching faith in Dana, the Earth Mother, but the sun god, really! Still, it could be a key to control them...and with them to help me, well ....I could even take on Senot with enough of them. Now that would be rough justice. Though Senot promises me the Ford for my help and fealty, he belittles me, just as Tarok always has, since childhood. Tarok shall not have the Ford. It will be mine! But, one step at a time. First the boy and Olwen. They will help me keep my hold on the outlander. Urak grinned, an expression not suited to the habitual set of his features, but an expression which had much in common with the well satisfied smirk of a pole cat leaving a partridge clutch.

Berin watched them return across the meadow. The rage he had felt when he had first learned of Urak's betrayal had dissipated and did not resurface at this, the ultimate proof of that treachery. Instead, Berin felt ice-cold determination. The bastards will not drive us out. Now I have the proof, father will listen to me, he thought. But why? Why should Urak do such a thing to his own people? As Urak and his men waded across the grassland, Berin sank back into the shadows, drawing the branches and leaves of his hide around him.

The three men passed well clear of Berin, heading for the spot from which they had first emerged from the forest. Berin decided to stay well hidden, his fear, the result of his last moment of inattention still tasted in the back of his throat. His caution was well justified, for as the outlander moved from beneath the oak tree, four watchers rose from hides in the grass and took station behind him.

Urak stopped to urinate. Just from sheer habit, built over a lifetime of hunting, the leading scout examined the lie of the stag and its hind. He had marked the place well and had no trouble identifying the place where the twig had snapped, but as he examined the scuff marks in the leaf mould, the bent and bruised stems of wood sorrel and crushed leaves of wintergreen, he was clearly puzzled. He cast about, finding tracks, tracing them to a fresh set of scuff marks. His partner watched silently, knowing what he was thinking, weighing the evidence in his own mind, nodding his agreement at the unspoken enquiry.

At the top of the slope, the leading scout stopped beneath a large beech, a landmark on the obvious route up the ridge; the wide umbrella sweep of its lower branches touched a ring of lesser growth, buckthorn, holly and elder, set amongst beech saplings. He motioned his confederate to stay, with a nod in the direction from which they had come, drawing his extended forefinger across his throat.

Berin, though anxious to reveal his news, was alert to the responsibility attached to it and to the risk of discovery. His recent fright was uppermost in his mind as he moved slowly, checking each advance before he made it, attuned to light and shade, sensing, testing the breeze, ears alert to any sound, eyes constantly searching, all senses reaching out to the inhabitants of the woods, feeling their fear at his passing, taking care not to provoke wild panic that would betray him. He paused at the foot of the slope, crouching in cover near his hide of the previous evening, and surveyed the ground ahead, particularly the cover at the top where, in what seemed to him now to have been a previous existence, he had stopped to check for a potentially fatal shadow. Satisfied, Berin rose and made his way up the hillside. As he reached the top, moving through the annulus of brush around the outer lower branches of a beech tree, a pigeon, flighting in crop-full to roost, suddenly

veered, nearly stalling in its wing clapping panic, to turn
and escape in darting flight, veering down the valley.

Berin started, then stared; a thin trickle of bark mould
and leaf fragments caught the light. As he looked up,
Urak's man launched himself at him, booting Berin's
shoulder, crushing him to the ground. Berin's spear fell
from his hand and skittered across the brown shiny leaves.
In a panic, he turned, rolling, searching for his attacker,
who was hurling himself at Berin as he lay, propped on one
elbow. Desperately Berin grasped his attacker's knife wrist,
feeling his hand slip in the sticky sweat of his own terror.
The bronze dagger gleamed perilously close to his throat.
The man's body smothered his own, bearing down. The face
above him was taught, teeth bared in a grimace of effort,
eyes glinting, sensing triumph, breath rasping with the
excitement of the kill. Desperately Berin held off the knife
hand, twisting his head to one side, sinews corded, muscles
straining, scrabbling with his other hand for purchase, to
roll, to do anything, fingers partly trapped under the
quiver. The attacker moved his left hand to his right on the
hilt of the dagger, bunching shoulders and biceps for the
death thrust. Berin scrabbled an arrow from the quiver and
holding it close to the head, drove it with all his might into
the side of the man's neck, pushing and pushing, grunting
and squealing with his effort and fright. He saw the flint,
slick with gore emerge below his assailant's ear, felt the
warmth spatter his face, tasted its metallic flatness. Berin
watched, time suspended, as surprise and shock coarsened
the man's features, watched the frantic scrabbling of
disbelieving bloody fingers at his assailant's throat, fingers
that Berin took in his own, twisting, rolling the man onto
his back, straddling him, both wrists pinned to the ground,
watching the life dim in his eyes, the blood pulse and
puddle, scarlet on the shiny brown of the beech leaves,

hearing the gurgle for breath, feeling beneath him the desperate chest heave, the death rattle, the final loosening.

Berin rolled retching, gasping for air, to lie beside the man he had killed. Then self preservation asserted itself. Quickly he grasped the bronze dagger, recovered his spear and stood shaking, shivering with reaction, his back to the smooth bark of the tree, leaning against it, taking it as ally to defend his back, his ears straining, hearing only the pounding of his own blood, eyes searching, darting from leaf fall to leaf fall. When he realised that only one had waited for him, Berin's breathing slowed and gradually returned to normal. The tremors subsided; he no longer wanted to run, to run headlong anywhere. Colour slowly returned to the pallor below the mud camouflage. Rationality re-established itself.

Urak and his guide retraced their steps, hurrying now, pausing only to scout carefully around the end of the picket line and emerged from the scrub on the edge of the West Way, just where it entered the thickly wooded valley which led down to the river. Ahead of them, tiny figures danced on the hill top, black against the sinking sun, throwing long shadows down the hill. From the valley, a chorus of disturbed bird calls, shouts and snatches of song sounded the arrival of a body of men on the march. My brother, Urak surmised, sitting on a stump. I shall wait for him. It will look well to arrive with Tarok.

Urak watched as the column of men emerged from the wooded valley. In the lead, his half-brother Tarok, Dorn's son by his first wife, as different to Urak as the sun to the moon. A big, broad, blond-headed man, muscular and powerful in body, but weak in the head, Urak reflected. A bully, Urak knew from bitter childhood experience, proud and a braggart. Yet, followed with slavish devotion by his subjects, the inhabitants of the settlements upstream of the ford, in particular those living at his headquarters, the outstation, a settlement established to control the rich fur trade with the river people. It was unthinkable that such a man should inherit the Ford...just because he was born first.

"Hah, Urak, well met," Tarok cried as he came up on the pair sitting at the way side. "Father said I would find you here. It's not like you to leave the comforts of home. What are you doing out in the far settlements?"

"Well brother, we must all serve as best we can. I have come to invoke the Mother's assistance for the new works and to dedicate a cairn to Belu and Ermid," Urak responded, nodding to the figures on the skyline, where a distinct cone was taking shape. "We are not all suited to playing soldiers."

"Damned shame, that, Belu I mean. I liked Belu," Tarok said bluffly, then called over his shoulder, "Go on, go on into camp. Hey Geran! March them on man. I'll talk a while with my brother. Take care to deliver Branwen and all her baggage to Com himself. He faced his half-brother. "Tell me," he said. "What's new here? Have they attacked again?"

"No, no attacks, in fact it has been very quiet. No sign of them at all. You've brought our sister then?"

"Aye. Father seems to be in an unseemly haste to consummate this match. I'm not sure that I like the deal. Com drove too hard a bargain, all those cattle and bondmen too. It makes him important above his station."

Father had little choice, Com is the key to the defence of the ford. He did what I would have done in his place, thought Urak, damn him, but said "Yes, it is preposterous, isn't it."

"Still, there was no arguing with him and I am to give Branwen to young Berin as soon as it can be arranged. Mind you, from the looks of her, it's not before time however soon it is. Our sister, it is said, has been casting her eye around and would be none too choosy if not bedded soon. A handful she'll be for young Berin."

"He's grown, Tarok. He's grown," said Urak, thinking that a wedding would provide reason for a day's feasting, for more distraction, more diversion of effort.

"I don't suppose they will attack again now, now we're here in force. I'd like to teach them a lesson. We should mount an expedition against them. Take the fight to them."

"Always the firebrand, brother," replied Urak mockingly, thinking on no account can he be allowed to do that, it would ruin everything. "Dorn's orders are to build the stronghold for the future, not crack a few heads for pleasure now."

"What's happened with the stronghold then?"

"Oh I think it has been marked out and they have experimented with building methods and so on. It really isn't my affair."

"Taking their time aren't they? Who's running things, old Com?"

"He's in charge, of course, but he suffers too much from his wound to do much. Berin seems to order most of the day to day affairs, helped by Aedd."

Tarok's face clouded at the mention of Aedd's name. Crossing the ford he had hastened, tingling in anticipation, to Anoeth's hut to pick up Ened, to bring with him for his enjoyment far from his interfering wife. His fury with the old man still smouldered, even after several hours of hard uphill marching. His disappointment at pleasures lost, or postponed, as he constantly reassured himself, was an ache in his groin.

"What, young Berin? Why he's nothing but a lad. It's a good thing I'm here to push things along then; five days since the raid and nothing done yet. Shouldn't be left to youngsters. You should have seen to it Urak. As for Aedd, well he's not one of the blood, is he. Can't rely on them. I want a word with him anyway."

Ever sensitive to nuances of tone, Urak glanced up at the edge to his half-brother's voice. "Then now's your chance, brother. There he is, supervising up at the burial site. As to what I should and should not do, you know my first duty is to the Mother. We overlook her needs at our peril," he threatened, grinning inwardly as he watched Tarok reach involuntarily for the soft leather pouch around his neck, which Urak knew contained a carved chalk figurine, a squatting, bloated, appallingly pregnant and grotesque representation of Dana. Superstitious fool, he laughed inwardly, hugging to himself the knowledge of how he had manipulated his overbearing older half-brother ever since, as a cowed and much bullied youth, he had discovered the depths of Tarok's credulity, his blind faith, his weakness.

Aedd, standing on the hilltop had watched the arrival of the column, recognising Urak and Tarok in conversation, feeling relief at the reappearance of the one in equal proportion to apprehension at the arrival of the other. Now as the brothers made their way up the slope towards him, he turned to Ened, who had lingered with him, enjoying his company and the rough banter of the workmen, feeling safe and warm in his huge ambience.

"Ened," he said softly to avoid being overheard, "Tarok's come. You'd best be off girl, back to the house. Go down that way," he said, pointing to a dip which developed in the far side of the hill. "Go down the gully. He won't see you. Stay out of sight when he's around."

With a sad smile, Ened gathered up the basket and now empty pitcher, the remains of Aedd's meal, and left. Aedd watched her, buttocks pulsing beneath the soft wool of her dress, the sensual, rhythmic invitation and promise subliminally directed at just one very special man amongst the many who watched. As she dropped from his sight, Aedd sighed.

The trench around the burial site, now nearly waist deep, was half completed. Aedd had started them off in four separate quadrants, each with two pick handlers working in opposite directions, so that eight faces were in operation at any one time; each face worker had his own shoveller, to excavate the loosened chalk and throw it onto the growing mound. The operation had already produced a startlingly white, flattened cone, with its top levelled, at about chest height.

"You're getting on well, Aedd," said Urak as he approached. "You know my brother Tarok."

"Aye, we've met."

"Yes, we have. Look here, I want to talk to you."

Aedd eyed the big man standing in front of him, every part of him a loud statement of the highborn, privileged origins of the man. Well-formed, handsome most would say,

210

though some would wonder if a weakness lurked somewhere, a weak chin, perhaps, disguised beneath the fashionably trimmed beard, or revealed by the over thick lips and their tendency to pout. His dress and ornament were magnificent, as befitted the heir to the High Chief; a rich blue cloak, fine white woollen shirt under a buckskin jerkin, short brown woollen hunting kilt, reaching to the knee, kid shoes. Each arm carried copper amulet and gold bracelet. A small, sweat darkened and much fingered pouch hung from its drawstring around his neck, below the clan necklace of polished greenstone and amber. A bronze dagger and axe hung at his belt. The spear which he carried was also tipped with bronze.

Tarok motioned Aedd aside, out of earshot, as Urak looked on quizzically.

"Aedd, now I know you are going to be reasonable about this, about Ened. You see I want her back...for my wife. She only sent her to Anoeth for him to look after. He had no business selling her bond, none at all. Give her back to me...er...her."

Aedd fixed his eyes firmly on Tarok's. "No," he answered.

"Aedd, Aedd," Tarok wheedled, "be reasonable. I don't mean give... I mean sell. Sell her bond to me. I'll make it worth your while. Here, choose. My axe?" Aedd's eyes lit for a moment, lifting Tarok's heart in triumph. "Yes, here, take my axe, go on, here," he said, drawing it from his belt and holding it out to Aedd.

"No," replied Aedd, hating himself for his momentary avarice.

"... and dagger."

"No."

"You drive a hard bargain, Aedd. Here, have all that you see. Axe, dagger, spear."

"No."

"Do you want jewellery, cattle? Name your price," Tarok pleaded, bemused by the evaporation of the momentary advantage that he had glimpsed in Aedd's eyes.

"No, nothing. I want nothing from you, " replied Aedd, grim faced. "You don't seem to understand. Ened's bond is not for sale, not anymore. She is not for sale again, ever. She has been traded enough. Now she stays with me."

Tarok sought to dominate as he had been used to doing all his life, using his bulk, his bearing, his birth right, so used to easy victory, but all useless against the flint hard eyes and unmoving mass of Aedd. His anger rose, turning his neck and face red. How dare this low born refuse him, Tarok of the blood of Harac.

"I mean to have her, Aedd," he spat.

"Not while I breathe, Tarok," Aedd replied, the outward coolness of tone belying the heated emotions within.

Tarok turned away, furious, but helpless in the face of Aedd's intransigence and determination and strode off down the hill to the settlement. Urak stared curiously from one to the other, then followed his half-brother.

CHAPTER 15

The sun hung, an orange disc, bright against the slate grey cloud which streaked the blushing western sky when Berin returned to the settlement along the stream bank. Once the fight was over, Berin had felt an overwhelming need to wash. With revulsion, he had discovered his hands and face slick, then cloying with the dead man's blood as it dried, caking and cracking on his skin. He had staggered straight down the valley side, heading for the stream, where the cleansing had assumed an almost ritual significance.

Berin had followed the stream up the valley, arriving at the picket line as the watch was being changed, but he barely exchanged a word, he was so tired and emotionally drained. Berin understood from Iowerth, who grumbled away about his night duty, that a large herd had arrived from the ford, followed by Tarok and his men. Had he paid more attention, he would have learned that his bride to be, Branwen, had arrived with her half-brother, but that information passed him by.

Berin drew back the doorflap. Com, Aedd, Urak and Tarok sat in council around the hearth. Com scowled at his son as he came in.

"Father, I must talk with you..," Berin began but was interrupted by his father, loudly, aggressively, in a voice slurred by pain and the drink taken in quantity to dull its edge.

"Ah, there you are at last. Well you might as well know it now as later. Your little trollop has found a good master. I've given her to Urak."

Berin's face froze, deathly white but for two fever spots high on his cheeks. His heart thudded, his pulse skittered. He awaited an awakening from the nightmare, but none came. Instead Com continued, compounding the horror.

"He's offered and I've decided to accept. So now you can concentrate on your obligations. Better than she has any right to expect, though why Urak should offer for the likes of her, and take her brother's wardship into the bargain defeats my understanding. She's a lucky girl."

"But you can't father. You mustn't. You musn't give her, give anyone to that traitor," Berin shouted, pointing a quivering finger at Urak.

"Berin be silent," screamed Com, as Urak and Tarok jumped to their feet, knocking stools flying.

"Traitor!" Berin spat.

"What?" snarled Tarok, reaching for his dagger. Aedd, silently, unnoticed by the main protagonists, rose and positioned himself close behind the big man.

Urak stared spectre-like at Berin, mind racing. He followed me. He's seen. He knows; he knows everything. He frightened the stag. He's the reason Gawin didn't return. What did he see? He couldn't have heard any of the meeting. What was that Com said, 'his trollop'? So Berin has a fancy for Olwen. Relief flooded his startled thoughts. That's the way to play it, a thwarted rival. Aloud he said in as reasonable and well modulated a tone as he could muster "Berin, be reasonable. Although you favour the girl, you are to marry my sister. We..."

"You bastard. You shan't have her," Berin screeched as Com staggered to his feet, waving his good arm.

214

"Silence. Stop it. Stop it. I forbid you to talk this way," Com wailed.

But Berin was not to be stopped, not by Com, not by filial duty, not by custom, not by physical restraint, not by the Spirit of Darkness himself, had he appeared at that moment. "I saw you. I tracked you to your meeting with the outlander."

"What?" roared Tarok. "You dare to accuse one of the first blood. By the Mother I'll have your tongue for that." He lurched at Berin, but was brought to an abrupt halt by a firm grip on his belt.

"Put back your knife," Aedd demanded, "there will be no violation of hospitality at Com's hearth."

Tarok twisted his head to stare at Aedd. For an instant the quarrel going on around them muted, faded in the face of their search of each other's hostility in their eyes locked. Slowly Tarok replaced the blade, but Aedd recognised in that instant, in the venom that tainted the big man's baleful glance, that one day he would have to fight and perhaps kill him.

"Explain yourself Berin," Com raged, spittle flying, eyes popping, an altogether comical figure had the drama been less raw, the actors less enflamed and capable of detached analysis.

"This afternoon I tracked three men along the top and down into the valley at the bottom pasture, the one we didn't use this year. As they lay in cover I heard Urak's voice. I watched them meet the outlander."

Consciously calming body and voice, Urak interupted with all the candour he could muster. "Now wait brother," he said, looking to Tarok as he held up a hand. "I understand your anger, but let us remember our manners even if those around us are forgetting theirs. There is an explanation, if only we can find it. Berin, I know now that you feel thwarted in your affections, but it is monstrous to try to discredit me in such a way just to..."

"Aye, to keep your doxy. That's it, isn't it," Com raged. "You'd do anything, say anything to keep her by you."

".. Er... quite. As I was saying, this afternoon I went out to meet my brother on the West Way, so you must have been mistaken."

"Aye, that's right," Tarok interjected, "Why we came in together. Aedd saw us, is that not so Aedd?" Reluctantly Aedd nodded, seeing the pit opening beneath his friend.

"Withdraw Berin. Com, your son has insulted Urak. He must withdraw what he's said and apologise."

"I can prove it. I can prove your servant was there. He attacked me. I.. I killed him. I had to, it was him or me. He's lying out there now, beyond the picket line."

"You've done what?" snarled Urak. "You killed one of my men?"

"He was covering your retreat. He tried to kill me, to stop me from reporting your meeting."

"By the picket line, you say. Covering my retreat? What from, eh? From where I sat on the West Way waiting for my brother? You young fool. I sent Gawin to scout the tops. From what Aedd told me yesterday I was sure the pickets did not go far enough. I was worried we might be outflanked. I sent him to check. He no doubt thought you were an enemy, coming in from down the valley like you did. Now you've killed him. Of all the... the incompetent, insolent, jumped-up upstarts," spluttered Urak in feigned rage. "Com, I demand an apology. Tarok, what do you think? This stupid brat is to become our brother? We must go to father and demand that he draws back from this madness."

"Urak, Tarok, let's not be hasty," quavered Com, pasty faced.

"I agree brother," Tarok roared. "We will leave at first light, all of us. We cannot depend on them. Father seeks to please, compensate, protect them. He offers our sister, cattle, bondmen. Now they insult us."

"Berin, you will apologise now, "Com hissed. "Who ever you saw, who ever you heard, it was not Urak. On the evidence of Tarok... of Aedd, it could not be!"

"Er..," Berin hesitated, startled by the turn of events..." er..but..."

"Berin, you will apologise handsomely this instant and withdraw your accusation now," Com shouted, "or you are no son of mine. I shall disown you, aye banish you."

Berin's eyes flew wide in dismay and alarm. To be disowned, to be landless, was an unthinkable punishment, to lose birthright, name, land and clan, would leave him no alternative but to offer his bond to strangers, for none in the clan could have him. But banishment, with winter coming, meant almost certainly a lonely death in the outlands.

Berin looked around the circle, all eyes hostile except for Aedd's. Mutely Berin appealed to him for help. Aedd sadly, with the barest perceptible sideways movement of his head, reminded Berin of the frailty of the evidence which could be brought in support and the danger in which it would place his son and Anoeth. His father's face was closed to him, implacable, watching but would not see, hearing but would not listen. Nothing would change that now. Urak's involvement of Olwen had seen to that.

Berin turned to Urak. Unable to face the triumph he was certain he would find in his enemy's eyes, he spoke from the shelter of downcast lids, trembling with rage and humiliation.

" It seems I was mistaken. The man I saw could not have been you; the voice I heard could not have been yours, since you were at the West Way. I ask you to accept my apology. I was wrong to accuse you before my father," Berin said, raising his eyes, locking them on Urak's. The edge with which the last words were spoken was lost on everybody but Urak, who knew from that moment that he was in a fight to the finish.

"I accept your apology," answered Urak cooly, receiving the unspoken challenge, confident that he would have the chance to repay the shock he had just suffered, that he would be able to make Berin pay for his discomfiture. "As to my man, well it is embarrassing to have one's servant attack the son of one's host. If you, Berin, will accept my apology in Gawin's stead for his excess of zeal, for which he has paid the ultimate price, I'm sure you will agree, then we'll say no more."

"Handsomely spoken," interjected Com. "Well Berin?"

Sick and humiliated to his roots, Berin wanted desperately to escape from the room, to find Olwen, run, hide. His father would never believe Urak's treachery. Berin was willing to do, to say anything to leave, to escape.

"I accept," he muttered sullenly, shamed by his own tacit approval of the lie as much as by his parent's transparent cupidity to which all had to be sacrificed.

"Father, may I take my leave?"

"Yes, I wish you would."

There was a silence after Berin left the room, which Com rushed to fill. The nightmare of the ruination of his magnificent deal with Dorn was slowly dissipating, but was still real enough to keep him tense and nervous. "I am so sorry, Urak, that you should have been treated in such a way in my house, and by my own son."

"Please, we must forget it and concentrate on our plans. Berin was clearly overwrought, his head quite turned by passion," Urak urged, adopting a conciliatory manner and tone, wanting desperately to get away from the subject. Urak didn't want Com to think back over events, knowing he had escaped by the skin of his teeth. He picked up the mead pitcher and refilled Com's bowl, making a play of filling his own. Com drank deeply.

"Yet Berin saw and followed someone," Aedd interjected.

"Aye," agreed Tarok, half wondering that he should have found something to agree with Aedd. "There's spies about that are getting around our picket line. We must send out more scouts and extend the line."

" Yes, yes," muttered Urak impatiently, wanting to turn the conversation. "Of course the outlander will be spying on us. You'll see to it Tarok, won't you. But Com, returning to Berin for the moment, I too have... well it will not do for Berin to see my woman alone again."

"You're right. You should take Olwen away, back to the ford as quickly as possible, if you really want her, that is. She's no match for you. I wouldn't want Dorn to think I had... well palmed her off on you."

"I wouldn't worry. I will of course not take Olwen as my first wife. Father has not yet made a choice, but meanwhile I feel the need for certain comforts."

Com smiled a worldly smile. "Of course."

"Hah ! and I thought your comforts lay elsewhere, brother," ventured Tarok with a sly smirk.

Com looked puzzled as Urak glared at his half-brother, before turning back to Com. "Yes I should get her away as soon as possible, but meanwhile, I wonder if they may not try... Berin is so headstrong. Should he not be watched? Now that Olwen is promised to me it would not do...and it would be such an insult to Branwen and Dorn if they... Well I've set my man to guard Olwen and the boy. They are in my quarters."

"Oh, I see what you mean. Yes of course. Aedd, find Berin, tell him that I order him to stay in his room. A guard on his doorway if you please. See to it at once."

"Of course the guards should be drawn from amongst my men from the ford, or from Tarok's. I shall see to that, with your permission Com," Urak said, joining Aedd as he rose to leave the hearth.

Com nodded his approval, turning to Tarok. "I would be pleased if you would take charge of our defences. We have little experience of war here on the West Way. I think this mess shows that well enough. Oh, Berin has done what he can, and has some good ideas, especially about the water supply, and the actual construction, but we need the sort of experience you must have from keeping all those savages in control at the outstation. Besides which, he's probably not going to be too reliable for the next few days."

"I'd be glad to Com. I shall see to it first thing tomorrow. We must get started building the defences. I'll set my men to it at first light. Dorn's and your men can join me when they've finished the tomb. That should be by sundown tomorrow. With your permission, I'll leave now and check that my men are settled in. Oh and thank you for your hospitality, but I have my tent and staff. I shall be quite comfortable with my own men and better able to keep an eye on things."

Aye, and better able to have my way with that slut Ened, he thought malignantly, when I get my hands on her.

CHAPTER 16

Aedd clamped his lips firmly together, biting back angry retort. He turned away from Tarok, who was standing, hands on hips, in the centre of the rising stronghold, damning the man, damning Com for putting him in charge over Berin, over them all. Why, Tarok behaved as though they were all bondmen, not freemen and landowners. Still, he had to admit, grudgingly, that no one could claim that Tarok had not achieved results. The top of the hill was now almost enclosed by high white walls, a row of shelters was being thatched, one of the cisterns was complete and already partly filled with water. At the other, Aedd could see the youngsters bending and dipping, puddling clay and plastering it on the chalk base and on themselves.

Piles of sling stones and bundles of arrows were being collected. Each evening, Aedd, in common with nearly everyone at the settlement, hammered and cracked, split and pressed, flake after flake to make yet more arrow heads. He cut, dried, straightened, notched, fletched and married shafts to points. No works of art these; no carefully crafted high precision missiles where accuracy turned on balance and trueness and accuracy meant the difference between full or empty stomachs. No, these were simple firepower, destined to be hurled as rapidly as possible into a massed attack, a crude but effective, spiteful response to aggression.

The settlement and encampment were littered with flint shards. In the mine men and boys toiled night and day, sunset and sunrise indistinguishable from one another in the dark belly of the hill, prising out nodules, delving deeper and deeper under the hillside. It was dangerous work. There had already been one bad fall. Kar had been dragged out by his heels from beneath a roof collapse, bruised and choking, but luckily otherwise unhurt, except for his dignity, and Brys had passed out in the foul air. It was always the same. Just when they reached the better flint, they had trouble with foul air and roof falls. Soon they would have to start a fresh gallery.

The argument with Tarok still rankled. Aedd had set the gateposts himself. Four massive oak beams through which the gate was to slide, were set deep into pits in the chalk and braced by angled beams, also fixed deep in the bedrock. He had taken so much trouble with the plumb line. Damn the man. The posts were strong enough and matched, well almost. Admittedly the one was a little thinner, but still adequate for the purpose. They had even begun to fill in the gap in the bank around the posts. Now Aedd was ordered to take an axe party and bring back a stouter beam to replace the thinner one. The nearest oak of any size was up the far hillside, a hard day's work to fell, trim and transport, even with the oxen, even if they all had bronze axes like the one Tarok had thrust at him as he told him abruptly to get on with it. Aedd looked at the axe more closely, thumbing the cutting edge, hefting the weight; admiring the properties of the wondrous material.

Aedd looked up as a growing shadow pressaged approaching footsteps behind him. He turned and saw that it was Berin.

"How is he?" Aedd asked.

"On the way out, I should say; Rh'on has sent for that bastard Urak. She seems to think his medicine might work where hers has failed. She's at her wits' end. Nothing she

223

does has any effect on the fever; she can't stop the infection either."

"Sounds bad."

"It is. Rh'on is frightened, really frightened. I've never seen mother like that before. She thinks he's going to die. He raves in his fever. Mostly at me; talks to Belu; romances on about the West Way, the old days of the drovers and the axe trade."

"I'm sorry."

"Don't be. Well not on my account. I know he's my father, but there's little left between us. Not after what he did to Olwen. I was going to wed Branwen anyway. He knew that. He had no call to do such a thing, give her to that bastard Urak. I know it was him I tracked that day."

"Well it was his bondman we buried," interjected Aedd grimly.

"I was going to run, you know, that night; grab Olwen and take our chances in the outlands. He put guards on me; on me, his own son."

"Aye, it was Urak that was behind that."

"And on her too. Next day she was gone." Berin sighed. "I've just got to get her away from him."

"She'll be well guarded at the ford. You couldn't bring her back here. Com would banish you if you stole her back, or worse, give you up to Dorn. Dorn would be bound to demand them back. Then Urak would get to punish you."

"Not if they didn't know it was me. If it looked like she and Oranc escaped. I could hide them in the outlands. Take food to them."

"You are treading a dangerous path my friend."

"Damn him. Rh'on loves him still. The Mother knows, but I find little to love in him now. I could wish him dead."

"He's our chief and your father. Right or wrong, you can't change that. I'll look in on Rh'on on my way."

"Why, where are you off to?"

"That Tarok wants me to replace one of the gate posts. I'll have to cut another from the east grove. It'll take all day."

"Shall I have a word?"

"Nah, save your breath," Aedd answered contemptuously. "There's no point. Com put him in charge and in charge he is. Doesn't everyone have to know it."

Berin was silent, reflecting on his recent displacement as captain, his curious position, in disgrace, with no authority or responsibility, ignored by Tarok, yet as heir to Com, so vulnerable on his sick bed, so close to overall command that none dared command him.

"How a nice old boy like Dorn could spawn such a pair as him and Urak beats me," Aedd added. "Young Branwen seems nice enough though."

Aedd glanced slyly at his friend to gauge the effect of his words. Berin thought back to the formal introduction in his father's hall. He had to admit that she was very pretty, with merry little eyes, which twinkled at surface and flashed promise in their depths, a complexion as dark as Olwen's was fair, her dark, stiffly curling hair springing back from her intelligent, finely formed features. A fine nose, high cheek bones, a firm chin with a hint of a dimple, a generous mouth. She smelt nice too, he had noticed, clean and fresh. She had trembled as she had stood before him. He had seen her arms, which carried a fine dark down, shake as she clasped her hands in front of her. Her shape was hidden by cape and long skirt, but her breasts pushed suggestively at the front of her soft woolen bodice, a promise of grace hidden beneath.

Before Olwen he would have been attracted, he knew that, in fact he would have been blessing the Mother for his good luck. But she was not before Olwen, his Olwen, who was lost to him, his own father's sacrifice to Urak.

"Aye," Berin said, dragging his mind back to the present. "She's alright."

"Aedd, Aedd, are you going to stand chattering like an old woman all day? Get on with it man."

Tarok's rough tone tugged Aedd's normally genial features into a grimace. With a brief handclasp and a shrug of the shoulders he set off back to the settlement, calling to his work party as he went. Berin stared after Aedd, yet did not see his friend, his eyes were unfocused, his mind was already at the ford, searching out Olwen. There could be no better time than now, with Urak on his way to doctor his father.

CHAPTER 17

Olwen was afraid, very afraid. Barac, Urak's bondsman, was pushing her to his master. She could sense his hope that she would resist so that he would have an excuse to misuse her. Her cheeks burned hot and red, shamed at the memory of the night they had come from Com's settlement and from the anticipation of what was to come.

"Come here," he had said that night, his voice menacing the silence left by Barac's departure.

"At once," he had snapped, slapping the side of his boot with a hazel switch.

She had stood proudly, looking directly at him. He had walked around her, silently, eyeing her, examining her. She had flinched as the switch touched under her chin.

"I have summoned you to tell you what I expect of you," he had said finally, after a long pause. "I want and expect only one thing from you; obedience. Do you understand me?"

Mutely she had nodded her head, not trusting herself to speak, following him with wide eyes.

Urak had smiled thinly and moved the stick slowly down across her breasts, making her nipples rise, making her shiver. He had pressed the switch over the slight swell of her belly, across her thighs to the hem of her shift. He had hooked it underneath and lifted.

"Lift it."

Olwen had flushed, looking at him in disbelief.

"For your first lesson in obedience, you are not doing very well. If you prefer, I shall have Barac help you. He would enjoy that."

Olwen had dropped her hands to the hem of her skirt and lifted it to her knees.

"Higher."

Hesitantly she had raised her skirt across her thighs, stopping, looking at him pleadingly, her defiance fading.

"I said pull it up," he had reminded her, quietly but uncompromisingly.

The stick had cut her buttocks, stinging, shocking. She had started, bitten back a cry and slowly raised her skirt to her waist, hanging her head, shamed, humiliated, tears welling, coursing hot and itchy over her cheeks, eyes fixed beyond the blur of her wretchedness, on her hands gripping the cloth.

Urak had been silent for a long time. He had stared at her. She had felt his eyes penetrate her privacy, parting, unfolding, debasing.

"I am going to ask you some questions which you will answer truthfully. Do you understand?"

"Yes," Olwen had muttered in reply.

"Speak up girl."

"Yes."

"A little respect would not go amiss," he had said. "You shall address me as sire or master!"

"Yes sire," she had muttered.

"What is said about me in Com's settlement?"

"Why nothing," Olwen had said hopefully, hope dying, choked by her screech of pain as the scourge slashed her legs, and by the sobbing as he had pushed the hazel switch between her thighs, pressing up against her core.

"I shall ask you just one more time, Olwen," Urak had said menacingly, slowly drawing out the whip. "What is said about me? What has Berin said of me?"

"Berin has said nothing...but...Aedd...Aedd wanted me to watch you. To report what you did," she had gabbled in panic when he raised his arm.

"Why? Tell me everything."

Urak had watched her closely, seeing her eyes following the switch. He had raised it slightly, hearing her intake of breath, smelling her fear.

"Oh please, I don't know anything. I don't know why. Aedd just asked me to keep an eye on who you met... to report what I might overhear you say. That's all."

"You are sure that is all."

"Yes."

He had run the tip of the switch from the neckline to the skirt bunched at her waist.

"Take this off," he had said.

"But..."

Her briefest of protest had died as he had stepped forward and slapped her, first on one cheek and then back-handed on the other. Tears had welled, coursing smarting over her cheeks.

"No buts woman," he had said, "not to me, not ever."

She had stifled her sobs and lifted the shift over her head, dropping it on the floor beside her, covering her sex with her hands, trying to conceal her raised nipples behind her arms.

"Put your arms at your side," he had ordered.

All thoughts of rebellion had evaporated with the slightest twitch of the scourge in Urak's hand. She had done as he had commanded, aware how vulnerable she was, how exposed she was to his gaze, to his whim.

He had moved behind her. She had felt his fingers close on her nipples. She had squealed as his fingers had twisted and pulled her.

"You will be silent," he had hissed in her ear. She had cursed the weakness of her own flesh, standing proud in its betrayal. His fingers had touched and probed everywhere, as though asserting their proprietary rights. She had cursed the weakness of her own flesh, yielding in moist betrayal of its true master. She had raised just a whimper of protest, just the once, when her final keep of privacy had been breeched by Urak's assault. But Urak had slapped her buttocks and she had re-learned that resistance brought pain.

"Turn around," he had said.

Fearfully she had turned to face her tormentor. She had flinched as he had touched her again with the switch, stroking her between the thighs, but had swallowed the cry of terror that had welled into her throat.

"Good, you are learning," he had said and she had found a glimmer of relief at the undertone of pleasure she had detected in his voice.

"Do you have anything more to tell me?"

"No," she had answered.

He had cut her six times across the buttocks, scourge whistling, cracking on her soft white flesh, biting, raising welts, her startled scream choked off each time by the breath-stealing shock of pain.

"Understand this: there is no mercy in me for those of mine who do not obey me," he had said, icily "...and you are mine now. You are mine to do with as I please."

She had been dismissed, locked alone in a bare room, without food, water or any comfort. She had been sore, hungry, thirsty, tired, very cold, confused and very, very frightened, when Barac had come for her the following day and each day thereafter. For days now she had attended Urak, summoned for a repeat of her shameful humiliation, ordered to expose herself then beaten on the slightest pretext, at Urak's whim. She had always been obedient, even trying hard to anticipate his wants to put off what seemed to have been inevitable punishment. She had quickly learnt that pain could only be avoided by instant obedience. She had learnt to look for the slightest sign that he was pleased, learning that his pleasure postponed pain and brought her a drink of water or some food. She had told him everything. Every word that Aedd had said by Belu's tomb, every whispered confidence shared with her by Berin. Each night she had been returned to her comfortless cell.

At first she had sustained herself on dreams, dreams of Berin, of their love-making, dreams of their baby as she lay curled, as the baby would lie, but one night she had not been able to remember Berin's face. She had wept. Then she had sustained herself on thoughts of revenge, thoughts of Urak lying vulnerable, open to her punishment. Last night she had dreamt of Berin again, but his face had been Urak's.

"Ah, there you are," said Urak as Barac pushed her roughly through the doorway. "You may leave us Barac. Prepare me for a visit to Com. Pack my medicine bag. You will accompany me. We shall be away one night, two at the most."

When they were alone, Urak turned to Olwen. "You would like to come with me, wouldn't you?"

Olwen's heart lurched. "Oh yes please," she gasped.

"Did I give you permission to speak?" he asked.

"No sire… sorry Master."

She prostrated herself before him, looking up at him, waiting for a sign, for an instruction, desperate not to give offence, to keep alive the faintest of hopes that she might be able to find kindness again at Com's settlement, perhaps even a brief glimpse of Berin. Urak stood silent, watching. It amused him to see hope light her expression. Her training was progressing well, yet she still had hope. That must be eliminated, he thought. Perhaps she was ready for the next stage. Perhaps he would not present her to the outlander after all. It would be amusing to see if she could learn to please him. He hadn't thought to try his techniques with a wench before. The boy was hopeless. He was rebellious beyond all conditioning. He would be glad to be rid of him. But hold and control the girl and he would control Berin, troublesome, bothersome Berin. Besides, it would be a fine revenge for the fright Berin had given him.

"Stand," he commanded.

Olwen stood, arms at her side, silent, eyes downcast, unsure of what would be expected of her, fearing her own response. She knew that she would do anything, anything to find kindness again, if only for a while...even from Urak.

The silence lengthened. Olwen felt her knees begin to tremble, and nearly sagged as an overwhelming sense of weakness enveloped her. Staring directly at Urak, Olwen slowly and determinedly lifted her skirt to her waist, baring herself to him. She saw his eyes widen slightly, the first response she had noticed in him. She was sure now that he was enjoying her voluntary submission, sure that submission and obedience would bring her reward.

Urak allowed himself a smirk of self-satisfaction.

Olwen unlaced the top of her shift. She pulled the dress over jutting breasts, nipples rising, as though alert to her new knowledge. She dropped it on to the rush-covered floor and knelt before him.

Olwen looked down at his feet. "Command me Sire," she said softly and bent her head in submission.

He would have preferred the boy, even though he was a little older than his usual choice, but Oranc would die before he submitted. That was plain. Anyway, the girl was the key to Berin. He reached out and gently smoothed the hair at the back of her head. She looked up. He stroked her cheek, running his thumb across her lips. His touch was gentle, like a caress. Urak reached behind him for a beaker of water and raised it to her lips. She drank greedily, spilling some down her chin, feeling it drip onto her breasts. He took a barley cake and dipped it in honey and offered it to her. She ate greedily and licked the last traces from his fingers. Urak was reminded of his childhood puppy, his best, his only friend, which had suckled on his

233

fingers in the same way; the same puppy that Torak had cast in the river. Oh how he was going to pay for that and all the slights since. Urak pressed his fingers between Olwen's lips. She opened her mouth and sucked them. Olwen looked up at him so that she could affirm her submission to him; acknowledge its exchange rate in the currency of kindness. She would find kindness by pleasing him. She knew it. Urak felt himself harden at the signs of her willing submission. Power...such pleasure in power.

"Hold your hands behind you."

Olwen complied, startled, wondering what was to come. Urak produced a cord and tied it tightly around her wrists, pinching the skin white. Olwen winced.

"Lie down," he commanded, "there, by the pillar," he said, jerking the cord roughly, forcing her, toppling her on to her side on the rushes. Urak wound the free end of the cord around her ankles, binding them together, bending her knees, tying ankles to wrists and finally to the oak support.

Urak stepped over her. Olwen looked from booted foot in close focus at her breast, upwards along the legs which bridged her, to the face at the pinnacle of power, a dark mask against the backlight, blurred by her tears of pain. Olwen acknowledged his power over her and the futility of her dreams. She was swamped by a sense of her own weakness. She had no hope but for a small kindness from her master. She must learn to please him...she would learn to please him. She cursed herself. What had she done to anger him? He had been kind...hadn't he? So kind... the soft touch of his thumb on her on her lips...

"Now can I can trust you?" he asked. "Trust you to be ready to please me when I return? Well, can I?" he asked, stirring her breast with the toe of his boot.

"Yes master," she heard herself saying and knew that she meant it.

Olwen heard the beam drop across the door. Slowly, from her depths, she began to sob, because he was gone.

CHAPTER 18

Ened hummed happily, if tunelessly, as she skipped from Com's house, feeling a sense of release, glad to be out of the sick room, with its pervasive stench of decay which overlay even the clean pungency of woundwort. She was glad to leave the oppressive feeling of hopelessness. Soon she would see her own man, care for him, feed him. She welcomed the burden of the basket, with its weight of barley cakes, lamb bone and ale that would sustain her Aedd. She had never known such happiness, not even at home amongst her own kin. Not even with her immediate family, had she found such a sense of belonging, of trust given and received, of shared confidences, laughter and dreams and of course never had she experienced the sensual joys and fulfilment which she had found with Aedd. She stopped humming to smile at the memory of the previous night's love-making.

Now she hurried, for she was late and her man would be hungry. The first batch of cakes which she had baked had burned when she had rushed to answer Rh'on's anxious call, to find her, with Gwyn and Cigfen, struggling to hold Com as he raged and thrashed in delirium, trying to restrain him, to prevent him from doing further damage to his injured arm. All but Rh'on recoiled from touching the bandage-swathed source of foul smelling yellow-green pus. Rh'on, her face drawn, with lines etched as deep as those of her patient, dark puffy half moons below sunken eyes, only Rh'on touched and soothed, bathed and dressed and spoke as gently as ever she had, as though unaware of Com as the pitiful bundle of clothes on the couch, as though she still saw the handsome, dashing chieftain to whom she had been given as a child bride all those years ago, before the world was turned on its head.

Ened easily followed the trail of crushed grasses, bent twigs and scuffed leaves. Occasional axe blazes left as guides by the felling party were quite unnecessary. It was dark in the woods, despite considerable leaf-fall and strangely silent, but for the soughing of the breeze and her breathing, which hammered in her ears as the slope steepened. Ened paused under a rowan, scarlet berries crushing beneath her feet amongst the discarded and fading yellow fronds and turned to look back the way she had come.

Rough arms encircled her, pinning her arms to her sides. A horny hand clamped down hard over her mouth, cutting off her startled shriek as it formed in her throat, stifling, suffocating. She felt herself lifted, felt male hardness pressed tight against the cleft of her buttocks. She struggled helplessly, kicking out futilely in panic, then she was dashed to the ground, the breath driven from her body. Dazed, she was suddenly incongruously aware of the smell of ale and the glugging sound it made as it spilled from the pitcher.

"So you thought to spurn me, eh?"

Tarok, she thought in terror. Oh Dana save me, it's Tarok. Helpless she felt him pinion her arms back under her body. One hand reached for her breasts. The other stayed clamped over her mouth. She kicked and writhed, then stopped in dismay and panic as the dampness of the leaves and crushed berries on her buttocks and the breeze on her thighs told her that she was open, exposed to him. Her own actions had rucked up her skirt. Tarok thrust a knee between her own and rudely felt her. She cringed, sobbing behind his hand thinking he mustn't, oh no he mustn't, it's Aedd's, its for Aedd alone. What will he think of me. Lasciviously, slowly, enjoying her helplessness, Tarok unlaced the neckline of her dress, pulling it from her shoulders, exposing her breasts and their tips, hardening to the breeze and Tarok's touch. Traitors, she screamed in her mind. Tarok forced her thighs apart and knelt between them. Ened's wide, terrified eyes watched in horror as he stared at her, a leer of anticipation on his face, a drop of spittle hanging from his lip that hung slack with lust. Tarok lent forward, his face only inches from hers.

"I will have you now," said Tarok thickly. The gob of spittle trembled as he spoke. Ened stared at it in fascination, watching it extend, wondering that it did not fall. "Yes, once you have known me, you will want none other."

Tarok took his hand from her mouth, replacing it with his lips in a prising, bruising parody of the kisses she knew. Filled with revulsion, Ened bit, hard and deep, tasting blood, seeking to close her teeth together. Tarok roared, reared and clubbed her with his fist. A white light exploded within Ened's head. Dimly she was aware of Tarok's hands on her and then fumbling at his belt. She arched her back, seeking to throw him off, to deny him entrance, then stopped in horror, realising that she was abetting, not hindering him. There was a roaring in her ears and a curious release as Tarok's weight lifted.

Aedd stood over her, but not the gentle Aedd she knew. This was a killer, blood-lust glinting in his eye; a bear raised up on its haunches, snarling rage and defiance in the defence of its mate. Aedd stepped over her to where Tarok had rolled from Aedd's first clubbing punch. Shaking his head slowly, Tarok was rising to his feet, a dazed and shaken survivor of a blow which would have crushed the skull of a lesser man. Aedd kicked, aiming for the groin, but finding Tarok's ribs instead. Aedd followed as Tarok slid down the slope. Tarok launched himself at Aedd's knees, bringing him down. The two giants rolled and thrashed, crushing the undergrowth, ramming into tree trunks, the fight madness upon them, kneeing at each other's groins, gouging for eyes, punching, butting, no rules but survival, no thought but to deal terminal injury.

Tarok, big as he was, soon realised that in Aedd he had met his match. He could never beat the implacable determination to kill which he read in Aedd's eyes. He knew he was fighting for survival and for the first time in his bullying life he felt fear. Mustering all his strength, as Aedd changed grip, he brought both elbows down on the base of Aedd's breast bone. Aedd went into spasm, searching for air. Tarok lumbered to his feet and crashed off down the hillside. Aedd staggered and made to go after him.

"Aedd. Aedd." Ened's piercing anguished cry reached through the blood hot fight rage. Aedd shook his head as though shaking off the madness and slowly climbed back.

Ened had pulled her dress back around her and now held it clutched in her crossed arms, hugging herself, shivering in reaction. Aedd went to her and held her in the great circle of his arms, gentling her, smoothing her hair, cradling her head.

"Are you all right," he asked her gently, touching her swollen cheek and bruised lip, where Tarok had hit her.

"Yes Aedd, just a ... he didn't ... you know..."

"Thank Dana I came back to find you. You were late. I was worried you might have fallen, or something."

"He didn't ..."

"Hush girl, it's all right."

"I couldn't have born it if he had taken what is yours."

Aedd smiled grimly, touched and wondering at her love for him, knowing that that which she had feared so much would have made no difference to his feelings for her; realising too that his view was not capable of explanation at that moment.

"I'll kill the bastard."

"No!"

Surprised, Aedd looked at her, startled by her vehemence.

"They'll kill you if you try. They'll probably kill you if you even appear back at the settlement. He's the High Chief's son, with three score men at his call."

"But he tried to..."

"To what? To have his way with a bondwoman? What's so terrible about that to the likes of him? Com can't protect you; he is near death. Berin's not in the settlement. Tarok's in charge. He'll have you killed. And then he'll have me." She shuddered in revulsion.

Aedd slowly shook his head, partly in perplexity at the turn of events, the position in which he now found himself, partly in wonderment at Ened's clarity of vision.

"You're right. Of course, I see now that we can't go back, leastwise not whilst Tarok's there. We'll have to hole up somewhere. Ilws? No they'll find us there too. The outlands then, but we'll need weapons and tools to make a shelter; warm clothes, some food to last until I can hunt."

"Surely your kin at Ilws will help?"

"Aye, but I must get there before them, and .."

"What is it?"

"I left two axes at the work site, one of them a bronze one of Tarok's. I'll have that for a start. You've food here," he said, stooping to pick up the basket, ruefully shaking the empty ale pitcher. "At least for tonight. Aye let's collect those axes and work our way around to Ilws. Auron will see me set up. But we will have to hurry. Tarok will be after us soon enough."

Urak wrinkled his nose in distaste while he carefully unwrapped the bandages from Com's arm. The stench of putrefaction, sweet and cloying, was almost palpable. Com lay stretched on his back on the couch, near comatose from the strong sleeping draught which Urak had administered earlier. Rh'on had demurred, protesting at its strength, but Urak had forced the bitter liquid into the mouth of his delirious patient anyway, explaining that Com had to be still to be examined properly and that anyway the drug would help to fight the fever. Urak had known, the moment he entered the sick room that Com was doomed and the strength of the draught was irrelevant. At least Com's passing would be eased and he would be unaware of his own decay.

Com twitched as the encrusted dressing caught. He moaned feebly, eyelids fluttering, his pallid complexion, a grey background to the dark slash of his open mouth and purple rings around sunken eyes, assumed a greasy sheen. Com's faint breathing barely stirred the lambskin cover.

Rh'on glanced at Urak, seeing concern written in his expression, frightened that her worst fears were about to be confirmed, yet strangely touched at sympathy from such an unexpected source. But Urak's thoughts took him outside the sick room, up the steep hillside south of the settlement, to where he had seen the white wall growing at the summit. Damn, he thought, they've moved quickly, too quickly. I cannot be sure that the outlander has gathered his forces yet. Damn Tarok for his efficiency. I must go up there and see the defences in detail. They can't be complete yet. There will be a weak spot, there always is. Perhaps the men of Afon'ken could be persuaded to raid, delay things a while. Maybe enough of the outlander's men are gathered, just waiting for the signal.

Com wailed pitifully and jerked his arm. Urak saw the corrupted flesh pull away with the cloth, revealing a glimpse of bone and tendon, startlingly white in its shiny black necrotic host. Hastily he replaced the dressing and rebound the wound in silence, quite satisfied that Com would die soon, bringing further confusion to help his cause.

Rh'on's pale face was set, eyebrows lifted, furrowing her brow, mouth twisted into a grimacing question mark, eyes soft brown, yet tensed and fearful, expecting the blow, dissolving when it came.

"He's dying Rh'on, said Urak, turning to her. "There's nothing we can do except ease his way. He was a strong man, a lesser man would have gone already. Just keep him still, give him more of the medicine when he wakens. He'll know no pain."

Rh'on slumped to her knees beside the cot as Urak silently left the room. She wrapped her arm defensively about her man, as though to ward off the outside world, to repel death's attack, as though unaware that the bitter enemy was already stealthily at work from within. She pressed her cheek to Com's chest, listening to the weak fluttering beat, where she had so often heard the strong pounding of his heart steady and slow with her own in the languor of after love. Her eyes brimmed with salt tears, her frame, thinned by sorrow and worry since the death of her first born and the mortal wounding of her husband, shook. Was this to be the end? Was this a just and fitting conclusion to so much happiness, bitter-sweet sadness, excitement of the hunt, exhilaration of battles survived, stories told and laughter, the wonder of love given and received, an end to the interwoven strands of the greatest adventure of all, that of a life shared? Was such a man among men to die enfeebled, rotting on his couch?

Rh'on felt a hand on the back of her head, gently stroking, gentling her as Com had always done. Startled, she looked up. Com's eyes were open, shockingly blue against the dark-ringed backdrop. They were fixed on her.

"It will be soon now, won't it," he said feebly.

Rh'on bit her lip, hesitating, wanting to prolong even what was left, not daring to frame an answer lest it fulfilled itself. After a long moment she nodded.

"I thought so," Com gasped. "It's time. This world is not mine anymore, a new age is come." His eyes clouded, and for a while he was silent, as though concentrating on each breath. "Send Berin to me," he asked.

"He's gone, Com. I don't know where."

He was silent for so long, his eyes still and unblinking, that Rh'on suddenly thought that he had slipped away, unnoticed, then she saw tears gather at the corners of his eyes, spilling over. "I was a proud man until now that I see my end coming," he whispered finally, so faintly that Rh'on had to strain to hear. "I must pay the price of pride. But when all is done, tell Berin that I have always loved him."

Rh'on sobbed and buried her face on his chest, unable to bear any longer the impenetrable sorrow she read in Com's eyes.

"Tell him to follow his heart in his age as truly as I have tried to follow my head in mine." Com's breath fluttered feebly. Rh'on bent closer. "Tell him that I wish him Dana's blessing, that I ask his forgiveness. I did what I did for the greater good, but after he had agreed to wed Branwen I did him wrong to send that girl away."

"Hush Com, my husband, you must rest," Rh'on soothed, her throat aching, her heart breaking at Com's inner pain.

"Aye, soon enough, for long enough," he croaked. "I love you Rh'on. Stay by me. Ah, but it will be good to see Belu again."

Urak gazed around him in awe, trying hard to keep the deep unease which he felt from showing on his face. The hill top had been transformed. The white chalk ramparts seemed unassailable from the steep hillside. Only a few gaps remained, where the gangs had started, working back to back, and at the gateway. As he watched, the residual causeways left across the outer ditch for access during the building, were being cut away by swarming gangs of workers, who dug, stacked and packed the chalk in the gaps in the wall. The cunning design of the wall on the break in slope would give the defender a fine advantage of a waist high protection whilst the attacker faced a sheer wall at least his own height, sometimes double, after a steep climb from the valley bottom, all the time exposed to the defenders' arrows and sling stones.

"Tarok means to raise the walls breast high by deepening the ditch still further and bevelling-off the outer shoulder. It will make the wall even more of an obstacle to an attacker," Amren explained. "He thought it best to have a complete defensive ring first though, just in case we get attacked meanwhile."

Urak cursed his brother's foresight. Within the area enclosed by the chalk walls, cattle and sheep grazed; there was water in one of the cisterns; bundles of arrows and piles of sling stones were growing as he watched and a well stocked granary sat on stilts amongst the shelters. They are already prepared for an attack. If the outlander does not move very soon this place will be impregnable, Urak worried. The weak spot is the gate side, on the ridge that leads to Ilws, where the wall is not yet high, but the slope has evened out. The outlander must move before that wall is completed and raised.

Amren's voice broke through his thoughts. "Hi there, what's going on?"

Urak turned to where Amren pointed. The workers were setting down their tools and gathering around Geran, Tarok's lieutenant, near the gate.

"No, its only Tarok's men I've been told to fetch," Geran was explaining to Iowerth. "I've never seen him so angry; in a terrible rage. I didn't hang about I can tell you. You should see him. His face is a right mess. Must have been in a hell of a fight."

"What's the trouble?" asked Urak authoritatively, as he and Amren approached. The chattering men fell silent and drew back, allowing Urak and Amren through to Geran.

"Ah Urak. It's Tarok. He's been attacked, by Aedd. Tarok wants his men to hunt him down; to take and punish him."

"What villainy is this?" shouted Urak, feigning anger, exhulting inwardly, hardly believing the stroke of good fortune presented to him as though in swift response to his gloomy thoughts of a moment before. A chance to create discord, interrupt the building, weaken the garrison.

"Not Aedd?" queried Amren. "Why he's as true as flint."

Iowerth was worried. "Are you sure it was Aedd, Geran? Aedd has given his oath to Com as a freeman just as Com has to Dorn. He'd never let Com down. He keeps his word. Everyone knows that."

"I know, I know. Tarok reckons he flew into a rage because his woman liked it when he flirted with her. Went berserk he did."

"Believe that and you'll believe anything," muttered Iowerth, wisely keeping his opinion to himself in Urak's earshot.

"But look here, I can't stand here all day," continued Geran. "I have my orders. Tarok wants the outstation men mustered in camp at once."

"Why Com's people are beyond help," Urak raged. A short while ago, I, Urak, son of Dorn of the first blood, was falsely accused by Berin of treachery. Now one of them has dared to assault my brother. We must find and take him. He must be punished. We must avenge these insults to our house and line and teach these louts a lesson. Iowerth, gather the men of the ford. I cannot let this last insult go unanswered."

Iowerth looked decidedly uncomfortable. "But Urak," he protested, "Dorn ordered me to give whatever help Com needed. The work here is so important. Tarok himself says so. There must be an explanation. I'm sure Aedd would not...."

"Do you question Tarok's word? Do you question me, Iowerth?" asked Urak quietly but menacingly, fixing the unfortunate captain with eyes that held no tolerance, no pity.

Iowerth dropped his gaze. "No sir," he answered, then turning to the men he shouted "All right lads, come on, leave your tools, arm yourselves and gather in the settlement."

The men of the ford and outstation streamed off down the slope behind Geran and Iowerth. Urak motioned Barac to him as he slowly followed.

"Do you know how it is now with the guards? Can you get a message to the outlander?"

"It is dangerous, sir. They are very alert and there are many more men out than there used to be. If Iowerth's and Tarok's men were pulled out I could."

"I'll see what can be done. Be ready. Tell the outlander that most of the men are withdrawn from the defences. He must attack at once. The weak spot is the slope near the gate on the Ilws side. Oh, and be sure to tell him that I have the boy and the woman for him, if he hurries."

Amren was left disconsolate and worried with the men of Com and Ilws, who gathered around him, flocking as though for mutual protection against further accusation, turning to stare after the threat as it made off down the hill, as heifers herd together to watch a dog.

"It's not right," stated Naf bluntly. "If Aedd hit him, he deserved it. He's had it in for old Aedd ever since he got here."

"That's as may be, but what are we going to do? What can we do?

"Might is right when it's seven to one," answered Kar. "Best hope he doesn't get taken."

"Can we warn him?" asked Auron. "He must realise that they'll come after him."

"Aedd's no fool," said Amren. "Tarok wants the girl. Aedd will know that he will have to hide her away; himself too. He'll know not to come back to the settlement. If it were me, I'd head for the outlands beyond the escarpment. There's water and game. You could hide away for ever."

"Aye, but he will need weapons and clothes," Naf said quietly.

"Then we'll have to see that he gets them, won't we," grinned Auron.

Amren wondered what Berin or Aedd would have done in his place, wishing that he had not had leadership thrust on him.

"Aye Auron. Get along home and fix it. The rest of us will stay and carry on as best we can 'til this madness is done. The outlander is still out there somewhere."

Urak laughed, a sound so rare, so misplaced that, just for an instant, Tarok was startled into forgetting his rage. "So brother," Urak sniggered, "you have met your match." Urak stared at his brother's battered face. His bruised and massively swollen lip was outlined by the unmistakable

248

punctures of a human bite. "Why, she clearly adores you. A love bite, my brother. She loves you enough to want to eat you."

"What the fuck would you know about it, you little ponce," Tarok snarled viciously, shifting his position on the stool to ease one of his many aches. "I'll show the little bitch when I've settled with him. I'll make the bastard pay."

"Quite so brother, said Urak evenly, deliberately ignoring the obscenities, and inwardly exultant at Tarok's pain, just a small measure of recompense for a lifetime of bullying he had received from his half-brother. Why he could almost feel grateful to Berin.

"The insult we have endured at the hands of these yokels is too much to be born," he continued. "To think of father pandering to them so makes my blood boil."

"I'm going to catch those two. I'm going to cut his balls off and feed them to him."

"Why don't you take Iowerth and his men too. I've mustered them down here for you. And you could use the watchmen. There's been no sign for days now. Surely they won't attack whilst we are here in strength."

"You're right. Sneak thieves and cattle raiders, that's what the Afon'ken are. They'll never fight a proper battle. Geran. Damn your eyes, Geran, where are you?" he called. The captain hurried through the flap of Tarok's tent.

"Bring out the pickets too," Tarok ordered. "I want every man we've got on this job, except the locals that is, they can't be trusted. One party is to drive up the east side of the valley, one must loop through Ilws, he may well head there, and one is to head straight up the valley. The three

249

groups meet on the edge of the escarpment beyond the West Way. Is that clear?"

Geran nodded.

"Well see to it then and hurry, I want those two."

Urak caught the eye of his bondsman and slowly inclined his head in the direction of the valley. Barac nodded and followed Geran through the tent flap.

CHAPTER 19

Berin willed the sun down. Now that he had decided on a course of action he was impatient to put it into effect and he needed darkness to do that. Ever since he had seen Urak and his servant heading towards Com's settlement that morning, he was sure that his plan was the right one. Berin had felt sick at the sight of Urak. His private torment, the thought that night after night Urak would call her to him, strip off her clothes, touch her, lie with her, spread her thighs, enter her, had made him groan aloud, digging his fingers into the loam, retching until he had shaken the fervently erotic imagery from his head, seeing and fearing the beckoning route to madness.

Yet he had allowed Urak to pass unmolested, drawing back deeper into the shade and shelter of the dogwood and elder thicket, breathing slowly and deeply, searching for control, though his fingers had ached with the longing to choke the breath from Urak's throat. Then, long after they had passed out of bow shot, he had regretted not despatching the traitor to the underworld, with an arrow through the neck.

No, it must be dark when I arrive, he thought. It will not do to be recognised. There's no telling what instructions Urak has left. Anoeth and Alen will know what's going on. Alen will guide me. They may even know where Olwen and Oranc are lodged. They will be under guard, or locked-in somewhere, he thought. A stroke of luck, Urak leaving like that. I wonder what the bastard is up to. Some trickery, that's sure.

Berin measured the distance the sun had to travel to the horizon, setting it against the way he still had to walk to reach the ford at last light, to give him the greatest benefit, light by which to march and darkness to cover his arrival. The crimson magnificence of the sunset, a dramatic back light to the tracery of branches beginning to emerge from their autumn coats, was lost on him, having no place in his mental gymnastics, his ordering of time and space. Satisfied that the time was right, he slowly straightened and carefully made his way back to the path. Once in the open, he set off at a steady pace towards the ford.

At the valley bottom, he emerged slowly from the woods, checking for late travellers or a returning swineherd. There were none. Silently, flitting as a shadow, he set off across the farmland to the river bank, opting to follow its course to the ford rather than continue along the well worn path. That way he would reach Anoeth's hut without passing other houses, offering less risk of a chance encounter or of alert dogs or wary geese sounding an alarm.

Berin approached the ford silently. A heron, beadily intent on a late fish supper, suddenly realised the danger inherent in inattention. Disgusted with its own poor watch keeping, it launched itself majestically into slow beating flight to its roost in the bare upper branches of the dead elm.

Berin paused in the shadow of Anoeth's hut. He smelled wood smoke, overlain by stale urine, the reek of a nearby privy and cooking odours. His stomach groaned loudly, as though to remind him that, although in his distress his mind might judge to reject food, his stomach did not necessarily agree with or accept the verdict. The very human sounds of a community settling down for the night, voices raised in anger, the shrewish wife, the exasperated husband; voices raised in laughter; the cries of a baby in pain; the distinctive whine of an indulged, over-tired child echoed from the houses on the terrace above the ford. There was no sound from Anoeth's bothy. A faint light showed around the door curtain. Berin quickly lifted the flap and slipped inside.

The hut was dimly lit by a flickering fire and a single taper. The fire, though no longer smoking, had done so earlier and by no means all the fumes had escaped through the smoke hole in the roof above the hearth. The resulting haze, rank with the smells of cooking, curing leather, and unwashed bodies, blurred the outline of the two figures hunched over the fire.

Alen started to his feet, slopping broth from the bowl he held, then relaxed as he recognised Berin.

"Why Berin," he called happily, glad to see a familiar face. Berin hissed him to silence. Anoeth turned his sightless face to Berin.

"Well met, Berin. I thought you wouldn't be long coming. Alen, some broth and bread for Berin. From the sounds his guts've been making whilst he's been checking us out these past moments, he's starving."

Berin looked at him in surprise. As though seeing Berin's reaction Anoeth chuckled, "Going blind don't affect the brain or the ears."

Alen tipped some broth into a bowl and handed it to Berin with a piece of bread. He made to sit down again in his place.

"Alen, to the door with you, there's a good lad. Keep watch. Our guest doesn't want it known that he's here, if I've judged him right."

"Aye that's right enough, Anoeth," Berin replied.

The door flap fell back behind Alen; his passing stirred the fug but did little to improve it. Berin ate appreciatively, suddenly realising his hunger.

"She's in Urak's private quarters. Oranc is locked in an outhouse by the rear gate of the compound. No guards, just the watchmen."

"You know what I'm here for? But how? " asked Berin in amazement.

"There's not much that would bring you in secret to the ford, to the home of your own High Chief. A pretty young woman is taken crying to Urak's quarters; her brother tries to stay with her and is beaten; she and her brother are locked away; then a young man comes in secret in the dark when Urak is away. Why I could make up the same story to tell a dozen different ways at any festival or wedding feast." With a smile he added," and each with a happy ending. As I said, my lad, blindness doesn't affect the brain."

Berin shook his head in disbelief at his own transparency. "I thought about appealing to Dorn, to lay all the information before him. You know Urak is betraying us to the outlander. Well I have proof. I tracked him, I'm sure it was him, although I didn't actually see him close up. I heard him speak though, and I saw the two of them together, but I couldn't even make my own father believe me."

"I wouldn't go to Dorn. It would only put folk here on the alert. Urak runs this place and his spies are everywhere. Since Com's visit it is said that he keeps the old man drugged. I doubt that you would get sense out of him. Anyway Dorn thinks his son makes the sun shine. No, if I were you, I'd steal her away like you plan. Alen will show you. You'd best take him with you when you go. There mustn't be any of Com's people here when Urak finds out they're gone. He's a bad bastard that one, a real wrong 'un."

"If he's harmed her, I'll kill him."

"By all accounts he's bent the other way, if you catch my meaning. He's more likely to have harmed the lad, though a bit old for his taste I'm told."

"The watchmen, what about him?"

"Old Rhynog will still have his feet under widow Merthws' bench at this time, downing her ale. There's a watchman in Urak's compound, he likes his ale too. You'd best put him to sleep. Alen can pass him some ale with one of my powders in it. Pretend it's a bribe to pass some food to Oranc."

"Alen," he called softly. The boy came through the flap and Anoeth motioned him over to his side. With their heads close together, Anoeth whispered his instructions. At one point Alen started up, pale, tears pricking, his eyes fixed on the old man. Anoeth held out a gnarled hand to the lad who took it between his own. Berin saw the old man's knuckles whiten as he squeezed. Anoeth pulled the boy's head back down closer to him and spoke earnestly.

Alen stood back from the old man and gazed at him for a long moment then rummaged on a shelf at the back of the bothy, returning with a small leather pouch. He stirred the contents into a jug of ale and left.

"He's a good lad. He would have made a great flint knapper, could have been as good as me, if I'd had him for a few years. He feels, he thinks of the flint, of its insides, what you don't see by looking. Ah well, its not to be. There's plenty that say flint is finished now that bronze is here, but how are we all going to pay for it, that's what I say?"

Berin stayed silent. There is no answer, he thought. Times are changing. Who can tell where it might end. The days of Anoeth, Com and Dorn were past and he could offer neither explanation nor comfort.

"See him safe to his father, Berin."

Berin nodded, absentmindedly staring at the fire, depressed by a strong but indefinable sense of immutability, then remembering Anoeth's blindness said "Yes, I'll do that."

Alen came through the door flap, his face split by a broad grin.

"Now be off the pair of you. Don't come back here, just go off to where ever you are going. No I don't want to know. What I don't know I can't tell. Have you got your things together, Alen? Here take an extra cloak. Get the bigger satchel, the new one," Anoeth fussed. "Put some of those cakes in and the ham bone."

Alen started to make his farewells but the old man just shook him, saying "It was not to be lad. Go now. Remember me to your father. Go with Dana Berin."

CHAPTER 20

The settlement was silent as Alen led Berin through the narrow lanes between the houses and walled compounds, stepping carefully over the gutters which drained household waste and rainwater. From their ripeness, a good rainfall was long overdue. They paused at the rear entrance to Urak's compound. Alen pulled at Berin's sleeve and pointed to where a darker shadow, outlined and emphasised by the glow from the taper wedged in the door jamb, showed the watchman slumped against the back portal of Urak's house. The ale jug lay on its side, just beyond his outstretched arm. They set down their packs. Berin linked his hands and made a step for Alen, hoisting him over the compound wall. Alen silently lifted the bar, slid the gate from its brackets and let Berin through. He dragged the packs in before barring the gate behind them.

Berin handed Alen his axe, motioning him to watch the guard, miming a blow. Alen nodded grimly and took up his station. Berin crossed to the hut set against the compound wall. Silently he lifted the bar and carefully removed the shutter. A foul animal stench rolled over him, making him gag.

"Oranc," he hissed.

"Who's that?" a barely recognisable voice croaked from the darkness.

"Berin."

"Berin... is it really you?"

"Are you all right?"

"I'm tied up," Oranc answered feebly. "Over here," he called as Berin stumbled in the darkness towards his voice.

"Thank Dana you've come," he groaned as Berin reached him, gripping his shoulder, searching for his bonds with one hand, drawing his knife with the other, holding his breath to avoid breathing in the stench of his friend's soiling.

"I thought I was going mad."

"Let's get you out of here," Berin said as he cut the last bonds, but Oranc was too numbed and cramped to move. Berin grasped him under the shoulders and dragged him to the fresh air. He rubbed his wrists and then his ankles, trying to restore circulation.

"Oranc, I must find Olwen. Can you manage?"

"Aye, I'm all right. You go on."

"Young Alen's guarding the watchman. When you are ready, help him. Wait for me there."

Berin glided silently across the swept, hard-packed dirt of the courtyard to the rear door. He passed the comatose figure of the watchman, who breathed heavily, oblivious to events taking place around him. He touched Alen briefly on the arm and indicated Oranc, still doubled over with the pain of returning circulation. When he was satisfied that Oranc and Alen were aware of each other, he turned and ducked through the door curtain.

Inside, it was as dark as death. "Olwen," he hissed. It was as silent as death too. Berin reached back through the door and took the taper.

A pale figure was slumped on the rushes next to the central post, curled into a still foetal ball. Berin's heart lurched. Holding the taper high for best illumination, he darted across the floor, nearly extinguishing the flame in his haste.

Olwen lay naked, bound, hair disordered. He drew in his breath sharply at the sight of the bruises and angry weals on her buttocks. Quickly he cut her bonds. She stirred, her eyelids fluttered then opened. She stared uncomprehendingly at him. Olwen saw only the light and the dark figure standing above her. She knew she must please. This time she was ready, she would please, give him pleasure. She wanted to. Her arms and legs spread as they were released from their bonds. She made no attempt to cover herself.

It was clear to Berin that she did not recognise him.

"It's me, Berin," he whispered, struggling to unsling his bow so that he could remove his cloak, to cover her.

"Berin?" she mumbled as though in a dream.

Berin finally managed to unpin his cloak. He wrapped it around her, sat her up and pulled her to him, holding her cloaked body to his. She began to tremble.

"Berin, is it really you?" she whispered through cracked dry lips, turning her face to look at him. He held the taper high. The light fell on his face. She raised her hand tentatively and touched his cheek. She began to weep, choking on deep wracking sobs, and buried her face in the folds of his cloak, pressing her head against his chest.
"Oh Berin, I thought I would never see you again."

They sat silent, unmoving for long moments, then Berin took her wrists and began to chafe the blood back into them, cursing inwardly at the deep grooves cut into her soft white skin by the cruelly tight bonds. He bent to repeat the treatment on her ankles.

"Olwen, we must go. Can you walk?"

"I think so. I'll try. My dress. Where are my clothes?"

Berin held the taper high. They saw her shift where she had dropped it. She hobbled across the room, clutching the cloak to her throat. Berin supported her with an arm around her waist.

Shyly, Olwen allowed him to take the cloak from her. She pulled the dress over her head and settled it around her hips.

"My boots. Oh they must still be where he kept me." Berin asked for directions, but Olwen would not let him leave her. She clung to him as they walked the passages to her cell. She leant on him to pull on her boots. Finally, she looked up and pressed close to kiss him, her lips dry and rough on his. He wrapped his cloak around her.

"Oranc," she suddenly remembered. "We must find Oranc."

"He's outside. Come, we must leave now. We must get as far away as possible before your escape is discovered."

They made their way to the door. Berin paused briefly to replace the taper. Olwen and Oranc embraced.

"Come on," Berin urged, kindly but firmly. "We mustn't delay."

Berin settled his bow across his back, handed his dagger to Oranc and took a firm grasp of his spear. He took Olwen by the hand and scouted the gate. All was quiet in the alley way. He motioned Oranc and Alen to follow. Alen hefted Berin's axe and looked at the watchman regretfully. He picked up the fallen pitcher and passed it to Oranc.

"We don't want it traced to Anoeth," he said. He waited until Oranc had passed through the gate, shut and barred it behind them then climbed the wall and dropped lightly beside the party waiting in the alley way.

"He'll have some explaining to do," he whispered with a grin, and a jerk of his thumb towards the recumbent guard. "Where now, Berin?" he asked.

"We'll work our way along the foot of the escarpment. They'll never be able to catch us in the outlands."

Olwen shivered. The outlands. Even the name provoked fear. The outlands were home to wild boar and wolf and bear and even wilder men, it was said. She knew that Berin hunted there from time to time, or rather hunted their edge, but to hide away, to live there, was a different matter.

Alen set off through the alleys and by ways. They saw no one but Rhynog, the watchman, as he staggered from widow Merthw's hearth. The noise of his fond and oft repeated farewells and loud praise of the widow's ale, and other charms, gave them ample warning and time enough to draw back into the shadows. Alen reckoned that the old fool was too drunk to see anyway. The watchman's blandishments roused some of the neighbours to shouted abuse, but no one came to investigate what was clearly commonplace in that neighbourhood.

When they came to the river, they paused. Alen kept watch as Berin rinsed the pitcher and filled it for Olwen to drink. She drank gratefully, wetting and rubbing her cracked lips. Oranc immersed himself in the river, intent on ridding himself of the stench of his imprisonment. Alen lent him his cloak to dry himself and clothes from his pack. The darkness hid Oranc's scarecrow appearance, his over-long limbs protruding far beyond the reach of any clothes that Alen could provide. Oranc wrung out his jerkin and britches. Berin hurried them on, wanting to be clear of all signs of settlement by dawn.

The path faded as they left the last of the cleared land. Berin led, picking a way through relatively open forest at the break in slope of the escarpment, avoiding the marshy low ground and the steep, brush-covered slopes. He pressed on, snagged by thorns, tripped by roots, slipping on moss-covered stones, skidding and sliding on wet leaves on the slope, knowing that he was pushing Olwen and Oranc to their limits, weakened as they were by their recent ordeal, but knowing too that they were leaving a clear trail. He was determined to reach relative safety before any pursuit could be organised. Finally, when Oranc could scarcely support his sister any longer, Berin called a halt.

It was drizzling. Berin cast around for shelter and settled on a leafy hollow beneath a fallen beech, partly sheltered by a spreading juniper bush. Setting down their arms and packs, they scraped some of the leaves and spread Alen's cape, huddling together for warmth. Berin pulled his cloak over them and then the leaves.

Olwen lay spooned in Berin's lap, her head resting on his upper arm. She fell asleep instantly, believing herself to be in her familiar dream as she kissed the arm on which she lay. She wriggled her buttocks against him and, searching for the edge of the cloak to pull around her, found his hand and pressed it inside the neckline of her shift, hugging his palm to her warm breast.

Olwen lay still, eyes closed, unsure. Was she dreaming? In which case she was asleep and dreaming of being awake. She was cold; the bed was hard; that much at least was familiar. Berin was pressed to her back, his arm wrapped around her, his hand cradling her breast; that too was familiar, a regular feature of her dreams, but this time the dream was so real, she could feel his warmth, smell him; and she was covered, that was new. The air was fresh, not the fetid, tired stuff of her cell; a draft stirred the hair at her temple, tickling her face. She raised her hand to smooth it back in place, breaking the spell.

Olwen opened her eyes, realising in a glorious flood of happiness that she was awake. There was no dream. She was free and in Berin's arms. Fine droplets of light rain or dew spangled the nap of the cloak, reflecting the faint dawn light. Drops had collected in the curled, shiny brown beech leaves, coalescing and running from her as she moved her arm. A spider's web, an intricate dew-silvered tracery, hung between the stems of a clump of nettles, a trap for the unwary. The web's owner waited splay legged in the centre, as patient as any fisherman. As Olwen watched, a moth searching for a hiding place ahead of the advancing dawn, blundered into the net. The moth thrashed its wings in panic. The white markings on the wings fluttered as though waving for help. But there was no escape from the sticky threads which held it. Slowly, ruthlessly, the spider stalked the helpless moth. Olwen thought of Urak and shuddered.

"What is it?" Berin asked anxiously, sitting up, instantly alert.

"Nothing. I just thought.... I remembered Urak."

"Well you don't have to worry about him anymore," Berin answered, as she crushed herself to him. "Not ever"

"But what are we going to do?" she asked plaintively.

"We'll hide in the outlands. I know a really good place. I found it when I was hunting.... the day we were attacked."

They both fell silent at the memory. The day the world turned upside down; the day her father and his brother died.

"But when can we go home?" she asked.

Berin was silent, brow furrowed, brought back to reality, the awful responsibility of leadership, of decision, of action and reaction. What am I to answer? he thought. Olwen can never go back openly whilst Urak lives, so much is certain. But how am I to explain that to her? How can I go back myself if Urak links my absence from the settlement with the escape? If Com dies, as his heir and chief in Com's place, I might brazen it out, so long as Olwen stays hidden in the outlands. Dorn would never allow Urak to war against us. But Com is alive and in his present mood, he would hand me over to Urak and by all accounts, Dorn is now a man of straw, a token chief, ruled and manipulated by Urak with his potions. Urak would pit clan against clan for his own ends and destroy us all in his vanity and lust for power. I have to stop Urak's plans, whatever they might be. My people depend on me. I have to go back, at least to establish contact, but Olwen...?

"Berin? What is it? You look ...you look so worried."

"I was thinking how to answer you."

The sound of their voices woke Alen and Oranc, who emerged from beneath the leaf-covered cloak, scratching and stretching to straighten sleep cramped limbs.

Olwen laughed at the sight of her brother, gawky as a pond skater, his long scrawny arms and legs protruding well past the scanty protection offered by Alen's limited wardrobe. Berin welcomed the interruption, but was pleased when the two lads wandered off, rustling through the leaves, to relieve the early morning pressure on their bladders.

"Olwen, I don't think that you and Oranc can go back; not whilst Urak lives."

Olwen's face fell.

"He won't give up. He'll keep on until he has you. You must know better than I how evil he is."

Olwen nodded, dumbly waiting for her worst fear to be confirmed. Her happiness would prove to be short lived and Berin would soon leave her. Leave her to a lonely life as an outcast.

"But I can't go back either.... well not openly."

Olwen gasped. Had she heard correctly? She prayed silently but fervently.

"I must go back, in secret, to find out what's happening. After all, when Com dies, I shall be chief; but I can't go back openly whilst Com lives. He would turn me over to Urak if that devil asked for me. Even as chief I won't be safe from Urak. He rules the ford now. He keeps Dorn stupefied with drugs and he's plotting something with the outlander.... I'm not sure what, but it will be our ruin, for certain. I must try and find out his plans and stop him."

265

"Then we really will be together?" Olwen asked breathlessly.

"Aye, it looks like it," he said, turning to her, seeing her simple love for him declared openly in every nuance of expression, the questioning arch of the eyebrow, the shining eyes, the lifted corners of the mouth, the parted moist lips, her ragged breathing. Berin captured her, his thumb caressing her downy cheek, the angle of her jaw. He lifted her face to his, pressing his lips to hers. Her lips parted, her tongue tip darted, agile and teasing against him. He accepted the challenge, pressing her back, claiming her now wide open mouth as his own.

A studied, well rehearsed cough brought Berin and Olwen bolt upright. Alen and Oranc, grinning widely, were rummaging in Alen's pack and soon set about carving chunks from the cured hock and breaking the barley cakes. Olwen, with a shy smile, accepted her share and ate breakfast where she sat. Berin, with some difficulty, disentangled himself from the cloak, took his share and wandered off to view the day and cover his embarrassment.

The sun had not yet risen, or if it had, it refused to show itself through the gloom. A lighter patch of sky in the east suggested its passage, but cast no shadow. The light beneath the dripping trees was gloomy, damp and heavy. The forest hindered vision, but Berin felt, from glimpses of tree tops and distant sky, that the main escarpment pulled back to his left in an embayment, which was occupied by low, gently rolling hills. Peering to the north, he could see the densely wooded wetlands which bordered the Great River and in the foreground, a linear ridge rising from the marshes, like an offshore island at the mouth of a bay.

Berin recognised the edge of his normal hunting territory. He now knew that the gully which led to his destination lay just beyond the far end of the ridge which marked the mouth of the embayment. For a moment Berin considered cutting across. It would be shorter, much shorter. Then he remembered the last time he had stumbled into valley bottoms, where choked, cress-filled streams, fed by springs at the foot of the escarpment, meandered through sedge bogs and thickets of willow and alder saplings. He decided against it. Speed was of the essence. They would make very slow progress taking the direct route. It would be much quicker to stay on the dry uplands of the escarpment.

Berin turned back to his party. His companions had finished breakfast and were repacking Alen's satchel. He accepted a swig of water from the pitcher gratefully.

"Oranc, are you fit enough to scout up the slope a bit, say a hundred paces ahead of us?" Berin asked. "Just in case they come on us from the West Way. Here, take my bow," he added, as Oranc nodded his agreement.

"No need," Oranc replied, swinging a stone in a leather sling.

Berin grinned. Oranc had not been idle. He would be much better protected with the sling. "Where did you get the leather?" he asked.

"Oh, off the bottom of Alen's jerkin," he laughed. Alen looked a little uncertain about the propriety of the arrangement. Grumpily he shook out his cloak and rolled it, wrapping the woollen cocoon around his shoulders before slinging his pack.

Berin enveloped Olwen in his cape, drawing her to him as he fastened it at her throat.

"Ready?" he asked.

"Yes," she smiled back at him. "Now I am... for anything."

They had scrambled lop-sided along the hill side for two thousand paces or more and were crossing a steep-sided, brush-filled gully, when a low whistle from Oranc sent the three of them to ground.

"Stay here until I call," Berin hissed, unslinging his bow. "Here, you take the spear, Alen." Berin snaked forward, climbing up towards Oranc, who crouched at the edge of the escarpment, peering through the bushy hawthorn which Oranc had chosen for cover. Berin crawled to his friend's side and sighted along Oranc's outstretched arm and pointing finger. Later he would swear that, just for an instant, his heart stopped.

Generations earlier, Com's ancestors had cleared the land at the top of the escarpment to make farms. Although long since fallen into disuse, the old fields were still recognisable, their return to wilderness delayed by sporadic use as pasture by Com's herds and by those which passed along the nearby West Way. The grasses and self-seeded barley and oats had grown long and rank, but only a few thorn bushes, briar patches and junipers had managed to establish themselves, leaving the view of the chalk uplands clear and unrestricted.

The white cone of Belu and Ermid's tomb crowned the skyline, barely a thousand paces away. A tall black silhouette, stood on top of the monument, a living menhir. As he watched, a line of men rose on the western slope of the skyline, to be halted by a gesture from the figure on top of the cairn. Shortly afterwards, more men appeared on the sloping ridge which fell away to the West Way on the east side of the tomb, to be halted on the skyline by a signal from the controller. Another gesture sent the men at the eastern end of the line forward again. Men at the far end of the line walked faster than those nearer the cairn, so that they executed a great sweep across the grasslands, centred on the cairn.

"It's Tarok and his men," Berin whispered hoarsely in alarm. "He's driving, but why? We have no need for meat. And where are the hunters with the nets? This is not for game. This is for us!"

A covey of partridges broke ahead of the advancing men, whirred and swooped in a contour hugging glide into a hollow and out of sight. Two hares sped in zigzag panic, white tails flashing their alarm. They stopped and turned to face the line of advancing men, dark eyes bulging, black-tipped ears twitching, then dived into the safety of a briar patch. For a moment, Berin felt an unreasonable envy. If only escape was so easy.

"How can the news have come to him so quickly? What lies has Urak told to persuade Tarok to do this? We can't get around the end of the line; too risky. We could run into men following from the ford. We'll have to outrun them.... straight down into the wetlands. Come on."

Oranc and Berin slithered back below the lip of the escarpment and scrambled back to their companions.

"Tarok and his men are driving for us," he said grimly. "We must run ahead of them, down to the wetlands and take our chances there. We'll never get around them."

Berin led the way, plunging down the steep gully, heedless of scratches, careless of leaving spoor, determined only to put distance between them and their pursuers.

Olwen, Oranc and Alen followed as best they could. As the floor of the gully began to widen and flatten, a line of springs seeped water into the valley. Their way was choked by the closely growing stems of osier and willow and alders, still green and fresh amongst the dying orange and brown. Foot-catching creeping willow, which rose no higher than a man's knee from a tangle of stems, concealed pot holes, rotted stumps and bog.

A fetid smell arose as they plunged on, through cloying mud and pulpy masses of rotting leaf fall, scrambling over fallen trees. Bluish green sedge and the dark feathery heads of reeds marked standing water, which they skirted, the still surface decorated with rosettes of water starwort and round water lily pads. A frog, alarmed by their crashing haste, leapt in a light brown arc, its dark brown-barred hind legs stretched far behind, before it sounded with a loud splash, searching for safety in the mud at the bottom of the pool, leaving only the widening circles of ripples to mark its panic.

Berin berated himself. He should have pressed on across the embayment at first light. It was a natural hide out. Of course any pursuit would sweep it. He had thrown away the advantage of the early start and now still had to travel across the difficult country, but now with the pursuit baying at their heels. Dogs... at least there were no dogs. But how had Tarok learned of their flight so soon? Even if their flight had been discovered almost immediately there would scarcely have been time to raise Tarok at his encampment.

Berin's puzzlement was interrupted by a cry from Olwen. Berin turned to see her lying white-faced with pain and exhaustion, one leg buried to the thigh in bog, the other bent back beneath her. Her dress clung wet, limp and mired to her body. Her hair, darkened by sweat and the drizzling rain was plastered to her head and streaked across her face. Before Berin could get back to her, Oranc and Alen took her under the shoulders and heaved her upright. Her leg came free with a loud sucking noise. Her leg was covered in sulphurous grey-black mud. Her foot was bootless. She looked at Berin in alarm. Oranc lay full length and plunged his arm into the mire where her leg had been, but it was no use. Her boot was lost.

"Can't stop to look for it," Berin said. "Here, wrap this around your foot," he added, taking a shirt from his pack. Hurriedly he pulled the tie thong from the lace holes, wrapped the soft leather around her foot and bound it with the thong.

"All right?" he asked, standing up, taking her by the arms. "Anything hurt?"

"No, I'm all right. I'll manage. I'm sorry. Don't worry about me."

Berin turned to lead the way. Far behind them, near the edge of the escarpment, they heard a shout, repeated at diminishing volume as the news of the discovery of the fugitives' spoor was passed along the line. The runaways started down the valley with renewed urgency. A near stagnant stream emerged from the lower bank of the pond. They followed its course and soon it began to flow, at first just a hand span deep across a chalky mud bottom. Watercress grew thick, greening the surface, confining the current to the centre of the stream.

A side stream barred the way. Alen and Oranc searched upstream. The stream narrowed between high earthen banks. A branch, fallen from an overhanging willow long years since, spanned the trench. Berin turned to guard their tracks as Alen, followed by Olwen and then Oranc felt their way shakily across the bark, slippery with green mould, fearing the still waters beneath and hidden sharp snags. The bough bent and creaked under Oranc. Berin inched his way across the sagging bough, arms outstretched, eyes fixed on the far bank, wanting to hurry, knowing haste could so easily finish his flight. The branch yielded with a groan. Berin made a wild leap for safety, scrabbling frenetically at the earth at the top of the bank, searching for foothold on the steep loam wall. He felt himself sliding and lunged desperately for a willow root, gripping with one hand, feeling the rootlets straining, snapping. Earth showered over his hair, in his eyes, the wet earth smell as strong as the stench of his fear. Alen and Oranc grasped his wrist. Olwen held their belts. They heaved and scrabbling with one hand, feet flailing, Berin was beached.

Not a word was said. The four fugitives, panting and white faced, regarded each other in silence as they regained their breath. Once more they set off, Berin gaining some comfort from the thought that the stream they had just crossed would delay pursuit. The ground began to rise. Berin sensed that they were approaching the ridge which marked the western headland of the embayment he had spotted that morning. He knew that the gully he had used that day, a lifetime earlier, when he had carried the deer carcass up the escarpment, lay just the other side of the ridge. Once in the gully, he could pick up the route he had followed when he tracked the buck to the kill.

Travelling was easier at the foot of the ridge. The better-drained ground above the spring line supported beech and rowan, field maple, elder, thickets of dogwood and buckthorn. The growth, though dense enough to give cover, did not impede progress, provided they avoided the clumps of dogwood, where blood-red shoots and crimson leaves competed with the golden glory of the maples. Berin resisted the temptation to climb to the relatively open ground near the top of the ridge. Any hunter worthy of the name would have rushed scouts ahead, along the clearer ground on the ridge top, as soon as their trail had been discovered. Even now the chase might be waiting for them.

But they reached the edge of the wetlands without further alarm. Berin refused to relent and pressed on, driving them all past their limits. Crafty now, using all the tricks of hunter and hunted, he covered their tracks, backtracking, going forward again, each time ending in a pool of water until at last he made each of them enter the marsh at a different place, stripping off their clothes, carrying them in a bundle above their heads. Olwen protested feebly from modesty then conceded to necessity, stripping as white and as vulnerable as her companions. Berin made sure that they only moved through water, half crawling, half swimming, shivering with cold. They stayed within sight and sound of each other, but only came together after several hundred paces. The boys turned their backs to hide their cold-shrunk pride as much as out of concern for Olwen's modesty, when she stumbled from the water, trying to cover herself and keep her bundle dry at the same time.

They dressed quickly. Berin followed the route the buck had shown him, a narrow twisting totally unmarked course through quaking bog, from tussock to tussock, beneath a cover of osier and willow. A snake the length of Berin's outstretched arms, as thick as his wrist, slid sinuously into the water ahead of them, its passage marked by a V-shaped ripple. Berin shuddered, even though he recognised that the snake was harmless, that his fear was irrational. He was relieved that they had no further cause to return to the water.

Berin identified the sedge bank where he had lain the day he had stalked the buck. They were safe. He had snatched Olwen from Urak and had escaped pursuit. They would never catch them now. No one could find their way through the marshes. He made his way to the brook with renewed strength spewing from his elation, knowing that his goal was close, feeling a curious sense of homecoming. He turned and smiled encouragement at Olwen, holding out his hand to her as she came, wan, slack shouldered and tremble-kneed, limping on her bootless foot to stand at his side on the pebbly stream bed, the first reasonably sound footing either had felt since they had left the escarpment. She dropped her head on his shoulder in exhaustion. He put his arms around her, patting her back.

"It's not far now, just up stream a bit and around the bend."

As they approached the sheltered bowl, carved from the chalk hillside by the slow but pernicious undermining of the spring, Berin tensed, nostrils dilating. A swirl of the breeze sent leaves fluttering, dropping from the ever more skeletal branches, whirling up from the ground, and brought with it a scent of danger.

"Boar," Berin called, recognising the rank pungency. "Alen, bring my spear." Alen came forward and handed it to him. Berin was relieved that his weapon was bronze tipped, but still did not relish the task in hand. He dropped into a defensive crouch as he advanced.

"Wait here," Berin commanded, unnecessarily, Oranc thought, as he was far from keen about advancing anywhere. Oranc, Olwen and Alen clustered together, futilely fingering knives and axe, knowing that good fortune was the only weapon effective against the most feared of all wild animals ahead of them.

Slowly, Berin pushed past the edge of a thicket of alder suckers and saplings and stepped from the stream on to the grassy floor of the hollow. Under the overhanging willow adjacent to the spring lay a huge boar. Berin froze, eyes locked on to his quarry, the huge curling tusks protruding above the long snout, curling back the pink and black upper lip, the long shaggy brown-black bristles on the head, matted in places, in others rising and dancing in the breeze, the massive hump of shoulders and withers, the downward slide to flanks and rump, the tail with its tuft of bristle. Berin looked for movement, at the flanks, the ears, the tail; there was none.

Berin trod cautiously towards the beast, his throat dry, his breathing light and rapid, knuckles white where they gripped the shaft of the spear, point placed protectively between him and the threat. As he approached, Berin saw blood on the tusks and snout, a spear in the tusker's breast and beneath it, the body of a youth.

Berin covered the last few paces at a rush. The boar was clearly dead. Blood spread from its gaping jaw, matting the red-stained grass. The spear was broken, but it had been driven, at least an arm's length, deep into the boar's soft insides, no doubt by the ferocity of its own charge, entering just below the throat, penetrating the rib cavity, through to gut and liver. The perfect spear thrust to receive a boar's charge, Berin noted with admiration. The youth, slim, lithe, but muscular, fine-featured with short-

275

cropped hair, not yet old enough for a beard, was clearly dead too. Covered in blood, not yet congealed, he lay still, face pale, sprawled on his back, the broken shaft of the spear buried in the earth beneath his armpit, his lower body and legs hidden by the boar's dead-weight. More as a reflex action than with any hope, Berin pressed index and forefingers against the side of the lad's neck, searching for a pulse. To his surprise he felt the faintest quiver.

"Olwen, quick, Oranc, Alen, help me," Berin yelled. His friends arrived in a panic, relieved the instant they saw Berin upright and the boar felled.

"Here, Oranc, Alen. Grab hold," he ordered, taking the boar by the hock and pulling it back, trying to roll it off the still form. "He's still alive. We must get this brute off him."

As they rolled back the carcass, they saw the lad's britches were soaked in blood; the left leg was ripped and torn by deep wounds from which fresh blood still seeped from between the crusted gore. Berin took out his knife and began to cut away the leg of the britches just above the knee.

"Olwen, there is marsh woundwort growing where we joined the stream. Oranc, make a fire. You'll find spindle and blocks in my pack. Alen, fetch water."

"A fire will bring them on us, Berin," Oranc said reluctantly.

"He'll die if we can't warm and doctor him. Anyway, I'll doubt they will be able to follow us through the marsh," Berin answered. Oranc joined the others who despite their own hurts and exhaustion, went willingly to their tasks, recognising the emergency. Berin carefully peeled back the britches. He took the water proffered by Alen, pouring it gently, avoiding the wounds, except where muddied, watching the blood wash pink and thin into the grass. The leg was badly lacerated above and below the knee. The lower shin was massively swollen and bruised. The shin-bone was offset and clearly broken. Berin pulled gently at the boot. The lad moaned, an eerie keening sound. Berin took his knife and gently cut the boot free.

"Olwen," he said when she arrived breathless, a bunch of the narrow blade-shaped finely toothed leaves in her hand, "it's badly broken. Do you think you can set it?"

"Yes I think so," Olwen replied. "You'll have to pull his ankle for me. Like this."

The youth jerked convulsively when Berin pulled at his foot. Olwen set the bones. Berin looked at the youth, full of concern, seeing the pallor, reaching to touch the smooth skin of the youngster's face, feeling it cold and clammy.

"I think we're too late," he said.

He rose and cut down an alder sapling, stripping it of branches and leaves before cutting it into four equal lengths. Olwen crushed the woundwort leaves and stems, recoiling a little from the accustomed pungency. She covered the gashes with the woundwort and bound them loosely with strips torn from the discarded leg of the britches, which Alen had washed in the stream.

"He's very low. We must get him warm," Olwen said, taking the stakes from Berin. She placed them carefully around the lower leg and bound them tightly together.

Berin glanced at Oranc crouched over the spindle held upright between a hardwood block in one hand which put pressure on the softwood block on the ground whilst he sawed the spindle with his bow.

Olwen sat back on her heels. "That's all we can do," she said, looking up at Berin. "Except warm him up a bit. It's up to him then."

Carefully they lifted the youth to a dry sheltered spot next to the chalk bank, beneath the willow, setting him down on some tussocky grass. Olwen admired his leather jerkin, although she thought the lad a bit of a dandy, for the soft leather was decorated in a zigzag pattern of quills, variegated shells and mother of pearl, which gave protection to the torso.

"I wonder who he is; where he's from," she said, as she took Berin's cloak from around herself and wrapped it around their patient, thinking damp though it is, it's all that we've got and it's better than nothing.

"River folk, I'd say," answered Berin, "from the looks of him. They've all got that pale skin and dark hair. The clothes too. See, they're all leather, no cloth."

"But they're just savages," Olwen shuddered, remembering the stories told around winter fires; the tales used to frighten young children into obedience.

"Some savage. Look at the decoration, the workmanship. See those stitches; and where have you seen leather cured as well as that?"

The youth groaned. Olwen turned to him, placing a hand on his forehead. "He has a fever," she said, "Not surprising really. Look, get Oranc to lay a fire next to him. We must try to dry him out, warm him. I'll see if I can find some betony."

Berin walked over to Oranc, just as he finished sawing the spindle and dropped his head to blow on the small pile of tinder on the softwood block. A wisp of smoke thickened, the tinder glowed. Oranc tipped it from the charred block onto a pile of dry moss and twigs and continued to blow. The smoke thickened then swirled as a bright orange flame flickered upwards. Oranc drew back, adding progressively larger twigs from a pile which he and Alen had collected.

"When you've got some embers, light a fire next to our new friend. Get some cooking stones heated. Olwen will want to brew up some potions. I'm going to butcher that pig. Alen, come and give me a hand. Mother, I wish it would stop drizzling, so that we can dry out."

Working with practised ease, Berin and Alen rolled the boar onto its back, hind legs spread. Berin slit the body cavity and removed the guts, carefully cutting out the greenish gall bladder from the liver, discarding it with the viscera before placing the liver carefully on a clean tussock, adding the kidneys, after delving deep to the back bone. Berin then went to the head of the beast, admiring the thick curved tusks. What a trophy; he had rarely seen a finer pair. He wedged open the mouth, reached in and cut out the tongue. Berin sent Alen to cut and peel some green sticks, then cut up the liver, kidneys and tongue and skewered them on the sticks. As Berin set about butchering the rest of the beast, Alen started to grill the choice cuts.

Berin was hanging the last of the joints from a high branch when Olwen returned, her earlier exhaustion forgotten in the needs of the present, her face glowing with pleasure.

"Hey Berin, see what I've found. Betony, but look, just look at this," she said, holding out a bunch of tightly clustered pink flowers at the top of long leafy stems.

"What's that?"

"I'm sure it's what Rh'on used that time she tried to dye the wool and it went all wrong. It didn't dye at all, but it washed cleaner than anything I've ever seen." She laughed. "I thought we might use it, seeing the state we're in."

Berin looked at her in amazement, begrimed from the crown of her matted hair to leather-wrapped foot, her eyes shining through her exhaustion, her smile lighting her face, coaxing out an answering shaft of weak, watery sunlight from the brightening sky, and fell in love with her all over again.

Alen, squatting on his heels, turning the skewers of meat, proudly pronounced them done. The four of them discovered their ravenous hunger and fell upon the meat, eating without talking, but not in silence.

Olwen took a wooden bowl from Alen's pack, filled it with water from the pitcher and, using two of Alen's skewers, picked up heated stones from the fire and dropped them into the water until it simmered. She ripped up the betony leaves and added them to the bowl, stirring the brew with one of the sticks. When the liquid had taken on a full green colour, she scooped out the stones and leaves and set the bowl aside to cool.

Berin, Alen and Oranc busied themselves cutting and trimming aspen saplings. The thickest end was sharpened with an axe and driven into the ground on a circular base. The thin end was bent over and interwoven with the pole from the opposite side of the circle. Then, hazel and willow were used as a wickerwork, to weave the uprights together. The effect was an inverted basket, the same sort of bothy in which Alen had lodged with Anoeth.

Olwen watched contentedly; it felt like one of the droving trips she had made as a little girl with her father, when he had made just such a shelter, if not quite so grand, for their overnight accommodation. She felt her emotions slide at the memory of her father and pulled herself up with a smart mental rebuff. Quickly she tested the fever brew and finding that it had cooled she took it over to her patient.

The fire was burning brightly and Berin's cloak was beginning to steam. Olwen lifted the youth's head, cradling it in the crook of her arm. She held the bowl to his lips, crooning gently, "Drink now, it's so good for you. Come lad, drink." The boy, far away in his own world was unaware that he gagged in this one, spilling the liquid down his chin and throat and on to his chest. Some of it went down, Olwen thought, in fact a good part of it, setting him down again, wiping away the spillage, opening the front of his jerkin to dry him off.

Olwen sat back on her heels in surprise. Flattened by and disguised behind the protective decoration were burgeoning breasts. With a bemused smile, Olwen refastened the jerkin and pulled the cloak up to the girl's chin.

"Berin," she called. "Berin, come over here."

"What is it?" he asked, as he came and squatted beside her, putting an affectionate arm around her shoulders.

"Our lad is a lass."

"What?" he spluttered in amazement.

"Yes, a lass. No doubt about it. Behind that fancy decoration she's all woman; and no, you can't see for yourself," she admonished with a laugh, slapping his hand as he reached for the jerkin.

"Some girl," he said admiringly, "taking on a boar like that. I thought he was over pretty for a lad. Just as well you told me," he added, "I was going to have the boys cuddle up to him.. er.. her tonight, to keep him warm."

Looking at his broad smile, his eyes fixed on her, Olwen felt a sudden jolt of wanting, but despite the suddenly awakened desire, or maybe because of it, she was overtaken by a self-conscious awareness of her mired and stinking body and clothes, her tangled, matted hair. She thought too of Urak and what she had....

"Berin, I must get cleaned up. I feel so dirty."

"All right, why not. There's a good pool over there; the sun's warming up, it's a good chance to dry out too. The boys and I will finish the shelter.

Remembering the plant she had collected, Olwen returned to the fire. She repeated the process which she had used to make the medicine. When the liquid simmered it seemed to rise in the bowl, frothing into a green-tinged foam. Olwen glanced around. Berin was busy thatching the shelter with reeds which the boys were cutting and collecting. She took the bowl to the pool, setting the bowl on a stone to cool.

Olwen sank into the water, gasped at the initial chill shock, but relaxed as she became used to it, ducking her head under, soaking her hair, wiping her face, her muddied legs. She waded to the bank and scooped some of the liquid from the bowl. It felt greasy. She rubbed it into the bodice of her dress and watched the dirt rise from the cloth in the foam and rinse away. Soon she was rubbing the liquid into her hair, arms, legs, all over. Finally she submerged herself, emerging from a welter of suds clean and fresh, squeezing water from her hair and dress. She had never felt so good.

"Oh Berin, it's so good," she said as she approached. "I feel so clean."

Berin turned from his rough and ready thatching. The transformation was amazing; the cleansing had not just removed the grime; Olwen was revitalised. Her exhaustion, fear and pain had been washed away too.

"Hmm, good enough to eat," he said, lunging for her. She dodged him easily as he caught his foot in the supports of the bothy, measuring his height on the grass.

"Lying down on the job I see," laughed Oranc, throwing down a bundle of reeds. Alen hovered in the background, grinning.

It's really going to be all right, Olwen thought, looking from one to the other.

CHAPTER 21

Ened snuggled against the bulk of her man, searching for warmth to counter the cold draught, which had slipped into their sleeping skins as Aedd had rolled in his sleep. She had woken with a downward swoop and jerk of adrenaline and now she could not sleep. Above her spread a huge velvety black canopy with its crystal spangling of stars, an unaccustomed vastness into which, disorientated, she had felt herself falling. She wondered what had woken her. The long drawn out quavering call of an owl answered. A silent winged shadow swooping across the stars raised hairs on the back of her neck, sending her shivering to find comfort against Aedd's bulk.

Aedd snored gently and rhythmically, seemingly immune to the strangeness of their situation, oblivious to the stillness, the chill of the threatening frost; a man at peace with himself and with the world. Ened felt a prickle of annoyance, which she quickly suppressed. Of course he must rest.

What a nice man Auron is, she thought. A dried ham, barley cakes, oatmeal, salt, mead in a pitcher with the stopper sealed with birch gum, wooden bowls, sleeping skins, blankets, cloaks, a change of clothes, though she would have to remake Aedd's, for none could match his size, fire blocks, spindle and tinder, bow with arrows, a spear, even fish hooks, line and needle, all packed, all ready and waiting for them as they had arrived red-faced and panting.

Auron had told them of Tarok's rage, told them that he had mustered his men to search for Aedd and Ened; that he guessed that Tarok would drive the main valley sides that same afternoon. They had left at once with the blessing of Ilws, slowed by their packs, heading north, straight up the narrow dene behind the farmsteads, to the col on the escarpment, where the West Way crossed, hurrying, anxious to outflank the end of the drive. They had camped at the top of the hill on the west side of the col, in the grassy trench in the lee of a long barrow. Ened had demurred, fearing the spirits of the dead, but Aedd had laughed, saying that they were all relatives of his and if you couldn't rely on your kin to help you in times of trouble, who could you rely on. Besides the campsite offered near perfect visibility, shelter and an escape route.

He was right of course. They had watched the men from the outstation and ford drive the valley, or at least they had seen them appear in dying daylight on the open pasture land along the West Way, directed by a distant silhouette on top of the stark white cairn that marked Ermid's and Belu's grave. The nearest the line had come to them was the ridge on the opposite side of their gully, fully a thousand paces away.

Auron had come after nightfall to tell them that Tarok had sent a squad to Ilws to look for them. Of course everyone had denied seeing them. Tarok planned to drive from the West Way to the wetlands at dawn; they would be all right where they were until noon at least, he had said, though he had added that after that it would be anyone's guess.

Despite Aedd's gentling, she had slept only fitfully, waking in fright at the recurring nightmare of Tarok appearing through the barrow wall, suffocating her to submission. Aedd had understood so well; he had simply held her in his arms.

285

As dawn broke they had been alert, peering over the lip of the ditch, all packed, but sheltering from the drizzle in their sleeping skins. They had seen the line of men trudge up the valley from their encampment, spread out along the West Way and advance. They had watched as the right wing had described a great arc anchored on the white slash of the tomb, the rostrum from which Tarok conducted. The line had disappeared into a thickly wooded valley, the men emerging into the open pasture land of the chalk upland one by one, waiting to form up again before continuing the advance. As the sky had lightened to a paler shade of grey, Tarok had advanced the left and then after it had moved several hundred paces, the right wing too. There had been a curious fascination in the geometrical manoeuvres, in their precision. What power, Ened had thought, to direct so many men.

As the line on the right had reached the tree line at the lip of the escarpment, it had gone berserk, like ants in a nest that is poked with a stick. The left line halted, the right dissolved, swarming to a spot near the centre of the line. Suddenly the left had been sent scurrying forward, swinging around to line the edge of the escarpment where it made a turn to the north, whilst the swarming figures on the right had poured over the edge and into the trees.

Ened had looked at Aedd askance, but he had only shrugged. Auron had come again in the dark. Com had passed away in the night. A messenger had come from the ford; Urak had flown into a rage and had had the poor man flogged. "Pitiful to see, it was," Auron had said. "Not right at all." Urak had left for the ford in a rare bad temper. The search party had found tracks and had followed them down the escarpment to the marshes, where they had lost them. The searchers had come back very tired, dishevelled and

286

disgruntled. Iowerth had said he thought they were river folk after what they could steal. They always moved down river at this time of year, but Tarok had been really angry, sure that it was Aedd and Ened and that they were hiding out in the tangle of hills and gullies between the escarpment and the marshes. The men would drive the area again in the morning.

Ened felt sorry for Rh'on, such a dear sweet person, so much sadness all at once. Her first-born dead, and now her husband too. She wished that she could be there to comfort her. Aedd had been very quiet and thoughtful; and now the great lump slept whilst she worried. What was to become of them? At least now I have Aedd, dear Aedd, she thought, as she drifted into sleep.

Not too many long strides away, Olwen lay next to Berin, staring at the same sky, but seeing just a tiny part of it through the smoke hole in the roof of the bothy. She had woken as Berin had come in to end his watch, check on the patient, stoke the fire and wake Oranc to replace him. He had laid himself beside her; she had rolled over to hug him, searching for warmth and the blissful sliding return to sweet oblivion, but sleep had eluded her. Now Berin lay beside her in a deep sleep and she watched the sky and the flickering shadows chase each other around the bothy walls.

Oranc was outside, hunched in Alen's cloak over the campfire. From time to time she heard him move about to ease cramped muscles and once the rushing splash as he relieved himself. The scrunching of his feet suggested a frost was forming; certainly it was cold enough, despite the shelter and the fire, and the warm man beside her. At least they had been able to dry their clothes, but without anything to cover themselves, it was cold, even though they had shared out all the spare clothing from Alen's and Berin's packs. She glanced enviously at her patient, A'isa, warm and snug beneath Berin's cloak.

As they had moved the girl inside the shelter, she had groaned and opened her eyes, which at once had flown wide in fright, as she had jerked her head rapidly from Berin to Oranc to Alen, who had carried her. She had tensed, started to struggle and then had slumped with a shriek of pain as broken ends of bone had grated.

"Hush girl, lie still," Olwen had said, coming to her side, smoothing the hair from her forehead. "It's all right. We are just moving you into the shelter."

The girl had seemed reassured by Olwen's presence and soft tones, but had stayed wary as they had settled her by the fire. She had slowly relaxed as Oranc had knelt at her side, explaining how they had found her, dressed her wounds and set her leg. She had clearly warmed to him as he had admired the way she had tackled the boar, the perfection of her spear placement, fetching the tusks for her to see, talking on and on until Olwen had chased him away to feed the girl some broth with barley cake soaked in it.

She had said that her name was A'isa and that she was of the river people. Her brother had been sent on his test for initiation to manhood; his task was to track and kill a boar by himself. As a girl, she had been excluded from the rites, but she could do anything her brother could, she had said with a flash of anger and then a smile as she had fingered the tusks, stealing a sideways glance at them.

Olwen had made her drink more of the fever brew and she had drifted off again into a deep sleep.

Olwen rose and knelt by the fire, warming herself, throwing on small twigs until the bigger logs were awoken from their dull red slumber and blazed again merrily. She looked back at Berin's still form asleep on the pile of rushes. So long as he is with me, it's all right, she thought as she curled up beside him again. He makes everything right for us all, remembering the three of them lathering, splashing and ducking in the pool, like children, the trials and strains of the day forgotten. Berin rolled in his sleep, enveloping her in his arms, spooning her buttocks in his lap. In a pose as familiar now in reality as in her dreams, Olwen drifted from one to the other.

"Berin!"

Oranc's call pierced Berin's sleep. He started, instantly alert.

"Berin!"

The choked off call brought Berin to his feet, hands reaching for spear and dagger, and sent him racing to the door. Olwen rose in panic behind him. Alen sat up in his cloak, hair tousled, rubbing his eyes.

A cold clear light greeted Berin. Beneath a slowly bluing sky, clear but for orange-red wisps of cloud low on the eastern horizon, the grass was covered in frost. The stream steamed, adding to the mist which lay thick on the marsh beyond. Oranc was held from behind, a hand clamped over his mouth, a knife at his throat. Oranc's eyes bulged white, showing the fear and panic that he felt. The camp was encircled by grim-faced men, arrows notched or spears held at the ready. Slowly Berin let his spear and dagger slip from his fingers.

CHAPTER 22

"I wish Berin was here," Amren muttered. "Where the hell is he?"

"From the look on Urak's face before he had that messenger flogged, I reckon he's been and lifted Olwen and young Oranc. Good luck to him if he has," answered Auron.

"Aye it were a bad thing Com did that day. Just to pay Berin out too. Real spite it was. I pity anyone in the hands of that there Urak. He's a real wrong'n."

"Well Com's paid for it now, and for everything else, hasn't he. What a way to go."

"Aye, poor Rh'on. She's taken it real bad. First Belu and now Com; and Berin in disgrace."

"Not with me he ain't. He's a good 'n that lad. Always knows what to do. Plays everything straight he does. You know where you are with him."

"He's not in disgrace with me either, but young Olwen and Oranc are taken by that bugger. Berin's off somewhere when we need him here to lead us, and him not even knowing that he's chief now. There's that Branwen, pretty as a picture, just a dying to be wed to him for all the help Dorn has given, and what's to happen to that if he doesn't wed her. Even Aedd's gone, not daring to show his face on account of Tarok. You can't say its turning out well, can you?"

"You'll have to lead," said Auron emphatically. "You're senior on the council. You'll have to do it."

"We'll have to call a meeting of the elders to decide," Amren said hurriedly. "I can't take it on myself, just like that."

"If we've got time my friend, if we've time. Han said he saw smoke from five camp fires down the valley. That'll mean at least thirty camped down there. Besides, who's left out of the elders except you and me?"

"You're right. It looks like they're gathering to attack, but we're all right, with Tarok and Iowerth here, they'll never dare."

"Aye man, but Tarok's out there, ain't he, chasing Ened, and he's taken Iowerth and his men and the new bondmen with him. How would we fare if they attacked right now? Why, we've not even finished the wall and there're not enough of us to man it, even if we had."

"Aye," Amren agreed reluctantly, looking around him, his face pinched with worry, slitting his eyes against the glare of the early morning sunlight reflecting from the frost, already melting, yielding to the day. The stronghold was like an island in a sea of mist which filled the valley floor, hiding the settlement from view, and, Amren suddenly thought in panic, hiding any attackers too.

"With the pickets gone, we wouldn't know if they were coming until it was too late."

Two working parties were filling gaps in the wall next to the gate, but their number was pitifully small and the gaps large. Only eight men, apart from themselves, had reported for work.

"Look, why don't you go and talk to Aedd. I'll send a message to Tarok, tell him about the smoke, try and get him to come back."

By the time Auron reached the barrow of Ilws, the sun had burned off the mist, although frost still lingered in hollows and on north and west facing slopes. The day promised to be sunny and warm. Auron panted from the steep climb, glad to sink to a crawl for the last few yards, to avoid showing himself on the skyline.

Aedd greeted him, as Ened lay on the grassy bank, looking out towards the escarpment. "What is it Auron?" Aedd asked, taking Auron's arm and starting to walk around the barrow. "You took a risk coming here in daylight."

"We're worried. Me and Amren. There're just ten of us fighting men left at the fort. Han reckons there're five camp fires down the valley. I looks like they could be gathering for an attack. The wall's not finished. There're no pickets. Berin's gone. Tarok 'n Iowerth are gone. You're up here. What are we going to do Aedd? What are we going to do?"

Aedd pondered. "You'll have to send for Tarok. He'll see sense and send at least some men back. Besides, he must give up looking for us soon. Tarok's a good commander. He knows the value of the settlement to the ford, to the tribe. He'll send some people back."

"I hope you're right. But what if he doesn't?"

Aedd turned to stare out over the West Way, reflecting on the problem. He froze, then dropped to the ground, pulling Auron with him, then crawled to the lip of the ditch.

"What is it?" asked Auron. "What's wrong?"

"Look, over on the West Way, where it goes over the hill on the skyline."

Sunlight flashed on polished bronze. Diminished by distance, but threatening in a way neither man had experienced before, a column of men advanced relentlessly in close order over the brow of the hill. The leaders rode ponies, their feet nearly dragging on the ground. As they watched, the column broke ranks and the men settled down on either side of the trail to rest. Pack ponies followed, swaying as they picked a path down the slope under their ballooning loads. Behind the baggage train came a second, pitiful column, a raggle-taggle collection of humanity, hung-shouldered, head down in their individual misery, shambling in collective despair, a parody of the warriors' marching step. Their hands were bound and they were roped together at the neck. The leader of the column was roped to the tail of the last pack horse.

"Outlanders! Why there must be a score of them, or more; and slaves. Poor sods."

"Aye, that'll be our fate too, if we let them take us. Those outlanders aren't there to please us. They'll be up with us by noon. Tarok or no Tarok, we've got to clear Ilws now. Get them and the stock into the fort. Go, raise the alarm. We'll follow."

"But Tarok. He'll have you then."

"Look Auron, the first place the outlanders will make for is the highest ground around. That's right here. Then they'll sweep down on Ilws and along the ridge to the fort, probably the same time as an attack from the valley. Ened and I can't stay out here. We can't go north or east because of Tarok. We can't go south because of Afon'ken. Besides we're going to need every man we've got at the stronghold. No, we're coming in, Tarok or no Tarok."

"Rh'on, I don't want to upset you, but we must clear the settlement. Everyone has to go up to the fort."

"Amren, leave me alone. I just want to be alone," Rh'on sobbed, turning to throw herself over her husband's still form.

"Rh'on, if you won't come, how can I make the others go? You are our heart now. Com is dead. The Mother knows where Berin is. Our people need you."

"I just want to bury my man, to make my peace with Dana."

"Rh'on, there's no time to bury him now. What do you think they will do to you, to Com's body if they find you here? We can bury him with honour in the stronghold, his stronghold. It would be fitting, his last work."

Rh'on lifted her tired sunken face and stared blankly at Amren. Wearily she nodded. Of course, for a chief, it never ends, for him or for his family. Even in death they are responsible for their people.

"All right Amren. See to it will you."

Brys had found Tarok on a steep grassy headland on the escarpment overlooking the marshes. Brys scratched his head in perplexity, wondering how to deal with Tarok's indifference to his message.

"But Sire," he pleaded, "Amren says it's urgent. There's a lot of men camped down the valley. With no pickets out, they could take us any time." There was no response. "He's so worried he's ordered Ilws and Com's into the stronghold. We must have help."

"Run like women, bleat like sheep if you want. I expect nothing better from low born rabble. There is my task," Tarok said, pointing to where a thin column of smoke rose from the trees at the foot of an isolated hill, rising as an island from the wetlands, where banks of mist still lingered, grey rollers on the autumn-leafed sea. "There lies the insult to the house of Harac, and his slut. I will take them and they will pay."

"But Tarok," Iowerth protested, "we don't know that it's Aedd out there. The spoor back-tracked and separated before we lost it. Anyway it looked as if there were more than two of them. It's probably river people."

"It's him; I know it."

"It's a waste of time. None but the river people can travel the marshes. Our men are floundering down there. No one can find a way."

"It's him and I will have him."

"Can't you see the danger? You will sacrifice Com's people, open the way to the settlement at the ford, just for your pride."

Tarok glowered but remained silent, aloof, folding his arms across his chest as though to shut out dissent.

"Brys, I'll come," Iowerth said, turning to the anxious messenger.

"You disobey me, and Urak too?"

"I gave my oath to Dorn. He alone commands me. Dorn told me to help Com and help I will."

"Then go and be damned. Who needs you; but think on who succeeds Dorn," Tarok spat, turning to glare at the smoke once more.

"Served as he is by some, there will be nothing to succeed to," muttered Iowerth to Tarok's back, his anger rising. "Brys, you go back. Tell them what's happened. I'll follow with my men as soon as I can."

At the edge of the marsh, men were wading slowly in a line, searching for a passage, looking for a footing. From time to time the line broke as men rushed to help friends trapped and sinking in mud holes, to be pulled out, covered in stinking sulphurous mud, often shoe-less and once, to great hilarity and ribald comment, without britches. The golden spears of willow littered the water, but enough remained on the densely growing stems to obscure vision, even without the wafting banks of mist.

The men were already tired, although the day was still young, soaked and mud-spattered; the earlier mirth and rough jokes were passing into memory. Those men who knew Aedd liked him and did not relish their task. Men called to each other now for support and reassurance. Iowerth sensed they were becoming dispirited.

"All right, my men, muster over here," he called. "We're going back to the stronghold." There was a loud cheer.

"What about the rest of us?"

"Best ask Tarok, but he was of a mind to carry on when we spoke just now."

A collective groan rose and fell as the news was passed along the line.   Iowerth's men splashed their way out of the marsh and trudged gratefully back, assembling at the foot of the escarpment. The men from the outstation, splashing, slipping and sliding, cursed their separate ways into the gaps left by Iowerth's men, closing ranks.

Suddenly there was a cry. "Here Lairg, are you all right? Lairg? Hey, over here, give me a hand. It's Lairg, I think he's done for."

"He's drowned."

"Aye, dead as mutton."

Iowerth waded gingerly to a willow stump, cold water creeping to his crutch; he pulled himself up through the withies for a better view.

Tarok's men clustered around a body lying face down in a pool, his foot twisted in a tangle of osier roots. As they released the foot and rolled him over, the gash on the side of his head gaped, dribbling pink wash into the pool. Lairg's eyes were open, staring, startlingly blue, bluer than his lips and face.

"Bring him over here lads," Iowerth called. "We'll see to him."

Almost tenderly, the men of the outstation laid their comrade on the rough tussocky grass. They were silent, still, a collective private moment, each reflecting in their own way the frailty of their own hold on life.

"What's going on here?" roared Tarok, bursting through the undergrowth to stand arms akimbo, beard bristling. "Get back in the line."

"But Lairg's dead," ventured a callow youth.

"Aye, and so will you be if you give me any more lip," Tarok raged, spittle flying, catching on his beard. He glared at the poor boy then suddenly lost control and punched the unfortunate lad to the ground.

The men turned sullenly to their task. Two of them helped their mate to his feet, consoled him briefly and splashed despondently back to the marsh.

"Won't you call it off, Tarok?" pleaded Iowerth, indicating the still figure at his feet. "Lairg is dead. How many more will die for this madness."

"Madness is it?" Tarok roared. "We'll see. Be gone before you join him."

Two hundred paces out in the marsh, a mist bank swirled around Cynw as he stood on a clump of reeds, wondering which way to step next, the dark peaty water bubbling as it rose above his ankles. He waved to his brother in arms, twenty paces to his left.

"Hey," he called. "What's it like your way?"

"Wet, what do you think," was the laconic reply, as the white damp air wrapped around Cynw. Silly fart that Cynw, the next-in-line thought, starting at the splash of a frog jumping, the splash exaggerated by the mist. What did he think it was like.

The mist, floating at the beck and call of feckless airs, rolled back. Cynw was gone.

CHAPTER 23

Olwen and Alen crowded through the doorspace. The man holding Oranc pushed him to one side and motioned Berin, Olwen and Alen away from the shelter, with a sideways flick of his knife. Olwen and Alen looked at Berin questioningly; he nodded, moving slowly, deliberately, away from his fallen weapons, recognising the readiness, the battle tautness of the surrounding archers and spearmen.

The man was tall, thin and sinewy. His dark, greying hair hung straight to his shoulders, but was held off his forehead by a beaded leather band. The hair framed a face tanned and deeply lined by constant exposure to its world, an uncompromising face accustomed to obedience.

He was dressed in fine-cured buckskin, with no adornment. He carried no weapon but for the knife which he had held to Oranc's throat and which he now hung from a thong about his neck, before striding purposefully to the shelter and ducking inside. The watching guards stood their ground in silence. Sounds of shouting from the direction of the escarpment mewled faint on the still morning air.

"I said they'd see our smoke," Oranc volunteered, nodding towards the escarpment, his voice startlingly loud in the silence. A bowman took deliberate aim. A suddenly mute Oranc raised his hands, palm outwards.

A loud cry of pain from A'isa started Oranc towards the hut. He stopped as a grim spearman stepped in front of him. Oranc slumped back next to Berin, acknowledging defeat. Olwen took his hand.

The cry of pain was followed by a screech of outrage and a loud duet for treble and base in a sing-song dialect. The words were strange to Berin but the point and counter point of parent and offspring at odds were all too familiar. Whatever the meaning, it certainly pleased the guards, for they visibly relaxed, some smiling broadly at each other. Deep stern tones interrupted the girl in mid flow. The response was a shrill angry shout and what was clearly, in any language, a torrent of abuse.

The Chief, for such he clearly was, backed out of the shelter, beckoning to a near toothless old man, clad in buckskin so old it was worn as shiny as the top of his head, which was bald but for a few white wispy remnants. He carried a bulging leather satchel. After a brief whispered conversation, the old man ducked inside.

"My daughter is a wayward child," the Chief said, an indulgent smile cracking his normally austere face. He addressed Berin in the common tongue, with a quaint, old-fashioned phrasing and a lilting accent. "She is much given to inventing stories. She tells me that she killed a mighty boar which savaged her in its death throes. As she lay beneath the great beast, bleeding to death, you came and saved her. A fantasy of course, but clearly you have doctored and looked after her well, no doubt after she suffered some foolish accident of which she is too ashamed to tell. I am grateful to you."

Berin smiled. "You have a remarkable daughter. It is no fantasy. The truth is exactly as you have told it. See the skin?" Berin pointed to the hide pegged out on the ground, next to the tree from which the butchered joints hung. "Her spear point is still within the carcass. Her broken spear lies over there, next to the kill. Come, see for yourself."

Incredulity was the only possible description of the Chief's expression as he examined the huge size of the hide, the broken spearhead. He shook his head in disbelief whilst he read the signs in the trampled, blood-stained ground where A'isa had made her kill.

A sharp cry of pain hurried them back to the shelter. They were followed by Olwen, Oranc and Alen. No one moved to stop them. A'isa lay white-faced, wincing in pain. The shaman had taken off the dressings and was examining the injured leg.

"It is well done, sire," he said, looking up from his work as they came in. "Properly set, and treated with woundwort to stop it fouling, just as I would have done."

"Of course it is," snapped A'isa. "I told you so; and what's more, Berin and Olwen didn't hurt me like you do," she added spitefully, conveniently forgetting that she had been unconscious at the time.

"A'isa, why didn't you show your father the tusks? Your trophy," Berin asked gently.

"He didn't want to believe me," she said, tears gathering from a pain that didn't lie in her leg. "You didn't believe me, did you?" she added testily, looking directly at her father, challenging him, as he stood in whispered conversation with the shaman.

"Well show them to me now," the Chief said, shifting uncomfortably.

"There you are," A'isa announced proudly, pulling out the tusks from beneath Berin's cloak. "I bet they are bigger than Tark's."

Leaving A'isa to the ministrations of the shaman, Olwen, Alen and the ever attentive Oranc, the Chief

302

motioned Berin outside. "I am Talwch, Chief of the people of the river. As you can tell from the way I have spoiled her, A'isa, my daughter, is very dear to me. Harwch, our law keeper and medicine man tells me she would have died without your help. I thank you, but I would know whom I thank."

"I am Berin, heir to Com, of the line of Harac."

"Then as cousin, I bid you welcome, for the chiefs of the people of the river are also of the line of Harac, although we have little cause to be friends in this age."

"As to blood ties, they are told in our lore too. Yet I cannot pretend they have brought our two peoples friendship."

Talwch grunted. "What brings you here? It is not often that you farmers enter our river lands."

Berin pondered his answer. "Urak of the ford, son of Dorn, took someone dear to me and used her badly. I have taken her back, but we were pursued. I found this place once by accident when hunting, so I came here to find sanctuary."

"Why did Tarok of Dorn's settlement, which your people call the outstation, come to Com's?" Berin looked at him in surprise. "Little escapes us," Talwch added.

"We were attacked by outlanders and Afon'ken. Tarok is here to help us defend our lands."
"I see, then why does he pursue you?"

"I don't know. It took me by surprise. I suppose Urak persuaded him."

"Perhaps I have an answer for you, "Talwch said, turning to his men."Bring him," he ordered. Cynw, shaking and whimpering, terrified near out of his wits, was pushed forward. "My men took this fool in the marshes. Why don't you question him?"

"Oh Dana. Berin, save me Berin," Cynw gasped, scarcely believing the presence of a familiar face.

"I know you. You're one of Tarok's men aren't you? What's your name? What are you doing in the marsh?" Berin asked sternly.

"I'm Cynw. That Tarok, he's mad. It's all because of that wench Ened. Mad he is for her and to get back at Aedd."

"Start at the beginning," Berin interrupted.

"Aedd beat Tarok because he fooled with his woman, Ened. Tarok has had a fancy for her ever since his wife bought her from the savages," Cynw continued, oblivious to his gaffe. "Tarok took all his men, Iowerth's too..."

"What?" Berin cried, his face paling, "all the men. What about the stronghold, the pickets?"

"He took them all, pickets too. Only left Com's and Ilws folk. Said they couldn't be trusted."

"You mean he left the settlement unguarded? Com agreed to this?"

"Oh, don't you know? I thought that you of all people should know..." Cynw paused and shifted from foot to foot in embarrassment. "Com's dead," he blurted. Com dead. His father dead, finished, the source of his own being already a memory, the transition from substance to abstraction had happened without his knowledge.

"Anyway Tarok has had us tramping up and down, to and fro, hurry up and wait..." Cynw prattled on unfeelingly, as if floodgates had been released, unaware of his crassness.

Berin struggled to come to terms with the news. But there was so much still to say, he thought, nervously shying away from the edges of guilt beginning to gather as a black cloud in his mind.

"... too much for Iowerth. He dragged his men out. Lucky buggers. Took them back to the stronghold."

"Again Cynw. What was too much for Iowerth?" With an effort, Berin returned to Cynw's story.

"Well Lairg getting drowned like that. Iowerth just pulled his men out. There was one hell of a row with Tarok. Some said news had come that the settlement was in danger; some said Iowerth didn't believe it was Aedd's spoor we were following, but savages'. Anyway, his men pulled out and left us to it, then these buggers grabbed me. Scared the shit out of me I can tell you. They..."

"Enough Cynw. If you've any sense at all, you'll simply shut up."

Cynw subsided, his words drying up like a flood that had run its course. Nervously he glanced around, suddenly aware of hostility in the glares directed at him.

"I apologise for this oaf, Talwch," Berin said.

"It's not necessary. You are not responsible for his lack of wits or manners. Yet so are we regarded by Tarok and his people. We do not love them for it. This Ened he speaks of; she is the girl from the West bought from our people by Tarok's wife?"

"That was her story."

"I should not have allowed it; but the clan that found her is small and poor. I thought it better she found a place with her own kind, if not with her own kin."

"You were not to know."

"Aye, perhaps, but a chief is expected to know."

"Talwch, I must go to my people. My father... I am now chief.."

Talwch reached out and gripped Berin by the shoulder, staring him in the eye, searchingly.

"You are a good man, Berin," he said slowly after a long silence. "Yes you must go. Leave your woman and young friends here, they will be safe. I have a mind to stay a while anyway; the hunting here should be good now, for we have left this ground for a long time. Besides, A'isa should not be moved. But please, take this fool with you. His prattling is likely to shorten his life if he stays in our company."

"I must get to the settlement without meeting Tarok's men. I do not wish to have to explain how I came to be in the wet lands."

"I understand. Grwlch will guide you, "Talwch said, indicating a slight, but wiry figure, one of the two who had brought Cynw forward. Talwch spoke to him rapidly in his own dialect. Grwlch nodded from time to time, glancing at Berin as he did so.

"You should make your farewells," Talwch said, turning back to Berin. "Grwlch will come to you."

The parting was awkward. Olwen knew that he must go, that she must stay, yet found both inevitabilities hard to accept. The intrusion of A'isa, giggling with Oranc,

306

prevented the physical closeness they both wanted to use to underscore their feelings and as a salve to imminent separation. Yet they embraced and kissed.

At the marsh edge, when they had left the tribesmen behind, Grwlch stripped to a loincloth and wrapped his clothes tightly in a greased leather pouch. He produced another for Berin, who quickly followed suit, marvelling at the cunning arrangement of folds and grease which gave a water tight seal to the package. Cynw declined and was studiously ignored as a result.

Grwlch slipped into the water, sinking to his shoulders. He moved forward, and from side to side, feeling with his feet, then grunted, and stepped up, standing only calf deep in water. He motioned Berin towards him and pulled him up. Berin found that he was standing on a gravel bank. He could feel the pebbles move beneath the soft, water-logged leather of his boots. Grwlch moved off westwards, with a curious high stepping gait. Berin followed Grwlch through the willows, bogs and sedge banks, trying hard to emulate his guide, wondering at the ease of their progress along what was clearly an old river channel which now acted as a causeway. Cynw floundered, splashing behind until Grwlch turned and slipped back past Berin, unlooping a knife from around his neck.

"You will be silent," he hissed. From the shouts and splashing loud to their left, Berin guessed the reason for Grwlch's concern. They were passing around the end of Tarok's line. Cynw's Adam apple bobbed convulsively as he tried to swallow his panic; his eyes fixed on Grwlch's knife. From that point he made scarcely a ripple.

They paused briefly when they reached the stream, the movement of the water barely discernible, hardly distinguishable from the surrounding still pools. In fact, as cats' paws of the fitful breeze drove the curve-prowed willow leaves ahead of them, across and up the stream, it seemed to Berin sometimes as if the flow had been reversed. Grwlch led the way upstream. As they approached the escarpment, low banks emerged from the slough and the flow was more noticeable. An iridescent blue kingfisher darted ahead of them along the tunnel created by overhanging alders.

The banks heightened, water released from its gloomy damp suppression by earth, tinkled its joy at being free. The stream narrowed and shallowed, though deep pools, especially on the outside of bends, were a hazard to the unwary and foolish, as Cynw discovered. Grwlch turned to Berin with a wry look as Cynw floundered.

"I will leave you here. Follow the stream to the spring in the beech wood. Take the gully to your right. It is a steep climb, but it will bring you directly to the top of the escarpment. You will know it. You will be on the hill which marks the east side of the col where Com's valley joins the ridge. Take care that you are not betrayed by the fool. Go with Dana."

"Thank you Grwlch, may Dana bring you safely to your lodge," answered Berin in the traditional formal farewell.

"Praise the Mother! I'm glad to see the back of that savage. Cut your gizzard out as soon as look at you, I reckon. Tarok's right; you've got to be hard on them, keep them in order. Let them once take advantage and..."

"Shut up Cynw," Berin interrupted wearily, regretting his decision to return Cynw to his fellows, saving him from the people of the river. He really didn't want

Tarok to know the whereabouts of Olwen and Oranc. Cynw now knew how to reach them and Berin knew that there would be no way of holding his tongue short of cutting it out. Cynw would have to go with him to the settlement.

"There may be more of them about." Berin said maliciously. Cynw's eyes darted nervously from side to side. As a perch pursuing its minnow prey, slapped the surface of the pool, Cynw started, slipped on a slime-covered stone, and fell with a loud splash.

"You'd best come with me," Berin sighed. Cynw nodded in emphatic agreement.

"Mother, oh mother. I'm so ... there was so much that needed to be said; to be put right between us," Berin sobbed over Rh'on's shoulder, pressing her slight frame to him, trying to give comfort where none was possible; she understanding, as she understood everything, accepting the spirit of the giver. She drew back from her son and looked at him carefully, holding his cheeks in her warm palms, searching out the depths of truth or falsehood released by the intense emotion of the moment from the acquired and studied stoicism, learned in his life as a perpetual also ran.

"I loved him," Berin cried.

"I know you did and he you, " said Rh'on. Hesitantly, the words simply forming in her mind almost as she spoke them, she continued, "It was ever so. A tragedy; the greatest love shows least and hurts most."

"But I hated him when... when he gave Olwen to Urak... I wanted to... Well it's done now. She's safe and he's dead. There is no wrong anymore, no right. It's too late. I can't put right what was wrong between us."

309

"He wanted me to tell you that he loved you; no that's not it. I must remember it as it was. He had always loved you is what he said," Rh'on remembered, clutching her throat as though to smooth out a constriction. Tears coursed freely down her cheeks as the memory gained substance and the pain became more acute with increasing reality. "You are to follow your heart. I was to tell you he was sorry, he was wrong...about Olwen. I was to wish you Dana's blessing and to ask your forgiveness."

"Oh mother. There is nothing to forgive. He did what he thought was right, for our people, for the clan."

Berin turned to the body that was, had been his father, taking the cold and somehow fragile hand in his, remembering it warm and work hardened, enveloping his podgy, dimpled childhood fist.

"Yes, as you must too, now," she said, adding after a long silence, during which they both fought to regain their private selves.

"He asked for you at the end. He cried when you could not come. I never saw him cry before."

"Ah Aedd, How is it going? Berin asked, as Aedd's unmistakable shadow fell across the door way. "Excuse me mother."

"Of course. You are chief now."

"Well Aedd?" he asked, taking leave of Rh'on and walking with his friend and lieutenant around the perimeter of the defences, "How is it going?"

"All the people are in; most of their valuables too, they were quite well prepared. The stock's another matter. We've got the cattle from the yard, the ones that came from Dorn and our own, and the sheep from our side of the West

Way, but the Ilws flock we left and that in the lower pasture too. It would have taken too long to bring them in."

"How many fighting men?"

"With Iowerth's score and Branwen's bondsmen there are forty two of us."

"You say there are two score outlanders?"

"Aye, but at least that number again down the valley, judging from the camp fires."

"The outlanders are the ones that worry me. They are used to war, and they have bronze. I could wish that Tarok was here with his men. Perhaps I should send for him."

"Would he come?" Aedd asked doubtfully. "He didn't come when Brys went to him."

"Aye, he's obsessed with getting at you and Ened, but if we were actually attacked, surely he would come to our aid," Berin replied.

Aedd looked at Berin closely. "You have only to tell him I am here and he will come soon enough," he said.

"Aye, and then I would have to fight him as well as the outlanders, for I shall not give you or Ened up to him, my friend."

Aedd grimaced but relaxed a little. "I'm sorry, Berin. My temper has brought us to this."

"Don't be sorry Aedd. You have right on your side and you know it. Tarok behaved like an animal. He is wrong. Better we stand alone than side by side with him."

"But it could bring us down."

"With forty of us we can defend the bank against three times forty. It's the gate I'm worried about. How are those gaps coming on?"

"I've had hurdles put in for the moment; better than nothing. They're banking the dirt up against them as fast as they can. They should be all right."

"Aye, against flint, but bronze?"

Aedd was silent, remembering his own desperate struggle with the outlander, the power of the bronze swords. Now they were faced with two score of them.

"Berin, Ened and I must go. You must call for Tarok."

"He'll not come until he has you, that much is clear from what Iowerth reported. But I've got an idea. Tarok doesn't know that I won't give you up. If he was told that you were here, if he came for you and arrived after the outlanders had started to attack, who's side would he be on?"

Aedd grinned. "Aye, Brys knows where he is. I'll send him now, before the outlanders come."

"Good, do that. Tell Brys to wait until the attack starts. He's to tell Tarok that the fort is attacked and that you have found refuge in it. That should bring him running."

"Afterwards he'll expect Ened and me to be handed over to him."

"Afterwards is soon enough to worry. We might all be dead. I won't give you up, either of you."

"Its all right Rh'on," Branwen soothed, taking her arm. "Its only natural you should feel this way, but Berin only did what was best for us all," she added, looking up shyly at him, her head tilted to one side, thick hair hanging loose, cascading over one side of her face. She sought eye contact, approval and something more.

Rh'on braced herself, drawing a deep juddering breath to suppress her sobs.

"We've taken his bronze, kept him from his ancestors, his son. There seemed to be so little left to honour him with. He should be in the Great Barrow of Harac, or with Belu, which I'm sure is what he really wanted. It isn't fitting for a chief."

"Mother, I promise you we will re-bury him with my brother when we get a chance."

"We shouldn't have to disturb him again. He should be laid to rest," Rh'on sniffed.

"But mother, how could I have spared men to open Belu's tomb? How could I have taken the clan from a place of safety just as we are about to be attacked?"

"We could have waited."

"Mother, he's my father. I care too. Would you have wanted to risk leaving him unburied, open to desecration, like the rest of us if the outlanders win, when we had a chance to send him to Dana peacefully?"

Rh'on struggled with her tears, biting her lips, raising her eyes to his, seeing his pain blurred through her own, watching the aura of chieftaincy grow as she watched, feeling with a strange sense of inevitability, enormous sympathy for her son.

"Oh Berin, you're right. Forgive me."

Branwen led Rh'on away from the graveside, back to the shelters; Ened helped her, putting her arm around Rh'on supporting her from the other side. To Berin Rh'on's frame appeared suddenly crumpled and frail-looking.

Berin felt Aedd at his arm. "See the smoke," Aedd said, pointing. Berin followed the direction of Aedd's outstretched arm. A column of white smoke rose from the direction of Ilws. "They're burning Ilws, the bastards."

"No, I don't think so," Berin answered. "The colour's wrong. That's a fire with plenty of green on it. Someone is trying to make smoke. Look now, do you see that. It's a signal. Someone is making the smoke come in puffs."

"Aye, you're right," Aedd answered. "Look down the valley."

An answering smoke rose from the valley south of them, a silent exclamation mark, a mark of intent.

CHAPTER 24

Berin peered through the small gap at the side of the gate, straining his eyes for a glimpse of the outlanders. Amren had called him a lifetime ago, or so it seemed. Berin had watched the frightening methodical advance of the column along the ridge, sunlight glinting on bronze fittings, on body armour, helmets and shields, and on the spear points held aloft. The column had passed from sight behind the hump on the ridge, where the shepherds usually sat, and had not reappeared. Gnats swarmed in his line of sight, dancing in the still air, confusing his focus. The men, posted at intervals along the bank had long since forgotten the nervous banter which they had exchanged as they had taken their places. They had fallen into silence, a silence broken only by an occasional clatter of equipment, sometimes a sling stone dropped nervously back onto the pile and the rattle of a new one selected in its place; a quiver of arrows placed more handily; a cough, a deep breath. Each man had long since drawn in on himself, dry-mouthed, alone with his private fears, his fluttering stomach and loosening sphincter. A bright black and yellow hover fly swooped and stopped, reared, side-slipped, hung again, its high pitched whine sawing across Berin's nerves, stretched taught as a bow string, ready to hurl body into action.

The deep roar from the valley came almost as a relief. With an answering cry, a relief of pent up fright, the defenders leapt to their feet, hurling sling stones, shooting arrows.

"Stop!" Berin yelled. "Stop. Don't waste them. Wait until the bastards are in range, wait until you can hit them."

Shamefaced, the men obeyed, but the tension was released, they had started; they were in the fight. Now they were no longer alone; now they were comrades. They grinned at each other ruefully.

Berin peered over the edge of the bank. A ragged line of men had run from the cover of the trees in the steep-sided valley and were scrambling up the hill side. As the slope steepened, the attackers bent first to a crouch and then stumbled forward, using their hands to help themselves up, grabbing the wiry tussocks of grass, slipping, panting, cursing. The men were from Afon'ken, but here and there a bronze spear point or bronze-bound helmet or shield highlighted the owners' alliance with the outlanders.

Berin glanced swiftly behind him, towards the gate. There was still no sign of a move from the ridge. "The logs," Berin called softly, "at my signal."

He saw the men climbing, creeping now, closer and closer. Now they were within range of bow and sling. As he watched, there was a shout from the valley; a blue-cloaked, helmeted figure strode from the cover of the woods to stand tall and arrogant, bronze blade in hand, shield at his side, his black eye patch as prominent as a bull's eye on a target. The last rank of the attackers halted at the shouted command, bracing themselves against the hillside, notching arrows to their bows. The outlander waved his arm; a flight of arrows hissed and whirred over the parapet. The defenders dropped down, but a scream from behind them showed that one at least had found a mark.

"Now!" yelled Berin, watching the front ranks of Afon'ken crawling forward under the cover of their archers. Along the parapet, men heaved with levers at the tree trunks balanced on the edge. Naf fell back, his knees buckling, clutching his throat, feeling with disbelieving hands the arrow which his eyes could not make out through the rising blackness.

With a creak the first log dropped, bounced, cleared the ditch and rolled, gathering speed and a violent energy. It pulped the legs and pelvis of a spearman who tried vainly to fling himself from its path. His comrade stood to locate the danger and took it full on the chest as the log bounced again. His ribs crushed. The runaway tree trunk smashed him to the ground, dragging his torn body around like a wet rag, smearing the grass red, before releasing the broken, worn bundle in the search for fresh victims. The archer looked up from releasing a jammed arrow from his quiver, alarmed at the shaking of the earth and the cries of his brothers-at-arms. Face frozen in fear, he turned to run, but the log took his legs from under him, breaking them both below the knee, hurling him into the air.

The second log slipped, catching the lip of the trench and slewed around end-on to the slope, never gathering enough momentum to overcome the friction. Half-way down the hillside the bow wave of sods, flint and chalk brought it to a halt. The men in its path dodged and weaved and eventually found shelter in its bulk, as the defenders hurled a storm of arrows and sling stones amongst them, searching out the careless.

The third log created mayhem on the attackers' left, leaving in its flattened wake two still, red-stained heaps and three broken twitching cripples, shocked to silence, not yet aware that their end was merely postponed, not realising that their lease on life had run to term, that the earth would soon repossess its mortgage. The men of Com, Ilws and the ford hailed arrows and sling stones on their enemy, some jumping to the top of the bank in their eagerness. They roared their fierce joy and defiance as the ranks of Afon'ken broke and ran.

As the survivors found shelter in the valley, the defenders turned their attention to the wounded, picking them off one by one, each hit, the wet thwack of an arrow, the dust-raising smack of a sling stone, raising a cheer. Death came as a relief to the cruelly maimed.

Aedd gripped Berin by the arms; his face flushed with intense exhilaration, the battle fever. "We did the bastards. We mangled 'em. That was a great idea of yours. That'll teach the sods."

"It was just to test us, Aedd," Berin answered quietly. "We took them by surprise that time. We won't again. Look over there, they are watching everything." He pointed along the edge of the ridge to a spur which overlooked the slaughter field. Three outlanders stood in full view. As Berin watched, they turned and disappeared below the skyline.

"Here they come," Iowerth called. The men of Afon'ken advanced in two columns each two abreast. They followed the trails of destruction left by the logs. The leaders carried wicker hurdles. Every second rank carried a hurdle above their heads, each column carried a ladder. The advance was slow; the attackers slipped and slid under their burdens, constantly pausing to close up, to re-knit their collective protection as an individual floundered. Yet slow as the advance was, it was also relentless. Berin's throat constricted. What was he to do? There was no time to move the remaining logs, to align them with the attacking columns. They were almost in bow shot, but neither arrows nor sling stones would penetrate the hurdles.

318

The men of Afon'ken spread out and set out their hurdle shield. Bowmen took their places behind their protection, arrows clattered about the bank and hissed overhead. Conwen of the ford dropped to an arrow in the eye, Han, turning to help the twitching form, already beyond all help, thereby saved himself, taking a barb destined for his heart in the fleshy muscle of his upper arm. Kar, ducking behind his shield, exchanged part of an ear for an extension to life.

"Stay down," Berin yelled. "Keep below the bank until I say."

Berin ordered spear and axe men to the anticipated points of impact and bow and sling men to the flanks. The attackers struggled in the ditch and the first ladder thumped against the bank. The arrow storm subsided.

Berin gave the signal. The men of Com, Ilws and the ford rose from behind the bank, and fired arrow after arrow, hurled stone after stone in a furious onslaught on the attackers' flanks. At point blank range, the flint-tipped arrows split leather as skin, lanced through flesh, splintered on bone. Stones bruised, stunned, concussed, broke bones, smashed teeth. Frantic attackers thrust spears upwards, ahead of them, probing at the defenders who had leapt onto the parapet, finding belly and calf and groin; stabbing, slitting, splashing out white-hot agony. Red gore ran warm and slippery down to their hands on the shafts. Afon'ken roared aggression. The defenders howled their defiance, grunting with each blow, shrieking at each wound. The smell of blood rose from the red-green trampled turf, and with it the stench of fear, driving attackers and defenders alike, each now divorced from rational self, each in the grip of senses and instincts, to preserve his own precious life. All were equal, reduced to the same desperate panic.

A head appeared over the parapet, wild hair framing a wide-eyed staring face, contorted by battle lust. The man's mouth opened in a cry of bravado, which was cut off abruptly by a side swipe from Aedd's axe. The blow crushed his temple, spewing his eye from its socket in a mess of blood and bone. The body jammed in the rungs. Berin set his spear shaft against the ladder and heaved. Aedd joined him. The spear slipped, Berin and Aedd stumbled and fell. The ladder thumped back against the parapet and an attacker, an arrow with a broken shaft in his arm, straddled the bank top, thrusting at Berin with his spear. Sobbing, Berin scrabbled sideways, searching for his own weapon, his eyes fixed on the point coming at him. Berin dodged desperately, then felt the burning tear along his ribs. Sitting back to the parapet, Berin seized his opponent's spear with both hands, jerking it down, pulling the man off balance, into the stronghold, where he landed on hands and knees, supplicant to the three spears which pinned him.

The next man appeared over the top as Berin scrambled to his feet and joined Aedd in pushing back the ladder. A scream from the gate snapped his head around, white-faced in panic. The outlanders! With a desperate heave, he pushed the ladder over and back. It fell, shedding men of Afon'ken like over-ripe fruit, thumping on to the steep grassy slope far below, rolling bruised and broken.

"Iowerth, take charge here," Berin yelled. "I'll take the gate. To me, Com's, Ilws. To me!" he screamed. "To the gate."

The outlanders advanced at a trot, in silence but for the padding of their boots and the jingling of their arms. Aedd and Berin hurried their men to their positions, shouting instructions, encouragement, banal nonsense, anything to

320

divert minds from dwelling on the probability of death. Both ventured a glance from time to time at the din of battle behind them, then closed their minds to it, leaving it to Iowerth, concentrating on the menace to be faced ahead.

When the attackers were at twenty paces, the bows and slings let go a storm of missiles, aimed low as Berin instructed, at the vulnerable legs beneath the shields. Men fell, bringing down others, shouting oaths. For a moment, order was reduced to chaos, and the menace was shown to be vulnerable. The men of Com and Ilws took heart. They panted with exertion as they fired arrows, hurled stones into the sprawling attackers, where collective protection was ignored. Each was an individual again and struggled to cover his own soft vulnerability with his shield.

Purpose was restored by the outlander's leader. With a roar, the outlanders rushed the gate, making for the hastily plugged gaps at each side. Arec ran to brace the hurdle, which was bowing, threatening to fall inwards under the pressure of the attackers. A bronze spear tip smashed through the split hazel withies, slicing through viscera, slashing arteries, emerging in a bright red gob from his belly. Amazed, Arec stared at the brown metal leaf, grasped it with both hands, then screeched as the pain bit hard. Elin and Kar thrust at his assailant, but their flint spear heads splintered on the hurdle. Arec fell, trapping the spear. Its owner drew his blade. Shield slung at his side to allow greater power to his swing, he hacked two handed at the obstruction. White chips flew as the blade bit through the withies.

Berin thrust with desperate strength. Belu's spear sliced through the shredded hurdle. The blade man had time only to see his nemesis. He had no time to remember that he had been told that the barbarian did not have bronze before he took Berin's spear point below the chin.

Swiftly, Berin withdrew his spear; just as swiftly the enemy was replaced by another, stepping up on the corpse of his fallen comrade. Again Berin thrust, his hands jarred as his opponent parried with his shield. A second outlander appeared. Side by side they placed their shields against the mangled hurdle, set their shoulders to their shields and pushed. The hurdle fell inwards, the two outlanders stormed the breach, trampling Arec's body, to face a semi-circle of spears, thrusting at them from all angles. Others filled the gap, anxious to avoid the fire from the parapet, eager to get to grips with the real fighting.

Aedd, seeing the outlanders surge into the gap, arrogant in the knowledge of the superiority of their weapons and skills, felt a red rage explode within him. He leapt forward, taking a blade slash on his shield, wrenching it sideways. He pulled his man off balance, and buried his axe in the man's head, just behind the ear. With a wild shout, he leapt on the other, smashing shield against shield in a frenzied fury, crowding the outlander back against the gate, sensing Berin beside him pick up the fallen blade and face the breach. In vain Aedd's outlander tried to swing his blade in the restricted space between shield and bank. Spurning subtlety, Aedd kicked him in the crutch, catching briefly the shock of sick despair in the man's eyes as he sagged to his knees, before all expression, and all else, was ended by a spear thrust from Auron.

Aedd turned to see Amren buckling, felled by a blade slash, blood spurting from severed carotid artery, the blade smashing down through the collar bone, opening a gaping wedge. The outlander stepped over him, looking for another target. Kar turning from the parapet, buried an arrow to its flight in the outlander's armpit as he raised his hands in triumph, his battle cry choked by the frothing lung blood bursting from his mouth. Berin fended one attacker with his shield, hacking unfamiliarly with the captured blade at another. Madwg, who raised his spear to ward off a blade stroke from an outlander who had scaled the bank, watched in horror as his lopped forearm fell at his feet. Cadw at Madwg's side, thrust with all his might, shoving his spear up into the outlander's groin, screaming his blood hot joy at the horror on his enemy's face, at the fingers scrabbling uselessly at the awful end to manhood, to life.

A rush of Branwen's bondsmen pushed past Aedd, phalanx - like, pressing the outlanders back with their shields, with the impetus of their charge, filling the gap in the defences. Berin jumped to the parapet. A horn sounded, a figure on the ridge waved and the outlanders pulled back beyond bowshot. As quickly as the din and heat of battle had risen, they now receded.

Arms dropped, limbs began to shake in reaction, men began to take in the reality of what they had participated in, of what they had done.

"You there," Berin called to the leader of Branwen's bondmen. "Come here, what's your name?"

"Its Warwch," said a soft voice at his elbow, before the man could answer. Branwen stood beside him. "I thought I could help with the wounded, she said, indicating a basket of dressings." She stared at him in open admiration, her expression changing to shock and concern as she saw the blood crusting his side. "You're hurt."

"Nearly," he said, laughing, then serious. "You'd best see to Madwg, poor devil, if he still lives," pointing to where the men of Ilws gathered around their kinsman.

"Warwch," Berin said, "I thank you, all of you. Were it in my gift, I would free you for what you have done."

"It was mistress Branwen sent us."

"Oh," Berin said, nonplussed, turning to her, "then I must thank you too."

"And what favour would you bestow on me. Would you free me too?" Berin stared at her, reading simple adoration and invitation in her open face. Words, even thought failed him. He half wished the battle still raged, so great was his confusion. Branwen touched his arm, breaking the binding spell. "But it is in your gift, for they are yours too," she added, very quietly and seriously, "as I am."

"So be it. You are a free man."

The horn sounded again. Berin glanced to the knoll on the ridge. The sun, already well on the way to the horizon beyond the black silhouettes of the outlanders' commander and his trumpeter, cast their shadows like two dark fingers towards the stronghold. A grey cloud, pressing forward on the rising breeze, shrouded the sun and spilled gloom over them; Berin shivered, the breeze was suddenly chill.

The outlanders formed up into their columns and moved off up the ridge. The men on the parapet jeered, venting their anger, their fear. A second roar from the men of the ford told Berin that the men of Afon'ken had withdrawn too.

"Why did they stop?" Aedd asked.

"There's your answer," Berin replied, pointing beyond the settlement, to where a column of men marched with jerky jolting steps down the hill side, a dark hairy caterpillar on the grassy slope. "Brys fulfilled his mission. Tarok is come."

"Tarok. I beg you to join with us. Let's forget this feud or only the outlanders will be the winners."

"There's no help from me until you submit to my authority. Give me Aedd and my woman," Tarok roared, tipping his head back, beard flaring, arms akimbo, legs braced wide apart to support the pride, the arrogance of his posture. "There will be no help from me until you give them up."

"Aedd is a free man and not mine to give," Berin replied evenly, suppressing the tremor which tried to creep into his voice. Tarok, with his habit of command, his size, bearing and rich dress was enough to intimidate anyone, but, as Berin reminded himself, had he not just beaten off the outlanders and routed Afon'ken? He had not done all that only to kneel to a bully, aye and a rapist.

"And Olwen and the boy Oranc. You stole them," called Urak from Tarok's side. I demand you return them to my charge immediately."

"Olwen and Oranc are not here," Berin replied flatly, icy cold filaments of revenge reaching out to his heart from his head, freezing the hot murder lust which had welled up as he had spotted Urak, misting the picture of Olwen as he had found her, naked and bound, shutting out the thoughts of what must have gone before. Urak leant across and whispered in his brother's ear. Damn the man, Berin thought, what evil is he plotting now?

"You deny the authority of the High Chief, and of the lore keeper?" Tarok yelled, spitting in his fury. "You refuse to hand over the criminal who assaulted me? You refuse to return my wife's bondwoman, my brother's woman and his ward?"

"As chief of Com's and Ilws I acknowledge my father's vow to Dorn and accept the authority of Dorn as High Chief."

"Then acknowledge mine, for Dorn is dead and I am his heir," Tarok raged.   "Open the gate!"

A keening wail from close behind Berin unnerved him as he concentrated on Tarok.

"My gate is open to all whose purpose is peaceable," Berin responded, "but I shall not force a man to go where there can be no justice. It's true you bought Ened, or rather your wife did. But I am told her bond was given to Anoeth of the ford."

"That's a lie," Tarok shrieked, shaking with rage.

"Aedd bought that bond," continued Berin. "Ened became his woman. You forced yourself on her and were beaten, by Aedd. With good reason, most would agree. Tell me where the crime lies, Tarok, where justice lies, tell me."

"You are lying, you turd-eater. I only tried to take back that which is rightfully mine."

"Iowerth, did you witness the exchange of Ened's bond, between Tarok's wife and Anoeth?"

Iowerth stepped up to the parapet. Tarok paled as he recognised him. "Come out here," he yelled. "Hold your tongue."

"I did," Iowerth answered defiantly, eyeing Tarok's fury nervously.

"Creggan, did you witness the passing of Ened's bond from Anoeth to Aedd?"

"I did," Creggan answered determinedly.

"So Tarok..." Berin began.

"Iowerth, Creggan. Bring your men, Branwen and the bondmen out here immediately," Urak interrupted.

".. it seems, Tarok, that right is on Aedd's side," Berin continued as Iowerth and Creggan stood undecided at his side. "I'll not hand him over to you."

"As for you Urak, any man who whips his woman and leaves her bound and naked, tied to a post, without warmth, food or drink, while he travels, is not worthy of either the name or of the company of men, far less the right to command them."

Urak started and paled. The men around him drew away, muttering, disgust written plainly in their expressions.

"I order you as your High Chief..." Tarok raged.

"You do not have my vow, Tarok, nor will I give it, not to a rapist," Berin spat.

"Iowerth, Creggan, seize that man. Bring him to me," yelled Urak.

Iowerth and Creggan looked at each other, then at Berin, at Aedd and Ened, at Branwen, sobbing quietly, head buried in Ened's shoulder, not yet accepting her father's death, so callously announced. They fingered their arms nervously; they had given their oath to Dorn, and Tarok was his heir. Their men looked at them uncertainly, shuffling, watching each other, searching for a lead. Branwen's bondmen gathered around her. The survivors of Com's and Ilws dropped their heads in despair.

"Yes, enough of this treason. Men of the ford, do your duty," Tarok ordered.

Branwen looked up at Tarok's shouted command. High spots of colour flared on her cheek bones as she strode to the bank, dashing tears from her eyes with her sleeve. She pointed to her two half-brothers, shouting "All my life I have watched you Tarok, bully and bluster to get your way, and you Urak scheme and cheat, even deceive your own father. Do not go with them, men of the ford. I for one will not. My father gave me to Berin. I know him to be honest and true. We have seen today how courageous he is. I shall not leave him, especially now he needs us, all of us."

The crowd had fallen silent, even Tarok and Urak appeared momentarily mesmerised by the intensity of her sincerity.

"No, men of the ford, do not go with them," Branwen continued. "Whatever you owed my father died with him. These two," she spat contemptuously, pointing at them repeatedly as though wanting to stab them with her outstretched finger, "are not worthy of you. Why even their help in a battle we are fighting to save all of us, from here to the outstation and all the lands between, is withheld unless we bow the knee to them, submit in a way never demanded by my father, a way that is not our custom. Their help is withheld unless we bow to their proud blood. Well I am of the blood and Berin too, and we do not demand that any kneel to us. But we plead that those who value right above wrong fight on at our side."

As though suddenly embarrassed by her own eloquence, Branwen's throat dried, the words simply stopped. She stood staring blankly at the crowd gathered around her. She heard a roaring in her ears; the light had suddenly assumed an unreal quality; faintly, as though at a great distance, she heard a cheer, then Ened was at her side, hugging her and Aedd, hugely comforting, mumbling deep behind his beard, "Well said lass, well said."

CHAPTER 25

"You must keep still, Berin," Bronwen admonished as he jerked once more from the pain. "If you had only let me treat you at the beginning and let Aedd get on, you wouldn't have this trouble. Now look, the blood has dried and stuck your shirt to the wound. I'll have to cut it and then soak it off."

Berin grimaced as Aedd continued his report. Branwen cut and sponged.

"We've filled the gaps with timber braces. We took two logs off the wall. They'll not fall for that one again, more's the pity, and I put out that straw in the ditch like you told me."

"What about arrows and sling stones?" Berin asked.

"We've plenty, but I've had them re-stacked, especially around the gate.

"How many are we?"

"We lost eight all told, not counting poor Madwg here," he said, turning to look fondly but sadly at the ashen-faced man lying on the litter next to the fire. He was watched over patiently, lovingly, but despairingly, by Rhian, his wife, her drawn face already that of a mourner. "Rh'on says he'll probably not last the night. He lost too much blood. Then there was the shock when the wound was cauterised."

Berin winced at the memory of the agonising screams as Rh'on, gritting her teeth and shuddering, had held the heated stones to Madwg's raw stump. The poor wretch had threshed and screamed, nearly breaking his back with the violence of its arching, his pain mirrored in the sweating faces of his kinsmen and friends holding him down.

"The wounded are much the same as yourself; flesh wounds, able and willing to fight. None of the bad wounds still live; thirty three of us, no, thirty four counting Brys."

Silently, grimly they looked at each other, measuring the odds.

"Look Berin, if it's all the same to you, I'd like to go now, to Ened."

Berin looked at his friend. The thought had no need to be spoken; one more meeting, possibly the last chance to be together, to seek mutual reassurance in physical closeness. Berin felt an irrational surge of jealousy because Olwen was not there, but castigated himself. At least she was safe.

"Of course," Berin said. "You go now."

Berin winced as Branwen pulled the last of the blood-caked shirt away. Her hands were soft and gentle. She bathed the spear gash with a solution of woundwort, drawing in her breath at the sight of the flesh gaping, yet thrilling to the touch of his skin, the hard muscles beneath her finger tips.

Berin was the last of the wounded to be treated. Rh'on, Ened, Gwyn and Cigfen had long since tidied their things away and left, left Rhian to her lonely vigil with Madwg and Branwen to treat her Berin. The silence lengthened and became uncomfortable. Berin felt a tension between them. Branwen made a pad of woundwort and pressed it to the wound, reaching around Berin's waist to bandage it in place. As she did, she pressed herself to him. He felt her soft breasts crushed warm on his back, knowing now what before he had only suspected, knowing too that the tension was real and double-edged, not the product of his imagination, knowing that Branwen wanted, expected too.

"There, you should rest now. Go and lie down. I'll fetch you something to eat."

"But I should check..."

"How often must you check the same things. All the plans that can be made are made. The wounded are attended to, the dead are beyond help. The living are fed and are resting; the watch is set. Now it is time for you to rest. Your people need you tomorrow."

Berin went to his quarters reflecting on the good sense shown by someone so young. A fire had been lit and the furs spread beside it. Tapers had been wedged into a roof support. With a groan, Berin stretched on the furs, favouring his injured side, suddenly aware of his aches and pains and tiredness.

How are we going to survive the coming day, he thought? The outlanders are so strong with their bronze. If only that business with Tarok and Ened had not happened. If only Tarok and his men had stayed. It had always been a gamble calling Tarok back with that bad blood between him and Aedd. At least their arrival had helped them to survive the day. But it could not be undone now. Aedd had right on his side. Surely it had been proper not to hand Aedd and Ened over to Tarok. Could I have handled it differently, better? He wondered. Which ever way he looked at it, the result was the same, Tarok was gone and all his men with him. Tarok must be mad. Divided, the outlanders could pick them off settlement by settlement; enslave them all, like those poor devils Aedd had talked about. Tarok must have been mad to risk the entire tribe for his prick. Urak was behind it somewhere, that piece of bat shit. I

332

should have jumped the bank and slit the treacherous bastard's throat.

Thank Dana for Branwen. For a moment he had thought that Creggan and Iowerth were going to desert him. Branwen had changed all that, bless her. What a girl. She wanted him. She had made that clear enough. She had stayed out of love for him, persuaded the men of the ford to stay too.

The curtain lifted. Branwen came in, dropping the hide behind her, shutting out the night and breaking Berin's reverie. She handed Berin a dish laden with a flat cake of rough barley bread and a steaming pig's hock, and then a pitcher of ale. Berin discovered that he was famished. Branwen watched him eating. She was content for the moment with the small service she had done him.

Berin broke some bread for her and a piece of meat. She bit delicately with white teeth, licking lips clean of the glistening fat with the pinkest of tongues, not taking her eyes from him. As he licked his fingers, she bent over his feet, pulling at the heels of his boots. The neck of her shirt fell forward. Berin watched her small, proud breasts jostle each other as she struggled at her task. She looked up and followed his gaze. She coloured, but made no attempt to cover herself.

"Thank you Branwen. You should go now. You need to rest too."

She did not move or answer. The tension returned, an ultimatum to deeds not attempted, imploring speech. Berin put down his bowl. She reached to take it and their fingers touched. Gently Branwen took his hand and lifted captured fingers to her lips.

"I would like to stay, if you'll let me," Branwen mumbled, averting her eyes. "I'm afraid... afraid to be alone...I don't want to be alone tonight," she added, in a firmer voice, looking at him with renewed determination.

He should deny her, himself too, he admitted. There was Olwen, dear Olwen, but Olwen was safe and tomorrow Branwen and he could be raven's bait. Life viewed so foreshortened seemed all at once to be so sweet, so precious. He stroked her cheek with the backs of his fingers. Such a generous girl, kind and thoughtful, courageous, loving...loving, he thought, with an inward shrug of self deprecation. She had been sent to him, away from her own people, had given him her loyalty and support when he needed them most, though it might cost her life. Why should she love him when he had given her nothing but a lien on her soul.

Berin reached his hand around behind her curls to bring her lips to his. She approached at his urging, jerkily resistant, unsure, unwilling yet to admit too eagerly to wanting. They touched lips. Berin found them sweet, fragrant, soft, springing back at first then softening against his. Delicately he traced the inner edges of her lips with his tongue tip. She drew back, surprised, but at gentle pressure, returned to delight at the new sensation.

Berin stroked with open palm and then with finger tips from shoulder, down the back of her arm, raising gooseflesh. Imperceptibly at first, but with growing resonance, Branwen began to tremble. Gently Berin, as much entrapped by mood as Branwen, touched her breast, feeling it harden, firm and taut, the nipple pushing forward for attention. Branwen gasped and drew away again, half fearing her own reaction.

Berin took the bow tied in the drawstring of her shirt and pulled. Branwen moistened her lips, her breaths short and quick, her trembling pronounced, yet eagerly she pursued him to the furs, pressing her lips to his while Berin slowly, gently slid his hand over her throat, slipping sly finger tips beneath the open neck of her shirt, stealthily stalking, touching and finally capturing taught mound and pinnacle. Branwen opened herself to sensation, crushing herself to him, subduing her trembling against the protective bulk of his body.

Lying length to length, she drew breath sharply at the hot touch of his hardness on her soft belly. His fingers traced a trail of arousal from cheek to breast, teasing her erect bud before smoothing their way across her fluttering stomach to her secret cleft. Trembling again, she clasped his wrist, stopping him, even as her thighs writhed with wanting. She pulled his head tighter to hers, deepening their kiss, loving the now familiar exhilaration, fearful of dark secrets alluded to in giggled kitchen gossip. Branwen wanted to postpone the ugly, to prolong the sweet tender excitement.

Berin trapped her hand. Excited by her resistance, he ignored the whimpered protest from beneath his demanding lips, and was excited still further by his own mastery. Gently his fingers stroked through her springy fuzz, pressing a rigid proxy between her thighs, gently thrilling, fomenting anticipation until the promise became too great to be born. Branwen opened her thighs then spread them wide to his questing fingers.

Tangled fingers parted lips, helping longed-for access. A conspiracy of hips overcame the last, utterly futile, pretended resistance. A sharp pain was ignored in the twice welcomed possession, lost in sweet frisson, a pushing,

335

pressing, prolonged delicious friction, until febrile sensation overpowered all but the last desperate lunge, the hot rush to reaffirm faith in tomorrow.

CHAPTER 26

Olwen frowned in the darkness and sighed deeply. Since the taper had burned out, all she could see was the pale black of the smoke hole and a dull glow from the hearth. Sleep eluded her, though her eye-lids were heavy. Her eyes were itchy and her head thick, as though stuffed with wool. Resentfully, she listened to A'isa's deep regular breathing on the other side of the hearth. The dire mind pictures would not dissipate. Each time she blinked them away, they returned. Determinedly she thought of Berin. He was chief now. They could be wed, but where or when? How could they live together if she was to remain an outcast? How could she ever leave this place? Urak would come for her, take her. He would make her pay for her desertion. Olwen shivered.

Where was Berin? He should not have left her so soon. Was he well? Talwch had news of a party of outlanders travelling along the West Way, and of smoke from the direction of Ilws. Pray Dana he was safe. She could not bear it if he were lost to her now. What if he were wounded? Who would look after him? Rh'on or Branwen? Jealousy struck like an assassin's knife. Branwen was there, promised to him, fecund, his to take, and so pretty. Even now they could be... Olwen sat up with a start, the borrowed furs dropping from her; a chill draft from the doorway curled around her waist.

Feeling the familiar prickle and pressure, she padded through the door and raising her skirt, squatted. The watchman, crouched by the fire in his cloak, inclined his head sideways, a registration of her presence and turned his back. Sparks flew as he threw another log on to the fire

337

to warm himself and enliven the dark and cold lonely
night. It would have been frosty but for the clouded sky,
she thought, glad of the shelter of the bothey, which held so
much of the heat of the fire. She pitied the hunting party,
spread around the camp fires, wrapped into so many
cocoons in their skins and trade blankets. Only Talwch
slept peacefully in a tent. Shivering, Olwen ducked back
into the hut.

A'isa sat up. "What's the matter?" she asked sleepily.
"Are you all right?"

"Yes, go back to sleep."

"You're worried, aren't you; worried about Berin? Don't.
Father's sent men to watch. He'll be all right, you'll see.
He's wonderful," A'isa mumbled, already half-way back to
sleep.

"Yes, he is, isn't he," Olwen replied, snuggling back into
her furs, finding with relief the residual body warmth. She
remembered their first love-making as she curled into her
familiar sleeping position. She would give him a fine son.
Oh what a loving it had been that had made him; such
pleasure in her surrender. How he had held her to him,
filled her. She could feel him, smell him, taste him. As she
rolled restlessly on to her back the image flickered and
changed. Branwen reappeared briefly, then the familiar
frightening picture returned. She was lying on a rush
covered floor, bound, naked; it was cold and dark. The bar
on the door was removed and a shaft of light struck across
the room. Urak had returned to her. He stood over her,
dark and ominous, powerful. In her picture, she moaned,
knowing she would do anything to please him, anything he
demanded. In her waking dream, he released her bonds.
She sprawled before him, spreading her thighs, opening her

338

arms to show her breasts. He stirred her with his foot. She knelt before him, wanting...

Branwen did not want to sleep. She felt as if she never wanted to sleep again, unwilling to miss the smallest portion of the wonderful life revealed to her, a life so full, full to bursting with Berin. So that's what it's all about, she mused. No wonder there's so much fuss made about it. No wonder. She squeezed her thighs together, sending a delicious tremor coursing through her body. She felt unreal, light-headed, detached, so happy yet curiously threatened. She tried to analyse her mood. It was as if now she had something to lose. No, it was worse than that, as if she was going to lose something. Oh Dana, not Berin, she thought. I've only just found him. She pressed herself tighter to his warm body, wondering at the hard but fuzzy texture of his leg as she raised her smooth inner thigh along it, bending to kiss the base of his throat.

Berin stirred and grunted with pain as the movement caught the edges of his wound. He felt her lips, dry but soft on him, the wet tip of her tongue, her hair tickling his face, her arm and leg thrown over him, he could even feel her fragrance.

"What's the matter?" she asked. "Did I hurt you? I'm sorry."

"No, I'm all right; just caught a bit, that's all. Why aren't you asleep?"

"Can't. I'm not used to sharing a bed, I suppose."

"I'd better go then."

"Don't you dare. I'm going to keep you here for ever."

"What, here?"

"Mmmm, yes, just there."

"Berin?"

"Yes?"

"Do we have a chance tomorrow?"

"Of course."

"You don't have to lie to me."

"Shh, it'll be all right. We saw them off today; we'll see them off again."

"If we don't, if anything happens, I want you to know that you have made me very happy. I'm the happiest girl in the world. I love you."

Berin was silent, touched. They kissed, she opening her mouth wide to him, holding him frantically.

"I love you too," he said. He might have done too, at that moment, he thought, but anyway the lie was the least she deserved.

"You don't have to," she answered seriously, "say it, I mean. But I'm glad that you did, even if you don't mean it, even if it all ends tomorrow."

"It will be all right. We've a few surprises for them," he said quietly, thinking that lying was becoming a habit

"But then what? No one will come to help us. How many times can we hold them off?"

"As many as it takes. We have to. It's our land, our home."

"No, I mean what about next year, or the year after? There just aren't enough of us here to manage on our own. Sooner or later they'll get us."

"We could manage if we had bronze. We've only a few spears of our own and the things that we've taken from them."

"Can't we get some?"

"The outlanders and Sennot, Dana rot him, control the bronze trade on the Great River."

"Is there no other way?"

"Ened tells a tale of bronze makers in the far west, but all we have to trade is our cattle, wool and hunting dogs. We would have to travel the West Way with the herds. The outlanders would get us in no time."

"Berin, I have something to trade, something easily carried and very valuable. My mother gave it to me. Amber and jet, copper and gold. No listen to me," she hurried on as Berin tried to interrupt. "Warwch has it. He has my orders to give it to you if anything happens to me."

"Nothing will happen to you."

"Well anyway, you can trust Warwch. He was devoted to my mother. She brought him up. You made him your slave when you freed him."

"Branwen, I don't know what to say."

"Then say nothing my love. I am yours. It's natural that all I have is yours. Oh I wish we could just leave. Can't we leave, go somewhere else?"

"Leave? But this is our home, my inheritance. It's..." Berin struggled to express the depth of his sense of belonging, the enormity of what she was suggesting.

"Anyway, there's nowhere for us to go. The outstation is closed because I won't give up Aedd and Ened to Tarok's revenge. I can't go to the ford because of Olwen and Oranc. Urak will have me killed for what I did. You know that he's plotting with the outlander."

"Is he? I believe anything of him. He's so evil."

"I followed him. He met the outlander, the one who attacked us first."

"I heard about that. You had a dreadful row, you and Com and Urak."

"I'm sure he had something to do with stopping help from reaching us from the ford that first time, but I could never prove it, and father just wouldn't listen to me. Urak had him twisted around his little finger."

"He's like that, very persuasive. I'm sure he kept father drugged so he didn't know day from night. But what did he want with Olwen? I can guess what he wanted with....what's his name, Oranc? The girls said... well they said he's...he's the other way. He likes little boys."

"He kept them locked up; whipped her... and I don't like to think of what else. I had to free her."

"You love her very much, don't you?"

Berin was silent, nonplussed, not knowing where to look.

"It's all right, you know. I've known since the beginning. I mind of course, but I'll share you if I have to," she said softly then added fiercely, "only I want some of my share now," as she straddled him and began to rock.

CHAPTER 27

Aedd turned to Berin, his big, normally genial face reflecting his perplexity. "Maybe they've just buggered off," he ventured, unconvincingly.

Berin looked at him as if he had taken leave of his senses.

"Then why don't they attack?"

"I don't know. Maybe they think it's a trick, Tarok going like that last night."

"They probably just can't believe their luck."

"Perhaps they're worried he's going to sneak around and take them by surprise once they start their attack."

"That arrogant bastard. I should have killed him."

"What and have Urak as High Chief?"

Aedd grimaced.

"Anyway, they've given us time to get ready properly. You put out the resin and tallow and the torches are ready?"

"Aye, that's all done."

"The forked poles for the ladders?"

"Aye that too. That's the trouble, the men have too much time to think, too much time to remember and worry."

Berin pulled his cloak around him against the chill breeze, favouring his wounded side, praying that the dull greyness of the day did not portend rain. He glanced upwards. The paler patch of sky high in the south suggested it was mid-day.

"Why not stand them down. Let them eat. Just leave the watch."

"I'll see to it."

Aedd passed the word to the nearest group and crossed to the communal hall and kitchen, empty of wounded since Madwg died in the empty hours before dawn, as quietly and unobtrusively as he had lived. The men stacked their weapons and drifted after him.

Berin took off the bronze-bound helmet, setting it down on a ledge next to where his spear and shield lent against the bank. He hitched up his sword belt and straightened the leather jerkin sewn with bronze plates, running a finger around the seam, where it chafed under the armpit. If only all his men had arms and armour like these that he had taken from the outlanders, the outlanders would not be such a threat. With the advantage of the stronghold they would be able to wait, able to keep them at bay until they tired of their losses.

He gazed out over the ridge, the familiar path to Ilws, to friends and kin, now threatening instead of beckoning. A thin plume of smoke rose as it had all morning, showing that the houses were occupied. Berin felt anger rise, surging hot and acid in his throat, at the thought of them there, eating, sleeping in the houses built by Han and Kar, Arec and Madwg, dead now, killed by the defilers of their hearths.

Berin walked the rampart, checking the bracings here, a pile of sling-stones there, talking to the watchmen, pausing to look down on the settlement, his birthplace, his settlement now, the centre of his world. The long houses looked sad and lost without their people, grey and derelict without the smoke from their hearths, the cries of children, barking dogs, the call of an anxious mother. The gloomy skeletons of the beech wood provided a fitting frame.

"Berin, you should eat. Here, I've brought you some bread and cheese."

Berin turned to see his mother, wan and pale, her face deep etched by recent events, yet smiling her concern for him.

"Thank you mother, but I couldn't."

She put the food down and, smiling wryly at him, took his hands in hers, squeezing them, pressing the backs of his fingers with her thumbs. "What is it my son? What's the matter?"

Berin sighed, a lonely sound that caught at Rh'on's heart. "What isn't the matter, mother." He put his arm around her and turned to lean on the parapet. "Look, that's our home. There, by the big beech, father taught me to use a sling. Up there on the pasture, I made my first kill, a hare."

"I remember; it made a fine meal. You were so proud."

"There's where I used to sit when shepherding. You brought me my food then as you did just now. Up at the top there, where the gap in the trees is, that's where we found Belu in the snow. I thought we'd lost him, he was so still, cold and blue when we got him home."

"We nearly did."

"And now we have, and father too, and it's left to me. Am I to be the one after all the generations since Harac who have toiled here, made it, cared for it, loved it; am I to be the one who will lose our homes, our land, our lives to Afon'ken and the outlanders?"

Rh'on looked up, tears starting in her own eyes at the sight of those in her son's. She squeezed him. "What must be must be. Your father's advice was to trust to your heart, Berin. He knew of your capacity for love, it was not something he shared with you, or even understood, but he loved you; he loved our home, our people, our land as you do, and at the end he trusted you. Whatever you decide will be right. I have faith in you as your father had, as your people have."

"But I don't know what to do. I have followed my heart and this is where it has brought me. I wouldn't give up Aedd and Ened and so lost the help of Tarok. I had to free Olwen and Oranc and so lost the ford. Now we're alone and dying mother. Amren, Naf, Han, Kar, Arec, Madwg, the men of the ford. How many more must die following my heart?"

"I do not know. I know only that they will follow you gladly, whatever you decide. It makes me very proud."

The watchman's cry ended their conversation, sending Berin running to his arms at the gate, Rh'on hurrying to her bandages and salves, but not before she had reached up to kiss Berin, saying "May Dana watch over you, my son."

"Over all of us mother, over all of us," he had replied.

Berin rammed on his helmet and took up shield and spear. The enemy was massing on the knoll. At first there seemed no order to the ants' nest of soldiery, then the milling crowd coalesced into serried ranks of Afon'ken and two columns of outlanders. A horn sounded and the army advanced. Berin felt suddenly weak, enfeebled. How dared he oppose such force.

"They must be over a hundred strong," he muttered out of the side of his mouth to Aedd.

346

"Aye," answered Aedd, loud enough for their neighbours to hear, "but they can only come over the wall one leg behind the other, like anyone else."

A ripple of laughter spread around the parapet. A cheer went up; "For Berin, for Com's and Ilws and the ford."

Berin straightened, wondering at their simple faith in him. Little did they understand the frailty of his grip on himself, let alone on events.

As they came within bow shot, the ranks of Afon'ken planted their hurdle fence and their archers took up position. A horn sounded loud and startling and they loosed the first stabbing shower to envelop the parapet, the arrows clattering as they fell spent, or whistling into the enclosure beyond, some even hitting the thatch and the hurdle walls of the shelters, making mothers gather their children under their arms. Some found softer targets with a wet thwack. Men fell, clawing at their pain, staring in disbelief at their own blood, surprised at its redness, its heat, its slippery feel. Most dropped unhurt behind the bank, grasping their weapons tighter, for reassurance. Berin, watching at the gate, flashed a quick smile at Branwen, who had rushed forward, skirts flying, to the side of Cranwch, her bondman who had taken an arrow in the shoulder. His heart lifted and surged at her grin, at the glint in her eyes.

Berin waited until the first of the attackers were at the wall and the outlanders' arrow storm died for fear of hitting their own men.

"Now!" yelled Berin.

As one, the men of Com, Ilws and the ford rose above the parapet and hurled stones, shot arrows, not aiming, not needing to, for they could almost touch the seething

347

screaming maelstrom of aggression. Almost as automatons the defenders created a barrier of missiles between themselves and their attackers. Men of Afon'ken began to die, unable even to get to grips with their tormentors, without even having struck a blow. They buckled and fell, some with a screech, some with a moan, some silently. The living stumbled over the bleeding bruised bodies of their comrades, slipping in the blood where the dying was thickest. Yet three ladders were pushed through the heaving press of bodies and thumped against the bank. The horn sounded again, barely heard above the battle din. The outlanders trotted purposefully towards the ladders, menacing in their armour.

"Make ready," shouted Berin.

Iowerth, Warwch and his men pushed the forked poles under the topmost rungs of the ladders and heaved. Archers dropped their bows, sling men their slings, to stab and thrust with spears, hack with axes, desperation rising as more and yet more of Afon'ken struggled on to the bank. The defenders were lifted beyond panic to unthinking survival reflexes in a sickening orgiastic killing frenzy. Ladders toppled, but the outlanders were at the wall, setting them back again, rallying.

"Now!" Berin screeched.

Torches lit at Berin's warning arced hot and flaring, trailing smoke, sputtering sparks over the bank and into the ditch. The prepared thatching straw, tallow and resin caught alight and flared bright. In vain the attackers nearest to the torches, seeing the danger, stamped and danced on the spreading flames. They cried warnings to their fellows, scrambled, fell, pushed back away from the growing heat. Too little, too late. The ditch flashed in a blaze of orange-red heat, searing, scorching, curling up around blackening legs, blistering, frizzling hair. Those caught by the press of their brothers-at-arms briefly envied dead comrades at their feet, before joining them to add their fury to that of the fire. The din of battle changed pitch, from a low clashing roar to a shrill communal shriek. Attackers on the parapet, with flames at their backs, clothes singed, boots smoking, jumped into the stronghold to be surrounded by semi-circles of probing spears, wild beasts at bay. All knew there would be no mercy. Some died quivering, cowering, whimpering, skewered by half a dozen quick and merciful thrusts. Others fought, roaring their defiance, until Berin ordered the men back and the archers and sling men had their way. The bravest and stupidest paid the greatest premium in pain.

Slowly the madness faded in men's eyes; some gagged, retching at the enormity of the killing, the stench of roasting flesh, of burnt wool, leather and hair. Others began to shake at the force of their own adrenaline surging through them with no target to pursue, or simply at the horror of a battle cameo, a severed limb, a split skull, blood sticking fingers together. Almost guiltily they looked at one another, then realising they had survived, at least to fight the next round, they cheered and cheered until their throats ached with their pleasure in life.

Berin and Aedd cheered as mightily as the others, dancing and skipping, capering like fools at a summer festival, then Aedd stopped, as though struck, staring over Berin's shoulder. Berin turned; Rh'on walked towards them in hesitant rushes, arms outstretched, ready to hold, to comfort. He knew, with a sudden dread certainty he knew the full enormity of what had happened without a word being spoken. Rh'on's hands, her eyes, her very stance told

349

him. He ran, past Rh'on, past jubilant survivors, past crying, still frightened infants, past laughing, squabbling boys collecting spent arrows, to the hall. There, where she had tended so many, lay Branwen.

She lay on her side, so quiet, so still, pale beneath the blanket. Berin felt for a pulse at her throat, heart jumping in relief as he found it. She opened her eyes at his touch.

"What is it Branwen?"

"Berin, I'm glad you could come. You drove them off?"

"Aye, they're gone, for the moment anyway."

She struggled for breath, her lips bluing behind the russet- pink.

"Don't talk. Its all right, I'm here."

"Must talk; too late soon," she gasped, reaching a hand through the folds of the blanket, searching for him. He took her hand in his, it felt frail, feeble.

"No Branwen, you must rest. Rh'on will tell you to rest to help make you better," he said, trying to reassure her, and himself, but panicking, looking up as Rh'on came and stood on the other side of the cot.

Rh'on lifted the blanket and Berin saw the arrow, shaft broken off, the alien head buried deep, deep in soft, tender, vulnerable Branwen. Rh'on gently shook her head.

"Wanted to say... say farewell," she wheezed. "Remember Warwch. Look after yourself. Oh.." she moaned, gripping his hand. "Hold me Berin, like you did last night," she whispered as she pressed his hand to her breast. "Warm me, its getting so cold."

Berin, speechless, numb, held her, felt her heart fluttering beneath his hand. She raised up, pressing herself against him.

"I love you. I've had my share." She coughed, a gob of lung blood trickled from the corner of her mouth. The fluttering stopped.

Berin had sat, still, pale, stunned, simply holding Branwen as she was, feeling her body cool. He had not noticed as Rh'on had dropped the screens, pushing inquisitive well-wishers away, scolding gently. He had not noticed Aedd organising work parties to replace burnt hurdles, repair damaged walls, strip the fallen of their arms, bury the dead, their own with reverence in a communal grave next to Com; the enemy tipped unceremoniously into the ditch and incinerated. The sights sounds and smells of life, of survival, the grumbles, laughter and tears of the garrison, and of death, the charnel pit, already attracting the black harbingers of ill omen, hopping, flapping, croaking around its cooling edges, went unseen and unheard. Rh'on came with food and left, came again and removed the bowl of broth, cold and congealed, untouched. Berin noticed nothing.

There aren't enough of us here on our own. Sooner or later they'll get us. Can't we leave, go somewhere else? The words sang in his head, over and over and over again. Sooner or later they'll get us; get us; get us.

Berin cried.

Rh'on took his wrist and lifted it, limp and powerless from Branwen's cold breast. "Berin, we must bury her now."

He raised his face to her and she was shocked at the strain showing in the deep etched lines in his cheeks, the

351

dark, multi-ringed pouches, the pallor, but was hurt as only a mother can be at the pain she read in the depths of his eyes.

"Berin, the living need you now."

Wordlessly he reached behind his neck and unfastened the amber and greenstone clan necklace. He bent forward, tenderly lifting Branwen's curls and fastened it around her, settling the stones on her breast. Rh'on and Aedd glanced at each other, startled. The necklace was given to a man at his coming of age. It was a sign of his manhood, his clan, his tribe, but much more, it was his identity; it encapsulated his sense of belonging, of home, of place. No one ever took off a clan necklace.

Warwch stepped forward and bent to lift her. Berin reached out and touched his arm, motioning him to stop. He wanted to prolong the contact, to carry her on her last short journey himself. Warwch stood back, obedient to Berin's gesture, his head slumping, arms dropping uselessly at his sides. A tear fell on to the pile of his sheep skin jerkin, unnoticed except by Berin.

"Warwch, would you please carry your mistress?" Berin asked gently, recognising the pain in the man.

"Aedd, we must leave."

"But we beat them again today. They won't stay for much more of that sort of punishment. They'll give up."

"I doubt it. We lost another five ..."

"Four," interrupted Aedd.

"Well four then. We're less than thirty fighting men now."

"They lost a score today."

"Aye, but how many outlanders?"

"Five."

"We can't fight bronze with stone."

"We've done all right so far."

"So far, that's exactly my point. What happens the next time, next year, the year after, or any time we're taken by surprise? We are not strong enough to stand alone, not here, not without bronze, and they control the trade."

"But Berin, this is our land, our home. Our... well our ancestors... it's... everything," answered Aedd, stumbling over the words in his perplexity at having to express emotions he believed to be so universally held that they needed no word picture.

"So, are we all to die so that we can remain on it? Has there not been enough slaughter? Have you not seen enough blood? Wasn't little Cas, with the first flight of arrows on the first day enough? Olwen, Oranc, you and I rescued the little fellow from the outlander, remember? Now he's dead, next to his father. Branwen..." he caught his breath. "What had she done to pay such a price? Or slavery, what about that? How do you fancy Ened in one of those gangs you were telling us about?"

"Berin, please," Rh'on interjected. "Don't be so hard on Aedd, he's only saying what we're all thinking."

Berin grimaced a wry apology.

"But where would we go? The ford?" Aedd asked.

"No Urak rules there now, or Tarok. Either way its death to you and me."

"Our people could go," Rh'on said.

"Yes and be made slaves, mother, just as the outlanders will, if they take them alive. Dorn has gone. Tarok and Urak aren't the same as him. You should hear them talk. It's as if they are born with the right to be obeyed."

"Where then, Berin," Rh'on asked. "You must have some idea?"

"There's a hill out in the marshes," Berin began.

"What, the outlands, the wetlands? They're full of wild beasts and savages," Rh'on objected.

"There's a hill out in the marshes I found when I was hunting," Berin continued. "No one could attack us, unless they found the secret way and even then we could defend it easily. There's a sweet water spring, enough land to support us. We could take a few breeding stock, seed corn, ploughs, start again."

"What, abandon our herds?" queried Aedd, shocked.

"That, or our lives."

"But winter is coming," Rh'on quibbled.

"Together we would manage. There's still time to hunt game, smoke it. Plenty of wildfowl in the marshes. We wouldn't starve." Berin turned from them and looked down towards the settlement, then towards Ilws and then the inside of the fort, sweeping his arm around as though to embrace it all. "All my life is here. I love it dearly, but without the people, it's only grass and trees, air, earth and water. If we leave them, our houses will rot and fall; the fields will grow wild again and before a generation has passed, our being here will barely be noticed, except for this," he said, patting the bank, " and Belu's tomb. Both are a symbol of our doom."

There was a long silence, broken finally by Auron, "Well if you've decided Berin, that's good enough for me."

Aedd looked at Rh'on. "What do you say? You are our lore- keeper," he said.

"Man has always been discontented, greedy. The story of our fall from grace isn't just about a single event in the past. It's in our nature; we repeat it time after time, in different ways." She was silent for a while, frowning, concentrating on finding the right words. "Our ancestors were lucky. There was land enough for all. Too much if we look at what they have given back to Earth Mother. Men had enough to eat, to drink. All used the same tools, to farm, the same weapons to hunt. Each was as strong as the other; there was no need to fight. Men were content, perhaps too content. We have prospered, perhaps we have forgotten how to struggle." Rh'on sighed and smiled wearily at each of them. "Then the outlanders came with their bronze. It gives power to those who have it, leaves weakness with those who don't. Power begets a yearning for greater power, the strong dominate the weak. Senot seeks to dominate Dorn, Tarok seeks to dominate Com and Ilws. Because he is strong he feels above the law. Urak...well who can understand what drives him? We are in the middle of a fall from grace, the beginning of a new age."

"Yes Rh'on," Aedd pressed gently, "but what do we do?"

"I am of the old age, Aedd, and so I must follow Com. I think you have one foot in my age too, for you find it hard enough to accept what Berin has to tell us." She smiled affectionately at the huge man, his forehead creased with the effort of following Rh'on's reasoning. "Com entrusted us to Berin because he is his heir, it's true, but also because he recognised the good side of the new age in Berin. Com's advice to Berin was that he should follow his heart. I think that's what we should do."

The silence lengthened as Aedd pondered, weighing his misgivings against the advice and opinions of the other elders. He had no alternative suggestion to make. "So be it then," Aedd agreed.

The laden oxen led by their halters swayed through the gate. Last in the winding column of refugees, they were barely visible against the blackness beyond the reach of the fires. The cattle left behind lay quietly, lowing gently to their departing brethren, bemused at the unaccustomed nocturnal activity. The sheep lay still, lighter blobs in the dark. Pigs grunted and snored contentedly in their sties.

Berin regretted leaving the stock, but to drive them through the darkness would slow them down and dramatically increase the chances of discovery. As it was he was far from certain that he could bring the breeding pairs safely through the marshes, or find enough winter fodder for them once there. He started as a shadow flickered at his side. "Ah Warwch, so you come to say farewell too."

"The mistress said I should watch over you," he said simply.

"Then pray you are not busy tonight."

Berin turned to the mounds of newly turned earth, wanting to feel a bond, some continuing attachment to the tangible Branwen, but found just emptiness, an ache. The grave was just a grave. "Have you gone then already?" he whispered. "Rest with Dana, Branwen." Turning to Com's burial place he added "and you too father, but show me please, where is the heart I am to follow?"

CHAPTER 28

The spear thrust split bone. I fell, through an appalling bottomless blackness that reeked of burning. I became aware that I lay drenched with sweat on a bed, my bed. The dream had been so real that for a time I disputed reality; but the dim outline of the window in its customary place slowly registered in my befuddled senses and put me in my place. I rolled from beneath the covers and fumbled the window closed against the stale fumes of the bonfires. The night air was cold against my sweat. I switched on the light and reached for my bathrobe. The whiskey had left a sour taste. I really wanted a glass of water.

Pippa's light came on, a bright line beneath her bedroom door.

"Are you all right, Dad?"

"Yeah. Sorry to wake you. Go back to sleep."

"Are you sure?" she insisted.

"I'm fine. Just had a dream. Got up for a glass of water."

"What were you dreaming about? You were moaning away there like a good 'un. Like Mr Belcher's bull."

"Nothing really," I answered. "Just a bit of a Stone Age ding-dong. Too much yarning with Rebecca and too much whisky with Les, I reckon."

"Huh," she said with all the expression that a teenager manages to pack into a monosyllable. "Might have known Rapunzel would be in the story somewhere."

"Pippa," I said on a rising note of warning. Pippa's light went out.

"Yes Dad?" she answered innocently.

"Go to sleep."

"Yes Dad."

She was right though, I reflected as I settled back in bed. Rebecca did feature in the story, if not in the dream. I wished her success with her project. There was an alertness, a brightness, a 'can-do' attitude about her which attracted me as much as the curve of her welcoming smile... though it was the curve of her breast that filled my thoughts as I drifted back to sleep.

But the dreams didn't finish there. I entered one of those trance-like states in which you are either asleep and dream of being awake or you are actually awake, but so tired that you are incapable of rational thought. Sarah came to me some time before dawn. She sat on the side of my bed, inclined her head and smiled wistfully.

"Go home," she said.

I reached out to her. She shook her head, smiled sadly and vanished.

Go home echoed in my head.

"Hiyah Pops," Pippa greeted me, spreading Vegemite on the toast, which she waved in salute.

"What's the time," I answered somewhat ungraciously, rubbing the glue from my eyes and exploring my teeth with my tongue. My mouth felt as though a gerbil had made its nest there.

"Seven thirty. I'm late. Melanie and me..."

"And I. Melanie and I."

"Whatever. We're going cross country up on the Ridgeway. Last day before Mel has to go back to school, so it's our last chance for a decent ride."

"The Ridgeway? What's that?"

"Mel reckons it's an old drover's route up on the Downs. It follows the high ground and you have great views; and its real country. No cars. It sounds really cool."

"Are you going to be all right? What if something happens."

"What's going to happen?"

"I don't know: anything. The horse bucks you off. You get molested. It pours with rain. You get hungry. Your horse picks up a boy scout in its shoe. I don't know what happens to young girls out riding."

"Oh Dad. Nothing will happen. Mel rides there all the time. Viv and Les are cool about it. We're taking waterproofs and a packed lunch. And a mobile 'phone."

"Hmmh... well I suppose so."

"Great. Can I make you some breakfast?" Pippa asked.

I shook my head. "Coffee would be good."

Pippa looked at me knowingly. She began to say something, smiled and thought better of it.

"How would you feel about staying in England for a while, like three months or so, say until Christmas?" I asked.

Pippa was silent for a long moment. Her eyes widened as my words registered.

"What here?" she shrieked incredulously. "You're kidding. You are kidding, right? I mean what about school. No, no I can't believe I said that. Of course. Yes. Yes Yes!"

"As for school, we'll have to see about getting you in at Melanie's."

"Wow, yes. But what about your business?"

I shrugged my shoulders. "Steve will take care of the business. It seems to be going really well with him in charge. Your schooling...well your high school will still be there when we get back. People say travel broadens the mind. Let's see what it does to yours."

"Oh Dad, I couldn't think of anything nicer." She came to me and gave me a hug. She looked up, eyes shining, but not blinded. "Is everything all right... I mean... back home?"

"Sure," I lied easily. There seemed no reason why anyone needed to learn so young what shits so-called grown up people can be.

"It's very good of you to see me," I said, taking Father Dominic's proffered hand at the door to the vicarage.

"I normally try and have a quiet day on Monday," he said.

"I'm sorry," I said hurriedly. "Of course, how stupid of me, Sunday is your busy day. We can do this another time..."

"No no, now is fine. I was going to add that I can't resist delving into parish records and I do so love a mystery. Your 'phone call really whetted my appetite."

361

Father Dominic ushered me into his study. "What year are we looking for," he asked.

"I'm not entirely sure. Not long after the end of the war. About nineteen forty seven or eight. It could even be nine."

"Hmmm..." Father Dominic rummaged in a stack of bound registers. "Here we are. You look through this one and I'll try these. Remind me about your parents... What names are we looking for?"

"Louise Berry and Michael Allen."

Father Dominic shooed a fat marmalade coloured cat from a frayed wing-back chair and gestured to me to sit. The cat looked me up and down, decided I wasn't worthy of her attention, stretched and set her claws into the chair's upholstery.

Father Dominic sat at his battered leather-topped pedestal desk. I relaxed into the chair and started to turn the pages. Half an hour later, we had to admit defeat.

"Sorry," Dominic said, gesturing at the pile of registers. "Where ever they were married, it doesn't appear to have been at St Andrew's."

I nodded glumly in agreement. "I was so sure I would find a record of them."

"Don't despair. Look here, why don't I check these through again more systematically. Maybe there are pages missing or even a whole volume. Or perhaps they married in a Registry Office. You could try Abbotsford; it's the closest."

"I'll try, of course, but I don't think so." I remembered the dog-eared photograph of my mother and father, smiling self consciously from the shadow of an arched church doorway.

"I'll have another look and call you," Father Dominic said quietly as, we smiled our goodbyes at the doorway to the vicarage. I was grateful for his sympathetic tone, but I felt despondent, adrift in a place of strangers. Sarah's words from my dream rang in my mind.

Planting railway sleepers in muddy gravel is guaranteed to frustrate, exhaust and foul up a body. When Les suggested we knock off, shower and count our abrasions in the pub before supper at his place, I was more than happy to agree. Charlie and Harry, Rebecca's students, had stripped back the grass from quite an area of the orchard, and were laying out a survey grid.

"Found anything," I asked, like an angler returning along a river bank asking about a fellow enthusiast's catch.

"Load of old rubbish really," Charlie said, jerking a thumb towards a box. "Horse shoe, nails, a bolt, a bit of old harness buckle, some pieces of bottle glass and china. Usual stuff for the grass root horizon. It won't get interesting until the first lift when the boss gets back on the job tomorrow."

"Be sure to leave at least two metres around the fruit trees" I cautioned.

"Yeah, Beccy's already warned us."

'Beccy,' I thought, wondering at and feeling jealous at the implied familiarity.

There was no sign of Pippa in the Granary, or in Les and Viv's Aga-warm kitchen when I hauled my heavy bath-crinkled body through the door. But Les was there, brushed-up and welcoming. I savoured the scent of his pipe tobacco and the companionable silence, walking the few hundred metres to the pub. The warm air, redolent with spilt beer and tobacco that greeted us when Les held open the front door of 'The Crown', was equally comforting. The aseptic, refrigerated air of an Australian pub, with its melamine or zinc topped bar and glass fronted cooler cabinets lay hemispheres and generations of experience away.

· "Two pints of bitter, Cyril," Les demanded. "Quiet in here tonight," he added. We were the only customers.

"It was until you came in," Cyril, the landlord answered lugubriously, wiping an imaginary spillage from the highly polished bar top.

The door was flung back on its stop to admit a fresh-faced bespectacled pin-stripe suited commuter. Many women would have killed for his 'peaches and cream' complexion.

"What a day," the newcomer announced. "The usual please, Landlord. What a day."

"And what would the usual be Sir," Cyril asked. "And it's Cyril."

"Oh... I see... one of your little jokes. A half pint, please...ah... Cyril."

Cyril placed our pints on the drip mat. "That'll be three sixty," he said to Les. Cyril plucked a half pint glass from the rack above the bar. I motioned to Les that I would pay and pulled some change from my pocket.

"Have those on me, Les old boy," the newcomer said. "I'm sorry, we haven't met," he added holding out his hand. As I shook it, Les announced, "Mike Robinson, this is John Allen."

I should have guessed from the opening exchange and from the looks exchanged between Cyril and Les that Mike Robinson was not exactly entertainment of choice at the Crown. But I didn't and accepted his kind offer at face value, on Les's behalf.

"What a day," Robinson repeated, looking from face to face, begging the question. Les and Cyril were too experienced and I too much of a new boy to ask, so Robinson decided to tell us anyway.

"The seven twenty seven was late this morning, and when it finally arrived, it stopped in the wrong place on the platform. There was a real scrum at the door, I can tell you, but it was no use, I was too far back. The train was absolutely crammed with Swindon commuters, so no seat for yours truly. Then the escalators were out on the Bakerloo line. My secretary is off sick. The boss had a real moody. He'd been working all week-end. Another take over. No... don't ask, I can't tell you about it."

"Thank God for that," Les muttered.

Robinson failed to notice. "I think he's overworked. Anyway he pushed me damned hard all morning. I was so glad that I had an urgent lunch appointment. Even Clive, my boss..." he added by way of explanation "... couldn't object to a meeting with the tax auditor, even if actually it was only Trevor, my contact in the regional tax office. Clive will never know. Trevor will appreciate the lunch... rather good actually. But the second bottle of claret was too sleep-

365

making to go back to work on. So here I am," he said in triumph, beaming at us in turn. "Early home for once."

"So you are," Cyril said, and moved to the far end of the bar, where he busied himself polishing glasses.

"I say, you're the Australian fellow people have been talking about," Robinson exclaimed. I nodded in agreement. As the only Australian around, it seemed safe to assume I was the one that he meant out of a population of twenty million.

"You're not one of those bolshie types I've been reading about are you?" he asked. You know, republicans?

Something in his tone, perhaps the brusqueness of the question or his general supercilious air of condescension touched a nerve end somewhere in whichever part of the brain it is that deals with tribal memories and identity. I could also feel the tips of my ears burning, never a good sign.

"I don't know what you've been reading, but no, as it happens I'm not a republican. What about you?"

"The very idea," Robinson snorted. "No, of course I'm for the Her Majesty," he brayed. "How can you even begin to suppose…"

"There's been a fair amount of anti-royal family feeling flying around in the media over here recently," I replied. "The press…the TV…full of it!"

"There's no anti-royal feeling in England… well, not amongst people like us, anyway. I can't vouch for the great unwashed or the Scots… and the Welsh of course, have always been….well…Welsh."

"But…" I began.

"Just press talk. The lunatic left..." Robinson stated.

"So I imagined the Daily Mail articles, and Earl Spencer, and the crowd clapping..." I said quietly and maybe threateningly, because Cyril paused, glass in hand and glanced towards me.

"Well it's different over here. She's our Queen. We can express an opinion. It's ... like a family matter," Robinson waffled.

"So she's not Australia's Head of State?"

"Yes...yes she is."

"But she's not our Queen."

"Well no...not like she's our Queen."

"Strewth mate," I replied, affecting the broadest Australian accent I could muster. "At last I understand why ocker Aussies rate you Pommie dickheads a right load of anally retentive bastards."

Les snorted into his pint. Robinson turned pink.

"Well really..." he said indignantly. Robinson set his glass down on the bar and walked stiffly out of the door, as though living up to his new rubric.

Cyril walked back to our end of the bar, drew two pints and set them in front of us. "On the house," he said with a grin.

"You don't want to take any notice of Mike Robinson, Les soothed. "He's about as representative of people around here as..as ..." He gave up searching for a simile, defeated by the enormity of the problem.

"I blame it on in-breeding and too much self abuse at boarding school," Cyril interjected.

"But there again, most of us do accept our peculiar constitutional set-up," Les ventured, " and respect the Queen. Oh sure we wouldn't mind a bit of constitutional tinkering...say with hereditary peers and bishops losing the vote in the Lords, but we're pretty content on the whole. As for Australia, well I don't think we could give a toss whether you're a republic or not," Les concluded.

"That's good, because whatever the outcome of the republican debate, we Aussies couldn't give a toss about whether you give a toss or not," I retorted, feeling the long tendrils of tribal resentment twist and stir.

"What a lot of tossers," Cyril concluded.

Cyril deflated me immediately. We laughed. Les and I settled in the window alcove. I started to draw up a list of plants and price it up against a catalogue that Les had picked up at a local garden centre. "I'm sorry, Les," I said. "It seems very expensive. If only I could get trade price, I'm sure I could reduce the cost, but I just don't know my way around over here."

"Just give me the list," he said, "and I'll talk to some mates."

I scribbled a few more items and handed the list to him.

"How did you get on with the vicar? I forgot to ask."

"No luck, I'm afraid. They weren't married in Bernton."

"What about a Registry Office? Even if they weren't actually married there, they should have a record."

"The vicar suggested that. The problem is I remember a picture of their wedding, with the arched entrance of a church behind them. But I'll check it out later this week. Abbotsford... the Vicar said. I have to go anyway, to see the school."

We drew on our pints and Les sucked on his pipe. We fell into the companionable silence that is so familiar to men and anathema to women. At the bar, Cyril sucked his teeth and pondered yesterday's crossword puzzle.

The door crashed open. Rebecca burst into the room, saw us in the corner and embraced first Les and then me. I was tempted to hold on longer than I should, but over Rebecca's shoulder, I noticed Cyril eyeing us.

"Guys...I got it," Rebecca screamed. "Full funding. Field crew for two months, including a geophysics crew - not just resistivity, but ground penetrating radar too; laboratory time, carbon dating, differential thermal analysis, the lot. He even wants to do DNA tests on the local population. Yippee!"

Les and I looked on bemused as Rebecca capered and pranced in front of us. "Let me buy you a drink. Cyril, drinks all round," she commanded.

Cyril looked around and was confirmed in his pessimistic view of life. The last time anyone had ordered drinks all round in his pub had been to the account of Bob Maxwell, just before he left on a cruise. Cyril drew four pints and only just managed to feel optimistic about the fourth.

"He's completely lost it. Prof has been invited to comment on some TV show. Well it seems that the presenter picked up the story of that DNA study in Somerset... you know, the one I was telling you about the other night? About the Stone Age burial and the local community? Well... Prof obviously means to get top billing

369

with a story of his own. He wants me to take swabs of Bernton school children. It's such a long shot. I mean...really. Of course it will all be hushed up if it turns out negative. On the other hand, he could refute the other result. Yeah, that's what he'd do. But I've got my budget, so who cares. Who bloody well cares," she exclaimed, kissing Cyril as he set the drinks on the table. Well... I did, I realised, very much. Fancy kissing bloody Cyril. But when she'd done, she looked directly at me and held my eyes with hers.

CHAPTER 29

"Aha, the likely lads return," Viv announced as Les and I tumbled into the kitchen. I was relieved to see Pippa and Melanie perched side by side on the Aga. I still hadn't adjusted to the idea of my daughter being able to roam safely on the chalk uplands on the back of a very large powerful animal.

"Huh, more like men behaving badly," Melanie sniffed. Pippa giggled.

"Father Dominic phoned, John. Can you call him back," Viv said.

Viv shooed the girls from the Aga. "Will cheesy scrambled eggs do for supper?" she called, as I headed to the study.

"Father Dominic here."

"Ah hello. It's John Allen. You left a message for me to call you."

"Yes, Yes. Thanks for returning my call. Well I've checked the registers again, like I said I would, more systematically this time, in case something was missing. Unfortunately for you, they provide a continuous record for the period in question. No missing pages or volumes...nothing like that. I'm sorry."

"Oh..." I said foolishly, lost for words. "Oh... yes, of course. Well that seems to be that, then." I must have sounded as I felt, really glum, because he did his best to reassure me.

"Please try the Abbotsford Registry Office. That's where they would have been married in a civil service, assuming that is that they were married locally. Civil services were popular at that time, at the end of the war. Everyone wanted change..."

"Er.. yes, thank you Father Dominic," I interrupted, suddenly conscious that he had been speaking for a while without me having heard a word he had said. "I'll do that. Thank you for your trouble."

"Goodnight then, and God bless."

"Er...goodnight and thank you," I said awkwardly, wondering what I was to do with the blessing, or how I was to acknowledge it.

Les looked at me askance as I sat down at the table. I've never learnt to hide my feelings. I'd be hopeless at playing poker. Melanie and Pippa looked at me, then at each other and then down at their plates, clearly deciding it was not the moment for levity.

"There's no record of them being married here," I started to explain.

"What about a civil wedding?" Viv said helpfully as she put a plate of scrambled eggs in front of me. "Maybe they were married in a Registry Office. Abbotsford would be the nearest."

I struggled to contain my frustration. How many times would I be told that; how many times had I already been told that; yet their wedding photograph had clearly shown a church doorway in the background.

"You could look in tomorrow," Les added. "Aren't you planning to go into town anyway, to see Melanie's headmistress about Pippa going to St Margaret's?"

"Yeah, I suppose so...but their wedding photo shows a church door in the background. I don't hold out much hope."

"If you do go, the Registrar's office is in the council offices, right in the centre of town, off the market square. You go through the archway, opposite the old county hall. You can't miss that. It's a wonderful Restoration period building with an open arched undercroft."

I loved Abbotsford the moment I rounded the bend and crossed over the Thames. A glimpse from the bridge of the river, bounded by water meadows on one side and the town on the other bank; a tall church steeple, a squat fortress-like building, overhanging willows and Georgian red-brick houses, begged me to stop and stare, but the press of traffic launched me straight into the one way system and for a while I was too busy navigating safely to care. I ducked into a multi-storey car park with some relief, and decided to walk.

Melanie's school was a Victorian neo-gothic red brick pile that was partially covered in ivy. It was set amidst park-like lawns and trees. A circular drive in front of the main entrance enclosed a flower bed. The planting was so predictable that the grounds men clearly belonged to the local corporation school of gardening. I chided myself for being overcritical.

Mrs Belingham-Smythe, the headmistress was a formidable character, Dame Edna without the spectacles and of course without the accent. She greeted me effusively, asked after Viv, praised Melanie and said how happy she was to welcome Melanie's friend from Australia as a temporary day visitor. After I had thanked her for her kindness, I hesitantly outlined Pippa's predicament. Mrs Belingham-Smythe listened sympathetically, prompting me gently from time to time. I found myself pouring out the entire story; Sarah, Emily, Wayne and the larrikins, Dougie, Mr Mariner, the whole sorry saga. I stopped, suddenly aware that I'd let my mouth run away from me, worried that I'd completely queered Pippa's chances. I needn't have worried. Mrs Belingham-Smythe declared with a discrete sniff and with what seemed to me to be overly bright eyes, that she would be very happy to fit Pippa in for a term. Pippa would, however, have to wear uniform. She was sorry, but could make no exceptions. However I might care to take advantage of the second hand uniform shop run by the PTA. This seemed a particularly helpful suggestion after Mrs Belingham-Smythe had walked me over to the Bursar's office, where I was relieved of a cheque for two thousand pounds.

England is truly amazing, I thought, stepping from a Victorian street, straight back to medieval timbered buildings that hang over the pavement. All of these buildings, not just one, but a whole street full, are working shops, offices and homes. In Australia, I've seen bluestone cottages dating from mid Victorian times feted as ancient wonders and turned into museums. I stopped at the corner where St Thomas's sticks out into the traffic as though stepping out to call to it to pause and reflect. The market square opened in front of me, dominated by the old county hall standing tall on its arched undercroft, rising aloof from the traffic that passed it on three sides, like a stately galleon at anchor surrounded by bumboats. I could feel the stories of the thousands of people who had trod this way before me; such continuity; such a sense of community.

I turned to go through the archway towards the council offices. The pavement was freckled with the ubiquitous tired grey patches of discarded gum, and then suddenly with vibrant blots of colour from old confetti. I looked for its source and saw the doorway shown in the wedding photo. I was certain. I stood still for a moment to contain, control the surge of elation. I tried the door, the handle turned. Just a step took me from the traffic noise in to the cool calm interior. My footsteps on the tiled floor echoed around the arched colonnades which flanked the nave.

"Can I help you?" A young priest emerged from a door set in a carved wooden screen, to the left of the altar steps. He walked towards me down the central aisle, extending his hand. "I'm Father Rowland. Curate."

"Er... John Allen. I'm visiting from Australia...trying to trace my relatives. I think my parents were married here. At least I think your doorway is the one in their wedding photo."

"Ah... yes. Well that's not necessarily evidence that they were married here I'm afraid. You see lots of couples from the civil ceremony ... well they sort of borrow St Thomas's as a background for their wedding albums. I know I'm being un-Christian but they're really a bit of a pain. They leave all the confetti for us to clear up. Anyway, when would they have been married?"

"I'm not exactly sure...a few years after the end of the war...say nineteen forty seven to nineteen forty nine."

"Oh dear." Father Rowland's face fell. "Well we certainly won't be able to help. You see we had quite a nasty fire in nineteen fifty four. We lost all the records in the register that was current at that time, which sadly includes the time you're talking about" he reported. "I'm so sorry," he added, in response to my expression, "I am sure, because I was looking for the books from that timeframe myself, just the other day, for a couple about to celebrate their golden anniversary."

"Oh… I just don't seem to be having much luck," I blurted, wanting to escape the source of my disappointment, a disappointment that was all the sharper for my recently raised hopes. "Well…er… thank you for your help, anyway," I added, turning to re-enter the world.

"I'm sorry that I couldn't tell you what you wanted to hear. What about the other churches in Abingdon? Do you know where your parents were living? I could work out the parish from the address."

"They lived in Bernton."

"Both of them? Neither of them lived in Abingdon?"

"No, so far as I know, they both lived in Bernton."

"Oh well in that case we almost certainly didn't marry them. Either the bride or the groom had to be a parishioner."

"But the doorway," I repeated.

"I'd try the Registry Office, if I were you. As I said, most of the newly weds use us as a background for their photos. It was probably the same then."

My enquiry at the Registry Office, which was surprisingly upbeat considering my recent disappointment, was dampened in a typically English way.

"Look, we can't do it today," the large lady in the camel coloured dress said, looking up momentarily from her nails, which she had been buffing, before my enquiry from the counter, which in her view had clearly been categorised as an intemperate intrusion.

"Then when?" I asked impatiently.

"Three working days. You'll have to fill in a form," she added, heaving her considerable bulk from her chair, which creaked, probably in relief, I thought. She reached across her desk to a stack of trays to select a form, revealing far more pallid flesh in the process than I wanted to see. She pushed back her lank hair from her face and waddled to the counter. The half-dozen steps she took caused her to wheeze. She pushed the form across the counter and returned to her seat. It groaned as she sat down, her ample buttocks flowing over the edge of the seat.

"Where do they do the weddings?" I asked.

"Draper's Hall," she said. "Ooh it is lovely," she smiled, her drab face suddenly transfigured. "It's old...very old, but nice like; all wood beams and panels and oil paintings. I often go...as a witness; like when they're short. Either they didn't think or someone's late... you know. Then they mostly have their photos took outside, in front of St Thomas's."

She rested her chin on her hand and gazed dreamily into space, obviously reliving weddings past. In a brighter mood I turned to the administrative minutiae of names and dates in front of me, sure now that I was on the right track. She scarcely stirred as I drew her attention to the completed paperwork, but waved an acknowledgement and muttered "Three working days," as I left. I hoped there was someone out there for her. Come to that, I hoped there was someone out there for me.

I had a quick look around the old County Hall, mainly given over to a museum recording the history of

Abbotsford. A pity, I thought as I ducked down a narrow street in the direction of the church which I had seen from the bridge, that so little imagination had been given to the display. The authors had so much material, such a long and fascinating history, such a wonderful setting at their disposal and yet had produced such a pedestrian exhibition.

I was thinking how much more Australian curators achieved with much less to work with when I heard a shrill shout of surprise and pain. I ran towards the sound. A narrow alley led to the riverside, between the churchyard and a row of almshouses. A woman crouched on her knees on the cobbles. A man stood over her, tugging at her handbag. As I watched he hit her in the face.

"Oi you!" I shouted, not very originally, and ran at him. He looked up from his victim. A pale pinched startled face stared at me from the open hood of a jogging top. He gave the bag one more tug, more in hope than expectation. The strap broke, but the woman held on to the body of the bag with both hands. Her assailant ran off, ducking around the corner. I raced after him, but pursuit was futile. The riverside path was empty. He could have dived through any of half a dozen doorways or on to one of the many boats at their moorings. I turned back to the woman. Madge was back on her feet. She interrupted her brushing and patting into place to smile at me in rueful gratitude.

"Oh thank you. Thank you!" she said shakily.

"Are you hurt?"

"No, not really, just a bit shaken," she said.

"I bet you are. Are you sure you're alright? Can I take you to a doctor."

"No, no Mr Allen. Thank you very much, but don't fuss. Thanks to you, I'm not badly hurt and he didn't take anything. Just as well, because Ethel's pension is in my bag, as well as my own."

"Well let me take you home. Or at least buy you a cup of tea. And it's Jim, by the way, please," I added.

The door of a nearby almshouse was opened by a frail bent elderly lady. She wore a blue and white spotted dress, black stockings, carpet slippers and several layers of knitted woollen cardigans. Her sparse white hair blew around her face, mottled with age. Her eyes were bright with anger and defiance.

" 'ere you. Clear off. Leave the lady alone. I'll 'ave the law on you, you see if I don't," the old lady piped querulously.

"I'm alright Ethel," Madge called. "This nice young man is helping me." She turned back to me. "I was just on my way to see her when that… that man jumped on me. I bring her her pension, have a cup of tea and a chat and run a few errands once a week," she explained. "I'll just pop in and have a bit of a sit down and a cup of tea with her and then I'll be as right as rain."

"What about the police?" I asked.

"No…I don't think there's much point. They won't do much except take statements, because there's no harm done, really, apart from a few scrapes and bruises."

"I hate to think of him getting away with it," I said. "I could give them quite a good description."

"More trouble than it's worth, I'm afraid, all that taking statements and asking if you want counselling. Then even if they do catch him and can prove he did it, he'll only get off with probation or community service." Madge replied resignedly, "but thank you. Thank you," she repeated, laying her hand on my arm. I led her to Ethel's door and left the pair of them to fuss over each other.

The orchard was an irresistible attraction. Okay, I'm lying. Beccy was an irresistible attraction. I wandered over, beer in hand to watch the dig. The students were scattered in the new trenches, but Beccy was where I had seen her last, in the first trench. She was standing, hands on hips, head bowed in thought, concentrating deeply. I hunkered down on my heels and watched. She must either have heard me or caught sight of my shadow, for she looked up, smiled and came and sat next to me.

"Can a girl have a drink?" she asked with a smile, reaching for the bottle in my hand, taking it without waiting for an answer. She raised it to her lips and drank thirstily, as a man would, and without wiping the neck of the bottle first, an act that was surprisingly intimate. She passed the bottle back to me and I took a swig. I swear that I tasted Beccy and not beer and that that had been her intention.

"Penny for them?" I offered. She looked startled. She blushed and turned her head to look back at the trench. "You were so lost in thought when I arrived," I added, by way of explanation.

"Oh…er…yes. These post holes…I was just wondering if they're curving round. I was trying to figure out how best to check that they form a circle without stripping too much of the orchard."

"Is a circle good?" I asked, content in my ignorance.

"It could be, if the date is right. Circular houses are typical of the Iron Age and were certainly common in the main part of the Bronze Age. The earliest circular houses appeared at the beginning of the Bronze Age."

"What were the houses like before that?"

"Not many well preserved examples have been excavated, but most houses seem to have been rectangular; a bit like present day tribal longhouses. So rectangular would be better if I get a lot of Neolithic finds. The funny thing is that the shape of the houses changed at the same time as the way they buried their dead. The Neolithic tombs are rectangular or trapezoid and the Bronze Age burials are in circular tombs."

"What's funny about that?" I enquired insouciantly. "Houses for the dead and houses for the living; what's so odd about that?"

Beccy looked at me as though I'd said something really profound.

"How can you test their age?" I asked to cover my confusion. Her direct focused gaze was quite disconcerting.

"Oh I suppose that ideally I'll get a radiocarbon date from some hearth material. Look, here. I'm sure this is the beginning of a hearth," she said, rising to her feet and pointing to a discoloured area of soil at the edge of the trench. "But I'll be happy to, find some pottery shards or other artefact at the bottom of a post hole or in the drainage ditch.".

She bent down and scraped with her trowel. I was content to drink my beer, feel the warm sun on my face and watch Beccy bent at her work, her jeans stretched tight across her buttocks and thighs.

"How does that genetic testing, you were talking about work?" I asked.

"I'll show you. You'll be my guinea pig," she laughed, jumping up again. She recovered her rucksack from beneath a nearby apple tree and took out a re-sealable transparent plastic bag. From this she took a pre-numbered transparent specimen tube.

"See," she said. "This adhesive label is in two parts, with the same number on each. I record your name and the date on one half and stick it in my note book. That way, I know which sample belongs to which victim." She said the last word with too much relish, "but only I know. The laboratory just has the numbered specimen which is completely anonymous.

She unclipped the top of the specimen tube which was attached to a cotton bud that fitted inside the tube. I must have looked very apprehensive, for she said, "Don't be such a baby, for God's sake. Open your mouth."

I did as I was told. She scraped the inside of my cheeks with the cotton bud.

"Close your mouth," she said. I did as I was told and she kissed me full on the lips.

"There, that wasn't bad, was it?" she said, and resealed the tube. I had to admit that she was right.

"Okay, that's how it's done, but how does it work?"

"The laboratory isolates the DNA and tries to match it with DNA recovered from the burial. A very close match shows relationship; and then of course there's mitochondrial DNA.

"What?"

It's a form of DNA, but what's special about it is that it seems to evolve through mutation at a constant rate over time and is passed on only through the mother. It's great for charting population histories. Like, for instance, if most of the people here are descendants of Vikings or Saxons. This was frontier land at the time of Alfred, you know."

"Do you want to take another sample, for the mito-thingummy?" I asked hopefully.

She moved toward me, putting her hands on my arms, tilting her head back...

"Beccy, come and have a look at this," one of the students called. She pulled back and grinned wryly.

At supper, Viv and the girls were full of plans to fit Pippa out with a uniform. Melanie could supply much of it and the PTA second hand shop most of what remained. As Viv explained, there was no point in buying new just for a term. The rest they could pick up from High Street stores. The details were quite lost on me, so I was relieved when I was called to the 'phone.

"...I was so disappointed that we hadn't found a record of your parent's marriage, that I couldn't settle. Then it came to me..."

What? I nearly screamed aloud.

"The baptism register. I can't imagine why I didn't think of it before. It took me ages, because I had to guess when your mother was born, but eventually I found Louise Berry in the book for nineteen eighteen. But that's not all." His voice rose and cracked. "A boy, born to Corporal Michael Allen and Louise Allen, née Berry, was baptised John in nineteen forty nine."

That was me. I was stunned. I had found more than just traces of my parents, I had found my own beginnings. I was speechless.

"Thanks Father Dominic. Oh thank you so much."

CHAPTER 30

"Hello Mary, John Allen here. I wonder if you can spare me a few moments," I asked.

"Oh Mr Allen. Yes, yes of course, especially after what you did for Madge."

"Oh you've heard..."

"The whole village has heard. You're quite the local hero, chasing off that mugger."

"It was nothing. I only ran at him and he ran away. I didn't actually do anything."

"You did too. Stopped her getting robbed and badly beaten, you did. Anyway what can I do for you?"

"It's about my mum, Louise Berry."

The silence spread, cold empty and inhospitable. I rushed to fill it.

"You see the vicar found her baptism record, and mine too..."

"You'd better talk to Madge."

"But you were so certain before I spoke to Madge the last time and she..."

"You'll have to talk to Madge. I can't help you young man. I'm sorry I have to go now. I'd like to help you but I just can't. You talk to that Madge Barnard."

"You tell him right now, Madge. It's not right. Making out that I was forgetting....just because you don't want to remember that you were sweet on that soldier... his father.

You know it was him... must have been. And this nice young man saving you from that larrikin and you treating him the way you are. Shame on you Madge Barnard."

Mary Bynam's lips tightened as she pressed out those last words. She turned and walked stiff backed up the path to her cottage.

I had bumped into the twin doyennes of village as I had walked back from a lonely beer and ploughman's lunch at the pub. Les and Viv were in Oxford for the day. The girls were at school. Beccy, I called her that now, at least to myself, was busy somewhere, probably taking DNA samples. She hadn't put in an appearance in the orchard that day, I knew that, for I had been waiting and hoping she would for long enough. Now I faced Madge.

"Walk me home", she said, still limping a little, an aftermath of the mugging. Her eyes peeped from yellow and blue bruises. We walked a few metres in silence. I didn't know how to broach the subject. I didn't have to.

"I should have known. You're very like him," she sighed. "I should have seen it when you came into my shop. So you're their son," she said. "Hmmh... you turned out all right. Yes, it's true. I set my cap at your father, but he chose Louise. It was on the night of the dance, after the harvest supper."

She fell silent again. We stopped next to a paling fence surrounding an orchard. Chickens scratched in the unkempt grass. A bonfire smouldered.

"He was a handsome devil. That's where he used to live. Lavender Cottage, it was called; belonged to Joe Pierce who had the pub. Your father rented it for his mother when the bombing started in London. It's gone now, all gone; burnt down after you all went off to Australia. His mother, your grandmother, went into the old folks' home. No one is going to get me into one of those places," she added fiercely. Seeing her eyes flash, I didn't fancy the chances of anyone brave enough or stupid enough to try.

"Some say it was Sid Pierce, who inherited the pub from his uncle. Some say he was after the insurance. Others say he wanted to build," she said when we moved on. "There was a lot of money in building houses after the war, but he couldn't build with your grandmother there as a sitting tenant. Anyway, in the end the Council wouldn't let him. Old man Berry, Louise's father put a stop to it. He was a big landowner and the local magistrate and councillor. He lived over in Heathcote manor."

I stayed silent. I didn't want to interrupt the flow, but neither did I know how to respond to her revelations.

"Old man Berry didn't think very much of your father. Thought he was common... not good enough for his Louise. She was the apple of his eye. He would have liked me to marry your father...he would have liked anyone to marry him, anyone except his Louise. He threw her out, you know, when they got married. Not in the church. No, he put a stop to that. He wouldn't have his daughter parading her disobedience on his home turf. Imagine that. What a thing to do to your own daughter. But she had defied him. He cut her off without a penny. Mean old sod. I laughed when I heard. I was jealous, see. Sorry," she said, turning to me. I saw the glint of tears in her eye.

"That's all right, "I mumbled.

Either she didn't hear me, or didn't care to acknowledge that she had.

"Anyway, Louise and her soldier moved in with his Mum. When he was demobbed he worked at the army base.

She had a baby...a boy. I suppose that was you. We never made up, Louise and I...."

She started to cry. She stopped and pulled a lace-edged handkerchief from her pocket. I smelled lavender.

"I'm sorry to be such a goose..." she sniffed and sighed. "Such a.... You see we had been such good friends... through school, in the Land Army, all the way through the war, until your father came on the scene. Around here, after the war, the only work was on the farms, or at the army base. When that closed and old man Berry wouldn't give Mickey a job, they went to Australia."

"What happened to the Berry's. Do any still live around here?"

"I suppose some would say they got what was coming to them. No, there are none here now. He had a son, but he was killed. Louise was his only daughter. The old man had a change of heart when his Louise left. He did look after Mickey's mother, I'll say that for him. But he went to pieces when his son was killed in Korea... took to drinking. He killed himself and his wife in a car crash. Drunk as a lord, they said. He smashed his Bentley into the railway bridge at Eastmoor."

We stopped outside the shop. I wanted to thank her but couldn't find words to express my thoughts of family found and lost again so quickly.

"I'm glad you are here, young man," she said, turning to go in. "You and your lovely daughter. I'm so glad that something good came of it all and that you have come back."

A family found and lost again. But Bernton had held only bitter memories for my mother and father. No wonder they had never talked of family and home. There had been nothing for them here. I realised that I had been hoping for connections in Bernton that I could weave into strong bonds, into a sense of belonging. The sense of rejection induced in me by Sarah's family and by Pippa's school and so-called friends had fermented and simmered. I had been looking for another home, a comfort zone from which I could in turn reject those who had rejected Pippa and me. But Madge had told me another tale of rejection, a story that showed up my search for what it was, a self-deceiving illusion. The connections through my mother were barren, sterile, a trail long cooled. All vestiges of family, of kith and kin had long since been swept away. There was nothing left of our family to tie Pippa and me to Bernton.

CHAPTER 31

"Any sign of them?"

"No, it's been quiet since nightfall," Iowerth answered.

"How's the evacuation going?"

"The tail-enders are heading up the valley now. I want to be ready to cross the marshes at first light."

"Will you get there in time?"

"With time to spare, Dana willing, but I don't want to be waiting for anyone in daylight."

Iowerth turned back to contemplating the familiar long houses of Ilws, briefly lit in the flaring of the watch fire as the sentry threw a on log in a fountain of sparks, his loneliness and boredom common to watchmen and sentries everywhere, codified by the stoop of his shoulders and the doleful droop of his head. Berin watched over Iowerth's shoulder.

"They bed down early," Iowerth ventured. "No scouts out.... well none that we've seen, anyway."

"What about Afon'ken?"

"That lot," Iowerth spat in disgust, "are pissed out of their brains. We'll not see them out tonight."

"The outlanders must be sure of themselves, sure that we won't come out," Berin said.

"Well we wouldn't would we, even if we weren't running."

"Not you too, Iowerth," Berin said resignedly. "Look, I explained all that."

"I know, I know. But after giving them such a hiding, twice, and all those good men dead.... well it just hurts, that's all."

"Should more die just to end in the same result? We cannot hold our ground without the men of the ford and the outstation to help."

"Oh, you're right I suppose," Iowerth admitted grudgingly. "But what about me and my men? We've got families back at the ford. With Com's and Ilws fallen, the ford will be next. We've got to go back."

"Of course you must," Berin agreed, "but watch out for Urak, he doesn't love you for standing by us."

"Ruler or not, our kin won't stand for it if he moves against us. Besides, he needs us to defend the ford."

"Don't be too sure. He plotted our doom with the outlander, that I do know."

"Aye, but he can't mean to lose his own fief, can he?"

Berin fell silent, the threads of argument knotted and tangled. His tired and bruised mind balked at the mental skein. Iowerth was so right. There could be no point in Urak plotting the downfall of the ford. But he had. He was... Where... what was the inconsistency?

"Look, if its all right with you," Iowerth continued, "we'll watch your back until you're up and over the West Way, then we'll pull out to the ford. I don't want to be around when that lot are up and about."

Berin reached out and gripped Iowerth by the shoulder. "Thanks, you've been a good friend. We will never forget your help. Our hearths are always open to you."

"Let's hope we'll have no use for them," Iowerth replied grimly, as they cautiously slid back from their vantage point overlooking Illws and set off on the trail of the clan

The refugees had left their mark. The signs of their passage cut a broad path through the bruised turf, down the steep slope to the valley floor, past the settlement, forlorn and lonely, past the still beech wood and the silent flint mine, through the home paddocks and up the valley. The stock had slotted the route with their spoor and spattered it with dung; the oxen had carved their wide, splay-toed tracks.

As the valley steepened, Berin stumbled over more traces of their passing; discarded loom weights, a quern, a hide bag of partly shaped flints. He caught up with the slowly plodding oxen just as they crossed the West Way. Auron, stolid and resigned, plodded head down and swinging, ox-like at their side. Auron looked up briefly as Berin overtook him. He sniffed loudly, a determined protest at a never to be forgotten slight. For a moment, Berin was tempted to make amends, then thought better of it. Silly fart, anyone could see that Amren's oxen were the best. Auron would just have to put up with it.

Ahead of the oxen, Naf's cow in calf swayed hugely, raising its tail stiffly, spattering the ground. Cigfen, cried-out and dry eyed, led it determinedly by a rawhide halter. Berin gave her a quick peck on the cheek as he passed. "Good girl," he said and was rewarded with a wan smile, the first since Naf had fallen.

Berin's dogs, tails wagging, ran to him as he approached, momentarily abandoning the small flock of breeding ewes and the ram at its head, led by Rh'on, shepherdess for the night. "Go by," Berin growled at them, waving them back to their task.

"All right Mother?"

"Yes, we're managing fine. The mothers with the youngsters worry me. Especially those... well those who've lost their men, like Angharad and Rhiann. That Camren is a little terror; and then there's Blodwen; she's carrying and nearly due."

"I'll look out for them."

Aedd bulked even larger than usual at the head of the column. Camren rode his back, stick-like legs astride Aedd's neck, lolling forward, thumb in mouth, onto Aedd's head. Ened, walking at her man's side, led two children by the hand. For once the normally genial giant was morose, silent and withdrawn, eyes fixed firmly at his feet, clearly discouraging any approach. Berin turned and hurried back to the tired, floundering fugitives, to encourage and help, threaten and cajole, hurt by his big friend's silence, glad that he had not ventured a word to be rebuffed.

"Oh Aedd, you shouldn't have," Ened admonished gently once Berin was safely out of earshot. "You're his friend."

"I know, I know. I just can't help it. We beat them. He did it; it was all his ideas, the logs, the fire; he gave the leadership too. His blade, his spear his shield were everywhere. The men would follow him anywhere. We beat them, but we're running away. The men don't like it. I don't like it."

"Just think what he's left behind. His father, his brother, his wife-to-be, his herds, land, he's lost more than anyone."

"That's just it. Why should he, why should any of us leave our land, our cattle, our dead? Our forebears worked

393

for it, hacked it from the forest. We love it; it's ours, our life."

"He sees more clearly than we do. He sees what must be done if the clan is to live, not just tomorrow, or through the winter, but next year and every year after that. Look I know and have suffered from these outlanders. I've seen the work of the new chiefs who have befriended them and use their power. I know he's right."

"I'm sorry Ened. You've lost so much. I've only Alen to worry about and he's safe with Olwen and Oranc. It's just that I feel so cut off. Somehow it feels worse because I agreed to do it, and wasn't forced. It's like betraying everything I know."

"Well now we are two of a kind, homeless waifs."

Aedd smiled wryly and bent to kiss her. His young passenger, falling in his dreams, grabbed handsfull of beard and sent a warm stream running under Aedd's shirt.

"The little bugger's pissed on me."

"How many children are you planning I should have?" Ened asked, with a mischievous grin. Aedd reverted to silence.

"Warwch, you and your men cover us." Berin drew the man back as Cigfen jumped from the path of the cow which was sliding splay-legged down the steep slope, bellowing in alarm.

"Yes sire."

Berin glanced anxiously along the gully. The stark branches were clearly visible against the dark sky. Dawn was coming and with it the outlanders.

"Just follow the stream. Someone will show you where to leave it."

As Warwch nodded, and set about placing his men, Berin fought his way past the skidding, white-eyed oxen and their cursing, floundering keeper, down to the stream. He splashed through the cold water to the head of the column, which Aedd had moved on to prevent too much bunching at the spring. There was no talk now, no repartee or laughter when someone tripped and suffered a drenching for their inattention. The mood of the mothers feeling their way over the stony stream bed, skirts wet, hems held up to free their feet, and of the men bowed under their loads, seemed to Berin to match that of the children; the whining petulance which comes to children when they are overtired and to adults whenever they feel like it. By the time Berin caught up, Aedd stood at the edge of the marsh, contemplating the black still water between reed and osier beds, mist rising and curling eerily in the pale dawn light.

Angrily he turned to Berin. "Now what, damn it. The enemy at our back, a trail a blind man could follow on a dark night and an impassable marsh ahead."

"I said there is a way, and there is." Berin looked around, trying to fix his bearings, masking his anxiety. A little further, he thought, pushing on downstream, probing with the butt of his spear. He turned to his right, only to sink to his knees in a bog. Aedd took the end of his spear and pulled him out.

A low whistle set Aedd on guard, the rising caustic remark choked off by the urgency of alarm. A small, slight, but wiry figure, naked but for a loin cloth and the mist which wreathed around it, stood, apparently on the water.

"Hold your fire," Berin snapped as Elin and Brys notched arrows to their bows.

"But it's a savage..."

"And your tongue too. He's my friend."

"Greetings Berin," the figure called.

"Greetings Grwlch."

"You are many and armed."

"We are all that is left. We seek sanctuary. The outlanders will not be far behind."

"It is said there has been much slaughter at your place of walls. Twice you have beaten them. What need do you have of sanctuary?"

"It is true that we have beaten them, but at such cost. Most of our force abandoned us. We are too few to stay on our own."

"Ai'ee so when you tire of killing you come to us. For today you are welcome. As for tomorrow, that is for Talwch and the council to decide. Come, it seems that you have a short memory," Grwlch said with a smile, indicating Berin's mired britches. "My men will mark the path."

Grwlch whistled, a lilting bird song. Men appeared, seemingly from nowhere, rising in sedge banks, from swirls of mist, from the water itself it seemed to Aedd, Brys and Elin.

Olwen, hair flying wild, with no thoughts of braids, ran into Berin's arms when he stepped into the clearing. She threw her arms around his neck, pressing her cheek to his chest, thrusting herself against him, warm, vibrant, nearly knocking him off balance in her eagerness for closeness. She pulled back and looked at him, her bright shining face dimming, her eyes clouding with concern as she read the strain in his face and ... and just a ghost of something else. He smiled weakly, taking her by the upper arms, kissing her.

"It's so good to see you," she said, "to have you safe again."

"I wish it were the same for everyone."

Olwen's face fell. "Talwch said there were battles, are there many..."

"Yes, I'm afraid so," he answered, lowering his eyes.

"Oh no, who?"

"Amren, Naf, little Cas, Han, Arec, Kar, Madwg, Branwen," his voice caught, showing his pain, "two of the bondmen and several from the ford. I never even learnt their names."

She hugged him tight, as though to squeeze the hurt from him, yet wanting to be soft, to soothe; slowly she released him as he stood unresponsive, unyielding. She could not reach him.

Alen brushed past, flying to Aedd, throwing his arms about his father's bulk. Gently Aedd took the just awakened Camren from his shoulders and set him on the ground, where he stared in wide- eyed amazement at the river-men. Aedd ruffled his son's hair and hugged him in return. Ened put her arm around his shoulders, bent and kissed him. Olwen, looking past Berin found herself smiling at their joy in each other, yet feeling strangely empty, cheated.

"You are much better," Berin said, almost formally.

"Me, oh I'm fine, but you, you're exhausted. Come, come and ..."

"No, I must see Talwch; there is much to do. See if you can help Rh'on. Blodwen is near her time. We'll talk later."

Talwch ducked out through the doorway of his tent as Grwlch held back the flap for him. He straightened and looked at Berin sternly and then frowning, beyond him to the bedraggled survivors of Com and Ilws as they staggered into the clearing, travel stained, weary, setting down their bundles, falling to the grass, relieved to be on firm footing once more but apprehensive, casting worried looks at the river men.

"You are welcome Berin," Talwch announced, unconvincingly, "But I did not expect you to bring so many guests. At least they have brought their own supper," he added, indicating the stock.

"Talwch, forgive me. I did not mean to presume... I ...I had no chance to get a message to you. Please let me explain."

Talwch folded his arms across his chest and nodded, stern and uncompromising.

"Dorn has died," Berin began. "Tarok is now High Chief. He demanded that we submit to him, hand over a free man and his bondwoman for his punishment. It was Aedd and Ened, the two we spoke of before, the ones he was chasing. But they had done nothing wrong. He wanted the woman for himself and to take his revenge on Aedd. I could not do it. He means to rule, not as Dorn did, wisely, by listening to and taking advice of elders and with the consent of the people, but as master of us. When I refused, he abandoned us to the outlanders. We would have been finished then except Branwen, she is daughter of Dorn and was promised to me as wife... well she stayed with her bondmen and other men of the ford loyal to her. We fought for two days..." Berin fell silent as the memories flooded back.

"I know of your battles. You inflicted two great defeats on the outlanders. Why then leave your homes to them to despoil? There will be nothing left when you return."

"Talwch, its true that we hurt them, hurt them badly. Maybe they would have left us alone today, but next year they would be back, or the year after. We are only a small part of a greater war. The outlanders come back each year in greater numbers. Not just for trade. Chiefs become powerful with their help. The more powerful they become, the more they command and the less they listen. The old ways we are used to are dying." Berin hesitated then went on, his voice hardening as his throat constricted at the hurt. "So few of us are left. We cannot survive without the help of Tarok or the men of the ford. But the price of that help is submission. We would no longer be free men. So many good men have died. My wife-to-be, who had so much to offer life, died too, though she could have returned to the ford in safety. All died in the name of our freedom." Berin paused, taking a deep breath, searching out Talwch's eyes, holding them, before adding softly "I cannot betray their memory, their sacrifice."

"Then you do not mean to return," Talwch said grimly, his eyes boring into Berin's.

Berin straightened, meeting Talwch's glare. "I hoped that we could stay here," he admitted.

"You presume a great deal; perhaps too much," Talwch answered grimly. "It is a matter for the Council. I shall not cast you out while your enemies pursue you, but for the future, we must see."

"Oh don't worry Olwen. I think it's a terrific idea. It'll be fine; I'll talk him round, you'll see." A'isa sat up on her couch, smiling, her whole young body animated, a picture of vibrant enthusiasm. "He's always grumpy about a new idea at first."

"It's not just him, though, is it. He said he must call a council of chiefs. Berin said he was far from happy," Olwen answered.

"I'll persuade him. He'll persuade the chiefs, you'll see."

"Fetch me my comb," she commanded Oranc, and smiled impishly, raising her shoulders in delight at his back as he leapt to fulfil her wish.

"I'm not at all sure. Berin says he was very grim when they arrived," Olwen observed gloomily, sipping the hot infusion of rose hips which she had made for the two of them and the ladies clustered about Blodwen.

"He doesn't like farmers much, none of us do. Oh you're different of course," she added hastily. "Mind you, I don't know how you can stand to have all those smelly animals around you all the time and live in one place. It's... Oh we're just different, that's all." She gave up trying to explain and with the total unconcern only displayed by young people secure in their privilege, ignored the problem and began to comb out her short, but thick dark hair.

"If only he does agree, it could work so well," Olwen ventured. "You trade with Tarok now, for cloth and grain, especially in the bad winters. You could trade with us instead. You say you don't like Tarok because he treats you so roughly."

"I'll work on father, it'll be all right, you'll see."

A sharp cry from Blodwen brought Olwen to her feet. "She's started. I must help Rh'on. Make yourself scarce, Oranc. This will be no place for you, before long."

A pile of packs, weapons, tools and household baggage stood in the centre of the clearing. Aedd paced next to it, directing, haranguing, cajoling the weary men and women who were cutting poles and withies and forming more of the bothys.

"Look Brys," Aedd said as Berin walked over to join him, "I know you don't want to be here; neither do I, but we are, so lets make the best of it. Let's at least sleep under cover tonight."

Stony-faced, Berin brushed past Aedd and reached up to pull down the pole which Brys was struggling ineffectually to bend into the roof of the hut. Aedd looked up, surprised at Berin's sudden appearance. He grimaced, shame-faced at Brys, and with a parting shrug of his huge shoulders, he moved off to the next gang. Berin lashed the pole to its opposite number and worked on, trying to sublimate in physical effort the pressure he felt building within him.

Berin's anger had not cooled as he lay in his sleeping skins, nor would his racing thoughts still. Olwen's back was turned to him, stiff and resentful as only a spurned lover can be. He doubted that she slept, for now and then a sniff and deep sigh betrayed her wakefulness and invited conciliation. He could no more explain to Olwen how he could not make love to her, with any hope that she would understand, than he could convince the men folk of the rightness of their flight from the stronghold.

Damn, what else could he have done. Anyone could see that they had only survived behind their defences by using surprise tactics, that wouldn't work a second time. A sustained attack by the outlanders and Afon'ken could have taken them at any time. Why, the outlanders breached the wall almost without effort the first time they tried and then they had only been probing for weaknesses; it hadn't even been a full-scale attack. But they won't see what they don't want to, will they. They think we're wrong to run away. They hate to leave their land, their ancestors. As if you don't. You've left all those dead, little Cas, Amren, Naf, Han, Arec, Kar and Madwg, and Belu, Ermid and Com before them. The familiar faces flitted before him, all his friends, all his responsibility. Should he have added to them? Why should he be blamed for saving what was left; and there was Branwen; quickly he suppressed the sharpest pain of all. How could he make love with their spirits all watching, with the feel and smell and taste of Branwen still so strong.

Berin sighed and rolled over, breaking the thought train. Olwen jerked the covers back over herself, pulling back her foot as if it had been scalded by the inadvertent touch of his toes.

Poor Blodwen. The screams still resounded in his ears. Olwen had said that the child had to be turned before birth, but the contractions had been too strong. Blodwen, white-faced, limp and exhausted from contractions, torn and worn by pushing, had finally expelled the baby boy still born, strangled by his own cord. The news had travelled like wildfire. It was a bad omen, a sign from Earth Mother, they had said. At least they were spared another funeral; there had been so many. Rh'on had quietly disposed of the little bundle without Blodwen seeing it, as was the custom.

It has all come so quickly. Why only a moon ago he had stood on this very spot and all had been well with his world. His father and brother had still lived; he had not even dreamed of the cares and worries of chieftaincy. How had it all changed? How had it all come to this?

Images crystallised, kaleidoscoping through his mind; the outlander; Aedd voicing his suspicions; the undergrowth as he listened to Urak's voice; the meeting of two figures under the solitary oak; the arrow head splitting the skin of Gawin's throat; confrontation and humiliation; Olwen's buttocks, bruised and wealed, spreading her body to him when he released her bonds; Madwg staring at his lopped arm; Branwen warm and alive crouched over him; Branwen cold and dead. One cause, one theme, one cancer threaded its way through the images. "Urak!" without realising it, he spoke the name aloud. The name seared, brought bile surging. Olwen raised her head briefly, then settled back with an angry snort.

"Mmm, that's nice," Ened purred, pressing herself sinuously against Aedd. She bent her left leg at the knee and slid it over Aedd's thigh as he rubbed with the index finger of his left hand, the vertebrae in the small of her back. She raised her face and pulling back the hair which fell forward over her face, lightly kissed his lips.

Aedd lay on his back staring at the night sky, watching the clouds scud across the stars now fading as the moon rose. The breeze eddied, gently cold and fresh on his face, yet snuggled together as they were in the sleeping skin, in the lee of a juniper bush, as far from the camp as they could go without falling into the marsh, they were warm and cosy, heartbeats slowing, breaths stilling. Even the release of love-making could not completely dissipate Aedd's disquiet.

"What is it?" Ened asked, sensing his mood.

Aedd stared at the spiky fronds of juniper outlined against the sky as though they might suddenly reveal an answer. "Oh I don't know," he answered. "I just feel restless, that's all. I can't get used to the idea of leaving the old place, I suppose."

"It is nice here," Ened said. It has a really comfortable feel about it."

"Hmm, not for everyone," Aedd replied, moving his hip from the root which was probing his buttock through the skins.

"Oh... I see, not that you great lummock," she laughed. "I hope Talwch lets us stay. I can't explain it but I get a really good feeling about this place. That clearing around the spring, the hill, all hidden away safely behind the marshes, well it just feels right."

"That's the point. It all feels so ready to be settled, almost asking us, as if it's time. Yet I don't feel ready. Maybe there's just been too much excitement recently."

"Yes, excitement we could do without."

"We did all right considering."

"Considering what?"

"Well, seeing that we didn't have many bronze weapons. Our flint just isn't a match against bronze in a fight. We're never really going to be safe, can't really settle safely anywhere until we've got enough bronze of our own." Aedd paused, taking a deep breath before continuing. "Ened, I

404

was thinking about our first night together. Do you remember telling me your story?"

"Hmm, yes I do," she smiled, kissing his throat, "and the things you made me do, you brute."

Aedd felt himself quicken. Ened shifted her thigh languorously in response.

"Well you told me about men from the West who once traded bronze with your people. Not outlanders, but people like us."

"Oh, you mean the people from the end of the world. Well, not quite like us, actually, but near enough."

"Well don't you see? We don't have to trade with the outlanders. We can trade with the...oh, them, the world-enders or whatever you call them."

"We'll have to find them first."

"That shouldn't be too difficult, judging from your father's story. Once we get to the West Sea we just keep on following the coast until we come to them. That's what he said, isn't it?"

"You're forgetting about all the wars and raiding parties, the slaving along the West Way."

"There must be a different way to get to the West Sea without travelling the West Way and passing by your old home."

"Old home. You called it my old home. It is funny to think of it like that." Ened fell silent, surrendering to memories.

"I'm sorry," Aedd said, palming her back, smoothing her buttocks, fingering the cleft, realising that a wrong word could so easily return her to a bout of introspective

405

depression which had been so common in the early days of their relationship.

"No, don't be. It's true. My home is with you now. Do you really want to go to the end of the world?"

"Yes, I'd like to give it a try; then we could settle down and at least know that it couldn't be done, but that we'd tried."

"You said we; can I come?"

"Not without some effort."

She nuzzled his throat and kissed his chest, gently straddling him, accommodating him with a sigh.

"Now I think you might, eventually."

"Oh Aedd, you are a lovely, lovely man."

CHAPTER 32

Berin shivered as he stood one-legged at the edge of the marsh, pulling at his britches. The cold breeze curled around his thighs, tightening, shrinking, reached across his torso, chasing away body warmth, parting chest hair, raising his nipples. The cold suited his mood. Methodically, Berin wrapped his clothes and bow string in the waterproof pouch which Grwlch had given him, and set out on the now familiar watery way he had taken when he had followed the buck to the spring and brought Olwen to safety.

The ice-cold marsh cramped his muscles. Mud squeezed through his toes. Water-logged branches stabbed at the hard soles of his feet, tore at the softer targets of his calves and ankles. From time to time he slipped and doused himself. Once he missed his way and swam across a pool to regain the route. Total immersion was almost preferable to being wet and exposed. He shivered, teeth chattering as he rose to check his whereabouts, baring his streaming skin to the chilling breeze. He started as a flight of duck sprang straight from the water with a splash and a whirring of wings, quacking their alarm and annoyance, white undersides glowing pink as they banked in the light flooding warm from the huge rosy ball of the sun which hung over Berin's destination.

A dog fox, which had carefully stalked the mallard along the marsh's edge, flattening his red-brown fur into the sedge, dirtying and hiding the stark white flash at his chest and throat, raised his sharp pointed mask, ears pricked, damp nostrils twitching, searching the reed banks with his bright amber eyes. Man scent came to him on an eddy. In disgust he turned and trotted away.

On firm ground once more, Berin dried himself on his cloak and dressed. He checked his weapons carefully and restrung his bow. There was a ruthless, single-minded determination about his actions. For the moment all thought of man the chief, warrior, farmer, even the lover were forgotten; he was man the hunter again.

Olwen awoke with a gloomy sense of foreboding. She lay for a moment wondering if she were awake or dreaming, trying to pin down in her thoughts the cause of her unease. Of course it was that silly row with Berin. How stupid of her to get so huffy when he had so much on his mind. She rolled over to embrace him, only to find his place empty and cold. She sat up in alarm. Quickly she dressed and rushed to the door of the shelter.

Life was slowly making itself known around the clearing. Sleepy figures made their ways to the privy, mothers carrying young children. In one of the shelters a woman's voice was raised in shrill scolding, suddenly punctuated by a smack and a child's wail, underlain by a soothing bass. Older children were drawing water from the pool at the spring and downstream the early risers were at their morning bath. Other figures bent to coax flames from smouldering fires or stood and scratched, eyes glazed, slowly, gently, coming to terms with the start of a new day. There was no sign of Berin.

Aedd and Ened, hand in hand, sleeping skin slung over their shoulders, stood for a while at the top of the slope above the clearing, watching the camp awaken before they zig-zaged their way down through the juniper. Olwen felt a pang of jealousy at their closeness, their transparent joy in each other. So it was once and should still be between her and Berin, she thought.

"Have you seen Berin?" Olwen asked anxiously.

"No, why, what's wrong?" Ened replied, sensitive to the edge to Olwen's voice.

"Nothing, I hope. Oh, we had a row last night and he's not here this morning. I can't find him anywhere. No one's seen him."

"Are his arms there?" Aedd asked, ever practical.

"I didn't look," she answered.

"Well let's check that first, then I'll check with the watch at the causeway. He's probably just gone off to scout. He's sure to have passed the watch."

Moments later Olwen emerged from her shelter, white-faced and clearly shaken. "All his arms are gone, everything; and he's taken the left-overs from supper. Why should he go without telling me? Where's he gone?"

Ened put her arm around her. "You're worrying about nothing, Olwen. He's just gone off to scout as Aedd said. He didn't want to disturb you, that's all. I mean... well you did have a row after all is said and done."

"Oh I know I'm just being silly. It's just that I've got this awful feeling that something dreadful is going to happen."

Ened motioned to Aedd, waving him in the direction of the watchman. "Look, whilst Aedd finds out where he's gone, let's see how Blodwen and A'isa are, and get some breakfast. I could do with some hot rosehip."

Aedd was puzzled as he pushed his way through the open door flap and stood still for a moment as his eyes adjusted to the gloom. Blodwen lay tearful, pale and drawn on one side of the hut, comforted by Rh'on, Cigfen and Gwyn. A'isa, smiling animatedly, flashing teeth and eyes, held court on the other, with Olwen and Ened in attendance. They looked up as his bulk blotted out the light, leaving only the vertical beam from the smoke hole. Olwen's face fell the moment she saw him. "What is it Aedd?"

"He didn't leave by the causeway, that's certain," Aedd answered. "The watchman saw no trace of him; he's not anywhere on the hill, so he must have left another way. I found some tracks down the stream a bit, that could... "

"Of course," Olwen cried, "that's it. That's the way we came the first time. It's the route he took when he first found this place. But where has he gone, and why?"

"Look here, what was it you two argued about last night?" Ened asked. "Maybe there's a clue in that."

"We were talking about going back home. Well I was and he was telling me all sorts of reasons why we couldn't, not ever. I suppose I was very upset. Anyway I cried and he said I was just like all the rest and when would we all wake up to ourselves, or something like that, so I didn't even try to make up and he just lay there. I thought he would be all right in the morning, after a night's sleep. I couldn't sleep for ages and I know he was just lying there, wide awake. At one point he yells out 'Urak', just that, nothing else...Oh no, you don't think he's..."

Olwen's voice trailed off into a miserable silence, her face ashen.

"Aye, you could be right," Aedd said.

"Has what?" A'isa asked, staring in amazement, eyes darting from one to the other. "Where's Berin gone?"

"Gone to kill Urak," Aedd replied. "We've all given him a hard time. Now he thinks we're all against him and he's

410

lost his father, brother, wi... er his inheritance," Aedd added hastily as Ened looked as if she had just swallowed sour milk. "Urak took and abused you, Olwen. Urak caused the final break up between him and his father. Urak has betrayed us to the outlanders at every step. He hates Urak and blames him for everything. Us going against him was the last straw. He's going to kill him... well try to... the fool. They'll cut him down first."

Olwen started to sob. Ened looked at Aedd in exasperation as she tried to comfort Olwen. So big, she thought, so wonderful, but so little brain sometimes. "Can you get him back," she asked, "before he goes too far?"

"I can try," Aedd answered.

When Aedd left, A'isa called for Grwlch.

The promise of a fine day had long been broken as Urak strode through the drizzle-dampened beech wood. Faithful Barak loped to heel. The light, but persistent rain, streaked the smooth bare silver-grey and mould-greened trunks and branches black. The soft dim light of summer was replaced by a harsher brighter light, despite the dullness of the day, because the once soft green canopy now lay brittle and brown on the ground. Holly bushes grew thick in the undergrowth, their livery of dark smooth green and brilliant red adding life to the otherwise gloomy scene. Foraging pigs scuttled from their path, forgoing the sweet oily beech nuts hidden in the leaf fall, sensing the welling anger, the malignant spirit passing by.

Urak was furious. That Berin's people had survived the onslaught was surprise enough; the news that Berin had escaped was simply unbelievable, a monstrous joke in the worst possible taste. Urak hesitated as he came to the beginning of the West Way. He looked around him, undecided.

"I thought you said we were to meet here," he grumbled.

Barak plucked at his sleeve and pointed up the trail. The outlander stepped from behind a tree. Urak, no stranger to wickedness and brutality, shuddered involuntarily. The man was clearly dangerous, not just in an obvious physical sense, although the arms he carried so confidently underlined that view, but everything about his stance and expression spoke of malevolence and malicious self-interest.

"What happened," Urak asked angrily without introduction or any pretence of politeness.

"You say they is just farmers, no fighters, no bronze, easy," the outlander spat. "Hah! I tell you they fight like best soldiers. My friend - is first in attack- takes bronze spear here," he shouted, making a slitting motion below his chin. "Is dead. Bronze, you hear? You say no bronze."

"I said very little bronze, and that is true. Look here, I kept my side of the bargain. I arranged for most of their men to leave. I delayed the building, leaving gaps in the wall. Why couldn't you finish them?"

"Pah! You fight as good you talk we win no trouble," the outlander exclaimed, disgust spilling over at the level reserved by all men of action to address those in authority with no first hand involvement in their world. "They fight good. They roll big logs, kill, break bones. Men frightened to go back. Men not fight good when frightened. Then fire. That is good idea." The outlander smiled evily. Urak was sure that two further tricks had recently been added to the outlander's already extensive professional repertoire. "But is bad for us. We lose many. Not just Senot men. My people, my friends, is bad. We ready to take them next day. No more surprises, then pouff, in night they go, all go, mens, childrens, womans, leave only cows and sheeps."

"But how? Why didn't you stop them?"

"We not expect leave shelter. Helos not there in night. We not fight in dark. Helos not there to take. If you die, go to dark world."

Stupid superstition again, Urak thought, the ruination of so many rational, well laid plans.

"My friend dead. His men angry. They is promise easy fight, plenty womans, slaves. Fight is hard, no womans, no slaves, only cows and sheeps."

"Why don't you chase them? They can't have gone far. They can't move quickly with women and children."

"We follow trail, it leads to stream and then nothing. Stream goes to marsh. No sign."

"But they can't just disappear," Urak shouted.

"Then you go look," the outlander said, suddenly dangerously quiet. Urak recognised a time for discrete silence.

"What you do now?" the outlander said sharply.

"What do you mean, what am I going to do? Why nothing of course. Everything has changed now anyway. Dorn is dead. My brother, the new High Chief, prefers to live at the outstation and will soon go back there. When he does I will be in charge at the ford and can deliver it to Senot, just as Senot wanted, but without a battle. Most satisfactory, I should say."

"Where boy and woman? Why you not bring?"

Urak failed narrowly to look as uncomfortable as he felt. "Er...you can have them when you capture or kill Com's people. That was the deal."

"Want now. No deal. You bring."

"Senot will not be happy that they have escaped. You get your reward when they are all killed or captured."

"Hah, this Senot, he promise plenty. You promise plenty slaves. You promise me boy, woman. You give me," the outlander shouted, tendons cording in his neck, a thick blue vein throbbing with the suddenly rising pressure.

"I gave you slaves," Urak said, beginning to back away. "You lost them."

The outlander's single eye fixed on Urak, who quailed before the malevolence of the implacable purpose he read in it. "You give me slaves, he said, suddenly quiet, in a tone which frightened Urak more than his rage of a moment before, "You give me or I take!"

CHAPTER 33

Aedd cursed foully and fluently as he stopped at the edge of the marsh to draw breath. He damned Berin for his anger, for his hurt. He cursed the marsh and everything which swam in, floundered on, crawled under, or flew over it. He swore at the breeze, the clouds which banked up in a conspiracy to hide the feeble warmth of the sun from him, the brambles which caught at his foot. He cursed himself for his generosity, his sense of loyalty to his friend and finally, as he set off once more at a lumbering, but deceptively fast pace along the clear trail left by Berin, he began to curse his own stupidity.

Of course Berin was right, Aedd thought. He had worked wonders at the stronghold; they had fought well and deserved their victories, but without bronze, without hope of reinforcement from the ford or from Tarok, they were doomed. The hill in the marshes offered a perfect haven. As to the future, well it seemed he was right there too. Any attack on the settlement could be their last, even if they survived the present campaign. At least the hill in the swamp offered some sort of permanence, even if they did have to start all over again. Aedd regretted his coldness. No wonder the poor man felt so hurt and angry. He had saved the clan and they had turned on him, himself included. But damn the man, why did he have to go off after Urak by himself.

Berin's tracks guided Aedd up the side of a ridge, climbing slowly and steadily through woodland, following first one game trail then another, switching for each advantage of height gained, taking the easiest route to the top of the escarpment. Near the lip, Berin had swung towards the sunrise, keeping just below the ridge in cover, avoiding the more dangerous open ground of the chalk upland. Aedd pushed on for a short distance to check the open ground. On the far skyline he saw the stark memorial to Belu and Ermid. A buzzard swooped and soared, sailing the air currents which swirled over the escarpment, hunting the grazing land, the only movement in a lonely landscape, its mewing cry the only sound.

Aedd pressed on, reassured that his right flank was secure, anxious to catch up with Berin before he reached the ford and any help that he might be able to offer would come too late. It began to drizzle, a cold, deceptively penetrating dampness. Automatically Aedd wrapped himself against the rain in his cloak, then let it fall, easing his wet britches where they chafed at the crutch. His passage through the marsh had wet him as thoroughly as any rain ever would.

A solitary crow perched high in the stark branches of an elm, a look-out over the broad expanses of the valley of the Great River croaked its annoyance and flapped lazily into the air as Aedd approached. Idly Aedd watched it riding the breeze, tipping air from its fanned wing tips, turning, side-slipping, to land in an ash tree, a few hundred paces further along the ridge. As the crow stalled, shedding air, flapping its wings which it had turned to slow its flight, it twisted abruptly, clattering a way out through the outer branches, falling twigs and a lone black feather, marking to its panic.

Aedd unslung his shield from his back and threw back the cloak from his shoulders, freeing his arms. Half-crouched, he advanced stealthily, carefully placing each foot before trusting it with his weight, rushing across open spaces, keeping a tangled briar patch between him and the bole of the ash tree, his eyes restlessly darting from side to side, watching for signs of movement, his senses heightened, his pulse and breathing rates quickened, feeling the pulsing of his blood, hearing the rasping of his breath.

"Aedd! What are you doing here?" Berin's shocked voice hissed from above and behind him. Aedd whirled around to find himself staring end on at a drawn arrow, the quivering point only a few paces from his throat. Berin crouched in the lower limbs of an elm, his body tensed as taught as the string of the bow he bent in his hands.

Aedd expelled breath explosively as Berin relaxed, easing the bow string and jumped down. "I saw the crow rise and then shy at me," he said by way of explanation. "Where are you going?"

"I would ask you the same question except I don't think I would like the answer," Aedd said grimly. "Look, you've scared me enough for one day. Why not forget all this nonsense about Urak and come back."

"You guessed then."

"It wasn't hard. You cried out last night. Olwen heard you. Come back with me now man, she's worried sick."

"I can't, Aedd."

"Berin, I was wrong. All right, I admit it. I'm sorry, we were all wrong. Now give up this foolishness and come back to us."

"There's more to it than that, Aedd."

"We need you Berin."

"Not really, not now. Talwch will let you stay. Even if he doesn't, you can fight him. You would have to fight him,

417

because you've nowhere else to go. He knows that, that's why he'll let you stay. You're all safe now in the marshes. You can get by without me."

"If not for us, then come back for Olwen. She loves you Berin."

"That's not fair, Aedd."

"It's Branwen, isn't it?"

Berin was silent. "Yes," he sighed finally, "yes it is, but more, much more than that. Think what he did to Olwen? I can't bear to. It's father and Belu; all of our dead and suffering, the end of generations of our way of life; the betrayal of our ancestors. It's a monstrous treachery that must be punished. I have to kill him, Aedd. I'll not be able to live with myself unless I do."

"Then I'll come with you."

"No Aedd, thanks, but you have Alen to think of and Ened. The people will look to you if anything happens to me."

"Now who's being unfair? I'll not be able to live with myself if anything happens to you and I had not stopped you. I'm coming."

"Then welcome," Berin said, grinning, suddenly feeling lighter than he had in days.

Before them lay a steep-sided brush-filled valley, which cut back into the chalk of the escarpment. Beyond the far ridge lay the defile which carried West Way down from the uplands to the ford. The going was hard. Their boots slipped on the green-slimed chalk rubble beneath the leaves. Briars and brambles caught at them; they were both panting as side by side they reached the crest of the ridge, dropping to their bellies to wriggle the last few paces, anxious to avoid showing themselves until sure that the West Way was clear. A pair of magpies flew off down the slope ahead of them, long wedge-shaped tails trailing behind, laughing hoarsely, as though at some private joke. Aedd and Berin pressed themselves to the ground and froze, eyes darting nervously from cover to cover. Berin put his lips to Aedd's ear and whispered "We'll stay here a while, just to be sure. There's no hurry. We should wait until nightfall anyway before we go on to the ford."

The ground fell away steeply in front of them, through thickets of dogwood and elder to the beech forest below. Pigs grunted and squealed between the trees, rooting through the leaf mould, rustling the brittle brown fall. Idly they watched them. Visions of roast pork, the skin bubbling crisp and salt, formed in Aedd's mind. His stomach rumbled in response, reminding him that he'd missed breakfast. A watery sun found a thin spot in the grey gloom and for a while tried to brighten the outlook, then gave up and drabness returned and Aedd dozed.

The pigs scattered. Someone was approaching from the direction of the ford. Alert, Berin prodded Aedd awake and together they saw a figure rise from behind a holly bush and around the side of a beech tree, to stride purposefully down the West Way. They looked at each other and nodded in unspoken agreement; it was the outlander and he was meeting someone from the ford.

Stealthily they began the stalk, inching forward from cover to cover, checking, double checking before each movement. As they reached the holly bush where the outlander had lain, Berin was uncomfortably aware that there was something he should remember, something vitally important, but the answer eluded him. Then, as he peered down the track everything but revenge was driven from his mind by the hot red rage that jarred him at the sight of the outlander talking to Urak. He started to his feet, reaching for bow and arrow. Aedd gripped him by the arm, holding, pulling him down. Sanity returned, the storm clouds of fury cleared.

The stance of the two familiar hated figures sparked his memory. Suddenly he recalled the mind picture which had eluded him; a meeting under a solitary oak tree, the departure of Urak and his bondsmen, four watchers rising from their hiding places in the waist high grass. He turned to Aedd to warn him, but his alarm call was lost in a scurrying rush of crackling beech leaves, a sudden press of bodies, a blinding pain in his head and a spinning image, blurred by tears, of Aedd clubbed to his knees, his bronze-bound leather helmet slipping incongruously over one eye, before he fell full length face down in the leaves.

Berin's arms were pulled sharply behind him. The thongs twisted the soft skin on the inside of his wrists, burning, biting. The tendons of his arms cracked with the strain. Dimly he heard shouting above him and as though from a far world, an echo before he skidded into the black void of unconsciousness.

Excruciating pain in his groin brought Berin back to reality, retching, sucking back acrid bile in a frantic search for breath, its bitter taste almost unnoticed amidst the greater bitterness at his own foolishness. Berin struggled to rise, but was dragged up by the hair and slammed against the bole of the beech tree. His vision cleared. Urak and the outlander, flanked by Barak and their assailants loomed in a semi-circle, the crazy perspective giving the impression of their heads meeting at the apex of a cone.

The inert mound of Aedd lay beside him, blood trickling from a patch of matted hair behind his ear.

"This is the cause of your problems," Urak said, "Berin, son of Com, chief in his place now I suppose, now that Com is dead."

The outlander grunted and stepped forward, driving his boot into Berin's kidneys. "For logs," he said, as Berin slumped onto his side, pulling up his knees, trying to roll into a ball. The outlander knelt at his side and pulled Berin's head up by the hair, smacking his head against the tree before smashing his tightly balled fist into Berin's face. Berin felt his nose crunch and spread, his lip split against a loosened tooth. He tasted blood, warm, metallic, felt it run, hot and sticky down his chin. Faintly, through the humming in his ears he heard the outlander say "For the fire. You see I pay, I pay good."

"Where are they Berin?" Urak asked.

"Where you'll never find them, turd-eater," Berin answered thickly, lisping awkwardly from between puffed lips. Barak drove the butt of his spear into Berin's kidney. Pain lanced through him. He laughed, loud and mocking in his mind. In reality his voice was weak and cracked.

"They're dead," he said. "They are all drowned in the quicksand. I killed them," he shrieked as Barak drove the spear end into him again. "Dana forgive me," he sobbed, not feigning the anguish in his voice or the tears as the pain stabbed, flashing and darting, rolling and aching. "I led them the wrong way in the marshes. I led them to quicksand. We're all that's left. We came to kill you…" he laughed dementedly, the act not all that far from reality at that point.

Urak looked uncertainly at the outlander, who pursed his lips reflectively.

"Maybe he speaks the truth," the outlander said, then grinned, "If I him, I want kill you too."

"How can we be sure?" Urak asked.

"I find out," he answered. "Wake big man," he said to his men. "Get thorns."

Urak turned back to Berin. "So, you thought you would defy me, eh? Well you will pay for your impertinence."

"Kill me if you will Urak, there's nothing left for me now," Berin mumbled.

"What, not even my half-sister or that other slut of yours. Did she spurn you then I wonder before you drowned her? Perhaps the habits of obedience she learned from me..."

"You bastard!" Berin tried to rise, to hurl himself at Urak, only to be knocked sprawling by Barak.

"... are too rich a fare for her to be satisfied by lesser ranks," Urak laughed. "Oh you'll tell us where they are, where your slut is. No, you'll not pay with your life. You obviously value that too little. No, it's this freedom of yours that we'll take. Agron here will have you both as slaves, Olwen and Oranc too. You can amuse yourself thinking of him enjoying the little tricks I taught Olwen. What say you Agron, will you take these two as an advance payment?"

"Is good. The big one, he fetch good price, very strong, but I not forget woman and boy," he said, touching the black patch over his eye. "You bring me."

"You shall have them as I said, when we are finished."

The vileness of Urak's treachery hit Berin harder than any blow. Woman and boy; so that was why Urak wanted them, for the outlander. A picture formed of Olwen and Oranc on the hill above the settlement, just before the men from Ilws arrived. A sling shot, the outlander clasping his eye. Of course, he wanted them to revenge his eye. The thought of Olwen and Oranc in the outlander's power, open to his cruelties, hardened Berin's determination.

The outlander had roused Aedd, who lay back against the hillside, trussed hand and foot, helpless. One of Agron's men knelt, holding Aedd's hand, fingers extended. Another selected a thorn from a blackthorn branch. He looked to the outlander for confirmation and at his nod, thrust it hard under the nail of Aedd's index finger. Aedd's body heaved, back arching; he screamed, an awesomely desolate bellow, like that of a bull as it received the death thrust.

Agron turned back to Berin, judging his reaction to Aedd's pain in his eyes, pressing his face close to Berin's. "Tell me truth."

"Kill me," Berin answered. "Kill me and have done with it. I have told you the truth."

Agron smiled, he had his answer. No one wished for death so soon. He turned and nodded to his man. Again Aedd bucked and roared in pain.

"You'll never get them."

Agron held his silence, watching carefully, knowing it was better to let the talk flow.

"They're all safe from you. The woman and boy too. You'll not have the woman or the boy." Berin saw the outlander's eyes widen slightly. "The woman and the boy

Urak promised you. You'll not have them. I took them back from him, days agoThey are with the others."

Agron grabbed Berin's hair and battered his head against the tree. "You lie," he spat, peering closely at Berin, who smiled weakly through the pain, at the unfocused features before him, replying with the sincerity that only comes with the telling of a happy truth. "It's true. I took them back. You'll never have them now."
Agron rose and turned on Urak. "Is true what he say? Where boy and woman? You bring now."

Urak paled and backed away. "He's lying, don't listen to him. Don't you see what he's trying to do? He's trying to set us against each other."

Agron looked from Urak to Berin and back to Urak again. "No, he tell truth," he said coldly. "You lie." His hand reached for the dagger at his belt. Barak leapt between them, to fall twitching, choking on his own blood, spitted on a spear thrust through his side, dying, trying in that instant to work out what was happening to him, dying without the answer.

Agron, dagger drawn, advanced on Urak in a knife fighter's crouch, the dagger held low, underhand. Urak licked his lips, his mouth suddenly dry of spit, his eyes fixed in fascination on the threatening point.

"Agron, he's lying. What are you doing? Are you mad? I have Senot's protection. Do you hear? "Urak screamed, his voice rising, breaking in panic as he backed away. "I am Senot's man!"

The outlander's men spread out to encircle him, grinning wolfishly in anticipation.

"Fuck Senot," Agron jeered. "Next year we bring plenty ships, fuck Senot good." He slashed viciously at the terrified Urak who, backing away, tripped over Aedd's foot. The fall saved Urak from the full thrust of the dagger, but its sharp point caught him at the apogee of its upward flashing arc, slicing him from belly to breast bone. Urak instinctively clasped his hands to the stinging pain and stared in shocked disbelief at the blood welling between his fingers as he slowly buckled to his knees. His long black hair dropped over his face. With a reflex born of long habit, he brushed it back, smearing his face and hair with his blood, allowing the red-stained, shiny blue and white knotted tubes to protrude. He looked down in disbelief and tried to push them back, but they were slippery, and hard to control. Berin started to giggle, a curiously demented sound in the stillness broken otherwise only by the panting of the protagonists.

Agron stepped forward for the death thrust. One of his men cannoned into him and dropped at his feet, a feathered shaft protruding from between his shoulder blades. An arrow bruised Agron's breast and fell at his feet, its flint point shattered on the bronze rings of his jerkin. Agron jerked around, his head moving rapidly, unable to locate the danger. More arrows hummed and hissed; one plucked at his sleeve, another caught in his cloak. The second of his men fell, twitching, but dead the instant the arrow split his eye. A third swore loud and foully at the dart in his thigh, breaking off the shaft, but unable to rid himself of the biting stone within him. For the briefest of moments Agron stared at his fallen comrades, then instinct took over and sent him leaping and bounding up the West Way, shield held between him and the slope, his uninjured companion hard at his heels. The wounded man screamed his lonely despair to their backs and set off in hopeless pursuit, dragging his leg, to fall within five paces, pierced through and through.

Grwlch and his hunters emerged from their cover in dogwood, elder and holly stands, some seeming to rise from the ground, to solidify from the air itself. Gentle fingers plucked the thorns from Aedd's fingers and sharp knives cut their bonds. Strong but tender hands and arms lifted and supported. Grwlch pushed one of the corpses with his toe, grunting in satisfaction at the dead weight, then turned to Berin, who was being helped to his feet.

"My thanks, Grwlch, " Berin said shakily. "I thought I would see the Mother then, for sure."

"You tried hard my friend, you tried hard enough."

"How did you come to be here? Dana must think kindly of me."

"Not the Earth Mother, but mistress A'isa. She sent me to look for you."

"Then I am in your and her debt."

"No, I think rather that the scales are now better balanced," Grwlch answered. "Do you want me to finish this bat shit for you?" he asked, indicating Urak, thumbing the blade of his knife.

Berin laughed hollowly. "Not yet Grwlch. Let the bastard suffer. He's caused enough pain to others, Belu and Ermid, Com, little Cas, bless him, Amren, Naf, Han, Arec, Kar, Madwg, aye, even his own sister Branwen. Let the bastard hurt for the fatherless children, the widows, the lovers left alone." Berin choked back his sorrow, not wanting to dilute his hatred, the sweet heady drunkenness of raw revenge.

"Did you hear Aedd, that bit about Senot?" he asked,

as Aedd staggered to his feet, pale and shaken, clutching his damaged fingers in the comfort of his armpit.

"Aye, the treacherous bastard, "Aedd replied."Ah, but will you just look at him," he added with a grimace compounded of hatred, disgust and sympathy. Urak's intestines slipped and slid through his fingers. Dried leaves and dirt stuck to them.

"Finish him off man."

Urak looked up from juggling his viscera, his face drawn, all hope gone, the pain biting deep, suddenly aware that his span on earth was drawing to a close, as the blood ran in a wide stream over his britches. "Yes, Berin, finish me," he gasped.

"Not until you rot, as my father did."

"Ah it hurts," Urak screeched. "Finish me, please!" he begged.

"Ask Senot, your master."

"Kill me, quickly."

"Ask Olwen, she might, for the whippings you gave her, you foul turd-eater."

"No, not Olwen," Urak gasped, his face suddenly a caricature of cunning contorted by pain. "She'd sooner beg me for more of what I gave her."

With a scream of rage Berin snatched a spear from Grwlch and thrust it through the base of Urak's throat, tipping him back with the fury of his strike, leaning his weight against the shaft as he felt resistance, pinning Urak to the ground. The light dimmed in Urak's eyes and his face set in an expression as near to satisfaction as anyone had ever seen before, on a corpse.

CHAPTER 34

Berin felt the cold outside the sleeping furs; he could feel the air, icy on his nose, see his breath frost. The fire had died down; it still smouldered for he could smell the wraiths of smoke, but he could not see even the dullest red glow from the embers. The taper had long since guttered to extinction, yet it was not completely dark. It did not feel like dawn, yet there was a curious lightness about the sky visible through the smoke hole. The air was still, there was an unnatural silence, as though the normal night sounds of the camp were muffled.

Olwen stirred beside him, pressing her cheek to his chest, reaching an arm across him, tangling her leg with his. He hugged her warmth tight to him, gratefully taking the chance to stretch his arm, cramped from where she had lain. He wriggled his fingers to dissipate the tingling.

Talwch should be back soon, today even, he thought. Oh Dana, make him let us stay. This place is good. We can be safe here. Life will be hard, especially during this, the first winter, but there's plenty of timber for building, scrub and deadfall for firewood; plenty of game and if that should fail, there's always wildfowl and fish in the marshes. A pity Aedd is leaving; it won't be the same without him. Olwen will miss Ened, A'isa too; her leg has mended well. She'll go with Talwch this time, no doubt.

"Are you awake?" Olwen whispered softly, breaking in on his thoughts, as though on cue.

"Mmm... yes."

"It's very quiet."

"Yes, I think it has snowed."

"Brr... I hate the cold. I'm glad I'm not sleeping alone. You're lovely and warm," she said, raising her face, kissing his throat as she hugged him."

"Will Aedd and Ened still leave, now that it has snowed?" she asked.

"He seems set on going, whatever. I've tried to persuade him to wait until spring, but he won't have it. He's set on leaving as soon as possible. They would have had snow one day soon anyway. If he has any sense though, he'll wait until Talwch comes. The right word from him could help a lot."

"It's a terrible time to travel."

"Try telling that to Aedd."

Olwen was silent, glad that she would not be setting out on such a journey." Do you think there's anything in Ened's story?"

"We'll see, won't we. Aedd feels he has to try; this trip of his could be our salvation if it comes off."

"But it's so dangerous; all those tales of war bands and slaving gangs. Can't you persuade him to leave young Alen behind?"

Berin chuckled ruefully, "Who would be his gaoler? They should be all right. I expect the slavers will be stopping about now. They'll be too busy setting up winter camps. Anyway, Aedd plans to go around all that trouble."

"But how will he find his way?"

"Grwlch has promised to give him a guide. It seems the river people know the West Sea. Grwlch told him that beyond the hills at the headwaters of the Great River, there's a salt river which rises and falls like the sea. The people there told him it was an arm of the sea and not really a river at all."

"We're so lucky to have something to trade... Oh Berin, I'm sorry. I didn't mean it to sound like that." Olwen hugged him tightly, hating herself for her stupidity.

Berin was silent.

"Berin, I'm sorry."

"It's all right. You are right; we are lucky. I had no idea how lucky until Warwch brought Bronwen's gift to me. The jet and amber are beautiful. The gold and those blue stones, well I really didn't expect anything like them. They'll fetch a good price in bronze, I'm sure, if they find any."

"Did you love her?" The words simply slipped out, almost without her knowing.

Berin was silent for so long that but for his gentle fingers caressing the soft rise of her hip, she would have thought him asleep, or worse, withdrawn from her. She damned her foolishness, but she had to know, she just had to.

"She saved us. She stood up to Tarok and Urak; made them look small in front of their men. Her example made Iowerth stay. We would all be crow bait but for that. She brought me Warwch and the other bondmen, well freemen now. They saved us the first time the outlanders breached the wall. She was so young, so alive..." Berin drifted into silence as the memories flickered. Olwen lay still, hardly daring to breath.

"She wanted so little, you see. She did her duty as she had been taught. She stood by her husband to be, even against her own brothers and stayed to face what seemed at the time to be certain death or slavery, though she could have left. She loved me; in the end died for me and even now, after death may save me and mine," Berin sighed.

"She knew of my love for you; accepted it; knew that at best she could only share me. She wanted so little, was happy with less. Yes I loved her, for a very short time I truly did."

Berin was silent; for a moment he was in another bed; another soft body warmed him. Olwen's wet lashes on his chest, the shaking of her suppressed sobs brought him back to the present.

"What is it Olwen?" he asked gently, lifting her chin, kissing her salt tears. "You know that I love you before all else"

"I'm sorry, I'm so ashamed. I have all of you now and have done so little. She did so much and has nothing."

"No, don't be so hard on yourself," he said softly. "Who ever knows how something will end. We all have to do what we feel we have to do. It's how we live, how we do what we have to do that matters. Besides, she has a place forever with all of us that were there. And if Aedd manages to trade well, then with all those that weren't there too."

Olwen's arm snaked around his neck, drawing his lips to hers, pulling him on to her, exulting in his weight on her, his hardness so quickly roused, spreading her thighs to receive him, to offer the ultimate comfort within a woman's gift, rejoicing in the gift so readily, so joyfully accepted, finally simply surrendering to passion.

Berin awoke as Olwen, already dressed and wrapped in a cloak against the cold, knelt by the fire, cheeks bellowing, trying to coax a flame from the dry grass and tinder she had heaped on the embers. He hopped awkwardly from the furs, shivering and dressed as quickly as he could, stooping to kiss Olwen's smudged forehead as she sat back on her heels to draw breath.

He blinked in the bright light. The camp, barely astir, was covered with a smooth white blanket. Columns rose from the smoke holes of the huts which sheltered early risers, through the still air, dark grey against the bluing sky. The ground around the watch fire was trampled where the disgruntled sentries had stamped their cold feet in the night. A few tracks led in the direction of the privy; birds had left their cuneiform signs, but otherwise the white surface was pure and unbroken. Icicles hung from the thatch, reflecting the light from the sun's bright orange disc, rising over the ford. Even the stark black branches were softened by the purity of their icy burden.

A gagging sound made him turn. Olwen had followed him out and was doubled over by the doorway, retching.

"What is it?" he asked anxiously, putting his arm around her, feeling her muscles tense, her stomach heave. "What's the matter?"

Olwen wiped her face on her sleeve and stood up, pale, shaking slightly, but smiling broadly, her eyes shining.

"Oh don't look so worried," she said, resting her hand on his arm. "It's all right. Rh'on says it's normal."

"What?" Berin asked, still puzzled.

"I'm going to have our baby."

Grwlch announced that Talwch would arrive that day. When Berin asked Grwlch how he knew, the river man

433

shook his head and grinned. It was a mystery how the river men seemed to know each others' whereabouts, a mystery as deep as their uncanny ability to vanish into a landscape.

Grwlch had persuaded Aedd to delay his departure so that he could travel the river men's domain with Talwch's blessing. Berin was sure that what Grwlch really wanted was to get Talwch's permission to send the guide. Berin had tried to persuade Aedd not to go at all, but he and Ened were packed and ready.

A'isa too was packed. Grwlch had gathered her few possessions against her shrill protests, but she was far from ready to go anywhere. The reason was clear for all to see. Oranc moped and mooned at her side, a pain to all around him, except A'isa, and she no longer had any judgement in the matter. The transformation wrought in A'isa by her impending departure was amazing. For days she had imperiously ordered the doting Oranc around as a bondman, dismissing him when it suited her, which was often. Now she would do anything, it seemed to stay with him. They were not fit for the company of others, so they kept their own, holding hands, gazing soulfully into each others' eyes.

Grwlch and his men had also bundled up the dried and smoked meat which the hunters had gathered. The efforts of Berin and his men still hung in the branches, puny in comparison, but still a sop to winter hunger.

Talwch came at noon, appearing as river men always did, from nowhere. Berin, Aedd, Auron, Talwch and Grwlch sat around the watch fire, now blazing, banked up to offer warmth.

"I have taken counsel from my chiefs and elders," Talwch began. "We do not like the changes which are happening all around us..."

Berin tensed, staring at his feet, inspecting his boots muddied by the slush melting around the fire. This is it, he thought. Where to go from here? Fight Talwch or submit to Tarok? Aye, with Aedd and Ened gone it is a possibility. At least survival lies that way. Tarok might welcome some experienced fighting men. We could get terms...

"We do not welcome you to our lands. You came unbidden, seeking sanctuary and asked to stay, asked for land. Now you ask for our help to search for bronze in the west, to make trade. If you succeed, more people will come, many of these will want land too. In time, the game will be frightened away, our hunting will fail, our way of life will die. I see all this." Talwch paused, looking from one to the other, his dark eyes filled with the pain of his vision.

"Yet I cannot change the world," he continued after a while. "If not you, there will be others, crueller than you, stronger than us. If we must lose our lands, we would rather give willingly to our friends than have them taken by foes who despoil, who do not even honour the Earth Mother. We have agreed to help you."

Relief surged over Berin, warming him as no fire ever could. His son would be born free.

"You may have whatever land you can hold against Senot and the outlanders on this side of the river between this place, the ford and the place which you call the outstation. It is not all marsh. There are hills which rise above the water which I'm sure you will find suitable for your farms. We will show you the paths. We will also help Aedd in his quest and permit trade under our protection if he is successful." He paused, looking at each of them in turn. This is it, Berin thought, the trade.

"In return," Talwch continued, "you will be our ally, against Senot, the outlanders, the madness in the West, even against Tarok if need be. Our enemies will be your enemies. We will also receive half of Aedd's trade," he added. "Is it agreed, Berin?"

Berin looked at Aedd and Auron, the two remaining elders. They slowly, barely perceptibly, nodded their heads. "Aye Talwch, it is agreed."

Most of the river men had already filed out of sight, leaving a trampled muddy path on the white surface of the hillside, when Talwch turned to Berin. "It is time for us to return to winter camp. If you have need, you know where to find us," he said. "Perhaps you should use Oranc as a messenger," he grinned, pointing to where Oranc slumped, morosely contemplating the end of his world.

"I wish you would take him with you," Berin laughed, "He will be no use to us like that."

"Work him hard," Talwch grinned. "He will still have an easier time with you than dancing attendance on my daughter. Better he stays with you. The winter is a good test of puppy love."

A'isa, from the look she darted at her father, clearly contemplated patricide.

"Farewell Talwch," Berin said, "and thank you."

"No thanks are necessary. It must be so," he answered, taking A'isa by the elbow. They began to move off, A'isa looking soulfully back over her shoulder at Oranc.

Aedd, enormous in his furs and pack turned to Berin, holding out his hand. "I'll be off then. See you when I see you, I suppose, there's no telling how long it will take," he said, masking his feelings in inanity, a device recognised and accepted by them both.

Berin took Aedd's massive mittened hand in both hands. "Good luck Aedd, Ened, you too; young Alen, take care of them for us. May Dana go with you all, may she bless your venture and bring you back safely to us."

"May she stay with you too, Berin," Ened cried, kissing him on the cheek, before throwing her arms around Olwen, hugging her. "I'm going to miss you. I'll try to get back in time for the little one."

A'isa broke from her father's restraining hand and ran back to Berin, looking up at him from sad, dark, yet somehow still mischievous eyes. "Thank you Berin," she said, reaching to peck briefly at his cheek, suddenly bashful, colouring at her temerity. She hugged Olwen tightly to cover her confusion. "I'll come and see you all as often as father allows me. Take care," she said, tears starting as she took both of her friend's hands in hers and leant back at arm's length to inspect her, as though to impress Olwen on her memory. A'isa turned finally to Oranc. She took his face gently between her palms and pressed her lips firmly to his. She drew back, silent, her expression serious, intense, the fierce possessiveness of her look said everything. She turned and ran back to her father as Oranc stood stunned, still and mute. He slowly lifted his fingers as though in farewell then pressed them in wonder to his lips. A'isa resisted the urge to look back. She knew that she had just lit a fire which would warm them both throughout the winter.

Berin and Olwen turned to the rest of their people who had gathered to wish the travellers good luck. Oranc stood as though he had grown from the spot, staring at the tracks left behind long after the last dark head had disappeared around the white rim of the hill.

"Look, whilst you are all here," Berin announced self-consciously, "I should tell you what's going on and what needs to be done. As you probably know by now, Talwch has given us land, everything we can hold between here, the ford and the outstation." The delighted smiles and nods of the company confirmed that those out of earshot of his earlier conversation with Talwch had quickly been informed by those near enough to have heard. "As you all know, I'm sure," Berin continued, "Aedd has gone off with some trade goods that... well that Branwen brought as her dowry, to see if he can find bronze weapons to trade. It's a slim chance, but if he does manage it... well, they will help us to hold on to this place." Berin glanced around him. "Life will not be easy. We'll have to fight to keep our new land. We'll have to work hard to make it produce for us. All we have is virgin ground, but as our forefathers managed, so can we. The alternative is to submit to Tarok and I'm damned if I'm going to do that."

Berin paused to draw breath. He felt pretentious. He hated making speeches, but his audience were all friends, kinfolk and from the sideways looks and nudges, most of what he was saying seemed to meet with their approval. Reassured, he went on. "There are some things which we must do. We have to survive this winter, as our forefathers did, without grain stocks, without the herds. That means we must gather as much food as we can; hunt and fish, dry and smoke the meat, like the river men. We must collect firewood, but most important of all, we have to clear the

438

ground and prepare it for spring planting. Then we have to build some decent houses to last, for generations."

"Hah," laughed Cadw, "you can tell who's just learned he's going to be a father."

"Aye, that's true enough," Berin responded, "and you can tell who wants to be one so much that he's forever practising."

Han's pretty young widow, Grainne, blushed and slapped him playfully. Cadw smiled uneasily, discomfited by the raucous laughter that Berin's remark raised about him. His determined pursuit of the young widow was the cause of most fireside gossip of the moment, yet he had believed himself to be so discrete.

"But there are things we must be careful not to do as well," Berin added grimly. "For the moment we are well protected by the marsh. We have to make sure that no one stumbles on the secrets of our paths through the swamp. No one leaves without me knowing about it. There's another thing. Gwyn here baked bread this morning. Enjoy it, all of you. It is the last we shall eat until we harvest our first crop. The corn we have left is for seed. Nor will any of the stock be slaughtered. Although we have no feed for them, we must hope that they can fend for themselves on the hill and survive to bear the young which most of them carry. They and the seed corn are our future. One last point," Berin added. "We have all lost loved ones, friends, our hearths, our possessions. We were rich and prosperous and are now poor, but let us be equally poor. Let us forget that the oxen were Amren's, that the sheep and dogs were mine, that the cow was Naf's and the sows Aedd's. It will be a struggle to survive. We must share what we were able to save, work together to make it through." There was a

439

general murmur of assent. Good, thought Berin, they've accepted it.

"Now for the work parties. Brys and I will hunt. Auron, you will take two of Warwch's men and the oxen and start to clear the ground at the top of the hill. Cadw, you will cut and haul the timber. Take Oranc and two of Warwch's men· you will have to use the oxen from time to time, arrange it with Auron. Elin, you take care of the building. Use Warwch and the rest of his men. Olwen and Gwyn will take charge of the smoking and drying. Rh'on, will you please organise the rest of the women and the children on the gathering...? Rh'on...? Mother, what is it?"

Rh'on was staring fixedly, almost trance-like towards the eastern horizon. She shuddered. "Oh nothing, I... just one of my turns I expect. Now what was it you wanted me to do, organise the gathering? Yes of course. I'll get the children involved too."

CHAPTER 35

When Berin rose, early the next morning, he saw Rh'on standing on the top of the slope above the camp, once again staring towards the east. Her face glowed bronze in the red light from the newly awakened sun. Concerned that she should be standing out in the cold, he trudged towards her, though the camp. He bent forward to the slope, his breath a white plume, the snow squeaking under his boots.

"Mother, what is it? You should..." Berin stopped as he saw the expression on Rh'on's face; it was as if she carried the sadness of a thousand generations. Slowly she lifted her arm, pointing towards the sun.

Berin turned; a smudge of black smoke spread thinly over the distant hills, fed by a twisting plume rising from the ford. "Oh Dana spare them," he muttered.

The men soon gathered as the news spread around the waking camp.

"What are we going to do, Berin?" Brys asked.

"Nothing. What can we do?"

"But they're our kin," Auron shouted. "Iowerth and Creggan helped us, fought for us."

"Aye, but if it's burning now, we're too late. Anyway, we are too few to make any difference."

"We can't just stay here and do nothing," Brys protested. Rh'on touched his sleeve gently, "What does your heart say, Berin?" she asked.

"They're our kin, we must save them," Auron yelled.

"Save? Save?" Berin yelled back. "There are hundreds of them and but a dozen of us."

"Listen to your heart," Rh'on whispered urgently at his side.

Berin looked from one to the other, eyeing their angry faces. As he stared their features blurred and were replaced by those of Branwen and Iowerth and Creggan. Berin's shoulders straightened. Of course they must do what they could.

"We'll go and see if any have escaped and help them if we can, but by Dana, you had better be ready to run."

Berin lay at the top of the escarpment, looking out over the open chalk uplands. He felt cold, numb and very vulnerable, a dark stain in the white winter landscape. Though he wrapped his cloak ever more tightly around him, the cold penetrated. His toes and fingers felt like ice. The men stretched in a line below him, to the bottom of the escarpment, each within sight of the next man in line, each, like himself, fighting the cold and boredom. Berin had approached as close as he dared. Now he was ready to go back. The days were short and darkness would come soon. Even if they left at once they would barely get home before nightfall.

There had been no movement on the uplands that long day; no human movement that is. A stag had trotted proudly from cover to paw at the snow, trying to uncover the grass. Berin had admired its noble head and antlers. Ten tines, a patriarch amongst the red deer, and then had damned his hunter's luck that the best quarry always seemed to tantalise, to appear when the chase was impossible. But he had marked it for a future occasion. The

442

stag had not settled. With the light wind coming from the settlement at the ford, it could not have caught his scent. Perhaps it was a whiff of burning or movement around the ford which had disturbed it.

A hare had hopped slowly across his line of sight, floundering in the snow, stopping occasionally to sit up and twist its long black-tipped ears, its incredibly mobile nostrils testing the breeze.

A scrabbling sound above him made Berin look up. Snow showered from the branches of the oak tree. Two squirrels, silky dark brown in their winter coats, oblivious to the watchers below, chased each other through the bare branches, scampering along the wider boughs, leaping through space, legs extended, bushy tails trailing, to crash into the outer branches of the neighbouring tree, then running head first down the trunk, claws scrabbling, gripping frantically at the ridged bark. As quickly as they had come, they were gone and there was silence.

A jay screeched. Berin peered through the closely laced branches, but saw nothing. He glanced down the slope to Brys below him. Brys was alert, staring along the slope. Then Berin heard, snapping twigs, a startled shout, a child's cry of pain, quickly smothered. Once more Berin raised his head above the lip. The uplands were as clear as ever, a smooth white expanse, even the bushes rounded by their coating of snow, turning blue-grey in the fading light. Berin hissed to attract Brys's attention, motioning him forward.

Seven people slipped and staggered in ragged line, grabbing on to saplings, roots, cannoning into tree trunks, falling, rising, skidding again on an icy branch beneath the snow, weaving an erratic path through the forest. Four were children, wide-eyed, frightened, led by the hand by two women, who had bunched their long skirts about the waist the better to free their legs, which now were scratched and muddied, mottled pink and blue-white beneath the dirt by the cold. The party was led by a man, supporting himself on a spear shaft, the point broken. His britches were torn and stained, blood oozed from a ragged hole where they covered his thigh and from beneath a rough bandage tied around his head. He had a haunted look as he peered behind them.

Berin barely recognised him. "Creggan," he hissed.

Creggan wheeled around, dropping automatically into a fighting stance, almost comical in his ragged, exhausted state, a pitiful parody of the man when fit and armed.

"Ah Berin, Dana be praised!" Take the women and children. I must get back to Iowerth."

"Brys, Berin commanded, "Take them to the camp."

"I heard fighting a few hundred paces back, nothing since. Senot's men, about ten. I must go to Iowerth and..."

"Here, go with Brys man, we'll see to it. Go, you can't help us now."

Berin watched the scurrying figures follow Brys along the side of the ridge, their steps still tired and uncertain, but their backs straightened by hope. A cry of pain jerked his head around. Iowerth and four men were running bent over, following the track left by their women and children. The last in line pitched forward, an arrow sticking from the back of his thigh. His comrades turned at his scream and made a shield wall about him, facing the approaching danger together.

Berin heard the fallen man plead with Iowerth to go on as the dark shapes gathered menacingly in front of them, slinking in like wolves along the trail, fanning out before the shields and spear points, jostling for position, searching for firm footing in the snow, trying to edge around, to outflank, to gain height, any trick to stack the already well stacked advantage before the kill.

The combatants faced each other grimly, triumph on the one side, sick despair on the other, a mutual recognition of this being the last confrontation. Berin loosed his arrow at the packed attackers, a man fell, sending a disturbance through the line, a ripple of fear as Senot's men searched out the new danger.

"To me Com and Ilws," Berin yelled as he launched himself down the slope, cloak flying behind him, sword and shield in hand. "Com and Ilws," his cry echoed through the forest as Auron and Elin, Cadw, Warwch and the rest of them ran to his support.

The attackers, so suddenly and unexpectedly attacked, turned, confused. Berin's downward rush crashed his shield into the end of the line; the man he hit stumbled and slipped, cursing, falling onto and tripping those further down the slope, who had turned to face Cadw, Warwch and his men. Iowerth's shield wall parted; Auron and Elin pushed through, their bronze blades slashing where moments before flint spear tips had defied. It was too much. The rout was complete.

"Stop," Berin yelled as Warwch set off in pursuit. "You'll bring a swarm of them about our ears if you're not careful. Just see they don't creep back."

"Iowerth, are there more of you out there?"

"No, none that are free, or live; not that I know of," Iowerth gasped. "I'm so glad to see you. I thought that would be my end."

"What's happened?" Auron asked.

"Later Auron," Berin interrupted. "We'll hear it all. We've got to get them to safety, us too come to that. Go on, get on man."

Berin heaved himself heavy-thighed up the hill to retrieve his bow and spear. As he straightened he saw a column of armed men trotting along the edge of the cleared ground towards him. "Outlanders!" he called, bounding down the slope. The party already jogging ahead of him, suddenly accelerated.

The fugitives retraced their steps in silence, saving their breath for their effort, running, equipment banging on back and thigh, feeling the cold air rasp in their lungs, the spit thickening in their mouths, hearing their hearts pounding, the panting of their comrades, the slip, the slither, the choked off curse. They stopped only to exchange bearers for the wounded man they carried, grateful of the chance to steal an extra breath into heaving chests. Their eyes never left the trail they had left in the snow behind them.

It was growing dark when they reached the edge of the marsh, where white-decked osiers and sedge banks rose from black and eerie pools. They paused for a moment, bent over or crouched on the ground to recover their wind. Out in the swamp they heard a splash and a cry as Brys led the women and children to safety. There was no sound of pursuit.

"They came at us from both sides at once," Iowerth said quietly, shaking his head. Sitting at Berin's hearth in borrowed clothes, rested, fed and cleaned, the lines of strain still showed stark and deep, etched deeper by the shadows cast by the flaring fire and the flickering tapers. "First reports came from the West Way," Iowerth continued. "The outlanders came in at dawn with the snow. Most of the watchmen were taken before our people even knew what was happening. Hiding away, I suppose, trying to keep warm. Well they paid a high price for their small comfort. By mid-morning all the upper farms had gone, but young Crynhew made it back to us at the settlement. Saw his whole family taken, poor lad." Iowerth sipped from his bowl of rose hip tea.

"Tarok sent Creggan out with a guard for the gorge, I'll say that for him. He was sure that Senot would be attacking at the same time. The rest of us were ordered to defend the settlement, but we'd already lost all the men from the outer farms and the men from the homesteads on the other bank hadn't yet assembled. The outlanders rounded up all the homesteaders on this side, just roped them all together and put them in the stockyard like cattle. Tarok tried and tried to drive them off, but they're buggers to fight." Iowerth wiped his face with the palm of his hand, as though wanting to wipe away the detail still so vivid in his memory. The rasping of his hand on his stubble sounded loud in the expectant silence.

"Out in the open like that, without a stronghold, we didn't stand a chance. Those great blades chop clean through a wicker and hide shield and an ash shaft. A wooden shield's all right though; sometimes if you give it a twist, you can catch a blade in it."

Berin ignored the digression and the silence which followed, knowing that Iowerth must go on at his own pace.

"They just cut us to pieces." Iowerth put down the bowl and buried his face in his hands. The silence lengthened, broken only by the crackling of the fire. Berin glanced at the flame reddened faces around him; Auron, Rh'on and Olwen, silent, smitten, sharing Iowerth's pain, recognising in it their own.

"Those of us with bronze, Tarok, me, we did all right, but the rest of them had a hard time, Dana rest them. We abandoned the settlement after noon and pulled back to the ford. We managed to get most of the women and children over. The ford was easier to hold, they could only come at us a few at a time, though we had the sun in our eyes later. That's when old Anoeth..." again Iowerth was silent. His shoulders shook and he started to sob. "The silly old sod just charged out of his hut straight at them, swinging his great flint axe. It was as if he'd decided it was time for him to go. That big bastard with the eye patch near cut him in two."

Berin felt his throat close, tears prick. Olwen's warm hand slid into his and squeezed.

"Then word came from Creggan. He'd been fighting Senot's men, hundreds of them, most of them with bronze. He had held them for ages in the gorge, but was being driven back; his squad was just about wiped out, not one of them not wounded. That Creggan," Iowerth shook his head in wonder, "what a fight it must have been. Anyway, what with Senot coming up in our rear, Tarok sends the women and children off with the wounded to the outstation, and me with a troop to help Creggan. We managed to hold Senot again at that narrow bit on the far bank, you know, where it gets really steep and the path overhangs the river on the bend.

The outlanders broke across the ford just before sundown. They used rafts to put some men across upstream. We had to pull back then, with them in our rear and Senot pressing hard. We thought we were all done for; it was very mixed up, small parties fighting everywhere. Tarok had formed a rearguard and was fighting his way back to the outstation. Creggan and I managed to keep some of the men together and fought our way out of the gorge, but we couldn't break through to join Tarok. Outlanders and Senot's men were everywhere, rounding up our people, sacking the farmsteads. Some managed escape to the outstation; we did save some. Dana be praised, we found our own hiding at the House of the Dead, looking for us, bless them for their faith. But not many got away, none of those who stayed to fight it out at their farms. We were cut off from the main party, so we swam the river. Mother it was cold. We hid out at the foot of the escarpment overnight and started to make our way here at first light. Then Senot's men found our trail. We ... well you know what..."

There was a collective sigh as Iowerth's voice petered out to silence. Olwen felt detached, floating, finding it hard to establish reference points in the emptiness left by the news of the destruction of the centre of their lives; the settlement at the ford, seat of the High Chief, resting place of their ancestors, home of their legends. Now, quite suddenly and brutally it was gone; taken and abused by strangers, soiled.

"Why, how could it happen?" Auron asked, his voice emphasising the confusion he too was experiencing. "Coms and Ilws I can understand now. We were so few and stuck

449

out there miles from anyone. But the ford; why they are... were so many, so rich, so powerful."

"So blind," said Rh'on. "You missed out so blind."

"What do you mean?" asked Olwen.

"Berin knows, don't you my son. He's tried to tell us all many times these last moons; and Talwch of the river people sees it too."

"You tell them, mother" Berin said, sadly.

Rh'on was silent for a long moment as she arranged her thoughts. Olwen stood and replaced a taper and heated more water, the stones hissing, the steam joining the wood smoke on its curling trip to the roof.

"I had never thought to add this chapter to clan lore," she said sadly. "We became rich and contented, it is true, by controlling trade, the furs, cattle and sheep, wool and hides, stone axes, greenstone, flint, amber, jet and salt. Our market was the biggest and most famous throughout the chalk lands. Anyone who travelled or traded along the West Way or the Great River passed through the ford. But we enjoyed our prosperity too much. We became complacent and blind. We ignored the fact that the outlanders had come. At first we saw them as a curiosity, but our neighbours were dealing with them. We didn't see that trade was changing. We ignored the danger of bronze, the power it gives and the craving for more power which it provokes. We ignored how Senot grew in power by befriending the outlanders."

"But how did the ford come to fall? We were so many and not bad fighters either," Auron persisted.

"Many, but widespread. Good warriors yes, but each fighting for himself. We live each in our own separate

450

homesteads or hamlets. Yes, we owe allegiance to a chief, and through him to the High Chief. We have bondmen and women, its true, but mainly we are free to live our separate lives, offering our allegiance only where we feel it is deserved. It is our great strength, but also our weakness."

"But I still don't see..." puzzled Auron.

"We have no proper defence against a powerful attacker like Senot because we have never seen the need and whilst everyone else, all the other clans lived like us, there was no need." Rh'on explained patiently. "Senot, as he grew in power was able to command men to service. He became rich enough to feed them and to pay them and arm them with bronze. Senot formed a permanent war band, and an alliance with those devils the outlanders. We did not, do not have a war band. Before Berin saw the need, we did not even have a stronghold to run to."

"Our defence lies with levies which come when they are called, if they are called in time and if they agree," Berin stated. "Iowerth, how many men stayed on their farms to defend them and were taken one by one?"

"Many Berin, far too many."
Now do you see?" Rh'on asked gently.

"I think so," Auron answered.

Rh'on looked at each of them in turn. "We thought that Tarok was taking too much to himself, the way he commanded obedience, right or wrong. The power he sought is as nothing next to that which Senot now commands. Our world has not seen the like of it before. Mark my words. What has happened since the harvest is not the end of Com, Ilws or of the settlement of the ford, for these are but places and will endure for ever. What has happened is the end of a way of life, maybe for ever."

CHAPTER 36

The sweat dropped on to the freshly split timber, spreading, sinking into the grain. Berin wiped his wrist across his forehead and reached for a thicker oak wedge, pressing it into the widening crack, driving it home with sharp blows from the back of the greenstone axe. Some things made of stone were still better than bronze, he reflected; not many though. He grunted as he hammered the wedge home. The log split. He picked up the fallen plank, putting it to one side, and reset the log in the trestles, starting another split with his bronze axe.

Oranc, grinning happily, hefted the plank and dropped it beside Elin, who stood in a sea of shavings, shaping the planks with an adze. Elin grunted and reached for the water pitcher.

"You can put that one up," he said.

Oranc fitted the plank across the beams and climbed up the short ladder. He secured the plank by driving hardwood pegs through the prepared holes. Oranc was as happy as he could remember. A'isa was waiting, the sun was hot on his back, they would soon break from work on the granary and he would be with her again.

"Are you going to have a break now?" Olwen asked, standing next to Berin, watching him work, admiring the glistening bunched muscles of his bared back.

"One more," Berin grunted through his hammering then stood with a sigh of relief, straightening his back, as the split ran the length of the log with a loud crack. He looked towards Olwen, bright eyes shining her love for him and for their son Garth, greedily sucking at her breast, pummelling with tiny clenched fists, the warm white milk squirting through the corner of his lips, his long-lashed eyes closed in ecstatic fulfilment.

Tenderly Berin touched his son's cheek with the back of his forefinger, marvelling once again at the softness and, as Garth grabbed his finger, at the perfection of the tiny pink nails at the ends of overlong fingers.

"He's so greedy, sucking away like that."

"He's his father's son," Olwen replied archly.

"He's just gorgeous," A'isa pronounced emphatically, appearing suddenly, as quick, fresh and elusive as stream water running through fingers, leaning across to kiss Garth, flashing a wide-mouthed smile at Oranc, who grinned back and jumped down from the ladder.

Berin caught her sun-warm young womanly scent and for a moment felt, not jealousy exactly, but a pang for time passing, for time already past, for a memory of a grassy bank and of Olwen sitting quietly at his side.

"Come on Oranc," A'isa called, holding out her hand. "I've brought your meal in the basket. Let's go up the hill."

The two of them raced off hand in hand, Aisa's skirts flying, swirling and dancing in time to her excited chatter. Elin set down his adze and stared wistfully after them.

"She's a girl and a half, that Aisa," he said. "That there Oranc's a lucky lad."

Berin put his arm around Olwen, their hips bumped companionably as they strolled.

"Aye, Elin. I hope we have time to get a brew ready before we need to feast them. It'll not be long."

"It will be good to have some ale again. I've had a long dry year."

"We're brewing as fast as we can," Olwen protested laughingly. "You men are all the same."

"I enjoy having bread again most," Berin said, "and nice fat pork. I've eaten enough lean, dry game this past year to last me a lifetime."

"Aye, those sows of Aedd's gave us some good litters. Mind you, it doesn't taste the same without the beech forest for them to root in," Elin remarked.

The threshers set down their flails and brushed the chaff from their clothes whilst they waited their turn to drink from the pitchers, leaning back to gulp the cool spring water, satisfying thirst and settling the prickling dust. Gwyn, her huge buttocks and bosoms quivering, stood in the puddle of her own shadow and tossed grain on the woven rush tray. A cloud of dust and chaff hung for a while, some sticking to her damp red face, to the hair plastered on her forehead and to her meaty arms; most was whisked away by a cooling swirl of breeze. Gwyn tipped the grain on to a growing pale yellow cone.

Berin paused for a moment to assess the harvest; the pile of grain at Gwyn's side, the stacked sheaves beside the threshing floor, measuring them in his mind against the areas cut and the corn still standing. It was good. The first harvest on new ground often was; they wouldn't be hungry before the next harvest and they would have plenty left for seed corn.

Rh'on greeted them with a smile which broadened as she took the sleeping form of little Garth from Olwen. There were moments during the long cold winter, especially in the times of the hard frosts and long nights and again during the depressing grey time, cold and wet, when winter refused to acknowledge spring, when Berin had feared for his mother. It had been as if she were waiting to be called. She had often spoken of being of another time. But since her grandson was born as the grain ripened, it was as if she had been given new life too; now she spoke only of the future.

"It will be good to have Aedd back," Berin announced as he sat on a stool and accepted a bowl of stew and a piece of bread. "He must have done some trade to have two pack ponies with him."

"I'm so excited," Olwen said. "I wonder what he's brought. They'll be so surprised when they see this place, what we've done. So much has happened since they left. Oh it will be so good to see Ened, and show her Garth. What else did Talwch's messenger say?"

"Oh, there was news of Tarok. Well rumours really. Some river people traded there this spring. He's turned the hill at the outstation into a refuge, like the one we had at Coms; he's moved the main settlement to the bend in the river below the hill, where the river almost loops back on itself; and he's built a bank and ditch across the open side. He's brought everyone in from the outlying farmsteads. They didn't want to, but he made them. Quite the master is Tarok by all accounts. Senot's people keep raiding, so now all the people live inside the walls and only go out to work the fields."

Aisa and Oranc chatted happily as they strode, arms swinging between the two rows of longhouses, past the spring and up the well-worn track to the top of the hill. Cattle and sheep grazed the stubble, kept back from the standing corn by hurdles. Auron and his gang were still at work, stooped, advancing in line, gathering a bundle of stalks in one hand, sawing near the base with the curved sickle, letting the cut corn fall to the women and children following behind, who bundled and bound with nimble fingers. As A'isa and Oranc passed with a wave, the harvesters stopped work gratefully and trooped off to their meal.

"I wonder when Aedd and Ened will get here," Oranc said.
"And Alen, don't forget Alen, he's so sweet. I've really missed him. Father said any day now, when I last saw him, and that was two days ago."

"I'll bet they have some stories to tell. I wonder if they got to the end of the world. What a journey. I hope they found us some bronze."

"The scout said they are leading two ponies. They must have done well. They've got something heavy; it must be bronze. It's so exciting. Let's go to our place and watch out for them."

A'isa settled in the warm, sun-filled grassy hollow on the western edge of the hill; totally unselfconscious, lying on her back, head on her hands, watching the dot of the skylark high above her. As she lifted her knees, her skirt rode high on her smooth tanned legs. Oranc squatted awkwardly beside her, interrupting her chatter with the touch of his trembling hand on her shoulder. She turned her face to him, squinting through sun-dazzled eyes, seeing the seriousness of his expression. He didn't move, he simply looked at her; suddenly the wanting and waiting became too much and she lifted her arms to him. Neither noticed the two heavily laden ponies, their coats mired and matted splash from the osiers, or the three travel-stained and figures who led them.

Aedd, Ened and Alen paused at the top of the slope. The neat fields and partly harvested crops, the small herd and growing flock which they had just passed, so different to the wild scrubland and rangy beasts they had left at the first snows, had prepared them for signs of order and settlement. The sight which greeted them was totally unexpected. Where only rough shelters had been, a bright white chalk bank topped by a palisade enclosed two rows of roundhouses, a granary and by the looks, a second which was being built. Beyond the houses were pig pens and a stockyard.

Ened pressed her bent fingers into the small of her back, kneading, leaning against the pull of her swollen belly, glad to have reached journey's end. "Why Aedd, it's so different to when we left, so...so settled," she said in amazement. A dog barked. Aedd recognised Berin's hounds racing towards them. He saw Berin duck out through his doorway and look up the hill, point and shout. He saw his kinfolk and his friends pour from their houses and flood up the hill side, an excited jostling crowd.

"Different or not, we're home, lass," he said, pounding Alen on the back in delight, "we're home!"

CHAPTER 37

The end of planting is always a moment for reflection. The hard work is over, but the scars still show; the scar of our revetments around the pond; the scars of Beccy's back-filled trenches criss-crossing the old orchard. You need faith and a leap of imagination to envisage what the planting will look like after several seasons' growth. I had planted a willow next to the sarsen stone. I could imagine the water bubbling from beneath its shade, its drooping branches brushing the surface of the pond, playing with and scattering their own reflections. For now, the sturdy tree of my thoughts was but a feeble sapling. While I stood and stared, a single leaf dropped and floated, boat-like, on the pool.

The orchard, when I turned to look at it, looked like Glastonbury after the festival. But in the spring, it would be a mass of daffodils and fruit blossom and then give way to cowslips, fritillaries, poppies and vetch, clover, cornflowers and so much more.

Yesterday, I had been planning to go back to Australia, back to the warmth, fleeing the drab wet greyness of November in England; searching for the warmth of the sun and for the familiar; for my job, for my life really, leaving a trail of family as cold and desolate as November. But when I told Les and Viv, they had looked dismayed.

Les had said "The Morgans are thinking of selling their barn conversion. They want to downsize and move back to her family in Cardiff. I was going to suggest that it would make a great place for a horticultural business. Plenty of outbuildings and about three acres; just enough for a pony."

"But why," Viv had asked plaintively. "Pippa just loves it here and she gets on so well with Melanie and is a real hit at school. We were really hoping you would stay for good," she had said, looking at Les. The full extent of their plotting had become clear.

"Oh I don't know," I had said, flapping my hands at my side. "There's my wife's family in Sydney to think about; they're the only family Pippa's got. It's where we belong."

"Belong," Viv had snorted. "Where your own family report you to social services and the school doesn't want a sweet girl like Pippa?"

"My family here are all long gone. And it wasn't a happy place for my parents," I had floundered in reply.

"And why should that affect whether you go or stay. Aren't you happy here?" Viv had asked exasperatedly.

"Well yes…yes I suppose I am," I had said, thinking of Les and Viv's welcome, of Pippa's ecstatic expression when I had said we would stay for a term and of course thinking of Beccy.

"Well then," she had sniffed, looking at Les again.

Les had had the last word on the subject, though from the look Viv had thrown at him perhaps he shouldn't have.

"You'll be missed," he had said, demonstrating once more just how smart he is.

Because when I told Beccy what I was planning, as I was tidying away the tools, she had turned away from me, muttering "just when everything was perfect." I had reached out my hand to touch her shoulder. She had turned, a wry smile on her face, a tear glistening at the corner of one eye. "I'll miss you," she had said.

"Will you?" I had replied gormlessly.

"Yes, you idiot. Don't you men know anything?" she had said and kissed me. I had kissed her back and had just begun to kiss her with growing enthusiasm when Pippa and Melanie had surprised us, running from around the side of the barn. Their mouths had each shaped an Oh, but no sound had emerged. They had looked at each other and then at us; their faces unskilled in deception had briefly parodied a Doris Day movie face, before their hands had been clapped to their mouths and they had dissolved into giggles.

That night I had gone to bed early, but not before I had a man to girl talk with my daughter.

"Oh Dad," she had said, interrupting me as I struggled with my apology, with my guilt about Sarah, my dead lover, her dead mother. "Oh Dad," she had said in a voice full of womanly wisdom, that belied her few years. She had smoothed the hair back from my forehead. "Rapunzel and me are like that," she had said, crossing fore and index fingers. "Mum is Mum and always will be. I know you can't forget her. I know I won't. I don't want to. I don't want you to. You don't have to either. I think Rebecca knows that."

"So you don't mind, then...if ..if.."

"All I can think of is what took you so long."

I lay awake in bed for a long time. I thought of Beccy and then, guiltily of Sarah, as though I was betraying her. When I had dreamt of Sarah, she had told me to go home. But Sarah was fifth generation Australian. The only home she had known was Australia and certainly the only home that we had known together had been our house in Sydney. Wouldn't she have said "come home" if she had meant me

461

to stay in Australia? I wished that Sarah would return and repeat the message, but she never did.

Today everything feels different, as though I have every reason to stay. It's true; we have found such kindness and sense of community in Bernton. Pippa is so relaxed, doing so well at school and is free of her bully boy cousin and his larrikin mates. She has her friendship with Melanie; her new-found love of horses. Our home in Sydney, with its memories of Sarah seems so far away, part of a different life. Somehow since my talk with Pippa last night, preserving the physical link to Sarah doesn't seem so important. She'll always be with us both and accepted by Beccy. And of course there is Beccy for me.

"Dad, Dad...! Guess what. You'll never guess. It's a scream."

I looked up. Pippa waved from the corner of the barn. Beccy stood next to her, her arm around my daughter's shoulder.

"Dad... those DNA samples. They found a match. Rap...Rebecca found a match. But guess what," she screeched. "It's you!"